WORLD EVOLUTION ONLINE

ONLINE

Book I

APOCALYPSE

Jason Kilpatrick

PROLOGUE
11/1/2020

As the large room's lights slowly turned from dark to dim, he could see several people sitting among their designated chairs. The massive circular table sat all of them wearing their usual silver masks to hide all the identities within the large room. The air was stale, yet it had a smugness about it as if the tides of the world would bend to their collective will. Meals were prepared and glasses of wine sat adorned in front of each member, yet no one dared take a bite. Not until instructed would anyone attempt such a move.

Internal fear was everywhere and distrust was apparent, however loyalty to the cause was as resolute as a mountain. It was 10:59 pm on a Wednesday night and the most pivotal meeting of their order was about to begin. From all over the globe they came to discuss their agenda. Normally these powerful anonymous individuals would meet via proxy or agents but today was different. Singular cell leaders amassing into a viper's fang of immense power, reach, and influence sat all around. Viper Eleven, however, was of no less skill or influence as compared to the others and he would soon show it. Secretly in the shadows they worked to change the paths of the world in all aspects. Tonight's agenda would be no different although to hear the Voice in person was different entirely. Then the clock struck 11:00!

Viper Eleven's distant thoughts abruptly ended as the gavel banged and the room was called to order. A tall man stood and began the proceedings of the meeting. As always, none of the faces could be seen under the masks however the man stood with authority and malevolence; there was no doubt that this was The Voice, the head of our secret order. The air of confidence radiated from him as if the temperature of the room had dropped twenty degrees when he began to speak. Arise my fellow Vipers, he said. All Twelve Vipers stood at once. The Voice bowed his head to all of them and all the masked Vipers repaid the gesture as a sign of respect. Although they were unknown equals; the Voice was the mastermind, brain, and calculator for scenarios upon scenarios without end. You may sit were the next words spoken and as silently as they arose; all twelve sat. All eyes of the twelve focused on the next words spoken.

The Voice uttered: As we look to the future, our actions will alter humanity as the world knows it. We are gathered here to make a better world in our own eyes as we see fit. The political and global landscapes are supercharged with strife and hatred. People are killing each other; rights continue to be ignored or violated. The time is now. Standing in our way will be nations, leaders, and the whole of humanity; but none can stand against Viper. The time has come to imitate the beginnings of the grand plan the Voice said. The time is coming so we must be prepared and ready to strike a decisive blow.

Viper One what is your update, the Voice said? As she began to speak, every other Viper focused on her words eagerly to garner even the smallest thread of what her part in this overall scheme was. After the mysterious woman's update came, Viper Two then spoke. Three then began, and then Four and so on around the table. Each one adding a piece here and there as Viper Eleven tried to formulate the secretive puzzle that had eluded him ever since he became one of the hidden Vipers in the order five years ago. Twelve there are plus the leader; never anymore and never any less.

As everyone spoke the time passed and one after another, they rose and talked. Now it was time for Viper Eleven's breakdown of what his group's part was. Weakness is not tolerated nor hesitance for the grand plan Viper Eleven thought. As he stood and gathered the air and confidence to speak, a quick glimpse of the room was gleaned from behind his mask. All the eerie heads turned towards his way as he looked upon them. They were impatiently awaiting the next update and as, he was sure, to piece together in their own minds what the overarching scheme would be. He began to vocalize in quick sharp sequences what his team had been working on while hitting on the high points but giving enough detail to satisfy them from thinking he was hiding information.

These people did not deserve to know the rest. Viper Eleven was the strongest and most vile of people and these snakes would quiver beneath his feet if he had the chance to make it so. So, for now he would play his part and do what needed to be done for the Viper cause and the Voice. One day that seat would be his. Once Viper Eleven sat down a quick nod from Viper Two and the Voice came his way. Questions came about scalability and execution on his part, but they quickly were answered without remorse or emotion. A soft "Well Done" could be heard from the Voice. Viper Eleven smiled from beneath his mask. In his mind he thought; thy time would come.

Fast forward to June 2023 as he was sitting in his office: Viper Eleven looked out at the city skyline disgusted with how aspects of dead flesh and decay rotting the world from the inside out exist within our global leaders and political organizations. One side versus the other or in many cases; no rival side at all. The world is ripe with distrust, and nobody is safe anywhere, he thought. Viper Eleven took a second to take confidence that their plan would accelerate Viper's credence for humanity: Submission, Obedience, and Evolution for Mankind.

It was an extremely warm and dark night in Austin, Tx. It was the middle of September when Mable began to feel very weak. At first, Mable just thought she was dehydrated even though she had been drinking water constantly over the last few months due to the heat wave. So, Mable did as anyone else would do. She filled up a glass of water from the tap and began to drink more. Except the weakness did not pass by but only got stronger. By midnight she was having trouble standing on her own and she made a call to her sister to take her to the hospital. By the time her sister had arrived, Mable was having trouble standing and you could see the unknown fear in her eyes. Sarah, her sister, got her into her Toyota Corolla and sped away at a breakneck speed. As Sarah drove in a manner that she had not attempted since she was seventeen in high school, she came screeching into the Emergency Room entrance with smoke following her tires and the noises of people screaming loudly. None of those noises reached Sarah's ears as she was totally focused on one thing: helping her sister, Mable.

Sarah ran into the Austin General hospital and screamed for help. As a few nurses and an orderly jogged outside to assist you could feel the fear reek from the female pair so much you could taste it. As they rushed her into the Emergency Room people cleared a path for the stretcher and group of people escorting her. Sarah was trying to describe the symptoms to the caretakers but was having a grim time focusing.

The symptoms sounded like a few common illnesses, however the lack of ability to put any weight on extremities is what caught the health care workers off guard. They radioed for the Emergency Room Dr. to look at her as soon as it was viable. Unfortunately, those departments can take a while with understaffing and a lack of urgency from some personnel. By the time the doctor arrived at the patient's room, Mable had deteriorated. Her skin looked ashen, her face appeared like it was starting to cave in on itself, and her limbs were now soft like a bowl of jelly that had just been sitting out too long from the fridge. At that point, the doctor tried to recall every class he took during medical school and nothing in his right mind seemed to fit the descriptions here. From that moment he quarantined the room, isolated anyone that had been exposed to this point to Mable and radioed the overhead speaker and two words came out of his mouth in a frenzy: CODE PURPLE!

The next few hours were a blur as Mable battled for life as her health deteriorated even more. Her limbs were softening like a horrific cartoon episode of some underwater sponge. Infectious Disease had intervened and could produce nothing as they tried to run all tests they could to help rule stuff out. X-Rays showed the bones were eroding at a massively rapid rate like a salt tablet being dissolved in hot water. Mable screamed about a heavy pressure on her lungs, but the medical staff could do nothing but look on in horror as her final gasp of air filled the room. Then the silence filled the air as the machines stopped their beeping.

Mable was now gone and all that remained was the eerie flatlining of machines, horror stunned expressions, and the deflated corpse of Mable Smith. From that point they tried to gather themselves and notate what they could try and determine what in the hell just happened. Unfortunately, that never happened as two more calls came from the Emergency Room ascertaining the same symptoms. The doctor knew at that moment this was a pandemic like he had never seen. He screamed to isolate the floor, evacuate everyone else, call the upper management levels, and he secretly sent words to his medical school friend who was now working for the World Health Organization. They would want to see this asap.

Within months, cases had surfaced worldwide with many of the poorer nations enforcing martial law and quarantines to prevent the spread. There seemed to be no rhyme or reason for who this new pandemic reached out for like a shadow. Rich, poor, young, old, and from any geographic region were all infected. Of course, it was more rampant in the poorer areas of the world, but it was non-biased, nonetheless. This disease was unlike anything else in history. It ate the bones and actively suppressed any immunities someone might have to bone or bone marrow issues. Nothing could stop it once the person or animal was infected and it took months to show but once visible it was incurable.

The World Health Organization worked around the clock in a race to see how people were infected when by a remote chance a researcher by the name of Gustov Sworlijen asked the question: Who is not infected? What similarities do they inhabit? After a few months of reverse engineering the issue, Gustov produced a viable hypothesis. It was the communal water supply around the world. Hidden as that fact was since it was well placed away from discovery. Upon reporting that discovery and finally deciding he would be better served to finally get some rest as he was averaging 20 hours a day for the last few weeks, he ended his day and was walking to his car when he asked himself the questions that he was dreading: By this point was it too late for humanity as we know it? Unfortunately, it was the last thought in his head as he felt an explosion of pain erupt from his chest. He then looked down to see a hole gushing blood; then it all went dark.

CHAPTER ONE

What a Mess

My name is Mitch and I can say without a doubt that we live in a crap storm. As I look out the window of my home into the cold, cloudy, and windy night that ripples the trees; you can still smell the light acrid scent of distant fires that rage around the country as the entire cloudscape reeks of it and has for months. Even in our country home, which was once a nice area about 40 miles south of Memphis, we have been unable to escape the pending apocalypse. The silence all around has always been the case with only the chirping sound of locust and frogs, however now it just seems eerie with the orangish hues in the far away skyline.

It is July 2024 and the world is pretty much a cluster. No way to call it any different than that. In late 2023, a few months before the US presidential election primaries began which was supercharged to begin with; we had the honor of having a biological weapon released worldwide. This was a hard counter to any political result that could have been and was as nasty as the name it adopted: Soul Crusher. The technical name is Osteo-Ush Syndrome, which is a plague that means Bone Death. The biological weapon was introduced via the communal water supply around the globe. No organization or at fault party has ever been found.

When ingested it begins to slowly eat away at the marrow and inner cells of the bones until they cannot support a person's weight. Then the body's mass utterly crushes itself into a floppy mess without any structural support. There is no current cure hence why it got its moniker. Once you get it, you are sentenced to a painful and miserable existence. The incubation period until death normally takes a few months. Anyone with well water or a dedicated source of H20 were able to mostly avoid the issue although it can transmit via body fluids. However, with that came its own set of issues with martial law and chaos spreading across the landscape. Looting, violence, and mass squatting ensued to forcibly attempt to take clean water from people's homes with wells or dedicated sources, and murder has become common. One would think we took a page right out of a civilized version of Road Warrior for all the bullshit that was happening.

Most families were scattered geographically but with cellular and internet lines still working; people could communicate and coordinate. Those that had been able to quickly found a way to manage to secure and gather their necessary family and friends to centralized places, however this was only really viable if well water or a dedicated water tributary away from the general water supply could be secured. Luckily, I had one such place as we had well water. Once we realized the severity of this upcoming trash heap of a dumpster fire, I immediately targeted my friends and family to come and stay with me.

Once it was determined that the communal water supply was the reason, all forms of bottled water were savagely horded from the shelves at every store worldwide with people using that hardship to extort thousands of dollars for a single bottle. It was insane. That is when I forced the issue with friends and family to consider that we had a well and the more here the easier we could defend it upon an attack of any kind. The Soul Crusher virus had managed to absolutely ravage all third world countries and decimated most of the 1st and 2nd.

Medical centers had been unable to keep up with the population at large that was sick and had to make some tough decisions when a person reached finality. Burn or risk the spread. With tens of thousands dying daily around the world mass cremators had been placed in any city big enough to maintain one. There had been no answer to the virus, and the total world population has now fallen to only about 2 billion-ish. Then came the announcement that changed everything and seemed to give a glimmer of hope for the world.

The remaining governments of the world had come together to solicit a response to combat the virus and look to give humanity a fighting chance to survive this. A team of doctors, scientists, engineers, computer programmers, and developers collaborated to finally achieve a solution. Seclusion until remedied. One developer, a man by the name of Igor Romanovichky, who was considered the most eccentric person alive produced the answer for humanity. It was determined that the continuing efforts to medically reverse engineer the virus for a cure would take roughly 10-15 years while the current rate of infection would deteriorate humanity past the point of recovery would take an estimated 5 years. The 5 years was a best-case scenario, and humanity would have none of that hot mess. That is when the groundwork for WEO was born.

WEO, or its full name of World Evolution Online, was put together from the most adaptive and current gaming platforms, stasis machines, and top tier engineering hypothesis from all around the globe. Most of the underlying support had already been in the works from other projects and programs from all over so the inception could be processed and put into motion logistically faster than normal. It was very odd how quickly everything was ready for all of humanity, but who was I to criticize. It was up to Igor and his team to create a simulation or experience to keep humanity alive.

Somehow the AI known as Ecological & Human Strategic Protection Intelligence or better known as EHSPI was introduced to the world as a long-term protective measure against the logical outcome of a Point of No Return scenario until they developed a cure for the Soul Crusher virus. The AI made it a never-ending fantasy medieval scenario that is from a digital measurement perspective, is about the size of ten earths.

The remaining governments around the world would gather up all the remaining unaffected and transport them to impregnably fortified zones for them to report too. Each Immersion Zone is protected by a contingent of military forces that will remain on site and fully in reality to protect us against threats. The medical personnel that will be conducting research as well as the computer staff that will monitor the simulation and pods will also remain on site and out of stasis. Growth chambers for food and wells for water are situated within the compounds to provide ample means to keep everyone alive for years to come. They will be completely stocked and safe as each area is fully sufficient to supply itself and all its inhabitants.

For the people within the game simulation, a list of family and friends will be compiled so that they can connect and gather not only at the military zones but also inside the simulation. Names and contact information will also be collected to assist in this. Once gathered the population will be placed in state-of-the-art cryostasis machines. Our mental consciousness and physical bodies will be scanned and uploaded to the system so that the simulation has a baseline to begin with for each person. Food and water will not be necessary in the real world as we will be ice cubes for the near future. This way the medical and scientific teams can work for a cure while the engineers and computer-minded people can monitor the simulation and stasis pods without being hampered with the strain of having to feed and water thousands of people for such a long time.

I really am scared to think what will happen to our home during the time we are on so called "ICE." Will we ever be able to return and if we do; what will we be returning too? Will Earth be something we even want to return too? We are left with the cold, hard fact that we can only put our trust and faith in people we do not know and do not trust either. It is our only long-term remedy for everything that is going on. So, trust we will and hopefully I can hold my family and friends for real one day without mutants roaming the lands or twelve-foot-tall cockroaches chasing us. That is a nightmare I want nothing to do with.

We were told it will be an exciting fantasy online simulation where we can be anyone and do anything we desire. Be the best humanity can be or its worst. I guess we will see. Most people are scared to what comes next, especially since it is unknown and they are ultimately relinquishing control of their mortal bodies. That is something most humans find terrifying but if they consider the alternative timeline; It does not give them much choice even though they truly have one. We were advised that we would not physically age or wear as it would only be our consciousness that would be uploaded. We would continue our existence inside the system until we could be brought back out.

As a group we sat down in our little secure area of earth called our home and decided that we needed to discuss the next steps for our future. Everyone had the same information, so it was a bunch or scared people venting hell freezing over scenarios and judgement day ideas. The gamers of the group such as myself, my son, son-in-law, and many others were excited to a degree about the idea. Throughout the talks we were able to shed light on what everyone could expect in a general sense with regards to game play, classes, questions, etc. We also advised that we really have no idea what to expect since this was a new concept of full immersion. We also had a lot of questions, but we also knew we could not get answers until we made the leap. So, after a few hours of heated and emotional conversation, we all agreed to join WEO and exchanged predetermined character names that we produced that night as well as any back up names in case of duplicity. We made a point to share our info with each other so we can all be together in WEO.

Two months later: Finally, after three weeks having gone by, most of my surviving friends and family finally arrived at the so-called protected zone just outside of Monticello, Arkansas. There used to be an old WW2 POW camp there that was a worn-down field used by the local university cross-country running teams for practice until it was commandeered by the US military for Operation: Destitute Survival. That is what this mess is called officially.

Sitting on a cot within our cabin, my wife, Ellen, and I are waiting for all our family and friends who have survived to arrive with us from processing. The first to arrive is my son, Paul, and my daughter's family which consist of Celeste, Lee, and our grandbaby, Ophelia. I was so happy to see them that I just gathered them all up in a hug and said thank goodness you all arrived safe. After hugs and welcomes we all sat down to await the others.

Next to arriving there was Travis and his family with Josh, David, and their families in tow. After that, my parents slowly strolled in. I was worried about them since they are slow to move and elderly, so I was glad to have them make it. Many others arrived one after another until the last group arrived, which was Ellen's family. We were incredibly lucky to have them all make it since a portion of that geographical zone of their town was blocked into quarantine. They were in a mad rush to escape so overall we were incredibly lucky to have everyone there. The remaining members of our respective families were thought to be in other regionalized camps situated around the country waiting to unite within the game.

One month later: After days upon days of medical testing for clearance, pod fittings, endless meetings, poking, prodding of parts that are no longer considered private, and generally getting utterly pissed off by the runners of this damn show; we finally came to the day in which we were here for; launch day. We all had previously produced in game names for everyone to be able to communicate through even though we were assured our contacts would be uploaded. We wanted to make sure, so we tried to use the adage: Trust but Verify! Everyone in our group was nervous and not sure what to expect, however we had our game plan. As the lines started to split and break up to begin immersion, I gave all my family hugs and goodbyes, telling them I would see them very soon and I told my friends we would all meet up as soon as viable after character creation.

We were told the creation matrix could take a few hours, so everyone was a tad jittery. My main concern was Ophelia as she was just a toddler. The organizers advised us that she would remain in a special type of pod designed for children that would allow them to grow and develop at a normal rate. Children across the globe would be set into these pods so that they would continue to receive special nutrient mixes while inside WEO. This would allow their bodies to grow at a normal rate until maturity determined by the medical specialists. Once that threshold was met, they would enter the adult phase of stasis from that point on. This way when we re-entered the real world, their bodies would match their mind. They would go through continuous activity and physical regimens to ensure peak conditioning and health.

After saying my temporary goodbyes, I strolled down the cold and dimly lit corridor around then hit several curves and turns until I found my pod number which was SP08675309. I caught notice of the pod number, and I chuckled out loud at the id number. Suddenly, I started singing the 80's hit song. With regards to the pod, I thought isn't this a crappy home for the next ten to fifteen years. I mean no kitchen, tv, or bathroom. What the hell, I uttered to myself as I stepped in laughing. I stripped down to the standard outfits that were given to us to wear for stasis and I must say: it is not very flattering. Just the basic of twill cotton on bare skin. Thank goodness I was not nipping out hard I told myself.

I laid down into the pod and tried to get as comfortable as I could. There was a timer display on the pod that said T-10 minutes to stasis. At this point, the medical staff were attaching the mandatory nodes and connectors needed for the simulation as well as a cerebral link that would connect us in game. Once they finished with their hustle and bustle, I needed to control my heart rate as I could see on the displays that it was elevated. Not to mention I could feel it racing through the roof. Deep breaths were in order and as I calmed myself, I said a prayer that we would all make it through this alive and hopefully have a better world to come back to. Those damn specialists better create a viable cure were the prominent thoughts in my head right then and there.

With 2 minutes to go the pod doors began to close. The situation was getting real now, and you could hear the paranoid screams of various people throughout the halls. That certainly did not help considering it was the last thing humanity would hear in real life for the next decade. It certainly puts a damper on what would come next. Now that the door had closed and sealed, a recording started that startled me a bit as my thoughts had wondered. "Hello please remain still and calm as we begin the stasis process. Please be advised that you will feel hardly anything as the process takes effect. We will begin with a nanite injection to monitor all conditions and vitals. Once that is complete there will be a slight hum as the link synchronizes to WEO. Once the connection is complete and uploaded, the stasis process will commence. From then on you will begin your journey into World Evolution Online. Safe journeys and see you when you return.

Once the recording was over, I felt a slight prick as the nanite injection did its thing. Even though I knew it was coming it still surprised me. The humming widened my eyes a bit as well, but I tried to remain calm. My heart rate shot up again and I felt like I was drowning so I tried everything I could to not panic. Oh shit, oh shit, oh shit kept coming out of my mouth and then oh my goodness I am going to die hit my mind. I battled with those thoughts and as I did so, I did not even notice that the noise had stopped. I finally gathered my wits and got into a state of calmness as I focused on my family and friends I would see shortly. As I entered the meditative trance that I had practiced repeatedly it all froze and went black. The next thing I heard was a soft female voice saying: Welcome Mitch Gillespie to World Evolution Online!

CHAPTER TWO

Resignation

The voice was soft yet safe sounding as I recalled her statement: Welcome Mitch Gillespie to World Evolution Online. The only sensory receptor that was working was my ears. Everything was black and void. No sight, scent, or touch was near. It was like I was floating in an endless cloud of perpetual utter blackness. I felt internally like I was drowning in the darkest of night. What felt like an eternity was only a moment of time because shortly after the voice came alive once more.

The voice said: I see that your vitals are elevated so allow me to adjust the landscape in which we will continue. At that moment, a dim light grew from within the space I occupied. The area seemed to move about and form from out of nothing. First the soft white floor and walls appeared. Then the light magnified until it looked like it was covered in soft white hewed bulbs from lamps. Next the furniture came with a plush brown leather sofa appearing right behind me and a desk with an art deco white chair formed in front of me. The ceiling came next, which mirrored a cloudless fall afternoon with light blues as well as specks of browns and oranges. The air started moving now like air conditioning had been installed and it was set at a mere perfect 70 degrees. An archaic looking desktop computer that looked like a vacuum tube television from the late 70's appeared on top of the desk after that. Then finally of all things to appear was a gigantic water and coffee station with all the fixings. Then as soon as it was finished all of my senses returned and I was assaulted with everything from my feet on the cool floor, the wind from the air conditioning blowing against me, to the robust smell of coffee hitting my nose.

I felt thirsty for some reason, so I walked over to get a glass of water although it did make me hesitant due to the circumstances surrounding water. That voice returned as if they knew my thoughts and said: The water is 100% safe I assure you so please indulge. I figured why not. There were two mugs sitting there at the station. One was a mug that said: I Love My Cat while the other said I did not fart as it was the other guy. Obviously, I grabbed the latter one. I poured a glass and took a sip. Wow this stuff tasted so good. I downed that glass and poured another before heading over to the sofa and taking a seat.

About 30 seconds later a door appeared and opened. A young dark-skinned female entered the room and walked over to me. She extended her hand and stated that she was here to help and answer any questions that she was able to before the exams and character creation process started. She then sat at the desk and looked at me. She introduced herself as EHSPI's assistant, Alara. Please relax and be as comfortable as you can as we get prepared for your upcoming introduction into WEO. We hope you will achieve wonderful things in our world and want to do anything we can to alleviate any concerns or apprehensions you might be holding onto as you were transferred into the simulation; Alara said.

My first thoughts were holy hell what is happening here. This cannot be real. As I am sure she could see the utter dumbfounded look in my face, she smiled and said, let's begin with any questions you might have and then I will also go over some common anticipated questions I am expecting from the general populace. Especially since I am currently being replicated millions of times over at this very second conversing to each person that is going through the transfer process. It is my job to oversee and facilitate your initial introduction to WEO. There are several waves today of player uploads so we will have plenty of data to talk about if you choose. My jaw dropped at that revelation. My mind was blank, but I tried to quickly produce some preset questions that my group had come up with in advance. Okay, okay, okay, I mumbled as I tried to gather my bearings.

Question One: How does this game work? An excellent question she said. Well, it is an open world, and this environment or game will only be limited by creativity and imagination. You will make your way in this world however you choose as humanity has a fresh start here. Classes are unlimited however your class offerings list will be tailored to you specifically based on several factors. There will be a series of mental and physical challenges, tests, personality profile assessments, and scans of both physiological and mental aptitudes. This could take as little or as long to complete based on the individual, you will be offered classes and professions based on those results, but you can always pick something else although it is not advised as your experiences may suffer. You only have one character. Races can be any you choose from a qualified list based on the forementioned tests and scans while benefits of each will be listed to help you refine that decision. Does that make sense Mitch? Yes, I uttered. What is the next question?

Question Two: Will we ever return to Earth? Alara seemed to ponder this question although she did not seem surprised in the least. Mitch, that is certainly the game plan and goal EHSPI and all the world's governments are aspiring too for sure. Nobody can state for 100% certain that we will be able to, however we are extremely confident that ESPHI and the team behind this will make that a reality. I hope that helps alleviate your worries. What is your next question?

Question Three: What about children entering WEO? Another valuable question Mitch. As you should be aware from the briefings that all humanity were subjected to prior to emersion; all children under full maturity and age fourteen will be placed in a different pod style until they qualify for full cryostasis as any other adult. Within these special pods which will be calibrated for each child's age and gender will be tailored for optimal growth. They will receive nutritional injections with special activity regiments to keep their physical bodies growing to keep up with their mental aspects that will be growing within the game. Once they have seemed to reach full maturity they will seamlessly transfer into the full-time stasis. At no point will their simulation or game experience show even the slightest glitch or a change when this happens. It will be as if a blink of an eye happened and then they are just like every other adult. We will notify them of the change of course as it is about to happen, but it will not affect them in any way. Next question?

Question Four: How does death work? Excellent question. You will now be immortal during your time here in World Evolution Online, however there will be penalties. Pain is set at 100% human adaptiveness as compared to other games a non-pain or a dialed down pain tolerance. We here at World Evolution Online and ESPHI want people to be whatever and whoever they wish but we do not want digital anarchy. This is done to promote adventuring and exploration as well as to attempt to keep the act of death a painful and unpleasant outcome. We want everyone to enjoy their time while keeping humanity at the forefront. We know there will be outliers and that is where the good adventurers come in as they will protect others and deter that kind of behavior from non-player characters or better known as (NPCS), Monsters, and Fellow Players.

Not only is the pain an issue but there will also be a scaling severity on death that could and will hamper player development issues once a character has evolved past level 5. This will include possible stat reduction, respawn timer scalability, and experience loss that can potentially cause a loss of levels. Think smart, play smart, and make your wishes come true. Be whoever or whatever you choose but keep in mind; death is not something you will ever want to have happen and the experience accompanying it will collaborate that sentiment. Before we get to your next question please allow me to go over a few items regarding gameplay that we expect every player will be inclined to ask and will certainly want to know. Is that all right? Yes, I replied.

Alara began: As every player enters World Evolution Online, they will go through the same process that we are experiencing now at this moment. Afterwards one of my counterparts within

World Evolution Online will assist in conducting the necessary scans and tests from which your class and skill choices will be offered. More on that in a second. The programmers that are still outside of the game will act much like GMs to apply patches, troubleshoot issues, answer questions, and general oversight of the game simulation. They will be mostly invisible unless they are needed to interact within the game however their directive is to allow the game to progress normally as much as possible without interference. They will be introducing patches, changes, or updates based on need just like any other game scenario.

To grow in World Evolution Online Mitch every player begins at Level 1. As you explore, research, complete social and environmental quests, impact the world, undergo social and environmental challenges that can shape the landscape, and improve your classes and skills; you will be awarded experience points. So, everything in WEO will offer a player experience points towards their overall player level. When a player accumulates enough experience points to reach the next level's threshold then they receive a notification to what is called level up. Leveling up will notify you via prompt so that you can complete that process at the opportune time and not in the middle of something as that might be distracting. Once you level up you will have your choice of potential skill upgrades, new spells, actions, upgrades, and stat point allocations. Fairly common with most games from what I know about.

There are also Distinguished points. Distinguished Points are the so-called Fame growth that you might hear of in other game types. Distinguished Points in World Evolution Online can work in two ways. I would say like a good approach and a bad approach. By doing honorable deeds that impact a species, town, region, or world, you will be awarded points that will lean towards an illustrious persona. If, however, someone was to do things in an evil manner then that person would be awarded points that would scale on the notorious scaled side. This is an ever-flowing bar. The more honorable impacts you perform then the more well respected and revered you will become. The more heinous events you partake in then the more reviled and hated a person could be as well. These could have their own level achievements if enough points are attained on one side or the other. They might even have benefits themselves. Only you can see for yourself.

To touch back on the class, ability, and skill choice offerings; I will touch on each of these over the next few sections. It is highly recommended that you take your time to really think about those decisions as they will begin to not only shape your gameplay but have an impact on your views on the world and how the world can view you. This will help you round out who you wish to become and achieve in World Evolution Online.

Your class is a final decision and anything going forward will be based on that choice, so I ask you to deeply contemplate that decision. It is final as there is no chance to retest or seek out a change in your beginning class or any class going forth. Only in certain instances can that be a possibility until something called class evolutions happens and even that is based on factors including your current class. Take the time to weigh the pros and cons of each class and look inward to see how you would see yourself living that character type and what you really want to become and achieve during your time in World Evolution Online. As I stated earlier, your test results will potentially give you many options to choose from so be diligent in your research.

The possibilities are there for all classes to achieve great heights. As you level up with experience points you will be able to unlock abilities, spells, class evolutions, maneuvers, and other items based upon your playstyle and level. An example of this might be a warrior at level one might use a sword and shield but only be able to swing and block. At level 5 the same warrior might be able to use the shield as a special attack and so on as this person levels their class. Another important piece about class selection is that your available weapons that you will be proficient in will also be determined by your class and race. You will have a proficiency level in those weapons and items, and they will be able to level faster much like anything else. It will also open the door to use better higher tiered items of that same weapon or item type. That is not to say that a spell caster could not lug around a sword and shield, but they would do it very clumsily and never be particularly good at it. They would level it slower and be limited to what they could do. Please also keep that in mind when making your selection. So, get out in the world and make things happen. Do not be a little wuss she said with a smile and before I could even pick my jaw off the floor from her remark she had hastily moved on.

From a skills standpoint, each player will start with the ability to obtain a maximum of 10 skills where up to 4 are determined based upon your testing results while others will be from a qualified populated list. You may choose up to 6 more. Quite a few will be unknown and will need to be experimented with or sought out to discover. Not all have to be selected now, and others might become apparent later. Some might require that certain prerequisite thresholds be met to be able to use them. I advise you to read them thoroughly before making your populated choices.

In rare occasions there could be more, but the average player will be able to receive 10. Practice and hone your skills to level them to achieve even more potent variants or options. An example would be skill proficiency in acrobatics. At level 1 they might be able to make a roll look easy, however as they practice, they might be able to make a back flip at higher levels. Practice makes perfect I always say: She giggled. In the case where a player feels as if they really made a mistake in their skill selection they can be changed and a random list to choose the replacement from will appear. This could allow for an unlearning of old skills and a relearning of new ones but not without a steep cost of money and experience points.

The gold cost will depend on the number of times a person chooses to change their skills while the experience cost will be determined by the rarity of the skill that a person chooses to learn from the random list. The rarer the skill the higher the cost. I will touch on rarity in a few moments. Special teachers can be found across World Evolution Online that would be able to complete this for you. However, it will be expensive and not an unlimited venture. You have been warned. Are you able to follow along okay so far Mitch? I nodded and said please continue before I ask more questions.

CHAPTER THREE

Continuing Education

Now let us touch on abilities. Special abilities can be given to individual players that are non-skill or class based. Using them can also advance them via levels with experience points being allotted to the ability based on usage and how it is used based on situation. These can be given to players by achieving certain achievements within the game, performing well on the initial testing results, and special hidden gameplay milestones. These can truly be a game changer depending on how they are used as well as the ability type.

Next, I want to touch on what is commonly known as stats. In World Evolution Online each player will have seven different stats they can distribute into their character archetype. Every class within World Evolution Online will have primary stats that should be the main allocation focus to a player as well as a secondary stat preference as it would complement the primary skill choice and the class play style. An example would be as a wizard you would want to focus on intelligence as it would determine the power of your spells and the number of spells you are able to cast without depleting your energy to do so. A warrior might need high strength to ensure that they have a high chance to land hit when attacking. The base number of stats given to a player at each level is preset at five while your class or other items could give you more. Each stat will impact a character in a separate way. With every level a character achieves they will be given a set-based number of points to allocate how they see fit for their race, class, and gameplay. Depending on the class and race they choose they could receive extra points when leveling up. Mitch, how are we doing so far? I am still following. Will there be access to this information in game? Why yes, Alara said. All you have to do is think about it and it will give you the prompt. Anything in game can be done mentally such as casting a spell, needing to see a map or inventory, accessing the tutorial, etc. Let us proceed, she said as the stat types are listed below.

1. Intelligence = Determines the size of your energy pool for arcane classes, energy-based items such as spells, certain skills, particular social interactions, and so forth. This stat also determines how powerful arcane spells can be and how viable they will be to hit their target. If there is success or failing checks, the numbers will be calculated to determine the winner of the encounter. Primary for most arcane spell classes. Exp: Knowing that the item is an apple!

2. Wisdom = How mentally strong a creature will be. Will power incarnate. Refers to common sense and a primary focus for divine casters. This stat also determines how powerful divine spells can be and how viable they will be to actually hit their target. If there are success or failing checks, the numbers will be calculated to determine the winner of the encounter. Exp: Knowing whether the apple is edible or not. Determines energy pool for clerics or ranger base classes.

3. Hardiness = More commonly known as constitution. This determines the health pool size of players and resistance strength to certain poisons and spells. Certain armor types require certain levels of hardiness. Primary focus for certain front-line classes and a secondary focus for many classes. Exp: If the apple was rotten, high health would allow you to eat it without getting sick. Stamina is based off Hardiness.

4. Strength = Determines carrying weight, how strong a player will be, pure raw power, and a primary focus for most melee classes. Strength determines physical damage amount. Exp: How easily you can lift an apple.

5. Charisma = Determines your sparkling personality and how well people will listen to what you have to say as well as determining your potential influence. Primary focus for bardic classes as well as certain others. Charisa is a primary stat for social interactions and barter based skills. Exp: How cheap could you talk a salesperson into selling you the apple for?

6. Intuition = This stat is that gut feeling you have in the pit of your stomach, the sixth sense tingling on your arms, and a secondary focus for any spy, diplomatic or recon based stealth classes. This stat does not provide a primary class allocation currently. Exp: Your gut tells you the apple is poisoned.

7. Agility = This stat is the primary focus of rogue, ranger, nimble minded classes, as well as any physical performance-based classes. This is a secondary stat for most classes as it determines how well a person can move, dodge attacks, avoid traps, and quickness in all situations. Exp: How easily can you juggle an apple.

Place these stat points how you see fit to enhance the play style you want to achieve. Be thoughtful though as you only have so many to allocate.

There is no hard level progression cap for a player to max out with, however there will be a substantial percentage of increased experience costs to achieve the next attainable level. It will become extremely hard and a slow grind to fully reach incredible heights. Most players will eventually give up and accept their level gain as is and live their lives as they want while the rare select few will strive for a level of glory and continue to level to heights never seen before. Will this be you, Mitch? I remained silent as I digested the information but slowly nodded to her. Good she said we will await your greatness.

Now let us talk about rarities. About every aspect of the game will be categorized into rarities. Everything from classes, skills, professions, quests, trinkets, weapons, armor, pets, mounts, buildings, races, abilities, food, drink, NPCs, spells, world impacting events, etc. All will fall into a rarity column. They will be classified in the following order from the most mundane every day to the most powerful. They are as follows: Common, Uncommon, Rare, Very Rare, Legendary, Mythical, Divine Relic or Artifact. Some of these rarities will only be heard of by rumors and others will be commonplace. Mythical and Divine cannot be crafted as they can only be obtained as the spoils of the deadliest foes in World Evolution Online. Now we can happily return to any questions that you might have. We can take as much time as you need to go over any items before you begin your testing.

Thank you Alara, I said. It is appreciated. So, I do have a few more questions that I had thought of prior to immersion, and I might think of some more if that is okay. Alara nodded and said of course it is. Please ask away.

Question Five: You mentioned the word, Divine. So, am I to understand that there will be gods or deities within World Evolution Online? Yes, Mitch there will be. There are many gods or deities in World Evolution Online. Several are well represented and known, others are middling minor gods that dream to have major followings uplift their divine station and through the assistance of players and NPCs they can. Anything can happen. Then we have the others which are unknown or faded so long ago they have left recent memory. These will have to be discovered to understand what and who they are. Are they good or evil waiting to be released? Who knows. A deep investigation might be required to awaken or satisfy their requirements to return them to prominence. Unlike Earth, in World Evolution Online gods and deities are a physical thing and can have influence over the world and its followers albeit with restrictions.

Question Six: Can you please elaborate on whether there is a profession or job listing available? Sure, thing Mitch. Just like

Earth, people can apply trades of their choosing. They are also affected by the rarity system and sometimes trainers might be hard to find but there are trainers for all skills and professions. Each player will have a selection of two profession choices during their journey here in World Evolution Online. Most players will look to synchronize their choices to complement one another or their classes, but it is not mandatory. An example would be someone that chooses blacksmith to smelt the ore obtained from miners, and then finally an armor smith to create a finished product. A general blacksmith can create general tools if that is all they want or need. Professions can be whatever a player chooses if it is a viable trade or craft that is supplied within the simulation. There is a list during creation that goes over many of the professions although several will be hidden to train until the trainer is discovered. Also, some professions might require certain prerequisites be met to utilize that profession. The armor smith profession that we just discussed might not be an option unless a player's blacksmithing skill is of adequate level. Just like the skill system, if a player wishes to change a particular profession to another then they must first find a suitable trainer for the profession they wish to change to. Then by accessing the menu systems, a player can cancel the profession they wish to remove. All progress from that said profession will be permanently lost and the new profession will begin at zero. If there are any prerequisites for the said profession, then they will also go through a value check to ensure they are met.

Question Seven: How will I be able to connect with my family and friends? I know we submitted the list of everyone, but can you please elaborate further? I want to make sure I get to be with everyone that I hold dear. Of course, you can Mitch. How this part works is that every person submitted people they want to connect with inside. That information will be uploaded and synchronized with your player character. You will be able access them via the contact list, send them video calls in the game, emails, and coordinate your locations so that you all can get together in a specified location. Some might enter the world in your same location while others may not however, we will try to accommodate what we can. However, with so many people having others that are connected to thousands or millions of other people via separation, it is no tall order. Okay I said, so I will be able to contact them and coordinate from there? Yes, you can, Alara said. Is there a priority to that list I asked? She nodded and said that immediate family members are the top tier with secondary family, extended family, and then friends following that. With proper communication and coordination, you can get everyone together. Thank you, I said.

I felt better with that one being mostly cleared up because that was a huge worry of mine going into this crazy dilemma. I then looked at Alara and said you know this might be wildly off base but for 95% of our conversation you resemble a musty stale librarian but for that random 5% of our encounter you have a kinky little wild bear persona.

She laughed softly and then commented that she has been programmed to be as human as possible at this phase so it will be less of a shock to most. I tried to implore my spicy salsa side when I deemed it appropriate. I laughed and said "keep it up. I will do my best Mitch. Do you have any other questions? I honestly had no idea as my mind was flying all around. So, I figured I would just roll with it at this point and try to ask questions later if I was able. Finally, I looked at her and said you know what. The hell with it; let's go ahead and get this party started. No sense in prolonging the inevitable. She nodded and said as you wish.

Question Eight: What about anyone that is currently disabled. I have a family member who has lost the use of one of their extremities and I want to know how that will affect them. Alara looked intensely at me but did not say a word at first like she was processing the question in deep thought. Remarkably interesting she said but not unexpected considering your family's profile. Very well she said. Any person introduced into World Evolution Online will have full range of motion of their full body's capability. So hypothetically if they were missing a leg then the scans would mimic the muscle tone and make-up of the other leg and provide the said person with an alternate match. This way they would have both arms. We do strive to make World Evolution Online a magical place so that is something we can easily do.

Now the next phase will include the actual testing and scanning portion. This will enable the character and class creation to begin. I will assist you in getting set up and preparing you for the initiation. From then the testing will take as long as it takes you to complete it as each player will be different in both results, depth, and length of time. The better and deeper the testing is then the more of a symbiotic analysis it will offer. This could include more class options, rarer skills, a deeper compiling of race choices, etc. The better and more in depth you do the more you have to choose from. Do you understand? Yes, I said as I understood this portion.

I knew I wanted to take as long as possible since this could be a lifetime choice or at least a very real likelihood of over a decade. I wanted to be very thorough and take my sweet southern time to get this part right. I only had one chance at this. I was not going to mess that up. Alara then advised me to sit tight while the room adjusted to accommodate the next phase. My eyes perked up at that and then without a word, the room started zipping all around with pieces and parts flying around like I was the eye of a tornado. Nothing hit me thank goodness as everything seemed to mold around my presence.

The next thing I realized now, instead of a sofa; I was sitting on a medical table. There were scanners, lights, and thingamajigees that I had never seen before. When all the movement stopped it felt like I was in my local doctor's office. I even had the matching paper-thin white hospital garb that so attractively had my bare butt hanging out. I yelled, "what the hell? Alara smiled and said: Yes, this is my favorite part. Most everyone has an episode at this juncture. She laughed. I started to feel very exposed, and I am not really a modest person. She then approached me and softly stated: I will now leave you to my counterpart that will administer the test. He will not garner as much enjoyment out of this that I have and then she smiled. I do hope you scale to great heights, as I wish you the best in World Evolution Online. He will enter shortly.

Then a soft pop and she was nowhere to be seen or heard. So, I sat within my own thoughts for I honestly have no idea how long. One part of me was super excited for what could be on the horizon while the other side was like what the absolute hell did I just get myself into. I rarely went to the doctor to begin and never in a game. I guess I did understand why this seemed weird due to the situation but still. This better not be a Cell Block D Prison exam. I certainly have no desire to use references; Moon River or are you using two fingers? Lol I giggled but the fear was a real first world problem. No Dr. Jelly fingers for me today or any day.

CHAPTER FOUR

Testing

Just at that moment a man popped into existence ten feet in front of me without a sound. He managed a slight cough to get my attention and then said hello there Mitch. I jerked up at the voice and said wow okay hello. He looked amused but proceeded without waiting. He stated that his name was Dr. Tee and he will be with me through the next phase and assist me with character creation and the initial installation of my character in the game world. I nodded as this was understood and I could feel my gut start to churn with excitement like the morning of a race right before the start, That nervous feeling in the pit of your stomach. Whew I had not felt that in a while. Not since a more civilized time. Dr Tee then moved closer and said the physical exterior scan would take place now as he waved a glowing stick over me as I rotated around until every inch was covered which honestly took around 10-15 minutes. I did not realize I had that much to scan ha-ha. I just had to hit the movie quotes for at least one comment. I laughed and said: hey doc did you use two? He looked at me with both eyes, laughed, and said: now that Mr. Gillespie was a good one liner. I am impressed. Then just like that he was all stoic again and continued. I figured since now that my last name was used, I might want to watch my comments. This was not something I wanted to mess around with even though I just could not help myself. Once he seemed to be finished, he then raised an eyebrow and softly uttered something that sounded like, remarkably interesting. I asked what that was for and he just said nothing let us continue. He mentioned some of my past achievements in real life such as athletics, personal events, triathlons, global achievements, and work-related stuff to verify them and I answered them honestly. Dr Tee at that point asked me to lay back for the mental scanning portion of the phase. So, I did as he asked and lay backwards on the bed. A metal ring was placed on my head, and he asked me to close my eyes. When he started the machine, I could hear a hum like what I heard when the link was kickstarting in the stasis pod before I emerged here. Once again, I focused on calming techniques. I am not sure how long the machine was at work, but when the humming finally ceased, I opened my eyes. Dr Tee looked confused and stood there with his digital brow furrowed. I was worried at that point and started praying that I would not be offered the race of a rabbit from testing so low. He just sat there and said humm okay. I pleaded with him to tell me what that meant. All I could get out of him was that my results so far show remarkably interesting readings and that he will be paying close attention to my testing part. All I could do was gulp. He then asked a random question: Is Fletch your favorite movie? I was taken aback but quickly said no. I mean the 80's comedies are unlike any other, but it's not really in my top 10. He asked what was? I said, "well you can never go wrong with Revenge of the Nerds, Stripes, Caddyshack, Ghostbusters, or the Goonies; however, that science fiction movie with the laser swords was my favorite of all time. He laughed and said those are excellent choices, but have you ever looked at the similarities of those selections? I said humm this time and pondered his question. I knew the answer but wanted to think it through. I looked up and said looking into his eyes that each was about doing more than you were expected to and rising above what you were given on purpose or not. You just did what you needed to do and felt right and in doing so the characters in the movies made themselves somewhat of a hero to a degree. He stood there for a second as if he were pondering my response. Once again, he said interesting and then added that it was a perceptively astute response. I said thank you and then he continued.

Dr. Tee began speaking and stated now that the mental and physical scans are complete, the only testing part left to do is the in-depth exams. They will involve a multitude of scenarios or choices to help better define and narrow down what classes will serve you better and match your mindset. There is no wrong answer to anything as they are just choices. Different choices determine the different pathways and lengths the testing might route you too to extricate more refinement. As you no doubt learned earlier some players might finish in a minute while others might take hours. Pathways among pathways of exploration within these skill and aptitude tests are designed to give you the best options that you could be. So, in the spirit of that please take your time and respond as you normally would.

I knew the time had come when a couple of scans and tests would determine what my potential life would be for the next ten years. So much for a college degree and career day in high school. You know damn well a fire mage or tanky type holy warrior were not part of that line up during that show and tell. Lol Well hell let's get this shit rolling I muttered. Dr Tee nodded and said that you will now begin with a series of logical tests followed by quick response situations where your expedited responses and gut instincts will apply their trade. From there you will move to practical application testing in a virtual setting while being put into experiences to see how you respond. Possibly more. From the onset your decisions and choices determine how the testing proceeds. Good luck and do your best. I will see you on the other side. Please take a seat at this desk and access the desktop to begin. I will be here throughout the testing piece just like I am for everyone else during this phase.

So, I got up off the medical table and walked over with a glass of water in hand to the newly formed into existence desk and sat down. The prompts were already waiting on me. I stared at the screen and then began reading: Welcome Mitch Gillespie to the final testing of your character creation. Please verify your identity by inputting your date of birth and mother's family name. I was a little caught off guard by the mother's name part as I did not expect a security question you would see by trying to reset a password for an online banking account but whatever I decided to just go with it.

I inputted the information and as it was accepted, a new prompt arrived. Shall we begin testing? The first part will be a series of questions in which you will have options of multiple choice, essay responses, and yes or no. please click start when you are ready There will be a stop button at the lower left of the screen and you may cease any section at any time if you so choose. There is also no time limit. I took a deep breath and hit the start button.

CHAPTER FIVE

Testing Part 2

At first the questions seemed very simple, albeit random with yes and no answers like the question: Do you like puppets? I mean I didn't have anything against them and didn't dislike them, so I decided to hit yes. The questions kept on rolling in for what seemed like forever when the screen finally went blank and then vocalized that the yes and no portion was over. Now we were to proceed to the multiple-choice questions. I stopped for a second hoping that I had answered everything correctly in what had to have been 300 questions. I didn't know if I had taken a 3rd grade final exam or the FINRA Securities Series 6 & 7 exams to trade stocks. My brain hurt but I had to go on.

Next came the multiple-choice questions which also started out simple like what your favorite color or genre of music was. Quick and easy, I thought those were however they soon started upping the difficulty and began requiring some serious brain power that I wasn't sure I had. Plus, we still had the essay and virtual parts to go and no telling what else. Those continued for hours as it seemed and another 300-400 questions before this part too ended in a blank screen with a vocal prompt. How in the world would 120 million-ish people reasonably complete this stuff I thought as all of this is beyond my scope of understanding. Then I suppose many would just hit the stop button when enough was enough in their eyes. Two down and not sure how many to go!

I accepted the start of the essay portion and holy crap I could barely see straight. There is a reason the ACT or SAT were only four hours. This was absolutely insane. First, they seemed to be more on the business and logical reasoning perspective. Then it shifted to a personal moral compass type of questioning line. One question was would you kill your grandmother to free yourself from a cage and how would you if you did? I mean really who asks that sort of shit. That's some seriously morbid stuff. I just sat there staring into the screen wondering what the hell that was. Then after mowing through those personally morally objective questions, it shifted to all the usual subjects one would see in school. First it went to English, or I assume whatever language the person was from, then questions about history, social sciences like sociology, politics and civil scenarios. Then psychology, the sciences, and mathematics. Before I knew it, I was working out mathematical equations and scientific proofs that I hadn't seen in decades. So much of my mind wanted me to stop but I refused, knowing this was a one-shot deal.

I willed myself to persevere. Then it shifted to religion, theology, and a sprinkle of home economics. So now we are essaying about how to navigate the kitchen. Oh, dear sweet mother of all things holy I screamed internally. Thank goodness my mom taught me right I thought. With question after relentless question, I did my best to answer with detail until I finally got to the end of this part. That blank screen with the vocal recognition never sounded so good.

How long have I been at this? 20 hours, a full day, two days? No telling for sure. Wow they weren't kidding about how in depth it could be. I hoped I was doing alright considering the length it had taken so far. I got up to get some water even though I didn't feel thirsty but felt the need anyway. I gulped that glass of water down and felt at least a little better. Now I was hoping the question-and-answer session had finally ended. Or let's at least pray that it had. I sat back down and was joyfully rewarded with a new prompt: Are you ready to enter the virtual part of the assessments? Your questions are logged and the responses noted. Shall we proceed? Yes/No?

I couldn't hit that darn button fast enough. In that moment the world around me went vibrant with swirls of color. It was whipping around me like a silent cyclone absorbing all things close to me. A split second later I was standing in a desert oasis. The greenish colors of the palm tree leaves and the tan and brown hues from the trees and the sand assaulted my eyes after being confined to that testing room for so long. I had to shield them with my forearm until my eyes caught up with my surroundings. Then the newly felt dry wind of the desert whipped my little medical outfit like a flag flying in a thunderstorm. Wait a damn minute: I am still dressed in my darn paper thin white medical outfit while standing in a virtual desert!

It was hot and windy, and it felt like a warm piece of sandpaper was rubbing up against me. Not very pleasant to say the least. I was also barefooted. What the hell! A searing hotness hit my feet, and I began to hop back and forth. The game hates me and I am being punished was the first thing that popped into my head. So, I quickly and wittingly did the first thing that came into my mind. I took off the medical attire and went full nude up in this joint while I used the garb to make a jimmy rigged version of paper-thin shoes. Now here I am in the desert, naked, no idea where I am, with raggedy makeshift shoes. I guess it was trading one burn for the other and likely not my smartest idea but hey. I must be able to walk was my thought process. We will see how this plays out.

The first thing I did after trying my hand a being a shoemaker was to see about getting some form of shade made so that I could get out of the blistering sun. I could already feel my privates warming up and I was not so happy about the onslaught of charred skin approaching. I grabbed a rock that seemed to have some sort of angled edge and began beating the branches until they broke. Once that was done, I placed the group of branches into a tent-like formation and managed to tie them together at a few strategic points to keep them upright while allowing a small shallow entrance to escape the elements. I am sure as hell no boy scout and it was crude at best, but I was naked with only a rock and a bit of string left from the leftovers of my shoemaking adventures. It wouldn't hold well but hopefully enough for the sun to set. Luckily, I placed it where the wind was cut by the mass of trunks from the palm trees.

I plopped down on my butt and sighed. Then I laughed as I realized I had totally MacGyvered that shit. Who's da man! The Naked and Afraid show has nothing on this, I laughed. I sat there for what felt like about ten minutes to cool off and keep my privates from burning when I began hearing chirping sounds. At first, they seemed far away but then they kept getting louder and louder. Just effing great, I thought. The next minute there are two buzzard-like creatures about twenty yards in front of my pathetic tent slurping water from the oasis.

To claim they were buzzard-like was a friendly gesture to their species as they were clearly not from earth. They seemed to be about four feet in height with decent wing spans. They had three eyes with one directly in the center just above the mouth. The mouth, however, was not a typical beak of a bird as it had a frightening resemblance of a velociraptor's jaw. I honestly went rigid and I might have even peed a little, but I knew I had to do something soon.

They were utterly terrifying to look at. That would seriously hurt if either or both got a hold of me. I just stayed there remaining utterly quiet as they drank and squawked. For a hot minute I thought I might be in the clear but then one of them turned around and noticed me or maybe just the shaded spot but that didn't matter. What did matter to me was that suddenly it started tramping my way like it was on a mission. I quietly and slowly grabbed my rock and prepared myself for what was to come next. As soon as that horrifying snout breached the inside of my makeshift tent line, I smashed the rock into its jaw and face. It roared in pain but before it could even close its jaws, I had bashed it repeatedly.

Whatever it is called, the thing tried to snap at me, but I was fast enough to dodge its blow and came down with another crash. I then went all crazy on its ass. I took one hand and wrapped it around its neck and started slamming it on the ground from one side to another and soon it looked like a ping pong ball bouncing back and forth. I was covered in blood from the beating I had given it. Now that it was dead, I realized that I needed to use my new floppy weapon against its friend. I decided I needed to try the ole hammer throw approach by swinging it into the remaining bird. The other buzzard-like thing came at me in a rush and as it did, I gave him an introduction to his compadre. I took that dead bird and used it as a club until the other one stopped moving as well. I was not dying out here today.

CHAPTER SIX

Neanderthal

As I sat there panting for air, I realized that was something I did not expect when I woke up this morning in that rough make shit bed inside the housing units used prior to immersion. Different times call for different measures I suppose. My smile lasted but a brief time as I realized I still had blood all over me. The water was tempting but then I took a guess that something worse might be in there. Not something I wanted to tempt just yet. Somewhere in the back of my mind though I was developing a crazy idea. I decided to start tearing the meat and skin off the birds and set the portions on a few palm leaves that I could use as a wrap. When I was done, I took the skeletons and set them a short distance away as a possible deterrent from their kin or maybe other predators. I took some more time to remake my tent and then when I was finished, I wrapped the scraps in the palm leaves. I quickly darted into the water and washed myself as fast as I could and then I ran back to the tent until I was dry.

I sharpened a few branches into make-like spears and wedged them against the tent to act as the worst wooden palisade/ defensive structure you had ever seen. At least it was something. I waited until it was dark before I made my next move. I could see when I looked outside that the moon had cast a semi dim light upon the sandy ground and it was much cooler. That told me I could move if needed as I really wanted to find out what I needed to do next in this testing arena. It couldn't be made for me to just make a camp and chill. Something needed to be accomplished. There had to be a goal right.

Once night set in, I tied the palm leaf wrapped meat to my waist, grabbed a spear with one hand and instinctively I grabbed one of those beautiful skeletons with the other one and made my way west. For some reason I felt like I could use the skeleton for something. Thank goodness for the cooler temps as I could now walk swiftly without the heat seeping through the shoes I made. I walked for what seemed like hours until I noticed a small town about a mile or so ahead.

I could see a few torches and what looked like a wall. I am sure this was going to be entertaining as I was still butt naked. For better or worse it was about to get even more real. As I approached the wall I heard someone call out. I stopped immediately and did my best to remain calm. Two beings exited the gate and approached. They weren't human as they had four arms, but I could understand that they were speaking a form of broken English.

When they got to within twenty feet of me, they stopped, cocked their heads to the side, dropped their jaws, and then whispered to one another. I could barely make out what was said however the words naked and skeleton were mentioned. I quickly figured out that they were in no mood to even begin to understand why a naked looking bipedal with a bird skeleton and a spear stood outside their walls. In unison they lowered their spears into what looked like an attack stance. Then they charged.

Even twenty feet away, they erased the distance quickly. I had just enough time to sidestep the left spear and counter with a thrust of my own. I somehow landed a shallow hit into the guard's side, and I felt it sink into its flesh. The other guard attempted to flank me on the other side but by instinct I threw the skeleton into the guard's face. The bone carapace caused a gash along the face of the attacker, and he reared back to grab his face. As he attempted to bat the assaulting skinny bird's skeleton to the ground, it gave me time to send a heavy thrust of my spear into the unprotected neck of the fist guard. He seemed to be totally caught off kilter and utterly surprised that this naked man had just put a beatdown on him.

When I pulled back on the spear a spray of blood flew from his throat and as he grasped his throat, his legs gave way and he next crumbled to the ground gurgling bubbles of blood. Now it was one on one, and my skeleton assistant was a non-factor. The guard wiped the blood from his face and sneered. I looked at him ready to attack if needed. I said one sentence: I came in peace and you attacked without warning and that was not cool at all man. Once again, he repeated his actions earlier and disregarded me and rushed me.

This time I wasn't quite fast enough to avoid injury. Although I did manage to dodge most of the blow, the edge of his spear caught my outer arm and gave me a deep slice to deal with. As blood flowed down my arm and onto the sand, the guard smiled. It hurt like hell, but I had to focus so that I didn't let it distract me, especially now in this dire moment.

The guard lunged again but I was able to pivot and slam the butt of my spear against his head. As he faltered and took a step to right himself, I used the leverage of my spear to drive his weapon into the ground. At that moment I lashed out at the side of his knee with my leg, and you could hear the crunch as the full force of my weight took out his knee. Without being able to stabilize himself from being dazed, he hit the ground and then I grabbed his spear out of the sand and combined it with mine to have two weapons. I then drove them both into the gut of the guard who cried out in agony. I could tell it went deep into his stomach, and it was likely fatal. I went after his chest this time and landed two more thrusts into his chest. Now blood flowed freely from his front, and I knew he was done. As much as my inner teenager desired to seriously give this asshole a first-class teabag; my inner adult decided to refrain. I grabbed my skeleton and placed it on top of his chest as a calling card and said defiantly: this was completely unnecessary. Now you die.

As he finally died, I stood there catching my breath wondering why did that that have to happen. I was no threat and

I wasn't even given a chance to speak. I felt guilty about what I had been forced to do but in the end; it was their choice not mine. Once I looked up and took a step towards the village, the whole world went nuts. The swirls were back in another cyclone of mental assault. I tried to just stand still and weather the storm. I closed my eyes as to not get dizzy and as I stood there calmly the temperature and climate changed. I took a few deep breaths and then opened my eyes.

I was now in an open theatre arena much like you would see at any small outdoor stadium. The air was crisp and cool with just a slight breeze. On the stage stood Dr. Tee and adjacent to him looked like a table of drink and food. I was still naked and he appeared to realize this so with a snap of his fingers, I was clean and wearing what seemed to be basic pants, a shirt, and shoes. At least I was covered. I nodded and said thank you.

I asked what happened and he said that I had completed the virtual portion of the testing phase. Suddenly, a slight shimmer of force sent a wave out across the arena. Nothing was tossed or pushed over but you could feel the wave rippling my hair and clothing. Before I could ask what had happened, I looked at Dr. Tee. He shivered and looked like he was experiencing something when he looked at me and smiled. Now I didn't know if I had really finished the testing or if I was about to have a smackdown with the AI doctor.

When he spoke, I could tell something was different. His voice wasn't off per se really, but you could tell someone else was speaking as his pitch was a bit different and his tone seemed very interested in me. His volume dropped and he said to please approach. This is when everything changed.

CHAPTER SEVEN

Algorithm

He looked at me and said that he was Dr. Tee in a sense. He advised me that Dr. Tee is a digital entity that he created to assist with the testing phase to help him identify and locate anyone that would match the results he was looking for. I stood there confused and my silence proved how dumfounded I really was as he laughed. Dr. Tee said I can completely understand just how confusing this is so please allow me to explain as I need your help.

My real identity will remain unknown for now, but I am a programmer assigned to many parts of the game's upkeep and maintenance while the populous is inside its walls. I am inside the compound alive and well watching over the game as you all are inside. Will you listen to my proposal as I don't have much time? I said sure why not even though my mind was racing to understand why this was happening to me. Please tell me this isn't the matrix in real life. He said not that I am aware of.

Here is my problem so please pay attention as my time here is short. I scoured all test results looking for certain results, scores, skills, personality types, and potential so that I could narrow the case search down to one individual to help. You Mitch were determined to be that one soul in this game that has the ability and potential to help me right a wrong. I was still very confused. He raised his hands and said, "I know, I know, I know, I need to get to the point." I looked at him with a glare now and said yes you do.

He looked at me dead panned and said something was off about what this simulation is and why we are here. Something isn't right. There is no way it could have been developed this fast much less put into live go mode. He continued: As I was working on programming for certain parts of the gaming code, I realized that there were many things that didn't make sense. As the oddities started adding up, I took it upon myself to investigate.

I noticed things that were not right. It is hard to explain as I am still in the early stages of that investigation. I do know however that something is up and the only way to figure it all out was to have both the outside coding researched but also the internal game play. It can also give clues to what is going on and when those two are put together we should get a complete story in time. When I realized that, I created an algorithm for what type of individual I would need in game to help. I assisted with the testing development to mask this algorithm as a normal part of the testing phase when really it was my search for you. Inside the game I cannot do what needs to be done but you can.

Inside I am 3 things. My creation here administers the test. I can and will be a part time internal GM applying patches and updates. The main part I play is that I am a long forgotten dead dark god, Tikallnosis. I am a dark god of Undeath, Destruction, Chaos, and yes even a splash of Creation. The lore on my god avatar is just about forgotten however there is a way to kickstart a rebirth so to speak.

If you agree to assist me in finding out what is really happening here, I can offer you a path which no others can take. I will per the rules of the game offer you everything you would supposedly qualify for from your testing results here and now, however there will be a few character and race options that are one of a kind and there will be a potential divine chain quest in your quest log upon entering the game. Upon completing the first leg of the quest you will have some bonus choices due to you being my chosen. And to repeat yes, I said divine chain quest which is the highest rarity and gives the biggest rewards. I will cover those when we meet there unless you choose not to hear me out. I will offer you a quest that will instantly be uploaded into your quest log upon entry into the game.

There will be a torn down dilapidated church with a hidden cave not too terribly far from where you spawn into WEO. The cave currently doesn't exist in the world however it will generate upon reaching the area. Your quest log will automatically generate the cave upon reaching the area. Please just go there and hear me out as I cannot linger here. I look forward to discussing it all more when you reach the cave. Please at least allow me that much and I will make it more than worth your while. I nodded and said alright I can do that and then asked what now. He seemed to relax a little and said that now the AI version will resume the programs that it is designed for and will go through the character creation.

Before I go, he said I would ask that you proceed to the cave immediately as to not lose any progress for what I plan to enrich you with. I nodded and said I will keep that in mind. He said thank you and we will talk shortly. At that moment another shimmer of force appeared and just like that Dr. Tee the original was back.

The original Dr. Tee looked awkwardly and muttered to himself; now where was I. Oh yes you had very interesting test results and from which you will notice that you have many options for your class and race selection. It seems as if you have unlocked some very rare and unknown things as well. Would you like to proceed Mitch? I nodded and said yes, yes, sure thing; because after all that is why the testing and scans took place. Am I correct?

Even after saying that I could not get the recent conversation with the programmer out of my mind. It was distracting me so I decided to put it out of my mind for at least the timeframe I would dedicate to determining my class, skills, and race. So that is exactly what I decided to do. The questing in the future, the dropped bomb of something aloof, and supposed rewards will have to wait a few minutes longer. I cannot deny that I will hear him out if only to see what the rewards are. I mean who wouldn't want a divine quest chain? The rewards must be incredible; right?

As I turned my head back to the digital Dr. Tee; I confirmed the prompt to proceed and awaited the news. That became a complete let down as Dr. Tee furrowed his brow, looked at me confused, and then placed his virtual finger on his chin. He then muttered under his breath; now it was right here just a minute ago, how can that be? Upon hearing that a growing concern appeared on my face as I knew something was wrong. What did he just say, flashed in my mind.

Dr. Tee looked up from his pad and gave me a stare and looked as if he was dumbstruck. He then stated plainly: Well Mitch I could have sworn your results were right here ready to go over but for some reason it has an asterisk as it has an additional qualifier. It states that currently you qualify for one class only. Your only option is Classless. As far as skills and abilities go you also only have 1 selection instead of the customary allotment. You are Unskilled. It also clarifies that you are a non-ability designation. I have never seen this before Mitch. That is your only option, however the asterisk denotes that these issues are under review pending completion of additional information.

I stood there stunned and in utter disbelief. Then I considered what was said and it dawned on me what had just happened. Once that realization hit me, I became immediately pissed off beyond belief. That bastard of a developer hedged his bets to ensure I would do exactly what he wanted and seek him out. If I didn't go talk to him, I would be essentially unable to do anything in my new reality.

That son of a bitch! He comes to me for help and forces my hand. I was planning on doing his little quest anyway but now that ass just infuriated the one person that he needed help from. He would rest assuredly receive a profane laced mouthful from me when we talked.

It took everything I had to regain my senses and keep my anger under control. I looked at Dr. Tee fuming, but I flatly and coldly asked; what are my class options? He just said one word: Human. I said, "is that it? He looked again and said yes Mitch although there is an asterisk there as well, but you only have 1 choice to proceed with.

I sighed with an unsettling anger mixed with animosity at what I was just possibly screwed out of. Only one way to find out I suppose as I had no other option right now. I looked and said human it is. What now? Well now you will need to determine your physical appearance and then your final step is to create your player character's name. This name will be your identification within World Evolution Online. All my group had already decided on specific names and if there was duplicity we would use a surname. So, I vocalized my choice and verified. I placed a surname to make sure it took. Once that was complete, Dr. Tee advised me that the name was accepted, and I would now be known by Dookooze Darkbringer.

He then asked me: Do you accept or deny the race of human, unskilled, unclassed, and non-ability? I resigned myself to the answer and verified yes. Dr. Tee then said very well Mitch your selections have been selected and verified. You will now enter World Evolution Online at a predetermined spawn point. At least one of your designated contact list members will be in the same spot.

We here at World Evolution Online wish you the best in your journey here and we cannot wait to see what you can achieve. Mitch, please prepare for integration in 5, 4, 3, 2, 1, Enter! I just stood there wondering what the hell did I just get forced into. I am sure this is going to be an absolute hot mess. What choice did I have now? As he counted down past one, I felt my body expand into a million particles and then there was nothing. Everything went dark and quiet. The time seemed to stop and then suddenly, I materialized in a small grove with a few tents scattered around a campfire. Here I was at last. Time to get this show on the road.

CHAPTER EIGHT

Well Now Isn't This Cool

As I materialized into the game inside of the grove, I noticed people of a few different races milling about and I noticed name tags of players. They were in various tents talking with what I can only assume were the non-player characters of this world of better called NPCs. I decided to walk over and see what was going on and then suddenly, a prompt filled the bottom left side of my screen. I didn't know exactly what to expect with the quest system but now I knew so I decided to read it. Not like I had a choice anyway.

You have been offered a quest: Commune with the Forgotten God! Part one of the Divine Investigation. This is a unique Divine Level quest and has an unspecified number of parts.
Level Requirement: None
Rewards: Experience Points; Distinguished Points; Unlocking of Classes, Skills, Abilities, Class appropriate items and actions, and Races; Unknown?
Do you accept the quest? Yes/No

There was a mental prompt asking for my decision as I had been advised about that already before entry, I willed my answer and mentally said yes. It appeared that was all it took as the yes button glowed, and the quest then appeared to my right in the middle of a screen. That seemed simple enough. I figured I would try some other functions out before looking for anyone else.

I noticed to my bottom right that there was a small circle with some dots listed. From my experience with playing games all my life I quickly realized this was some form of a mapping system. The tents appeared to be shades of grey. The players appeared to be blue while the NPCs were of a purplish hue. Once again that seemed very straight forward and easy enough. I then willed myself to see my quest log. A second after I thought of it, a pop up entered a small portion of my screen and only one guest appeared. Obviously, it was the one I already accepted so there was no point in verifying it however it did ask if I wanted to set that as my primary quest. I selected yes and then immediately a goldish tint seemed to glow outside of the immediate area on my mini map.

I wanted my map to enlarge the zone and without prompting anything else it encompassed a larger part of my visual screen and in the distance, I could see a faint golden circle. I knew that to be the vicinity that the quest would be located. It didn't seem too terribly far and from my estimation it would be about a 15-20-minute journey there on foot. I did notice some other dots in different colors, but I decided to figure that out later.

The location did seem to be a bit sketchy as it looked like it was on a mountain covered by trees. There wasn't any sort of tracking arrow or line like some MMO or single player games. It was a small let down but considering it was a new reality for the next decade or so, I honestly really wasn't even considering it to be an option. So, to have a vicinity marker was a huge dynamic to help players complete stuff. There was no point in completely disappointing myself by looking at my character sheet, so I avoided that for now.

I willed my inventory and a series of slots appeared in front of me and of course it was empty. I told myself that I need to figure out a way to reduce the time that took and the visibility of that as that could be distracting in a hastened time of need. So, map-check, quest log-check, inventory-check. I then focused on the top left of the screen that showed a picture of me with three bars listed. One was greyed out but was labeled as Energy. The other two appeared to be Stamina and Health.

As I glanced at them, my mouth dropped. Are you shitting me I yelled? Not only did this dude lock me out of my classes and everything else but he only allowed me a single point of stamina and health each. I would literally die if the wind blew too hard. What the hell! With only one stamina I would have to slowly walk because I certainly can't run with that abysmal number. That douche pulled no punches in forcing me into his clutches, did he? There was nothing I could do about it now, but you can be damn certain I will address it very shortly. I decided that I will need to research more later when I had a real character sheet and not this barren description I had now. Plus, I would need to try it on skills, actions, etc. Once I had them of course. I am sure there was a ton I was missing but I would get there in time.

Next on the quick agenda was to search for any contacts that might be nearby. I once again willed up my thoughts of a contact screen. As determined earlier with the other functions, a list of about 80-90 player names popped up on my screen interface. I reached up to it with my hands and sure enough as I did so the list rotated up and down like a rolodex. Some names were not lit up which means that they apparently were not online while others were lit up in white. I could see about 90% of the names we had agreed upon and so that was good. There would be a lot more names that I would need to add due to extended family's trees but that would come later.

Next to each name was their level, race, class, location, and three methods of contact: Email, Private Message, or video Chat. I scrolled up to my name to identify where I was and noticed that I was in a place called, Inkwood Region Upper Forrest Camp. Okay so I now had a reference point to try and locate others. I scrolled the list for anyone that was at least in Inkwood. After a few short seconds I found my son. Luckily enough he was in the same camp and off to the west a bit. His typical gamer name of Jaceberlen was all I needed to see. I enlarged my screen and the question about what the orange-colored dots meant had now been answered. It was my contact list.

Once I focused on his dot, a name appeared albeit small.

It showed his name but no other initial details. I would have to see if I could discern more up close. I went to tap the video feature and the next thing I knew was dialing like a cell phone. A face answered and I laughed because it was close to his real face. I mean don't get me wrong; he had longer brown hair and pointy ears with a more chiseled jawline, so I figure he went with his usual High Elf race. I could also read that he in fact was a Paladin although the specifics were unclear. So far pretty par for the course with him. I was excited to see how all his testing stuff went but for starters I told him that I was in the camp and to please come meet me as I needed his help and would explain when he got there. He said no worries as he was just starting a quest and would be right there.

As I was waiting for Jaceberlen to arrive I took this time to soak up my surroundings finally. Every sensory type was sharp as I could not only smell the grass like it was freshly mowed, but I could taste the humidity in the air mixed with the earth. Obviously not overpowering but faint. Just on the edge of your taste buds. My eyes were sharp and I could see clearly for about 100 yards. In the real world I wore glasses and had them since I was a teenager, but here I no longer needed them. It was insane and I loved it.

The wind blew softly against my skin, and I could feel the beginning of goose bumps forming. It gave me a slight shiver, but it honestly felt great. The temp was not cold or hot but mild as one would think a forested area might be. The grass felt like it was yielding to my will with every step. Soft yet firm. The shades of all the earth tones really set the tone for the area we were in. This was so extremely lifelike. I could not believe it. I can only imagine what the rest of the zones would be like as this unfolds.

I reached down and placed my hand on the damp earth. My palm pressed into the ground for a quick moment then it hardened and stopped my progress. It was cool to touch, and the blades of grass tickled my fingers as I grazed them. Amazing was the first thing that I thought. This adventure could be truly amazing if I can get my shit unlocked and be something other than a glorified NPC at this point. As my son would be here in a second, I took a quick moment to talk to the three NPCs people that were manning the tents.

One guy's name was Fred and only Fred. He gave me a typical fetch quest to assist in picking mushrooms for food. The next person was a lady with white hair named Darlene that said I should see about finding some wood for a fire. The third person was a Corporal White. Okay so he was the first with two words attached to a name. He also gave me a clue quest to search the surrounding area for his missing Private. Well, I suppose there are three NPCs and three fetch-like quests. I am not surprised considering they must introduce a lot of non-gaming joes to a gaming simulation that would likely have no idea what any of this meant.

As a lifelong gamer this was about as simple of a start as you could imagine. The rewards appeared to be some small experience points and some basic gear and rations. The usual starter items so I accepted all without any hesitation and I moved on to wait at the edge of the camp from which Jaceberlen was approaching. We would tackle those quests after the so-called meeting.

I saw my son approach from the edge of the woods. He was a little taller than in real life and outside of the obvious Elven features he appeared to be a little leaner. He walked up to me, stopped, seemed to have a wildly curious look on his face and then said: dad what the hell is going on with your character? You're basically nothing. Did you bomb the testing or get in trouble somehow? I sighed and looked at him. I said no to the first and the jury is still out on the second part. I then very quietly touched on the major parts of my discussion with the programmer however I left out the parts that I wasn't sure needed to be shared just yet. I knew that he would be a part of whatever I would be a part of, but I figured I would let the anonymous programmer decide what to share with him. I told him about my one point of health and stamina due to forcing me to meet this god and my boy just facepalmed himself and laughed. Only you would crash a game on the first day. This could be an utter failure or something very world shifting. I agreed and we decided to set out.

CHAPTER NINE

Discovery Time

Upon looking at him more closely, I visualized inspecting him. Once I did that, I could see more of his character sheet.

Name: Jaceberlen
Race: High Elf
Class: Deliverance Paladin (which appeared to be the pissed off damage dealing type)
Level: One

That was all that I could see from my initial inspection so I wasn't sure what else could ever be available to discern without consent. He wielded a crude iron two-handed sword, wore a rickety iron chain shirt, boxer shorts, and a pair of cloth boots that looked like a salvage job. I asked him if he was waiting for a brothel or just getting gear from question or loot. He laughed and asked if I liked the look. I smiled and said totally. He advised me that the drops were minimal as expected but he felt he could at least get a full set of clothing and armor although it would be crude at best. Hell, it is better than a wanna be NPC like me. He concurred with a laugh.

We asked each other if any quests could be shared so I attempted to will my current quests up and tried to mentally share with my son. I guessed he already had them as none of the fetch quests synced. I tried to share my Divine quest, but I received an error message. It told me that this quest can only be issued by a higher power and that it was unique in nature. Well, I was hoping he could share in the wealth but maybe I can still leverage my anger to get something for him. I asked If he was ready and he nodded. Since he was going to be my bodyguard, I needed him to travel at my snail pace.

For the next ten to fifteen minutes during the slow walk we discussed the scanning and testing phases comparing notes. He seemed to also take a good while on the computer part of the testing. Not as long or in depth as me but still a considerable timeframe. He laughed and told me he was griping to his version of Dr. Tee about the length of time everything was taking but the good ole doctor just nodded and said okay. He was extremely dry in my son's opinion.

The boy's virtual part however was completely different as he was placed in a cave and had to identify things to help him get out. He discovered and notated ores and made a makeshift breastplate with a few pieces of wood and a strap of leather from a broken shield. He then had to bum rush two rat creatures that were watching the exit to the cave. After he had slain them and reached daylight, he morphed back to the theatre arena like I had.

He looked at me when he saw my eyebrows raised and asked me how much different mine was due to my surprised look. I then went into my ordeal in detail, and he just looked at me in amazement. The next words he said were: so, let me get this straight; you were by your own choice naked in a desert carrying around a dead veloci-buzzard thingy skeleton after you swung it around beating its brother to death with it? Then you took on two armed guards with one of the skeletons and a spear but still naked and flung your little boney companion at the face of one of them? And you survived? Dude, that's seriously savage. Dad, I love you but that is some cold murderous stuff right there. It's awesome. I then briefly touched on what happened afterwards and how pissed I am over it. He agreed and said that what he did was pretty crappy, but he guessed that the guy had to make sure I came. I could see that but the way he went about it was wrong. He also agreed.

As we approached the proximity of the golden circle we had

to veer off the pathway into the woods. It seemed we were still about three or four minutes from the area in question, but we could already tell the woods were looking to hide something. At first it just seemed like an ordinary forest. Once we got off the path and headed west that all changed. Suddenly, the trees were of a darker tint, and the leaves were largely trying to shade us from seeing its secrets. The roots were broader and windier, and we started having trouble getting around them. We both began to feel as if we were being watched by something just out of our sight.

Paul, my son, which I guess I need to start calling him by his character name unless otherwise needed, decided to take a stab at being a smartass and said: Aww be careful over there, Big Spoon as we can't have you dying by mosquito bites. Now is not the time you Jackwagon, was my quick response. I laughed but his statement was spot on considering my health bar, but we had no idea if mosquitos were even in this game. I really hope not as I despise those things. Growing up in the south was all you could do to avoid them. My blood was like Sweet Meat to those bad boys. Anyway, we continued to slowly navigate the terrain for a minute or two until we saw a clearing in the trees. I had expected to see a run-down church but wow! The only thing that even resembled a church was a half torn down archway, a few cobbled stones that I can only assume was the flooring, and one side of a building that is half decayed with rot and crumbled stone. The forest had certainly tried to take back the area all around this little gem of creation but for some reason the grass and roots were avoiding this building like the plague.

As we slowly crouched to take in our surroundings, we noticed that it was eerily quiet in the clearing. It looked as if the forest would not come an inch closer than it already was to the old building. Well, I said; this is our spot and I am sure we are walking into a mess, but this is the only way we can find out what is going on and I can get my character back from being hijacked. We looked around and decided to approach from the archway as there really wasn't much of a hidden advantage point for anything due to the degradation of the building.

So, we approached slowly and we made our way to the building. I knew from the quest description that once I was here, I would find a hidden door or cave entrance, so I advised Jaceberlen of what was needed and we both began to focus on searching. We both continued to search for a few minutes when suddenly, I saw a glowing light up against a rockface right behind the back of the church. It was something for sure and when we approached it, we both hesitated, scared at what might happen next.

I took the next small and light step forward to inspect the area but as if it was on cue, my foot somehow sunk slightly into the ground and we heard an audible click. Oh, shit were the next words said as we both rolled to each side of the rock. We were expecting a trap or an explosion that would surely send me to an instant death with my one hit point; however, nothing blew up. No poison darts, spikes, or monster ambushes. All that came next was the grinding of stone on stone as a small pathway inside of a newly visibly cave opened before us.

Without even a second glace my son, Jaceberlen looked at me and said, don't look at me like that as I am not going first. This quest is all you Mr. I got hijacked by a GM. He bowed his head and swung his arm out as if to say age before beauty. I just shook my head and whispered, "gee thanks", but do you happen to have a torch? He just kind of looked at me funny while avoiding my eyes like a puppy in trouble and said, oops my bad. I said, "if I die, I die and it's all your fault bodyguard". I took the first step towards the many uncertainties that were in front of us. As I slowly tried to walk along the edge of the cave wall quietly, I couldn't help but wonder what all of this was about. Why me of all people as I am nobody special. I am just your typical husband, father, boss, friend, etc. There are likely a million more qualified people than me for the effort that this GM has put me through to secure this meeting. Well, whatever it is he will hear some upcoming attitude about his actions and methods of procurement.

It seemed like we walked for about 40-60 meters when I could start to see a faint greenish-black glow from up around the corner. I reached out for Jaceberlen's chest behind me and tapped him to stop. As the shuffle of our feet went quiet, he peeked around my shoulder to catch a glimpse of the hue. He looked at me and asked if I was sure that I wanted to do this? I said no but there really isn't a choice for me, is there? Besides, I have my boy here and there is nothing we can't do. Don't ever forget that. Jaceberlen smiled, nodded, and then finally shrugged and I knew the moment was now. I took a deep breath, inhaled the stale air that tasted like gym clothes, then I exhaled to harden my resolve as we moved forward. I lifted my chin and was ready to hear what all the commotion was about.

I wonder what would happen if I refused him. I should probably hear what he has to say first. At that moment we entered what appeared to be some sort of ancient burial room with a black obsidian altar in the middle radiating a smoky light greenish-black aura. Jaceberlen stopped immediately and whispered; dad, are you sure this is worth it? This is likely not a game anymore. I contemplated both remarks and he had a point. This wasn't like some run of the mill game with monitors, virtual reality headsets, or receptors attached. This was as real as our bodies could make it. Something the world hasn't really seen much of. I admit I was scared but I knew I had to get my character unlocked and if this was as monumental as I was hoping; we would be greatly rewarded for doing this.

As soon as we approached the altar, I felt the familiar wave of force that I had felt in the theatre arena after completing the virtual assessments of my testing. Jaceberlen, however, was not familiar with the sensation and took a few steps back. I looked back at him and nodded to come closer. Then I noticed his eyes got a little wider and he seemed to freeze in place horrified. His hand instinctively reached for the pommel of his sword, but I held up my hands to stop him. I mouthed to him: Let's see how this plays out. He reluctantly nodded and placed his arms back near his sides.

When I turned around to face the altar, I quickly understood my son's protectiveness. I was facing what appeared to be a 15-

foot undead divine creature wearing black and gold laced robes with a crown that radiated an aura that I couldn't even begin to comprehend. It permeated uneasiness and a will to control all. It took everything I had to muster up the words to remind him he was an asshole. I rose up to look him square in the eye and angrily yelled: Hey dickhead I am here for your meeting that you obviously made sure I came too so knock that shit off and talk to me before I use the one point of stamina you gave me to run up and shove my foot up your ass!

For a brief second, it seemed as if he was glowering at me. I said no, no, no sassy pants you don't get to do that crap after the stunt you pulled with my character. You forced me to come here with no health as a glorified NPC so quit with the aura and the foreboding look of death. Ironically, he laughed in a low echoey voice and said very well Mitch. It was kind of an awkward look coming from a 15-foot undead skeleton. He then proceeded to tell me that while in this form he is the long forgotten ancient god called, Tikallnosis. I remembered the name mentioned from our previous meeting, but it still was a bit different to see it in person. I figured I could ponder on that later and wanted to get straight to the point.

Okay man now can you please explain why the hell you pulled a hijack on my character and why all of this is so important? He honestly looked defensive or as much as a skeleton could really look with any emotion and asked why my son was there? It took me by surprise but then it came to me that they have our family contacts and profiles, so it would likely be very easy for him to know who ever person's character's name is so I got over my shock and responded.

Well first you left me with one hit point, and I needed a guard to help me get here. Secondly, he is my right hand and anything I encounter in this game he will be right alongside me. Don't worry, I didn't tell him much as I decided to let you disclose what you felt appropriate, but I won't hide anything from him. Lastly, I figured I needed someone I fully trust that is also a gamer like me.

Tikallnosis seemed to ponder that and after a few tense moments said that he understood and that he would disclose what he could to him. The rest is for you. I said fair enough and Jaceberlen came to stand right beside me. I then asked to have my character unlocked. Tikallnosis just said okay, but hear me out first and yes, I know I did you dirty at the start, but I needed to guarantee that you would come. My apologies.

I smirked and informed him that all he really had to do was ask and I would likely have come. Please get on with this. Tikallnosis looked at me, lowered his skull, then said okay. Tikallnosis began with going back over what he had discovered during the programming phase when he would come across periodical anomalies. At first, they seemed random, however as more were discovered, he noticed a hidden pattern to them. The more he looked the more he found until the point that he was convinced something was not right. None of the coding seemed to fit or even more so went against the vision of the simulation.

He knew that someone very smart had hidden the code so he wasn't sure if he could trust anyone within game development. He decided to keep investigating until he discovered enough that he could put a story together. This is where the theory of my character came into play, he said. As he kept finding stuff, he discovered that important fragments of the code were data files that were somehow stored away as high-level code within the game itself.

He continued, even as a GM I could not openly seek those codes out as it would tip my hand as they were coded as high-level NPCs as well as certain dungeon or raid bosses. He added again, I am not allowed to interfere with any of that code unless I have a way in. It is highly encrypted on my side. Now if certain players were to slay these said entities, then it would create a small gap in their firewalls from the inside. As soon as they are killed, I will have a few seconds to slip through the encryption and steal the data files before it seals itself. Between my efforts on the outside and your efforts on the inside, we can finally determine what is going on. Mitch, or AKA Dookooze, I cannot tell you enough how important this is. Something is not right with the simulation, and I believe it has a sinister ulterior motive, but I just can't figure it out yet. I need your help. Humanity could be at stake. Someone on the outside is pulling hidden strings and we need to find them.

I cannot trust anyone out here but there I must place my faith in you. My son and I sat slack jawed for a moment before we both looked at each other. Jaceberlen just uttered what the nut sack did you get us into. I just wanted to live and level in the game like we would normally do. I didn't expect this bomb to drop. I had to agree with him, and I just said son; you can't say it won't be epic, and the experience will hopefully be sweet. I need you man at my side if I am going to do this. Are you with me? Zach smiled and said of course, till the end and plus, this could be some intense stuff, so I am right here with you.

I looked up at Tikallnosis and asked, why me man? There must be better options out there. Tikallnosis took a second and then began. He started off by describing how he discovered the data files as bosses and NPCs. He realized that any hard-core gamer could kill most of them, but he needed a different attitude and a deeper approach. He then went into how he determined the various skills and traits that would be ideal in one person to help him with all the possible obstacles he would need.

The testing questions and scenarios were meant to reduce candidates and help identify potential people that met most if not all the skills and traits needed. First it was the leadership experience, then the athletic background throughout a person's lifetime being ingrained into a habit, then academics, the personality to influence, someone that wouldn't fly off the handle or react without thought, but pull the ruthless trigger when needed, and finally someone that had a future to fight for.

From your file you proactively recruited your family and friends to your home and created a compound. Most people across the globe were not that way but you protected all whom you care about. I need that. Humanity and your future outside of the game need that kind of forethought.

CHAPTER TEN

Acceptance

I stood there stunned and thought well shit; didn't he just whisper sweet nothings my way to sway me. Dammit. I looked again at Jaceberlen. Well Champ, here we go. I glanced back at Tikallnosis and said there are 2 things. What now and what about my character? Tikallnosis seemed to visibly ease with what appeared to by my acceptance to assist him in this global secret that we had to uncover. He commented that we still have much to go over but first I would still need to accept my chain quests and that he would share it with my son.

Nobody else for now can know the magnitude of the situation. To everyone else it will just be random quests to take out bosses, and certain high-level NPCs. Depending on the nature of what is needed you will have the ability to offer quests to other Earthen, AKA players, if you choose but it will be an altered description. When you need to contact me, we will do so in this form as my GM form is tracked. In your character contacts you will see a prayer button. Click that preferably at an altar devoted to me but anywhere will suffice to contact me. Nobody will hear our conversations, nonetheless. An altar is more secure though so that is a priority. You will be able to create them. If I need to contact, you then you will receive a prompt summoning me. I nodded with acknowledgement.

We will handle your character last as it will likely take the most time and I will give you some insight into things when we do. However, before anything your boy needs to get some damn pants on. Those He-Man boxers ae just too much champ. I don't care if you're muscular or not; Astral Elf chicken legs are not what I want to see right now. Please cover yourself as soon as possible. Jaceberlen looked almost offended then laughed and said, hey, now I am trying to pick up my gear as I quest so I don't have to buy any, but fine I will see if I can loot any.

The next item on the agenda is that once we start attacking the encrypted NPCs you will begin being noticed. We need you to gather your strength, unite your family and friends, build up your forces, and solidify your defenses. I have found a location of an isolated small town that could use a new leader to rebuild it and grow it into a formidable city. Grow, build, establish trade, and make it your home. I think you are up for the task regarding that. It is run by a bandit gang currently that is terrorizing the local populace. Their leader is also the first NPC we need to take out as he is an encrypted file holder.

That got my attention if nothing else did. I just wanted to verify: so, is there a cultivation and city development ability in this game? Tikallnosis nodded and said it is extremely rare to qualify for, but it is one or your abilities. That took me by surprise as I literally had no idea up to that point what anything regarding my character would look like. Now I knew this was a possibility for me to rule a city and I immediately was stoked. I couldn't wait for what else there was.

Tikallnosis next words out of his mouth brought me back into focus; As I will communicate with you in this form, it would conceivably make sense for you to be a champion of my faith. It is considered a dark religion and widely thought of as unnatural although it is not inherently so nor evil. Many might have a negative modifier to your character upon knowing this. Others might flock to your cause, and some might be let's say unsavory. Use your judgement and navigate your diplomatic ties and resources with caution. You will possibly have to put in extra effort to win some groups or people over. I will do my best to mitigate this through the unlocking of your character but ultimately the choice is yours. Does that make sense to you? I won't lie as it might be a steep challenge.

From being a lifelong gamer, I knew that some games had a negative stigma towards undead or anything related to being against the natural order of things. I can deal with that, if need be, I said and yes, I fully understand. Tikallnosis relaxed again as it seemed he was one step closer to obtaining his internal chess piece. He then said; Now you know what is at stake and what is needed. Will you agree to help and be my champion? If what he was saying is true, then how can I not regardless of the peril. I mean if I was immortal then sure but what if someone caught wind and deleted me from the server? I couldn't really worry about that. I knew what needed to be done so I looked up at Tikallnosis and told him I will do my part if he does his.

Well done and a wise choice the deity said. More importantly he said thank you as I know this is not what you had planned. As for you Paul, will you accept the quest and help your dad potentially save humanity? If you decide to become part of my faith it will ultimately alter your character. You essentially would become a dark version of what you already are. You would lose some abilities while gaining others in a darker form. Will you assist me too? My son looked up at me, whispered like father like son and then turned to Tikallnosis and said yes. The next thing that happened was apparently my son got the quest chain too.

Jaceberlen you have assisted with a hidden chain quest: Commune with the Forgotten God! Part one of the Divine Investigation. This is a unique Divine Level quest and has an unspecified number of parts. Since you have assisted with the completion of this part you will be rewarded accordingly and grandfathered into the quest line.

Level Requirement: None
Rewards: Expcrience Points; Distinguished Points; Alteration of deity from Cos (Goddess of Light and Detection) to Tikallnosis (God of Undeath, Darkness, and Chaos), Loss of Light-based skills, abilities, and spells, Adoption of Dark based skills, abilities,

and spells, class change from Paladin to the new Legendary class, Night Paladin, and possible new class path options.
Do you accept the quest? Yes/No

Jaceberlen's eyes widened a little as he read the quest prompt. He took a few minutes to read through everything and then everything changed with him. First a golden spark flashed above him. Then his demeanor took on a darker glint, his armor darkened, and a slight dark aura showed from below his feet, and I could feel a slight invigorating feeling. I decided to inspect him again.

Name: Jaceberlen
Race: Astral Elf
Class: Night Paladin (Shadow Vengeance Vow)
Level: Two

Once again that was all I could read about his description, but he will be giving me the scoop when this is completed. He looked at me and smiled. The only words out of his mouth were crap! Dad, I won't take away your experience, and I can't wait for us to compare notes, but this looks awesome. Then he faced Tikallnosis and said thank you. Tikallnosis nodded and said no thank you Jaceberlen. Your dad will need your help.

CHAPTER ELEVEN

My Turn

Tikallnosis then looked over to me. Now I believe we need to finish your character. We have a tough and dangerous road. I have faith in you Mitch, or should I say Dookooze. Are you ready? I was admittingly super excited now after seeing what happened to Jaceberlen. I said yes and then it finally came upon me like a tidal wave.

You have completed the quest: Commune with the Forgotten God! Part one of the Divine Investigation. This is a unique Divine Level quest and has an unspecified number of parts.
Level Requirement: None
Rewards: Experience Point 750; Distinguished Points 100, Unlocking of Classes, Skills, Abilities, Class appropriate items and actions (delayed until character creation), and Races; Unknown? (delayed until character creation)

Beginning character creation: First we will start with class options. Per your testing results you have unlocked a total of 217 out of the possible 230 class options. A few of these are hidden and extremely rare. You have also unlocked 1 Legendary class option and 3 Mythical options. Would you like to review all your class options now? Yes/No? I didn't hesitate to select yes. What a data overload.

Suddenly, a scrolling text of class designations appeared in the forefront of my interface with description links to all of them. Thankfully it allowed me to sort by rarity. I decided to quickly glance over the commons to see if there was anything that stood out. I started with the common classes, and my query populated 91 class options. As I glanced through them briefly it was as expected, the normal run of the mill classes like rogue, base fighter, and mage. I quickly dismissed those considering there were still 126 options to go. As I continued to scale up the rarity column I sorted through the 63 uncommon, 38 rare, and 21 very rare. Some seemed cool, but they just didn't feel right. That left the 4 remaining options. Next, I brought up the legendary option and 1 class appeared. Now it was time to focus.

Class Option: Defender
Rarity: Legendary
Base Description: A warrior who uses their shield for both attack and defense
Primary Attribute: Strength
Proficiencies: All armor, shields, simple and martial weapons
For a deeper inspection please click here

I immediately knew this wasn't for me as I am not normally a fan of sword and board playstyle or in this case a board and board play type. I decided to go ahead and take a stab to see what the Mythical tab had in store. I chose it and selected sort.

Then the three remaining options appeared. I just started at my internal interface all wide eyed. These options were listed in this order.

Class Option: Night Blade
Rarity: Mythical
Base Description: Part Spellcaster/Part Warrior and complete terror on the battlefield by wielding spells that sap hardiness while inflicting damaging poison effects.
Primary Attribute: Strength and Charisma
Proficiencies: Light and medium armor, simple weapons, battle

axes, great axes, great swords, longswords
For a deeper inspection please click here.

Class Option: Nightclad
Rarity: Mythical
Base Description: A genius inventor who taps into the realm of night and death to create mechanical armor and creations that horrify their enemies.
Primary Attribute: Intelligence
Proficiencies: All armor, shields, and simple weapons
For a deeper inspection please click here.

And finally, the last option.

Class Option: Moon Cleric
Rarity: Mythical
Base Description: A cleric that possesses the power of the moonlight to empower and heal while consuming the night to cast devastating spells and summon undead hordes upon their enemies
Primary Attribute: Wisdom and Charisma
Proficiencies: Light and medium armor, shields, simple weapons
For a deeper inspection please click here.

So, there we have it. These three options were amazing, and I can only imagine what Jaceberlen would say. As I looked over them, I felt as if I was doing them an injustice if I didn't read them more clearly although I already had a solid idea on what I was going to choose. So, I clicked on each one.

The Night Blade is a dark and very powerful spell sword who not only has an ongoing health sap but also can utilize a poison affliction damage over time effect at the same time. That is one bad combination, and I can only imagine what specializations there would be.

The Nightclad is very interesting as it seems to meld artificing and crafting into a juggernaut creator. Just imagine horrific suits of mechanical armor charging at an enemy. As cool as that is I want more from my character than that especially considering the task that is laid before me. I just don't see that class as being the best choice, so I dismissed that one.

The moon cleric on the other hand is something that intrigues me greatly. I decided to really take a deep dive here. As I hit on more of the class details, I immediately liked what I saw. In most of my games I have played either a summoner or a cleric, so to be able to possibly achieve both in one class certainly had my attention. It seems as if my light spells are limited but I could still cast healing spells to a degree so that was a plus. The initial listing shows that for level one I would gain a single targeted Heal spell that will do 8+skill level points of healing with a range of 20 meters plus a single targeted attack spell called Necrotic Ray that will do 10+skill level points of death damage. That also has a range of 20 meters. The allotment of 3 cantrips were also included from a list which is custom for a cleric class. The cantrips use minimal energy so they can be cast more repeatedly if need be although they were generally weaker. Certainly not bad for level 1.

As I took a last glance at the Night Blade. I had to concede the point that it was a bad ass class. It seemed to be a non-tank type fighter that focused on crowd control and burst damage output. That means that it is a damage focused warrior and not an attention or aggro seeker. As cool as that sounds, I just can't take my eyes away from the Moon Cleric. If I think about what the task is before me that includes building up a force, leading, and defending our own, it just makes more sense to go the Moon Cleric route.

So, with the last of my hesitations I selected Moon Cleric. The system asked for confirmation. Do you wish to select Moon Cleric as your base class? Yes/No? Please remember that this selection is final and cannot be altered. I selected yes and then a tingling sensation spread all over me. The next prompt appeared stating that it was now time to select a race. This was another monumental decision as I needed to find one that complimented my class.

Dookooze Darkbringer below you are the complete list of

races that you have qualified for. There are 111 options shown below and this will include all races, subraces, and hybrid races that you meet the testing qualifications for. They may be sorted by rarity if you choose. Please read thoroughly and select your option. This cannot be reset or changed as this decision is final. All races have the potential to evolve given specific hidden parameters though. I decided to take the same approach as I had done with the classes and sort by rarity starting with the common type.

This list contained roughly 35 or so races that were standard for any game a person would log into. Humans, Elves, Half-Orcs, Gnomes, and plus many others were all listed. I have a good idea of what they represent and I wasn't interested. Once I hit the uncommon list the choice selection got much larger with a total of 54. This included Kitsunes, Leonins, Half Giants, and the likes. I read through them briefly and a couple sounded decent, so I logged them into the back of my mind as I moved on.

Next came the rare options. This had a total of 20 listings. Drow Royals, Water Elfs, and even a rarer type of Kobold was listed here. Interesting indeed but nothing really stood out here. The Very Rare options only came up with 1 option, but it was my first look at a hybrid race. I read it as half Vampire and half Dragonborn. I looked at it, and I tried to even conceive what this would look like. Honestly a dragon vampire was a scary ass thought. Wow! I made a mental note to really consider this hybrid.

If my math was correct, then I had one option left to consider so I selected both the Legendary and Mythical options and selected them. Thankfully my math held true and 1 option populated. It was very interesting to say the least, but I was initially taken aback by the one I had just read. I needed to read this one to see why it was also labeled Mythical just like my class was. It was a half Darkened Aasimar and half Shadar-Kai.

The Aasimar were of a celestial bloodline that were humanoid as I had heard of them before. They mostly follow the benevolent route but not always and not evil except for the rarest of situations. That is good as evil is not what I was going for. Naturally they are a beautiful race and if you add darkened features which align them more with a shadowy feel, then I can only imagine how they look. The Shadar-Kai on the other hand are a race of elves from the shadow regions. They seem to exist somehow between the realms of life and death. Interesting for sure. From a class standpoint this choice seems to match what I will be in a seamless manner. I decided to click on the link to see the pros and cons of this class.

As the link opened it stated, as a being of two blended races you will receive a portion of both pros and cons. Below you will see what this blended being will obtain if selected.

Race: Half-Aasimar/Half-Shedar-Kai
Description: As an offspring of darkened humanoid creatures from both the Celestial and Elvin bloodlines you have made your way onto the material plane from the shadows to forge a path of your choosing. Both races resemble typical humanoid creatures but with potential elven or celestial features that are a bit off from your typical kin. You do meet the prerequisites for both the Elf and Aasimar subset.
Attribute Bonus: +2 Wisdom, +2 Charisma, -2 Hardiness, +1 attribute point to place where you choose. Due to your unique race, with each level increase you will receive +1 Wisdom and +1 to Charisma along with any standard increases.
Size: Medium
Speed: Normal
Darkvision. You can see in dim light within 60 feet of you as if it were bright light, and in darkness as if it were dim light. You discern colors in that darkness only as shades of gray.
Keen Senses. You have proficiency and +2 bonus in Diplomacy and Perception skills.
Necrotic Resistance. You have resistance to necrotic damage, charming, and sleep affects.
Night Cloud: Once per day you may cast this spell centered around a targeted point within 60 meters. This spell emits a

perpetual mass of spherical darkness surrounding your targeted point. The distance emitted will equal in meters to your character level plus skill level. Enemies within this darkness are blinded and considered flat footed. Night Cloud can dispel any light spell within the same area of equal or lower level. This spell can be negated by a higher-level magic spell.

Well now that was something to read. I was not a fan of having my Hardiness reduced but I had to admit that the other stat bonuses outweighed the con. It would seem this hybrid is tailor made for a shadowy type of cleric. I was trying not to salivate. I glanced again at the vampiric dragonborn and although it sounded awesome, it was just not the type of race that radiated a leader to save mankind. I went back to my selection and mentally hit the yes button. Do you wish to select Half Aasimar/Half Shadar-Kai as your permanent race? Yes/No? I confirmed and another tingle ran through my body. Congratulations and your base stat allocations have been adjusted for your race and class.

CHAPTER TWELVE

Full Characterization

Dookooze now that we have your class and race determined we can next move to the skill selection. Some of which are predetermined for you based on your test results while you will be able to select the rest from a qualified list. Would you like to see your predetermined list now or your qualified list? I selected the predetermined list first to see what I automatically got.

Automatically Granted Skills:
Structural Construction – Allows the concepts needed for building and development of settlements. As this skill increases more options will become available to develop
Conceptual Research – Permits the study of blueprints, recipes and schematics combinations to discover something new. Leveling this skill allows for more complex creations to emerge from combination.
Lore-Ancient – Initiates an understanding of ancient lore and history long forgotten to the world of WEO. As you find ancient or historical items and information this skill will increase. The higher the skill the more information gleamed from items
Leadership – As your decisions can impact societies this skill allows you to fine tune those abilities. Leveling up this skill will open evolutions for buffs that will apply to led groups, factions, or partners.

All of these were great skills to have, especially with what needed to be done. I loved city development in every game I played that allowed it. The research sounded good too. I had a feeling that the Lore-Ancient was something I specifically needed for my mythical quest line and Leadership made a ton of sense. Now that those were out of the way I decided to focus on the qualified list. I brought that up and it appeared to have over 200 options. I had an idea of some things I really either felt I needed or wanted so I looked for those first.

First thing I snagged up was Lore-Religion. It only made 100% sense considering I was a cleric and would need that. Next on my list were the usual Herbalism, Skinning, and Knowledge-Divine Spell Craft. Now that I was down to two initial options, it became trickier. If my goal was to really become a leader and developer of a potential metropolis, then I should have a good understanding of a few things. Agriculture seemed like a smart idea, so I knew how to feed everyone. I knew food played a role in WEO with the Earthen players so I would learn more however the NPCs I am sure needed to eat too. This would help. My final option would pair well with some of my others. I grabbed Administration. This would help me govern and understand the nuances better.

Once I placed the 6 chosen options into the bucket I was once asked again to confirm my choices. That tingling hit for a 3rd time once I did. Now there was only one thing left for me to decide or be advised on and that was if there were any abilities that I had received. My character creation screen must have been reading my thoughts because as soon as it popped into my head a prompt asked me if I would like to review my absorbed abilities. So of course, I clicked yes.

Dookooze Darkbringer, you have been granted the following abilities. They are passive non-skill nor race based. You may evolve these abilities like anything else, however it will depend on the usage as well as the situation in which you do so. This is also very rare. Please see your granted abilities below.

Higher Education – Based on your high assessment scores you have been granted the ability to have an accelerated learning speed. You will level all scalable weapons, armor, spells, skills, and abilities at a 10% increased rate. Your overall experience will have a 10% increased rate of accumulation.

Over Skilled – You have mastered the ability to learn skills. Therefore, you are no longer trapped by the maximum 10-skill limit and can learn another 25 skills of your choosing. Be warned as these selected skills cannot be changed or removed like your initial set. Once chosen they will stay. Think carefully about your choices. As you venture into the world you will be prompted to add or not add a skill when you utilize it.

You're A Secretive Lot Aren't You – You have decided that you do not want entities knowing your plans. You can place an Anti-Scrying enchantment either on yourself or a respawn town. This can only apply to one item at a time. If you wish to choose a different target, then you will need to cancel and re-cast. This can only be done once per day.

All of those will come in very handy with character progression. It was time to finalize my character and get this quest completed. I looked over at the prompt that asked me to verify my choices, took a deep breath, and selected yes. The tingling was much stronger now as my full character sheet appeared in front of me. I set it aside because I wanted to complete the quest first before I took my full glance at it. I minimized the screen and turned my focus back to Tikallnosis. He looked at me and said very nice choices, and they will compliment you well. Now let's conclude this meeting, complete your quest, update you on what's next and put everything into motion. I nodded and then I received the next prompt.

You have now completed character creation and fulfilled all the requirements to receive the rewards from your quest: Commune with the Forgotten God! Part one of the Divine Investigation. This is a unique Divine Level quest and has an unspecified number of parts. You have received the following rewards: 500 Experience points, 100 Distinguished Points - Illustrious, Unliving Armor Set- Evolution Set, Sickle of Minor Decay, Action – Prayer, Ability – Summon Companions

The next thing I saw as my eyes went wide were the flashes of an icon at the top right of my interface as I heard the chime: congratulations you have hit Level 2. You have 6 attribute points to allocate. You did not receive any other spells, evolutions, or actions at level 2.

In looking at the Summon Companions, I can only assume that was the unknown part of completing that quest. So, I decided to check that out.

Summon Companions: At level 1 you may summon 1 companion to be by your side. They will have a personality, communication abilities, and decision-making skills just as you would and they will develop a closer bond with you as time develops. At level 10 you may summon a 2nd companion and at level 20 you can summon a final 3rd companion. They will assist you in your quests and can be directed to perform other duties and functions. These companions will be randomly selected and will rank between Common to Mythical in rarity.

Upon reading the description I think I peed a little at how awesome this was. I looked up at Tikallnosis and whispered thank you. He nodded somberly and said thank you as well. I need your help Dookooze. We need to uncover what is going on. Your next tasks are simple. You need to gather as many of your friends and family as you can, then head to the town we discussed. Those are your next quests. Level up and get strong, understand what you are and do what must be done. The prompts then hit my screen.

You have been offered a quest: Gather the Followers Part Two of the Divine Investigation. This is a unique Divine Level quest and has an unspecified number of parts.

Level Requirement: None
Rewards: Experience Points; Distinguished Points; Class Appropriate Spell
Description: You are to communicate and coordinate at least 85% of your contacts list to meet you at the quest point or at your designated place of gathering. Percentage of group gathered – 2% 2/83
Do you accept the quest? Yes/No

You have been offered a quest: Homestead
Level Requirement: None
Rewards: Experience Points, Distinguished Points, Class Appropriate Spell, Appointment of Town Oversight for Settlement
Description: Head to the designated town, eliminate the brigands terrorizing the citizens and assume direct control over the town and its population. Brigands defeated 0/Unknown, Brigand Leader defeated 0/1
Do you accept this quest? Yes/No

Now it was time to finally look at my completed character sheet.

Name: Dookooze Darkbringer
Level: 2 (86% experience gained to next level)
Class: Moon Cleric
Race: Half Aasimar/Half Shadar-Kai
The Chosen of Tikallnosis
Stats: Intelligence – 10, Wisdom 16, Hardiness 10, Strength 12, Charisma 14; Intuition 10, Agility 10. You have 6 free stat points to allocate.
Health: 22 Regeneration Rate = 1 Per Second (Non-Combat)
Energy: 50 Regeneration Rate = 3 Per Second (Non-Combat)
Stamina: 22 Regeneration Rate = 1 Per Second (Non-Combat)
Distinguish Points: 100 Illustrious Level 1
Skills: Structural Construction, Conceptual Research, Lore-Ancient, Leadership, Lore-Religion, Herbalism, Skinning,

Knowledge-Divine Spell Craft, Agriculture, Administration. You have 25 open skill slots remaining.

Abilities: Higher Education, Over Skilled, You're A Secretive Lot Aren't You

Action: Prayer

Defense: 10 (Base)

Spells Cantrip:

Spare Death – Cast Time: 1 second, Range: Touch, Cool Down: Once Per Hour, Description: You touch a living creature stopping health loss to 1 remaining hit point in their pool. This will not stop death if wounded after nor if inflicted with a critical strike. This spell has no effect on undead or constructs.

Toll of the Dead - Cast Time: 1 second, Range: 20 meters, Cool Down: None, Energy Cost: 2 Description: You must visibly see the target to cast, and they must succeed at a Wisdom save or take 1D8 necrotic damage. Cover can negate damage.

Dark Flame – Cast Time: 1 second, Range: 20 meters, Cool Down: None, Energy Cost: 2, Description: A dark radiant flame emits from you towards a target. The target must succeed at an Agility save or take 1D8 dark radiant damage. Cover cannot negate this saving effect.

Spells By Level:

Heal – Cast Time: 1 second, Range: 20 meters, Cool Down: 3 seconds, Energy Cost: 8, Description: Heal a living creature in need of health for 1D8 + skill level of health point. This cannot exceed their maximum health pool limit.

Necrotic Ray – Cast Time: 3 seconds, Range: 20 meters, Cool Down: 5 seconds, Energy Cost: 8, Description: Produce a bolt of death and necrosis at an enemy for 1D10 + skill level necrotic damage. This spell has no effect on undead and constructs.

Spells Divine:

Absorption – Cast Time: Instant, Range: Self, Cool Down: 24 Hours, Energy Cost: 40, Description: Once per 24 hours you invoke the divine instinctively to prevent a death dealing blow you would otherwise normally receive. Your god looks down on you and will keep you alive with 1 hit point. Warning any subsequent successful attacks dealing damage will deal damage accordingly.

Spells Gifted:

Summon Companions – Cast Time: 1 Minute, Range: Self, Cool Down: None, Energy Cost: 30, Description: As a reward for assisting your god, you are given the ability to summon up to 3 companions to aide you in your pursuit of justice for your god, Tikallnosis. May summon 1 companion at level 1, another at level 10, and a final companion at level 20.

No weapons, jewelry, or armor descriptions available

Racial Abilities: Darkvision. You can see in dim light within 60 feet of you as if it were bright light, and in darkness as if it were dim light. You discern colors in that darkness only as shades of gray.

Keen Senses. You have proficiency and +2 bonus in Diplomacy and Perception skills.

Necrotic Resistance. You have resistance to necrotic damage, charming, and sleep affects.

Night Cloud: Once per day you may cast this spell centered around a targeted point within 60 meters. This spell emits a perpetual mass of spherical darkness surrounding your targeted point. The distance emitted will equal in meters to your character level plus skill level. Enemies within this darkness are blinded and considered flat footed. Night Cloud can dispel any light spell within the same area of equal or lower level. This spell can be negated by a higher-level magic spell.

Once I completed reading my stat sheet, I immediately added my available stats. I slapped 3 into Wisdom to bring it to 20. I put 1 Into Agility to help with my motions and help with my defense. The final points I into Charisma. I just felt like that would play a part. I approved the upgraded stats and noticed that my Energy had increased from 40 to 54. Every bit helps. So, my stat book looked like this: Intelligence - 10, Wisdom - 20, Hardiness - 10, Strength – 10, Charisma – 17, Intuition – 10, and Agility – 11.

Next, I decided to peek at my armor and get dressed finally.

Armor Set: Unliving Cowl – Armor 10, Unliving Spiked Chest Armor - 15, Unliving Spiked Gauntlets Armor – 8, Unliving Spiked Greaves Armor 10, Unliving Boots Armor – 8: Set Rarity: Rare, Full Set Bonus- Summoned companions or pets have a 10% attack speed and 10% increase in damage; Evolution Set – This set of armor designed to be donned by the mightiest of the lords of death but you have received this in its infancy. As you grow in skill and power this suit can be evolved to further protect and enhance you with powerful features at higher levels.
Weapon: Dual Sickles of Minor Decay – Type: Simple, Hand: Both Slots, Attack: +5/+3 rating, Rarity: Uncommon, Speed: Normal, Description: Sickles designed to slowly rot its enemies upon attack, Each will inflict 1D6 + Str modifier damage with a 15% chance to inflict Decay. Decay will cause 3 necrotic damage per 3 seconds for 12 seconds.

I immediately equipped both. My armor stood at a miniscule 51 . The armor felt like the wet moss of a cemetery as it was cool to the touch with a damp feel. This I will have to get used too. The sickle had a slight greenish hue to it. Jaceberlen just looked at me and said about time geez dad it has been like 20 minutes. So, what did you get he asked? I described it all in detail to him. His face dropped at the mythical class and race. As I described the spells, skills, abilities, weapon, and armor set he gawked. I guess it beats unclassed he laughed. I mentioned that I wanted to see his stuff as soon as we got out of here, but I had one thing to do first after we were done with Tikallnosis.

We both looked up at Tikallnosis. He shook his head at us and stated that his time was short as he must depart but follow the quest. Your objective is to liberate the town from brigands, assume control, and grow. Gather your people as quickly as you can. You will have enemies try to destroy what you have and wish to have. Go now and be safe. We shall talk soon. And just like that the wave happened again and he was gone.

The altar room was utterly quiet except for the sounds of both Jaceberlen and I. I looked at him and asked him to join me at the altar for a sec as I had a hunch. We both approached and knelt at the altar. When we did, I received a prompt: As this is an unprotected altar would you like to claim this for Tikallnosis? I had hoped for that and hit yes. Immediately the altar turned a metallic jet black. The air developed a greenish black tint as the air seemed to change colors slightly. Jaceberlen's eyes went wide upon reading the next note.

Congratulations you have sanctified a temple to Tikallnosis. This forgotten god has now been found and his religion is now available to spread to followers. Experience Points 100, Distinguished Points 50-Illustrious. We both bumped hands as he hit level 3 while I was now only 20 points away myself. That quest really helped me. My Distinguished Points were 5 away from level 2 as well. The final thing I needed to do was summon my first companion. Will it give me a choice, a role type, or just random. What were the options I wondered? I told him my plan, and he was more than eager to see how this went and what we received from it. He said hell yes let's do this. I looked up the spell, and it didn't give any more instruction, so I began.

I just knew innately how to cast it. As the chant came out of my mouth you could see a greenish black form on the ground in front of my feet. Jaceberlen instinctively backed up as it caught him off guard, but he quickly retook his place next to me. Then after a minute the chant was complete. At first it seemed as if nothing was happening; then the form took the shape of a circular orb. It then began stretching like a membrane about to release spiders. You could see the pushing and pulling as it tried to free itself. Then a tear appeared in the corner. A fluid seeped out and as it hit the floor it had an acrid fowl stench that made both Jaceberlen and I gag. We both turned around and lost our lunches. It was just damn gross.

As we turned around, we got our first glimpse of my new companion, and it looked at us both and muttered. Mommas hungry! We both stared at her stunned at the first words out of her mouth. Pick your jaws up before I smack you. You're a sassy little shit aren't you I said. Or should I say SPICY! She gurgled and said I prefer spicy as she looked at my son and told him, you're the bitch not me. I knew she would be able to possibly communicate but to outright talk was a shock. My son just sat there dumbfounded but finally smiled as he said. Who's my little spicy bitch? He then took a quick step back as the little booger swiped at him. I said that was enough even though I was inwardly laughing. The beast glanced over at me and said, whatever but stopped. That was all it took for us to bond. Finally, I inspected my companion.

Companion: Species: Displacement Beast, Rank: Kitten, Rarity: Rare, Level: 1, Armor: 45, Health: 15, Stats: Intelligence -5/ Wisdom – 12/ Hardiness – 15/ Strength – 10/ Charisma – 10/ Intuition – 10/ Agility – 17, Skills: Perception +3/Stealth +5, Abilities: Darkvision, Avoidance (1/2 damage on saving throws), Displacement (projects a magical illusion of itself within 10 feet of its position creating a -50% chance to be hit), Keen smell (+2 perception for issues relying on smell), Shifting Step (While displacement is active and an attack misses her she can teleport up to 5 feet without penalty), Magic Resistance +5, Attacks: Tentacles – Melee attack, Range: 10feet, Attack: +5, Damage: 1D4+3b Bite; 1D4 piercing, Description: This beast Is aggressive, fearsome, playful, unruly, apparently super spicy, normally evil in nature. They will on rare occasions be bound to a lord who is not. This is one such case as there is great potential for carnage. Loyalty: Somewhat Friendly. Name: Unnamed

She will be a great asset I said as I knelt to extend a hand. The beast looked at me like I was nuts, but she took a slow swipe at my paw and mumbled. Now feed me! Jaceberlen laughed and said yep, this ought to be fun but what name do we give her? I pondered that for a moment and tried to consider her personality. What about Wilfreda as in the cleaning service or Wraith? Jaceberlen was quiet for a second and then said; "You know what I think we should call her Mittens. Oh, that's a good one I said. Mittens it is. I then willed up my companion screen and focused on the name. and then I entered Mittens and confirmed my choice.

A female voice prompt ensued stating my companions name has been selected. Mittens looked up at me with a not so happy smile and said out of all names you must call me damn Mittens? Really! Oh, the travesty and kill me now were her next words as she rolled her eyes and advised Jaceberlen: You will pay for that! She then placed one of her black paws up against her forehead. Her little spikey tentacles then turned a little to face Jaceberlen and then he saw 2 beasts. Oh no you don't he said, so stop that right now Mittens. She growled low and said I will get you back. Then she chuckled if that was even possible. Aren't we a bit dramatic now huh Mittens? Jaceberlen snickered and said of course I will.

CHAPTER THIRTEEN

The Adventure Begins

As we exited the cave, I finally turned to my son and said, all right champ now you can tell me all about your character. He smiled and was like it isn't like we don't have the time. He looked at me and said tell me what you think of this.

Name: Jaceberlen Darkbringer
Race: Astral Elf
Class: Night Paladin (Dark Vengeance)
Level: 3 – (33% experience gained to next level)
Stats: Intelligence – 10 Adjusted 11), Wisdom 10, Hardiness 17, Strength 20, Charisma 17, Intuition 10, Agility 10.
Health: 55 Regeneration Rate = 3 Per Second (Non-Combat)
Energy: 49 Regeneration Rate = 2 Per Second (Non-Combat)
Stamina: 55 Regeneration Rate = 3 Per Second (Non-Combat)
Distinguish Points: 50 Illustrious Level 1
Proficiencies: All armor types, shields, martial and simple weapons
Skills: Mining, Smelting, Diplomacy, Principles of Metal Working, Keen Senses, Sense Motive, Noble Lore, Religious Lore, Bartering, Spell Craft.
Abilities: Charm Resistancc +5, Smite of Shadows (1/Per Day the paladin can target one enemy within sight. If the target is not of shadow or darkness then the paladin may add their charisma modifier to attack rolls/damage), Darkened Grace (add charisma

modifier to all saving throws), Immunity to Fear and all types of disease, Aura of Darkness (all allies gain +4 morale bonus for attacks and saves), Shadowed Hands (Number of times = to ½ level plus Charisma modifier you may heal 1D6 damage plus a calming affect for every 2 levels you possess)

Defense: 65

Spells: Cantrip Sacred Flame – Cast Time: 1 second, Range: 20 meters, Cool Down: None, Description: You create a small flame in your palm and when it hits an enemy it will deal 1D6 fire damage

Blessings Of Shadows - Cast Time: 1 second, Range: 20 meters, Cool Down: None, Energy Cost: 8

Description: As you blend yourself and others in the shadows it protects up to 4 allies including self with a +5 defense and +2 to all saves.

Protection From Good and Evil – Cast Time: 1 second, Range: 20 meters, Cool Down: None, Energy Cost: 8,

Description: Protects +5 defense against any entities of those alignments.

Thunder – Cast Time 3 seconds, Range: 20 meters, Cool Down: 1 minute, Energy: 20, Description: Raising your weapon in the air you summon thunder down on your enemies in a 20-foot area dealing 1D8 damage. Can cause a 3 second stun

Armor: Iron Cap – Armor 15 Rarity: Common, Chain Shirt – Armor 20 Rarity: Common, Leather Gauntlets – Armor 10 Rarity: Common, Leather Boots – Armor 10 Rarity: Common, Wooden Buckler – Armor 10 Rarity Common, Weapon: Iron Great sword – Type: Martial, Hand: Main Slot, Attack: +8 rating, Rarity: Common, Speed: Normal, Description: Basic common sword that deals 1D10 + Str modifier damage

After reading his information I looked up at him and said, man, that looks pretty sick and especially the new shadow-based stuff. You went vengeance I see? Mitens looked at him and said you still suck. He said yeah it fit him the best and now that we are in this thick plot it will only come in handier. I love the dark and shadowy tweaks that were made Jaceberlen said. I had to agree and nodded with a yep. Jaceberlen looked up at me and said, "So where too now? Well first off, I said, is that we need to knock out those remaining little quests that we left on the table from the camp. That way I can hit at least level 3, and we can finally hopefully get you some damn pants. I laughed out loud and finally he did too. I looked at him again and said as far as I know there are not any red-light dancer poles out here for you to twirl on so unless you want tips from the local goblins or whatever we need to make pants a priority. But first I need to message the rest of the group and tell them where to meet.

I mentally pulled up my contacts list, and it finally seemed that everyone was on. I typed a quick message for everyone to meet at what appeared to be a centralized village called Thatcherton that was about two days from where our goal was. It seemed like a day from us, so I said to meet there in two days' time so that everyone can level up and get their classes rolling. I hit send all to make sure everyone got it and it was done. Then I sent a few private messages to my wife, daughter, and a few others with more personal notes. Once that was done it was now time to get some questing done and find that boy some pants.

For the next few hours Mittens, Jaceberlen, and I completed quest after quest in the camp area. By that time the three NPCs manning the tented area had become extremely friendly with us. Fred didn't seem to have any quest progression as he just continuously asked us to gather more mushrooms. We did that one like five times until even our pockets were full of mushrooms. And yes, by that time the boy, Jaceberlen, had a pair of pants. He was whining an awful lot about them, so I was beginning to wonder if he was going to be some form of new undergarment paladin type lol. Thank goodness that was a big no.

Darlene had enough wood now to build a few houses if the fire didn't work out for her. Corporal White however did have a small chain questline. After the initial quest of finding the missing soldier, we had to track down and investigate what happened to him. After some lengthy questing and private detective work we finally discovered that it was in fact a small den of goblins that had killed the soldier. Our final quest of that chain and as time would have it that we were on this last portion now, was to assault the den and wipe out their ranks.

Mittens was overly eager to get all up in that business and I must admit that she held her own well so far over the last few hours. Even as a kitten that displacement thing she has is nasty to the unknowing. She would project herself on one side of the cave while we were in fact on the other. Once they fell for it, we would totally catch each small group off guard. It was easy picking after that. I think all in all we took out about twenty of them before their little chief came to play. He on the other hand did not fall for Mitten's trick.

Jaceberlen ended up tanking this affair by rushing in, letting his aura flood the area, and swinging his newly equipped bastard sword. Mittens then attacked from the rear, and I lit it up from afar. By this point I was very close to level 4 and Jaceberlen was on his way to 5, although my 10% experience boost was gaining on him rapidly. Mittens was also level four at that point. We continued to battle the chief and upon his defeat he dropped a nice pair of common chain boots that Jaceberlen immediately equipped and stashed the pair that he had back in his inventory. When the goblin chief was completely looted, I took immense amusement in being able to use my new level 3 spell for the first time; Raise Skeleton. I just haven't used it but this point in time was as good as any.

I raised both of my hands to the side and uttered the words: To serve in life is to serve anew in death! At that moment 3 pairs of boney hands clawed their way out of the ground. As they continued to rise from their slumber, I could tell that they only had a thread of intelligence. Enough to receive commands and respond but dialogue was basic at best. I looked at my 3 new minions, and I decided to inspect them.

Skeleton Minion Scrapper – Level 3, Health 30, Energy 0, Stamina 20, Defense 20, Weapons Claw (1D4 +2)(x2), Description: These basic skeletons can understand basic commands and execute them to the best of their ability. Tier 1 Skeleton, awakened until destroyed or dismissed.

They weren't much but these suckers would certainly be fodder and a distraction. I looked at them and asked if they understood me. They muttered a guttural yes, my lord! I told them good so now follow me and protect our group but do not attack or engage unless ordered to. Yessssss they said and fell in behind me.

As we made our way back to the encampment to turn our final quest in it was certainly weird listening to the clanking of bones as the skeletons walked behind us. After what seemed like thirty minutes, we finally entered the clearing where the tents and NPCs were located. As we approached, we were greeted with nods and waves. When we submitted the goblin head to conclude the quest we were immediately notified of a local event, The Goblin Retaliation. The skeletons started jerking around and immediately ran towards the woods. Corporal White advised us to get ready as this was their last stand. There were some newer players that looked at us and decided to run away foolishly. We yelled at them to get back to us but to no avail; they took off. Unfortunately for them, they ran right into another group of goblins that cut them down like shredded cheese.

As the skeletons engaged with their group of goblins it was the first time to really see them in action. It looked like a jumble of bone and steel. The skeletons were raking their claws against any goblin they could reach while the goblins were using short swords and shields to counter. That is when Jaceberlen and I joined the fight. As my son charged the group, I led with a necrotic ray followed by a toll of the dead spell. Both slammed into the outermost goblin, and he stumbled back and fell. As he rose, Jaceberlen's sword met his neck and the goblin dropped dead to the ground.

The next took a dark flame to the face and two of the skeletons jumped all over him until the goblin stopped moving. I decided to go attack the other group that was rushing Corporal White and the other two NPCs. I casted my racial gift, night cloud, over the area to hopefully buy us some time and it was a sight to see or should I say not see. The whole area near the goblins emerged into a cloud of darkness. You could hear them slow their charge and the fear was evident in their tones.

As Jaceberlen and the skeletons finished off the first group, they turned their attention to the darkness. He looked at me and smiled saying; way to buy the calvary some time boss man. We all got prepared for the fight and as I dismissed the cloud we engaged. Jaceberlen charged and evaded an overhand chop from the biggest goblin. I cast toll of the dead followed by a dark flame. I then finished one off with a necrotic ray.

Mittens portrayed an illusion of herself in the rear of a goblin and when they turned to attack it, their back was exposed to her attacks. The goblin had no chance. The skeletons were not idle either. They were clawing and ripping flesh with utter abandon. One of them caught a sword to the skull and dropped silent. I could feel the connection stop, and it caught me off guard, but I couldn't lose my concentration. I kept casting spell after spell. Jaceberlen had also been caught with a deep gash to the leg, so I guess the pants weren't good enough. I waited to heal as I didn't think he was in dire need and he was winning the fight. Mittens was entering that melee now so I had no doubts they would take the big boy down.

As the goblin fell, we noticed another large goblin enter the field. As if on cue, we got an updated notification that the final goblin boss, AKA the Goblin Warlord, was the final part to our quest chain. We didn't want to waste any time on this. Jaceberlen charged and I ordered my two remaining skeletons as well to attack. Mittens went all sassy rogue on us and disappeared into sneak mode. I began casting toll of the dead followed by a necrotic ray.

The toll of the dead splashed against the warlord's arm, and you could see the greenish black necrosis hit. The necrotic ray seemed to have been dodged, which was a surprise to me. I quickly regained my composure and sent a dark flame his way and the black flame charred away some of his topknot. Dodge that you prick, I yelled. Jaceberlen then channeled his lightning and that really looked like it hurt as it crackled all over him. The warlord physically seized and screamed in pain. That seemed to enrage him as he began to glow red. From our history of video games, we knew that it was likely enrage or a berserker skill. The time was at hand in putting this thing down. Mittens kept attacking its rear while dodging in and out. She would attack then teleport a few feet away and repeat the process. Only one of my skeletons was still fighting as a broad swipe of the warlord's weapon took out the 2nd one. The final skeleton wouldn't last long and sure enough a split second later, its head was removed from its bony shoulders in a backhanded swipe. The bones crumbled to the floor as Jaceberlen took on the full aggro from the warlord. I kept casting spell after spell and although the warlord was in a very bad necrotic state, it still wasn't down. Just as we were beginning to think we had bitten off more than we could chew we caught a break. Mittens yelled who's my bitch as she landed a critical hit to the hamstring of the goblin. He wobbled for a split second due to the hit and then his leg buckled and gave way. That was the only opening we needed to finish him off. I blasted another necrotic ray to the face and as his face turned rotten and green; Jaceberlen's sword split his skull in half. The goblin froze and went limp as his lifeless body hit the ground.

Verification of the warlord's death soon became official when we got a notification that the event had ended, and the warlord was slain. Not to mention the sparkling lights of all too sweet loot. The goblins who accompanied the warlord didn't have much to offer as spoils other than silver coins and poor-quality weapons and armor. Everything we already had was of equal or better quality, so we just took it to sell when we were able. The warlord, however, had a ring of strength that Jaceberlen took to help him. Next, we were to report to Corporal White for any rewards. There were other notifications flashing but I decided to address those later.

As Corporal White, Danielle, and Fred rushed over to check on us, we were out of breath but that didn't stop us. I immediately went to Jaceberlen and gave him a few heals to mend the leg and bring his health back up to full. Mittens was scratched up a little but one heal took care of her. As Corporal White began talking we received another quest icon stated that we had indeed completed the quest chain.

Local Event Complete: The Goblin Menace
As only 2 Earthen participated in this local event, your rewards have been adjusted accordingly. Experience Points – 750, Distinguished Points – 125, 100 Silver Coins, Belt of Wisdom +1, 5 Camp Rations

The belt was amazing and seemed self-explanatory as far as the benefit. The experience and distinguished points were great too although I don't really know yet what that entails. You can never have enough money or food. I then noticed that I had more icons flashing so I decided to go ahead and look at them now before we hit the road.

Ding! Congratulations you have hit level 5. You have 15 free stat points to allocate. You have new abilities, skill upgrades, or spell modifiers to decide.
Ding! Congratulations you have hit level 6. You have 20 free stat points to allocate.
Congratulations you have reached level 2 in Distinguished. Your name spreads among the lands and the world will now take more notice of you.
Congratulations Mittens has hit level 5

CHAPTER FOURTEEN

Gains

The gains were most certainly solid, and I had already caught up with my son in the experience department. I figured I would wait to dive deep in the upgrades for a few more minutes as I needed to see if there was anything else we needed to do here before resting and hitting the road. Jaceberlen and I made sure everything was closed out and sat for a few minutes to eat and drink so that we were at max health, energy, and stamina. While we took our quick rest, I decided to look deeper into the notifications I saw a few minutes ago. They were as follows:

Upon reaching level 5 your Raise Skeleton spell has evolved. Your minions have grown stronger, and you may now summon 4 skeletons. You may also choose from a new type of minion. You can specify the number of each mentally for a combined total of 4 as you cast the spell. Option 1. Scrapper – the base unit of the spell and is a front-line attacker with minimal intelligence. Option 2. Archer – a step above the scrapper and is a ranged unit armed with a bow and arrow. Their intelligence is slightly higher as they can scout, track, and communicate more effectively.

You have a new cleric spell: Bless – This spell allows you to target up to 3 allies and bless them +2 to attack and evasion. Range 30 meters, Duration 10 minutes, Cooldown 30 seconds.

Well, that was a good spell to add to the toolchest and the summon changes are great. Now I can add a ranged attacker and open the door to tracking and scouting. Heck maybe even assassination if need be. I couldn't wait to try this out and since I needed to resummon my group anyway, I decided to get on it immediately.

As I began to cast the spell, I mentally felt a tug in my mind asking me how I wanted my group. I decided to split them evenly for now with 2 scrappers and 2 archers. I could always tinker with it to find the right mix. As the skeletons emerged from the ground, they all looked different. The scrappers had evolved with thicker bones and some sort of medium crude chain shirt. Their claws seemed to have elongated into short daggers. Their health had gone from 30 to 50, their stamina was now 30, and their defense had jumped to 35 from 20. Their new melee attacks increased damage from 1D4 to 1D6+2 (x2). They were still as dumb as a can of corn but hey the gains were welcome.

The archers on the other hand looked downright awesome. They stood there in basic black leather armor, black cloaks, short bows, and quivers of matte black arrows. Their health was at 30, stamina 30, and defense 20. However, they had evasion and agility of 18. Stealth and sneak were also in their build. I can already see how I could use these.

Mittens had also grown stronger. Mitten's rank evolved from kitten to Junior. Across the board her stats seemed to increase. She sprouted 2 more legs which I was then assured that there would be no more of those surprises. She also seemed to have gotten a little bigger. Mittens purred in the fact that she could now inflict more damage on her enemies and Jaceberlen. He took a step back and said now we are all friends here. She just snickered.

I allocated my free stat points and was ready to get on the move. I addressed the group as I asked if they were ready to move out. The archers certainly responded more like a sentient being than the scrappers. The archers looked at me and stated in unison: What is our orders sir? The scrappers just nodded and with an elongated answer uttered yessss. After giving the archers, a forward scouting role and the scrappers protection detail I looked over at Jaceberlen and asked if he was ready. He nodded and then we said our goodbyes to Corporal White and the rest of the group. They waved and said we were always welcome back and then we were off to meet the rest of our group at the designated location. As we were leaving, I decided to take a quick peek at my stat sheet.

Name: Dookooze Darkbringer
Level: 6 (28% experience gained to next level)
Class: Moon Cleric
Race: Half Aasimar/Half Shadar-Kai
The Chosen of Tikallnosis
Stats: Intelligence – 12, Wisdom 30, Hardiness 14, Strength 10, Charisma 22, Intuition 14, Agility 14.
Health: 84
Health Regeneration Rate: 21 Per Minute (Non-Combat)
Energy: 180
Energy: 45 Regeneration Rate Per Minute (Non-Combat)
Stamina: 84
Stamina Regeneration Rate: 21 Per Minute (Non-Combat)
Distinguished Points: 225 Illustrious Level 2
Skills: Structural Construction, Conceptual Research, Lore-Ancient, Leadership, Lore-Religion, Herbalism, Skinning, Knowledge-Divine Spell Craft, Agriculture, Administration. You have 25 open skill slots remaining.
Abilities: Higher Education, Over Skilled, You're A Secretive Lot Aren't You
Divine Action: Prayer
Spells: Cantrip Spare Death – Cast Time: 1 second, Range: Touch, Cool Down: Once Per Hour
Toll of the Dead - Cast Time: 1 second, Range: 20 meters, Cool Down: None, Energy Cost: 2 Description: You must visibly see the target to cast, and they must succeed at a Wisdom save or take 1D8 necrotic damage. Cover can negate damage.

Dark Flame – Cast Time: 1 second, Range: 20 meters, Cool Down: None, Energy Cost: 2, Description: A dark radiant flame emits from you towards a target. The target must succeed at an Agility save or take 1D8 dark radiant damage.

Spells: By Level

Heal – Cast Time: 1 second, Range: 20 meters, Cool Down: 3 seconds, Energy Cost: 8, Description: Heal a living creature in need of health for 1D8 + skill level of health point.

Necrotic Ray – Cast Time: 3 seconds, Range: 20 meters, Cool Down: 5 seconds, Energy Cost: 8, Description: Produce a bolt of death and necrosis at an enemy for 1D10 + skill level necrotic damage. This spell has no effect on undead and constructs.

Bless – Cast Time: 3 seconds, Range: 30 meters, Cool Down: 30 minutes, Duration: 10 minutes, Cost: 20 Description: This spell allows you to target up to 3 allies and bless them +2 to attack and evasion.

Raise Skeleton – You can call upon the bones of vanquished enemies to serve you in death. You may summon a total of 4 skeletal minions and can be a pre-selected assortment of the following. Skeletal Scrapper – Level 5, Health 50, Energy 0, Stamina 30, Defense 35, Weapons Claw (1D6 +2)(x2), Description: These basic skeletons can understand basic commands and execute them to the best of their ability. Tier 1 Skeleton, awakened until destroyed or dismissed. Skeletal Archer – Level 5, Health 30, Energy 0, Stamina 30, Defense 20, Weapons Short bow (1D6+3), Description: A tier 2 minion and a step above the scrapper is a ranged unit armed with a bow and arrow. Their intelligence is slightly higher as they can scout, track, and communicate more effectively.

Spells: Divine Absorption – Cast Time: Instant, Range: Self, Cool Down: 24 Hours, Energy Cost: 40, Description: Once per 24 hours you invoke the divine instinctively to prevent a death dealing blow you would otherwise normally receive. Your god looks down on you and will keep you alive with 1 hit point. Warning any subsequent successful attacks dealing damage will deal damage accordingly.

Spells: Gifted Summon Companions – Cast Time: 1 Minute, Range: Self, Cool Down: None, Energy Cost: 30, Description: As a reward for assisting your god, you are given the ability to summon up to 3 companions to aide you in your pursuit of justice for your god, Tikallnosis. May summon 1 companion at level 1, another at level 10, and a final companion at level 20.

Armor Set: Unliving Cowl – Armor 10, Unliving Spiked Chest Armor - 15, Unliving Spiked Gauntlets Armor – 8, Unliving Spiked Greaves Armor 10, Unliving Boots Armor – 8: Set Rarity: Rare, Full Set Bonus- Summoned companions or pets have a 10% attack speed and 10% increase in damage; Evolution Set – This set of armor was designed to be worn by the mightiest of the lords of death, but you have received this in its infancy. As you grow in skill and power this suit can be evolved to further protect and enhance you with powerful features at higher levels. Total Defense 61

Belt of Wisdom +1

Weapon: Dual Sickles of Minor Decay – Type: Simple, Hand: Both Slots, Attack: +5/+3 rating, Rarity: Uncommon, Speed: Normal, Description: Sickles designed to slowly rot its enemies upon attack, each successful attack will inflict 1D6 + Str modifier damage with a 15% chance to inflict Decay. Decay will cause 3 necrotic damage per 3 seconds for 12 seconds

Racial Abilities: As an offspring of darkened humanoid creatures from both the Celestial and Elvin bloodlines you have made your way onto the material plane from the shadows to forge a path of your choosing. Both races resemble typical humanoid creatures but with potential elven or celestial features that are a bit off from your typical kin.
Darkvision. You can see in dim light within 60 feet of you as if it were bright light, and in darkness as if it were dim light. You discern colors in that darkness only as shades of gray.

Keen Senses. You have proficiency and +2 bonus in Diplomacy and Perception skills.

Necrotic Resistance. You have resistance to necrotic damage, charming, and sleep affects.

Night Cloud: Once per day you may cast this spell centered around a targeted point within 60 meters. This spell emits a perpetual mass of spherical darkness surrounding your targeted point. The distance emitted will equal in meters to your character level plus skill level. Enemies within this darkness are blinded and considered flat footed. Night Cloud can dispel any light spell within the same area of equal or lower level. This spell can be negated by a higher-level magic spell.

Companion (Mittens): Species: Displacement Beast, Rank: Junior, Rarity: Rare, Level: 5, Armor: 55, Health: 90, Stats: Intelligence -10/Wisdom – 12/ Hardiness – 18/ Strength – 10/ Charisma – 10/ Intuition – 10/ Agility – 21, Skills: Perception +5/Stealth +7, Abilities: Darkvision, Avoidance (1/2 damage on saving throws), Displacement (projects a magical illusion that creates an image of him within 10 feet of his position creating a -50% chance to be hit), Keen smell (+2 perception for issues relying on smell), Shifting Step (While displacement is active and an attack misses him he can teleport up to 5 feet without penalty), Magic Resistance +5, Attacks: Tentacles – Melee attack, Range: 10feet, Attack: +7, Damage: 1D6+3b Bite; 1D4 piercing,

CHAPTER FIFTEEN

More of the Gang

Tiger Lilly awoke to a chorus of noises in an active town hall. She looked around to see a bustling area full of people running around. As she took a second to calm her anxiety; she mentally thought to herself: I wonder who else was up and going? Suddenly, a translucent screen popped up in her field of vision with her contacts listed to see who was online and if anyone was nearby. Luckily there were quite a few in the same little village. Raven, Ophelia, and Laltag Duine were only steps from her, while Please Just Call Me Duck, Mimis, and Big Bear were on the other side of the building.

Through chat and just a raising of the voice; they were all able to group up together. Raven was the first in this group to finish her testing and had been waiting to see if anyone else would be spawning at her location. Tiger Lilly was certainly relieved that she had. Some of her nervousness receded with that knowledge. As they all stood there looking at each other's appearance; Laltag Duine finally said: So, what did everyone choose for classes and races? As the looks got a bit awkward Laltag decided to go ahead and spill the beans on his class. I am a human dual wielding warrior. See not that hard to talk. It's like we're not all family and friends; Geesh.

That comment seemed to loosen everyone else up and the rest began to chime in. Raven stated that she was a human ranger while Tiger Lilly stated she was also a ranger although she was a drow. Raven said that Ophelia was unclassified since she was still a toddler but was a human. Please Just Call Me Duck advised everyone that she was a gnome cleric even though Laltag Duine stated that the race was kind of obvious since she came up to everyone's waist. Everyone just laughed. Mimis and Big Bear were the two that looked the most awkward. As the parents of Mitch and the grandparents of Raven and Jaceberlen; They were nearly 80 years old and had no idea how to navigate this new reality. Mimis had been a nurse in her real life, so she naturally chose the healer class although she said she wanted to also try cooking. The race of human was the only choice for her since anything else was too much of an alteration from reality.

Big Bear on the other hand seemed to gush with excitement. Even though he seemed out of place with everything; he had been without one of his arms for almost thirty years. For him to have full function again of that limb made him so excited for the possibilities in this simulation. He looked up almost like a new man and said that he chose human as well but will be a two-handed warrior. They all looked at each other like they didn't know what to do next.

Laltag Duine and Please Just Call Me Duck were somewhat familiar with gaming as they had played them in real life to some degree. They had a good idea of what needed to happen next, so they began discussing with everyone how to group up, get quests, level up, and get stronger as they figured out what was next on the overall agenda. After about thirty to forty-five minutes of fumbling around the system trying to understand the controls and mental menus, they shared their experience to help the non-gamers understand. Finally, after another hour they all felt comfortable with the system's abilities.

The group decided to do some small quests around the town to get some experience and work to better understand the mechanics of their newfound bodies and abilities. Please Just Call Me Duck or as she quickly advised; Duck led the group around town talking to random merchants and townsfolk seeing if they needed help or assistance with anything that would remotely resemble a quest. When it was all said and done, they had obtained about six quests and decided to head out.

Tal'n opened his eyes and muttered hell yeah as he looked over himself and his surroundings. As an avid gamer in a regular online group with Dookooze, Captain Ahab, and Biggus Dikkus, he couldn't wait to see what this world had in store for them all. The first thing he did was try to mentally bring up his contacts list. After a few minutes of failing miserably he saw the screen in his field of vision. Once that was up, he noticed that Biggus Dikkus and Captain Ahab were both nearby as well as their families.

Dookooze was across the map somewhere he couldn't see and too far to reach right now but he had most of his peeps close. Tal'n messaged those around him to group up. Outside of those 3 and their respective families there were a total of 4 others nearby.

Altriox The Arcanist who was a friend of Jaceberlen joined them as well as Jackaboo, Jaceberlen's stepbrother, Gunthar, and ThreeBD. As they all greeted each other, they began disclosing their races and classes since everyone was eager to see what each other had gotten. Tal'n was a draconian war priest while Captain Ahab disclosed that he was a half drow/half human hybrid bard.

Everyone in attendance looked shocked as they stated they didn't get the option to have a hybrid race. They were like damn man that must be nice. Biggus Dikkus brought the conversation back around by telling everyone that he was a gold dwarf barbarian. Tal'n started cracking up and slapped Biggus on the back stating that he couldn't wait to see the crazy crap they were all going to get into now. ThreeBD advised everyone that he was a half giant paladin focusing on two handed weapons. Jackaboo was a regular dwarf with the artificer class. Altriox was a suli and a sorcerer. Gunthar looked at the group and giggled; I am an oread brawler focusing on these bad boy fists to wreck the land. The rest of the family members gave their updates as well and then they also decided to start questing to get some mechanical understanding of how this would all work. After getting some quests they all split up into smaller groups and headed out.

Gundham entered the world in a forest clearing next to a

wooden fort that was underneath the backdrop of a breathtaking mountain range. As he began to get his surroundings under control, he began hearing someone calling his name from about twenty meters away. He looked over to see what appeared to be his wife Belle and their three young girls. They had their prearranged names of Zippidy, the oldest, Boppady, the middle, and Dooppidy, the youngest. At least they were all together.

Just then they heard someone else walking over. It seemed to be Belle's parents: Priest and Nana. They also spotted Dookooze's brother and his family, so they waved them over. Once everyone was gathered around, just like every other group, they had a conversation about what each of them had chosen. They decided to go around the group and enlighten everyone to see what the composition of the small horde looked like. Killer, which was Dookooze's brother, started off by informing everyone that he was a human warrior focusing on sword and boards. The traditional tank class from earth games. His wife Tallulah, also a human, said she was a healer. Their two girls, Neelz & Birdz, were both human but Neelz who was 14, decided to be a two-handed Warrior. That must have been a decision based on her softball background ripping those home runs. Birdz was still too young to decide anything.

All three of Gundham's girls were too young as well so they too were all human and classless. Nana had chosen human as well and the class of oracle. Priest was of course the obvious as a human cleric. Belle stated that she was a wood elf druid wanting to focus on shapeshifting while Gundham was a wood elf ranger.

Dartonias was gazing around at the new world they had just entered and couldn't believe his eyes at the realism. It was like they were transported into another world, which they technically were. Being a social worker in the real world he saw a lot of things that were unimaginable to most humans, and he quietly feared that in something like this reality it could get worse. He hoped that he and his friends would stay together and work to make a lasting mark in this world. When Dookooze had initially reached out to him about coming to stay at his compound due to the worldwide pandemic; he was hesitant that it wouldn't help anything. He had already lost his wife to the Soul Crusher and had really nothing to live for anymore.

Dookooze and his other DND friends had helped change that. Dartonias whispered to himself that he would do everything he could to be stronger here than in real life to help and protect his friends. Speaking of those friends, two of them approached him and looked amazed at the landscape around them. Landoleer gave Dartonias a hug and said welcome to the new world man. Landoleer then advised them all that he had chosen the half assimar/half cat folk hybrid race and wanted to be a swashbuckler. Dartonias laughed and said of course you were my friend but then disclosed he was a draconian artificer.

Fandela whistled and said that sounded so cool. They both turned to her and asked what she had tested to be. Fandela let them know that she chose the yaddithian race while electing to be demonic summoner. All eyes went wide at that one, but they knew her personality, so it wasn't too much of a shock. Once they had completed their hellos another voice was heard. It was Jaceberlen's best friend, Smeeeagal. He looked extremely weird, and the darkness just seemed to wrap itself around him. He was smiling and giggling when he approached saying how awesome all of this was.

The group asked what his class and race were, so he decided to go ahead. Smeeeagal announced that he was a slayer class with the race of fetchling. Smeeeagal then told them that it is a race of humanoids descended from the plane of shadow. Although his skin was pale white it appeared to look like it was in a cloud of darkness. Smeeeagal laughed again and whispered isn't this cool. The others had to nod in agreement.

While everyone one that was connected to Dookooze in some form or fashion was not yet fully accounted for, the ones that had were busy questing and becoming familiar with the mechanics and interface. As they were all leveling and questing, they each had something in common happen at the same time; a message icon from Dookooze. As everyone connected with the groups stopped what they were doing, they all mentally summoned up their messages and read the following.

Hey everyone,
This is Mitch, aka Dookooze, and I am sure you are all excited about what is coming into our new world. I can't wait to see each one of you. Jaceberlen and I spawned into WEO together and let's just say it's been very intense. I can't say much more now but we need everyone to meet at the location included in this message. You can add the location to your map as a waypoint by mentally telling it to do so. It will then ping on your map, and you can set a course. We need everyone there in two days' time. I know for some of you it will be a long journey but believe me it will be worth it. I can go into more later, but this is a very important situation that needs to be handled delicately. Please make your way to this meeting point and from there we will go as a group to our ending destination. Use this time during your travels to level your character, quest, and hone your skills; we will need them. I cannot wait to see what everyone tested out to be both class wise and racial. The sky is the limit for us although there will be many challenges. I look forward to our reuniting in two days. See you soon. Mitch.

Tiger Lilly paused after reading the message and took a second to gather her thoughts. Everyone around her was silent but as she dismissed the message and set the waypoint for the location just as the message said, she looked up at her immediate group. Is it me or did my husband sound like he wanted to say more. Raven looked at her and agreed with the sentiment; Dad and Paul must have gotten into something, but we will need to head that way to find out more. Everyone else muttered acceptance along with them and as a group they decided to head back to the city to turn in the completed quests, get provisions, and head toward the meeting location.

CHAPTER SIXTEEN
The Journey to the Unknown

As Jaceberlen and I stood in front of the dungeon door we stopped to look at the progress of the other groups making their way to the meeting spot. All eighty or more people were making their way there and all seemed to be looking to be on time for the meeting point. We were still about six hours out and would make it in plenty of time even with all the stops we had been taking. There had been fights, detours, and several other stops we had made for levels and experience. This dungeon just a bit off the main path was just such a stop.

In some of our other fights with the local monster inhabitants, we had looted a message with a map stating that this was the spot for the Plains Master. It was the gnoll boss for this area. Gnolls were large hyena-like creatures with savage war-like ways. As we made our way through the area defeating all that we ran across while helping locals with quests; this was an exciting find. We had leveled up several times and were growing stronger with each kill.

As I approached the entrance to the cave, a system message appeared in my field of view: You are about to enter the dungeon, Den of Bones. Make your way through the Den of Bones and defeat the Plains Master. Rewards will be based upon participation and completion percentage. Captains slain 0/4; Dungeon boss slain 0/1. Level 12 recommended! Party up to five recommended!

When we both finished reading the dungeon description, I looked at Jaceberlen with a bit of doubt. I was almost level 10 while Jaceberlen had just hit level 9. We did have the addition of my minions so that was a bonus, however this would be a very tough run. After discussing it for a few minutes, we decided to give it a shot and if it came to the point where it became obvious that we were in over our heads, then the two of us would just leave and gather what rewards if any we had accumulated. Mittens just called us a pair of pansies and said she was hungry for Gnoll meat. Alright, we said as the group entered the dungeon.

As we crossed over into the dungeon area it seemed to feel like the party stepped into another area. Out of nowhere, it seemed transition to be a war camp of some sorts bristling with gnolls. It looked like the fort was broken into 5 camps with each being a separate point. The easiest way to explain it was like a square with the main camp in the middle. After discussing it for a moment Jaceberlen and I chose the first one on the left to begin with.

As the two of us approached you could see the wooden walls gloom over the plains around fifteen feet in height. Gnoll guards manned the walls and thank goodness they were not the smartest foes. Our group snuck down behind some logs to formulate a plan of action. After talking over some strategy and the simplicity of the makeup of everything, I decided to take one camp out at a time and do our best to pull the targets away from any other camps as to not be overwhelmed by numbers. I decided to have the archers begin the assault while Mittens snuck up towards the walls. Jaceberlen would show himself to draw their attention and I would sling spells.

Before Jaceberlen made his move I decided to cast bless on Mittens, Jaceberlen, and myself. This small ragtag group would take any help we could get. I gave the orders to the archers to open fire on the guards on the wall. All eyes were watching the wall as the thrum of the bowstrings sounded from the two skeleton archers behind the logs. We all tried to follow the arrows and as my eyesight caught up to them, I watched them hit their marks.

One of the arrows struck a gnoll guard in the throat and

before a gurgle could even leave its mouth it fell over the wall silently too it's death. The other arrow struck the adjacent gnoll in the chest and the force knocked him off the wall. The trajectory, however, was in the opposite direction and onto the ground within the camp. The gnoll landed hard as the group could hear it from our position. Suddenly, a cacophony of squeals and shouts came from inside the camp as their forces marshalled. Luckily no other camp seemed to notice. Our party seemed to have lucked out there.

The gates of the camp opened and what seemed to be about twenty gnolls emerged wearing chainmail and short swords. The group was searching for their targets which allowed the archers to fire a few more rounds. They ended up taking out a total of five more gnoll warriors before they began closing in on our party. Now the rest of the group joined the fight. Jaceberlen stepped out to meet them along with the two scrappers while still giving me and the archers freedom to attack from afar. The archers continued to release arrow after arrow taking down any of the enemies they could. I began casting as fast as I could with toll of the dead and necrotic ray. Bolts of sickly greenish black bolts struck gnoll after gnoll causing blackened decay to mar the enemies in front of them.

As the two sides finally engaged, a total of twelve gnolls were littering the field as corpses. The remaining eight attacked Jaceberlen and the scrappers with extreme savagery. The gnolls swung their swords in downward chops with most hitting the dry soil as plumes of dust filled the air from the impacts. Jaceberlen used one such attack to slide within the front gnolls guard and deliver a front thrust. The sword tip pierced through the chainmail and cut deep into the gnolls chest. Blood sprayed the ground as bubbles gathered in the gnolls mouth. Jaceberlen didn't have time though to reflect as another gnoll was charging. He took his boot and kicked the dying gnoll off his sword to prepare for the attack.

Just as the charging gnoll was about to strike it was struck by an arrow in the thigh and a dark flame on the face. It screamed in pain as it withdrew its arms to its face. In that moment

Jaceberlen took advantage of the distraction and drove his sword into the gut of the distracted gnoll. The enemy's eyes went wide and continued to scream as its fate was sealed. As the sword was removed blood sprayed everywhere. Just for good measure another arrow slammed into its skull to verify it was dead.

Mittens had hardly been idle. When she approached from behind them, the low intelligence level of the gnolls gave them literally no chance at figuring out her displacement spell. They were swinging at literal illusions and when they would go off balance she would pounce. The gnolls were being slaughtered from both sides. The scrappers were damaged but still holding their own well. One scrapper was missing an arm while the other one was not much better. Their armor was ragged but still intact.

As Jaceberlen took down the last of the gnolls with a reverse swipe that relocated its head onto the blood-soaked field, we heard a rally cry from with the camp. Just then a gnoll much larger than its predecessors emerged onto the field in scale mail and wielding a giant club. It had two other gnolls with it. As I tried to identify the beast, I saw a glimpse of what we would be facing: Gnoll Captain of the Western Camp. Level 13.

As we promptly began to prepare for the battle I gave Jaceberlen a quick heal to top him off and double checked the status of the scrappers. I doubted that either of them would survive this encounter, but it would be what it was. I didn't have the time to resummon new ones before the battle ensued. Once the glance over was complete I gave the order for the archers to fire as the beginning of a necrotic ray spell was developing. Arrows and the bolt of greenish black decay sped through the air as they came closer to their intended targets. The captain went to use his club as a makeshift shield, but nothing hit it. The other two gnolls, however, were not so lucky. The two arrows slammed into the gnoll on the right as the shafts were sticking out of the stomach and chest. The gnoll dropped to the ground, clutching its wounds but would likely never rise again. The gnoll on the left stumbled upon the impact to its chest as the sickly dark magic began to decay the flesh at the edge of its arm.

The captain saw the events take place and decided to close the distance rapidly as it seemed to realize that it was losing its support staff. The captain and the remaining gnoll charged at us. Jaceberlen and the gimpy scrappers took off in kind to meet them head on. Jaceberlen met the attack of the captain head-to-head while the scrappers veered to the remaining gnoll. The archers knocked and released arrows at the injured gnoll while I let loose a dark flame at the captain.

Jaceberlen blocked the captain's initial blow from the side and tried to parry with an upward thrust as well. The captain, however, was not a mere amateur with battle and side stepped the swing and countered with a crushing blow to Jaceberlen's exposed rib cage. The blow sent him back into the air about five meters and he landed with a thump. I immediately began charging to attempt to get near Jaceberlen to heal him. I tried casting toll of the dead while I was running and soon found out that it was more difficult than I had expected. Only one of my four spells that were cast seemed to land on the captain.

By the time I got to within in range to cast my healing spell, the captain had closed the ground on me. I barely had time to get the heal off when I had to immediately roll out of the way of an overhand attack. As realization dawned on me that I would now be too close to cast there was no other option than to see what those scythes of decay could finally do. This was certainly not something I would ever want to do as "hello I am a not a tank" type of a cleric/necromancer, but I was given the dual-wielding skill and the weapons so I might as well see what it was capable of at this early stage.

Somehow, I noticed out of the corner of his eye that Jaceberlen was getting to his feet as I dodged another attack. As I turned to face the boss and squared off against him, you could see the captain laughing, thinking it had an easy target. Then it noticed the greenish aura emanating from the blades and the smile left his face. The gnoll now seemed to take a more cautious approach now as it closed the distance. The attack began with a forward thrust from the club. I pushed it away with one of the scythes and swiped its leg with the other one. It connected with the first attack, and the blade cut flesh and the gnoll winced in pain as the decay took hold. The gash rapidly took a black and greyish appearance and the blood looked black. It seemed to slowly spread in a matter of seconds. That is a very nasty effect I thought to myself. I spun around to attempt to get the second attack to hit. The spin move was fast and just as the second scythe was about to hit its mark, it was deflected at the last moment by the gnolls club.

The gnoll was visibly in pain but appeared to shrug it off as it tried to stand up straight. As its focus was solely on me now the attacks seemed to hasten. It was like it knew that if this fight was not finished quickly, then whatever was spreading from the wound could be fatal. Attack after attack came at me and although I was able to dodge several, I was not without injuries. After refocusing my stance, I felt something in my ribs snap from a side swing of the club, and it took everything I could muster just to not drop one of the scythes. It was obvious that I was not a front-line fighter but dammit, I had to give everything I had. Time and time again I tried to quickly heal himself during several of the exchanges but the gnoll seemed to time his attacks perfectly. Every time I tried to cast it, it would interrupt my concentration. The momentum of the fight was turning for the captain even though the decay was still spreading.

Finally, out of nowhere Mittens joined the fight from behind. Her attack seemed to hamstring the captain and as it went off balance; Jaceberlen struck it in the back with a sword thrust. In seeing that exchange, I managed to get a second burst of adrenaline and then the onslaught was in full force. All three of us rotated as a team with attacks, feints, and a whirlwind of damage. Mittens got the final blow as she leaped on top of the gnoll and sunk her teeth into the skull. The captain twitched and spasmed but then fell to the ground and slowly stopped moving. Just at that moment we heard the remaining gnoll fall to the skeletons. Down now to only one scrapper and the two archers, it seemed an appropriate time to recast the summoning spell. I really need a more reliable warrior type of minion.

CHAPTER SEVENTEEN

Gnoll Party

With each camp seemingly to be its own little battle, we were afforded the luxury of time to rest. We now also had a solid idea of the mechanics of the four camps so in theory it would be an easier outing going forward to eliminate the remaining three camps. After healing up and resummoning my skeletons, we began to make their way to the northernmost camp.

As our group made its way methodically through the remaining three camps, the blueprint from the first encounter managed to hold true. The strategy was simple. The archers started the encounter followed by spells from yours truly. Then when the gnolls would come out from the gates the group would engage them with melee from Jaceberlen, the scrappers, and then Mittens. Rinse and repeat. The enemies did, however, gradually became more difficult, which challenged the team's skills. A constant resummoning of my minions after each battle was necessary but Mittens and Jaceberlen were more than up to the challenge regarding the close quarter fighting.

Recognizing that melee was not my best skill set, I tried to stay away from that aspect after the first captain, however I did have to dabble in it for a time or two more. The archers more than earned their tier two skeleton status as they were invaluable. I mentally told myself that I couldn't wait to see what the higher tiers had to offer. If the archers proved to be a quality scouting force, then Mittens could remain close to the group to remain safe or at the very least provide us with a multi-pronged scouting option in the future.

While the archers and Mittens were away scouting the central fort, Jaceberlen and I discussed the dungeon so far. Although all experience was paused until the end of the dungeon, we expected to see some nice gains from the levels and quality of the enemies so far. Not to mention the quantity. From our rough calculation we had killed hundreds of higher level gnolls so far between the roaming patrols and the encampments. It was an exciting event that we just happened to stumble on. Not to mention that we were becoming a well-oiled machine with team chemistry. The loot as well wasn't too bad.

There were plenty of swords, armor, and shields to go around. The sell value of all of those could potentially be nice. We had discussed also wanting to see if any of the people in our larger upcoming group could use any of it as well before we just sold the mess out of everything to a vendor. Jaceberlen did, however, loot a nice pair of gloves from the third captain. It was called the Gloves of Superior Defense and added a + 30 to defense which was much higher than what he currently had. It also gave a +1 to Hardiness which for him was vital. Both of us were excited to see how much experience we would finally receive after the dungeon was over. After looking at the dungeon quest one final time before the boss fight; we knew there should not be any new surprises except what the Plains Master might throw at them.

Den of Bones Dungeon Update: Captains slain – 4/4, Dungeon Boss Slain – 0/1

The scouts and Mittens could be seen in the distance returning so I decided to check my interface once more to see if there were any messages or travel updates. By this time everyone had made it into the simulation and there were several groups and many individuals making their way to the appointed location. A few messages were present, and most were just giving an update and confirmation of the receipt of the email. My wife, Tiger Lilly, also sent me a message stating that they were in route and Raven and company were with her. Oh, was I ready to reconnect with everyone.

Finally, the scouts returned and gave us their updates. The archers proved to be very proficient with scouting and much to my surprise, they gave a decent breakdown of what they observed. It included basic movement patterns, formations, and defenses. They didn't give anything too detailed but considering they were currently lower level that wasn't to be unexpected. Mitten's recount wasn't too far off but was a bit more detailed. She noticed that the numbers were greater and they had archers. That was a new wrinkle in the makeup of the forces that we would face. That could pose some serious trouble for our smaller party. With the knowledge now in hand, we came up with a sound strategy and figured that the bigger the risk, the bigger the reward.

It was now time to complete this dungeon and get back on the road to our meeting location. I looked at Jaceberlen and nodded to him. We didn't need to verbalize anything as both knew what was at stake. Jaceberlen bunched his lips into a flat line and nodded back in return. It was time to see what all this fuss was about. I advised Mittens to do her thing but wait for the attack to start and the forces to be flank able. Mittens also nodded her head and said time to kill shit. Both Jaceberlen and I chuckled but the sentiment was shared. I then ordered everyone to move and make their way to the designated positions.

Jaceberlen, the skeletons, Mittens, and I came to a stop just inside the range of the archers so they could begin with a strong advantage. Mittens went into stealth and made her way near the gates, Jaceberlen made his way to a tree stump, the scrappers hid within another fallen tree, the archers took their stances next to some bushes, and I took cover behind a boulder. When everyone was set and ready, I cast bless again on Jaceberlen, Mittens, and myself as that was my first order of business.

As soon as the spell was completed, I gave the order for the archers to target the bowmen on the top of the wall to the left.

My target would be the one on the right. The archers released the arrows, and I sent a necrotic ray to my target. All three landed with soft thumps and then unfortunately; loud squeals of alarm could be heard. You could see the bowmen reel from the impact and two appeared to fall off the wall although only one looked to have been fatally wounded. One of the archer's targets was still active and fired a return shot that missed an archer by a few feet. I then sent a toll of the dead spell its way that finished the job.

As more gnolls came up to the walls they were greeted by more arrows and spells. Mittens appeared to be correct in the fact that their numbers were far greater than the encampments. As our ranged party members continued to dwindle their numbers from a distance, the group certainly didn't go without injury. I took a nasty bow shot to the thigh that required a healing spell to staunch the bleeding. One of my archers had a few arrows sticking out of him as it fumbled to keep firing arrows in retaliation. I really need to name them when they get stronger.

I had just finished casting a dark flame spell when I felt a sharp pain in my stomach. Instinctively I looked down to see an arrow shaft sticking out of my gut with blood flowing down onto my legs. That damn well hurt. I took a quick look at my health bar and noticed that it was dropping much faster than I had thought so my focus immediately had to shift to healing rather than damage. At least until everyone was back in good shape. I then removed the arrow only to have blood splatter the ground and gush out of the wound. One spell would not fix this and so I began casting heal as fast as the cool downs would hopefully allow me to heal the injury. With my focus solely on healing, I didn't see the arrow shot that shattered the skull of the damaged archer. All I heard was the cracking of bones and then the sound of my minion crashing to the ground.

Upon seeing the turn of events, Jaceberlen began cussing the ground as they were still basically useless. At this point he decided to enter the battle by casting blessing of shadows on the party even though it was a few minutes too late. It would help with damage reduction going forward though. Jaceberlen also began attempting to do whatever damage he could with sacred flame. With his attacks it bought me some time to finally heal myself and resummon my skeletons. At this point I decided to recast bless on Jaceberlen, Mittens, and myself as its time limit was about to expire shortly so I figured I should refresh that before my concentration had to be on fighting.

Finally, after a few minutes more we could see that the tide of enemies was thinning out, and I knew the main encounter was about to hit another phase. As if the dungeon agreed with that thought, we all suddenly heard a loud roar and then an eerie quiet. The fort doors seemed to creak open with a sense of dread as a giant gnoll strolled out of the fort and looked directly at us. Saying it was a gnoll was not giving the sight justice. It looked to be nearly twenty feet tall and about as round as a door from Earth. It had fangs that were about a foot long.

The monstrosity also had a security force of about ten gnolls that were noticeably stronger than their predecessors. As before, I ordered the archers not to waste any more time and attack the accompanying gnolls. I then joined as well by casting a necrotic ray. Jaceberlen popped his main area of effect spell, thunder, and the area lit up with the crackling sparks of electricity. You could see the thunder spell causing damage all through the group and as soon as it hit, the party could see the stuns take hold on about half of the group. This allowed the archers to gain a short-lived tactical advantage on critical hits and the scrappers rushed to join the fray. Jaceberlen was right behind them. He tore into the gnolls on the flank of the Plains Master while the scrappers were on the other side. The archers targeted that group too to increase the pressure on them while I attacked the Plains Master itself.

Mittens was in full stealth mode while she was sneaking up on the Plains Master. I was trying to keep its attention away from noticing her and so far, it had been successful. I finally used my darkness spell on the area with the melee taking place. Mittens and Jaceberlen could both see in the darkness, so it wasn't very immobilizing for them but for the remaining gnolls; it was a different story all together. Their hearing was incredible, but their eyes were unable to see anything. Mittens then took that opportunity to use her displacement spell to create an illusion of herself about five feet away and to the side of her true self. It created a dark shadow within the spell's area of effect. As the Plains Master noticed the illusion and mistook it for an enemy the speed of the attack was mind boggling. I barely even saw the blade. Thank goodness it was just an illusion because I would make no claims that Mittens would have survived that attack if it were to have connected with her.

Now that the subordinate gnolls were finally down, everyone focused their fire on the Plains Master. As the group continued to harass it with arrows, spells, and melee attacks, you could see the damage piling up. So far everything was going according to plan; and that is when the crap hit the fan. It would seem the Plains Master had other ideas rather than just taking a beating.

What appeared to be the second phase of the battle began as the Plains Master suddenly charged out of the darkness cloud and emerged into the light right in front of the archers. The Plains Master then made a terrifying roar that shook everyone with what appeared to be a taunt mechanic. As they tried to scatter for better positioning, the urge to attack took over and won out as they stood there trying to fire arrows. The Plains Master hit one of the archers with a backhanded swing of his sword. The unfortunate archer exploded into a spray of bones and then it was no more. Once the Plains Master was done annihilating that archer, it turned its attention to the other one. The archer rattled off a shot or two before it was doing everything it could to dodge the incoming attack. When the sword was on it's decent to have a friendly conversation with the archer's head, it was met suddenly by Jaceberlen's sword.

Jaceberlen followed his block attempt by kicking the knee of the gigantic gnoll. He then cast smite of shadows to help with his damage output. As the two began to dodge and weave while exchanging blows, the scrappers arrived and started flanking from behind. Mittens then followed as well. The group was then able to regain its continuity once more as we dwindled down the health of the Plains Master once again. The group had survived the burst of entering phase two. We were still down an archer, but Jaceberlen's smite of shadows damage addition was helping to make up the difference.

The Plains Master began looking worse as the wounds began to pile up. Hope began to creep back into our party as the enemy looked to finally be ready to fall. Once again as if on cue, there appeared to be a third phase to this encounter. Suddenly, the Plains Master jumped up and then slammed its club on the ground. This move seemed to create a massive wave of force that knocked everyone back into the air and then onto the ground. The dungeon boss immediately took advantage of the chaos as it closed in on the prone skeletons. Before the group could gather their bearings, every single skeleton had been destroyed by several attacks from the boss. Now it was down to us three versus the boss.

The battle had truly reached its final stage as only one side would emerge standing. The Plains Master was reeking of decay from my spell's effects and weapon wounds while we were all suffering from numerous wounds, low energy, and a small tinge of fear that was beginning to creep in. Pushing that down we as a group reengaged the boss. Jaceberlen charged, Mittens tried to flank, and I opened with a volley of spells. Both sides were continuing to accumulate damage and finally after a club smash that crushed her leg; Mittens was out of the fight.

In a fleeting sense of panic, I immediately lost my concentration as I was obviously worried about her safety. I tried to refocus, but I lost sense of the battle raging on. In that moment, Jaceberlen then took a sweeping attack that left him off balance and he hit the ground. He tried to roll out of the way and mostly succeeded; however, the glancing blow still took a huge chunk of his health. Jaceberlen began spitting up blood as he continued to try to get away from the attacks. I, sensing that the party was about to lose and my son might die, I went into a rage, equipped my scythes, and charged. I needed to buy Jaceberlen a bit of time to heal himself.

As my rage infested charge came ever closer, I cast necrotic ray and sent it racing towards the Plains Master. This time the ray landed in the face of the Plains Master, and it reeled back in pain. I then struck with all the force that I could muster as I swung both scythes in a cris cross motion that cut deep into both sides of the Plains Master's hips. Immediately the decay took hold, and the Plains Master promptly took a few steps back. As blood and ooze spread from the wounds it could see that the wound was serious. At this point I was a wall of determination and fury as I refused to relent and went after it. Whether it was panic, skill, or just a sheer will to survive, I swung my weapons in several formational arcs to maim the boss.

CHAPTER EIGHTEEN
Dance of the Plains Master

Jaceberlen sat up and coughed up a handful of blood. He knew this was a bad injury, however he refused to lose and especially when he wasn't out of it yet. He also knew he would not allow his dad to fall or take all the glory. He cast shadowed hands to give himself a bit of healing to at least get him up and be operational. If they were going down, then he would use everything he had to tip the scales.

As Jaceberlen stood up he noticed some things. One was that Mittens was still down but slowly breathing. Secondly was that his dad, Dookooze, seemed to be holding his own although he knew Dookooze was no frontline warrior and if he did not rejoin quickly that the momentum could easily shift. As much as he was still hurt, he began moving as fast as he could towards the beast.

I kept landing attacks repeatedly to keep the boss off balance. The decay was encompassing its entire body and blood was oozing from several wounds. The Plains Master parried with a few attacks but was still on the defensive awaiting me to tire. Suddenly the Plains Master saw its chance. I overextended my attack which left my side wide open and the beast crashed its club into my exposed flank. As I fell back in pain the boss felt a surge of adrenaline take over it only to recognize that whatever the weapons carried on their blades had finally done their work. It was not adrenaline at all but a realization of fear. The decay had rotted most of the flesh and the open wounds were ripe with necrosis.

Just as the boss glanced down to see the wreck that was its body, the boss felt a searing pain in the back of its neck. Its eyes widened as it saw a blade sprout from the front of its neck. It tried to cry out but no sound was available. Then the sword was yanked out of the boss and was followed by a cross swipe to the back. As the beast fell to its knees, Jaceberlen stood behind it with a bloody sword. I was certainly happy to see him up and moving and grateful for the timely intervention. I then leaped to my feet as gingerly as I could muster and swung both of my blades on an arc towards each other that after meeting flesh; they continued their trajectory slicing through flesh until they finally touched each other in the middle of the beast's neck with a resounding clank.

The Plains Masters eyes went dark and lifeless as it fell to the ground. As Jaceberlen and I saw the final breath, we both rushed over to Mittens to assess the damage. Mittens was lying there breathing with her eyes closed. She was still alive thank goodness. I immediately cast a healing spell on her and did that several more times to bring her up to full health. As she opened her eyes, she looked at us with a stare that we had never seen before. Something had changed. Mittens gingerly got to her feet and looked at us and said just two words: thank you. I had been overtaken with worry but finally heaved a breath of relief and went over to Mittens and gave her a big hug. She tensed up at that since this was the first time I had really shown affection to her but as fast as the tense moment was, she relaxed and embraced it. She wrapped her tail around my waist and leaned into me. Truly something had changed between us. She even looked at Jaceberlen and whispered: okay I might let you live now. We all just laughed and we all fell to the ground exhausted and relieved.

Just as we seemed to relax, a blinking icon appeared in front of my vision alerting me to several notifications. It seemed like Jaceberlen also had something similar, so I decided to take a moment to read them.

You have successfully completed the dungeon: Den of Bones
You have earned a title of First Dungeoneer for being the first party to complete a dungeon in WEO. +10% gain of experience while in dungeons
Distinguished Points earned = 300. You have reached Illustrious level 4
Due to completing this dungeon with two Earthen members instead of five you will have an experience a reward multiplier added.
Experience Points earned = 10,600
Congratulations you have reached level 10, 11, 12, 13, 14, 15, and 16. First Dungeoneer title has been retro activated. You have 45 free points to allocate.
At level 10 you have unlocked Professions. You may select a total of two professions to specialize in at any given time. To progress in your professions, you must seek out trainers or skill books.

Congratulations! As the first Earthen to reach Level 15 you have been granted the title: Megalomaniac. This title gives a +5% increase to any Distinguished Points
You have new abilities, skill upgrades, class evolutions, or spell modifiers to decide.
You have earned two gold

As I finished reading that section of the notifications, I couldn't believe just how much we had gained. It was safe to say that dungeons might be the way to become as powerful as we needed to be for what was to come. Especially with the bonus experience gains from that title. My goal was to be the strongest person in this simulation as I feared that I had to be. Right as I was getting ready to look at my level gains, our conversation was cut short by the sudden trembling and shifting of the ground nearby. Everyone jumped away only to see the area next to the dead Plains Master churn and then suddenly, a large chest shot up from under the ground to rest next to the boss. That was the dungeon reward. We had forgotten to loot the boss as well.

As both Jaceberlen and I leaped to our feet with the excitement of the loot and rewards, we decided to loot the Plains Master first. As I touched the monster an icon appeared asking if I wanted to loot it. Naturally, I agreed and then realized I'd received 550 silver coins, a crafting material called Essence of Savagery—which I'd never looted before—and a Cloak of Protection +10 that boosted my defense by ten points. Not a useless item but I was hoping for more. I was pleading mentally that hopefully the chest would be better.

I then made my way to the chest and peeked inside. Now this was much better. As I went to inspect it all, I began to smile as I looked at the items; You have received ten gnoll leather (crafting material), Elixir of Progression (consumable potion offering +15% experience gain for 3 hours. Stacks with any ongoing effects), Bracelet of Control (All minions do 10% more damage)

I could not believe that this had dropped. The system must have an increased chance of lootable item drops based on classes. Not to mention the modifier for completing it with two people. The elixir was fantastic, and it would stack. I would have to save that for an opportune moment though. The craft able leather might prove useful to someone in our group, though I am not certain what leather items could be made with it but at this point, there is no way to know for sure. It is possible that I could wear something made from it. We would just have to see.

The bracelet on the other hand would be an absolute game changer. This would instantly make my minions stronger although I needed to see if it affected Mittens at all. I pulled up her stat sheet to do a quick comparison. As I equipped the bracelet, I was disappointed to see that she was unaffected. I guess since she was a companion and not a minion, the bracelet effects did not apply to her or any future companions. Oh well it was hopeful thinking. I unequipped it so I could see what the difference was when I summoned my minions again. That will happen shortly after I look over my levels and such.

Jaceberlen completed his looting and was excited to receive a Cloak of Brutality that increased his chance at a critical strike by

10%. He also snagged so other crafting materials, and a Cap of the Plains Beast (a cap infused with the Plains Master's savagery as well as a bit of its scalp. Defense +20, +1 Strength). Overall, according to him it was a genuinely nice looting experience.

Now was the time about which I was most excited. I really wanted to see what the gains had provided. As I pulled up the notifications again, I could not help but have a giddiness within my stomach. I needed to be the strongest period. So, I willed my progression so that I could see where to start.

Upon reaching level 10 your Raise Skeleton spell has evolved. Your minions have grown stronger, and you may now summon 5 skeletons. You can specify the number of each mentally for a combined total of 5 as you cast the spell. Option 1. Scrapper – the base unit of the spell and is a front-line attacker with minimal intelligence. Option 2. Archer – a step above the scrapper and is a ranged unit armed with a bow and arrow. Their intelligence is slightly higher as they can scout, track, and communicate more effectively.

You have unlocked your second companion.

Your spell Necrotic Ray has evolved. As you strengthen so does your magic. Necrotic Ray will now add a damage overtime effect of 2 damage per second for 5 seconds. This stacks with any other damaging spells and can stack with simultaneous Necrotic Ray spells. This is in addition to its normal damage output.

You have acquired a new Necromantic spell: Aura of Necrosis. This spell emits an aura of necrotic energy radiating from you in a 10-meter circular radius. Any ally will gain necrotic resistance while any enemy will take 5 points of necrotic damage every 3 seconds while within the area of effect. At higher levels, this spell can evolve. Cast Time: 5 seconds, Range: 10 meters, Duration: Passive until dismissed, Cool Down: None, Energy Cost: 30 initial and a reserved cost of 10 during use.

You have unlocked your second summon companion ability.

Upon reaching level 15 your Raise Skeleton spell has evolved. Your minions have grown stronger, and you may now summon 6 skeletons. You may also choose from a new type of minion. You can specify the number of each mentally for a combined total of 6 as you cast the spell. Option 1: Scrapper – the base unit of the spell and is a front-line attacker with minimal intelligence. Option 2: Archer – a step above the scrapper and is a ranged unit armed with a bow and arrow. Their intelligence is slightly higher as they can scout, track, and communicate more effectively. Option 3: Umbral Mage – A tier 3 minion that is more intelligent than their predecessors. They specialize in darkness and shadow magic and raining death, fear, and gloom to unsuspecting enemies. This type of unit can execute conversations with a full vocabulary.

You have a new cleric spell: Purge – This spell allows you to purge and remove up to 3 afflictions or poisons from a targeted individual. Ability to purge dependent upon level of ailment being removed. Range 30 meters, Duration Instant, Cooldown 120 seconds.

You have a new Necromantic spell: Summon Skeletal Bulwark – A tier 3 minion that is capable of frontline combat. This unit is of minimal intelligence although it can communicate. It has damage reduction and taunting capabilities with its shield and club. Only one bulwark can be summoned at one time.

Well now that was a helpful addition, I thought as it would allow Mittens more attack options as well as let Jaceberlen focus more on damage rather than tanking. I also just realized I hadn't added a single free point since level 6. I decided to get all of that taken care of as well as perform all my summoning prior to us leaving the dungeon. I couldn't wait to see the end results from not only the minions but my new companion option. I looked at my 45 free points and what appeared to my shortcomings from the recently completed dungeon. That was a good measuring stick as how to improve my overall development.

I started off by summoning my minions first and I decided to go with two scrappers, two archers, and two umbral mages. I really wanted to see what they all looked like as they had evolved. The mages really had me interested. As they emerged from the ground, I inspected them all.

Skeletal Scrapper – Level 15, Health 120, Energy 0, Stamina 70, Defense 65, Weapons: Claw (1D8 +2)(x2),. Tier 2 Skeleton evolution. Once again, they seemed to look more solid with their bone structure and had changed from the crude chain shirt to a charcoal dark scale mail armor. Their damage had increased by 2 per attack and I cannot wait to see what the bracelet adds.

Skeletal Archer – Level 15, Health 80, Energy 0, Stamina 80, Defense 45, Weapons: Crude Longbow (1D8+3), Description: Tier 2 minion that has strengthened. This ranged unit is now armed with a crude longbow and arrow. I noticed the armor looked sleeker and more shadowy.

Umbral Mage – Level 15, Health 65, Energy 100, Stamina 65, Defense 35, Weapon: Staff (1D6), Spells: Shadow Bolt – A bolt of shadow that does (1D8 + Int Modifier), Blindness – A dark magic spell that will temporarily blind a target from seeing. Any attacks toward the target gain a + 2 attack and +2 to damage as they are considered flat footed. Targets can resist if their resistance exceeds the spell strength. Description: This Tier 3 skeleton is a masters of darkness and shadow magic. They are intelligent, capable of creative thought, critical thinking, and high-level communication. As they formed in front of me all I could see was dark forms emersed in jet black robes, hoods, and a smokey shadowy mist creeping out from them. It was honestly creepy and awesome at the same time. These were going to be a huge bonus as now our party had more ranged damage but most of all some crowd control.

Skeletal Bulwark - Level 15, Health 155, Energy 0, Stamina 155, Defense 95, Weapon: Heavy Bone Club (1D10 + 3), Actions: Taunt – A roar that angers enemies and makes them focus on the bulwark, To the Last Bone – when injured down to 10% health the bulwark will enter a stance that reduces incoming damage to itself by 15%. This will last until either the bulwark is destroyed, or it is healed above the 10% threshold. You may summon one bulwark at any given time. These frontline warriors focus on taking the brunt of the damage from enemies. They are equipped with armor, a club, and a shield. They have minimal intelligence but can communicate. They will follow your commands to the best of their ability. They are frankly dumb brutes but will protect you with their bones. This big bag of bones came out of the shadow wearing what appeared to be matted dark chain mail. All you could really see were greenish eye sockets. The club looked like onyx bone. This was a scary sight, and I was glad on our side.

I decided to equip the bracelet, and I immediately saw that the damage had indeed increased by 10%. Oh yeah! This would certainly help. Now was the time to really get excited since I can now summon my second companion. Mittens has been incredible, so I was hoping for something comparable to her even though I know it is a completely random encounter. I did, however, give a quick prayer for a good result.

CHAPTER NINETEEN

Second Summoning

As I began the casting of the summoning spell I had Jaceberlen's full attention. Even he was super stoked to see what arrived this time. Mittens seemed to have a bit of sarcasm and a touch of jealousy, but she too was all eyes on the summoning spell. Once the spell was complete everything went quiet. Like eerily quiet and for a what seemed like a much longer period than when Mittens came. Suddenly there was a thunderous noise and the swirling vortex of shadow on the ground erupted like a geyser of music which caught everyone off guard. I jumped back in surprise and grabbed my ears as the sounds coming from the vortex were hurting my head but then as it reached a crescendo, it began to soften. I then removed my hands and looked up at the scene before us.

The vortex seemed to calm as what appeared to be a woman and a small girl stood in the epicenter. Whatever they were they radiated with power. The lady looked at me and nodded. She took a step forward and the air seemed to whisp around her like a cloak. She stopped before me and spoke. Are you Dookooze, the Chosen of Tikallnosis? My mind went racing as to why and how she knew that. I quickly gathered my thoughts and politely said; Yes, my lady I am. My name is Dookooze. It is an honor to meet you. I waived over to Jaceberlen and introduced him and advised her that he was my son. The lady just simply bowed to both of us and, likewise, said that it was an honor.

She cordially smiled and somehow seemed to read my mind. I am sure you are wondering how I knew your name and that you were the Chosen of Tikallnosis she said. I nodded and replied that I was. The lady then stated that she can explain although time is not limitless. She then began that she and her child are being hunted by evil shadow dragons from an alternate plane. Fearing that she could not protect both herself and her daughter, she reached out to Tikallnosis for assistance. Tikallnosis is a patron of Chaos, and they have been allies in the past. Tikallnosis agreed to help and asked her if his chosen could be honored with her daughter as a companion. The lady then explained that she and her daughter have discussed the issue and what is at stake. Both agree that the child being placed under the chosen's care is not only necessary to protect her, but also to assist in hiding her until it is time to fight and help her grow.

The apparent mother then looked directly at me and said in a very powerful yet endearing voice; Do you swear to protect, care, and teach the future of my lineage? I was dumbfounded at what I was hearing and like an idiot I just fumbled out of my mouth; what exactly are both of you? I mean you both look human but however I have a very strong gut feeling that neither of you are. I also know that our path will not be without danger. In fact, I wager that our group will have many perilous adventures if we are to complete the quest that Tikallnosis has given me. The lady cocked an eyebrow at me and then once again smiled. Yes, I am aware that you have a destiny ahead of you. She will need to be strong if she is to face what is ahead. As far as your question of what we are, I will give you a glimpse.

Within a fraction of a second the air began to ripple and what was a lady had now been transformed into something of myth and legend. Before us stood a beast of at least hundred feet in length, slender in stature with iridescent pewter and blue scales. This was a dragon and no ordinary dragon if that could even be a thing. You're a Dragon I blurted out a little too fast. What kind of majestic dragon are you, my lady? A few seconds later she had transformed back into her human-like appearance.

We are Song Dragons. My name is Essmereldythia, Matriarch of the Moonheart Tropics. That is our home. This is my daughter, Serenitianix. Our true form is not something we readily show due to obvious reasons. Our kind has the innate ability to transform into a humanlike creature. Serenitianix will be in this form as to remain undetected unless needed. Now that you have seen our true form I will ask again. As she is but a very young child, do you swear to protect, care, and teach the future of my lineage? I resisted the urge to kneel however I did bow and then the next words out of my mouth sealed it for me. Yes, my lady, I will.

Once the words left my lips the matriarch relaxed and softened her stance. She then ushered her daughter over who then looked up at me and smiled. I then advised Serenitianix that it was very nice to meet her. I introduced her to our entire party and yes even the scrappers and the bulwark since they didn't have names. They mostly stood stoic except for Mittens who just said, Well shit. Didn't this just get interesting. Jaceberlen took his chin up off the ground and introduced himself as well. You could tell that internally he was about to explode with giddiness as to what we were experiencing. I couldn't really argue with him, but I then realized we had to keep her alive and train her.

The lady then looked at me and ushered me close. Upon reaching her she whispered to please keep her daughter safe as she is entrusting their future in the faith that she has in my patron. I replied by telling her that my path is perilous, but I will do everything in our power to protect her, care for her, and train her. The matriarch bowed her head and uttered three words; Thank you chosen. The mother then wrapped her arms around her daughter, kissed her on the cheek, then stepped back into the center of the vortex, and disappeared. Just like that the awkward quiet of the situation returned.

Once the scene returned to somewhat of a normal state, we looked at our newest member in a state of shock. I asked her if I could inspect her and to get a better understanding of what the group had morphed into. Two eyes then seared into me like she was trying to read into the gesture but after a few moments of silence she consented. I went ahead to inspect her.

Companion (Serenitianix): Species: Song Dragon, Rank: Very Young, Rarity: Mythical, Alignment – Chaotic Good, Level: 15, Armor: 105, Health: 135, Stats: Intelligence -16/Wisdom – 17/ Hardiness – 18/ Strength – 17/ Charisma – 16/ Intuition – 15/ Agility – 12, Skills: Perception +17, Abilities: Dragon Sense, True Sight (Passive), Lightning Reflexes, Hover (Locked), Flyby Attack (Locked), Immunity (Electricity, Paralysis, Sleep) (Locked), Magic Resistance +10, Attacks: Breath – Magical attack (Locked), Range: 30feet cone, Attack: +11 DC16, Damage: 2D6 electrical, Bite Range: Melee Attack: +11 Damage: 1D8 +4. In her human form the bite is replaced with dragon bone sword x2. 1D6 +4

Once I had finished inspecting her, I look straight into her eyes and said that I would do everything to protect her. Jaceberlen followed my sentiment with a statement of his own. As she seemed to notice the sincerity in our voices the dragon appeared to relax. I then laughed and said welcome to the club. What do you want us to call you. She looked at me puzzled. I then rephrased my question as I realized that in all reality, she was still technically a child. She stated her name, and we all looked at each other as none of us wanted to continue to pronounce that name. It was a dead giveaway that something was afoot. I recommended Serenity to her, and I explained it was the name of the greatest spaceship in one of the best television entertainment shows from our world. Not to mention the following movie with the Serenity name. It was a very honorable and regal name. That seemed to win her over as she looked at all of us, smiled wide and agreed that Serenity would work.

Now that that was over, we needed to rest up and head out. Our timeline just got a lot tighter with the dungeon and the subsequent events taking longer than expected. I noticed a flashing icon in my field of view, so I mentally selected it: Congratulations upon reaching level 15. As you reach the peak of normal human existence you will notice that to strive to levels never seen, it will take a much more dedicated effort to become more. As levels 1-15 are expected for any Earthen, to progress past mortal limits going forward will have an increased experience requirement. I took a quick peek and sure enough it looked like the percentage of experience needed had increased. This was going to be a grind to say the last. Especially with no level cap. That was an issue that I couldn't control and that everyone would have to deal with. I asked Jaceberlen and Mittens how their gains and upgrades were. Jaceberlen was elated at how his progression was going. He was almost level 15, and I advised him of some things to expect like the new abilities and the newly discovered experience change. He frowned at that but stated that we will all have to navigate that issue. Mittens was also pleased and so was I as I looked her over. Once that was complete, I decided to go ahead and allocate my stats, look at my character sheet, and roll the hell out towards our meeting point. Once I was finished with all my increases, I decided to look it over one last time before we headed out.

Name: Dookooze Darkbringer
Level: 16 (49% experience gained to next level)
Class: Moon Cleric
Race: Half Aasimar/Half Shadar-Kai
The Chosen of Tikallnosis
Stats: Intelligence – 13, Wisdom 62, Hardiness 14, Strength 11, Charisma 59, Intuition 12, Agility 12.
Health: 140
Health Regeneration Rate: 45 Per Minute (Non-Combat)
Energy: 620
Energy: 155 Regeneration Rate Per Minute (Non-Combat)
Stamina: 140
Stamina Regeneration Rate: 45 Per Minute (Non-Combat)
Distinguish Points: 525 Illustrious Level 4
Skills: Structural Construction, Conceptual Research, Lore-Ancient, Leadership, Lore-Religion, Herbalism, Skinning, Knowledge-Divine Spell Craft, Agriculture, Administration. You

have 25 open skill slots remaining.

Abilities: Higher Education, Over Skilled, You're A Secretive Lot Aren't You

Titles: First Dungeoneer, Megalomaniac

Divine Action: Prayer

Spells: Cantrip Spare Death – Cast Time: 1 second, Range: Touch, Cool Down: Once Per Hour, Description: You touch a living creature stopping heath loss to 1 remaining hit point. This will not stop death if wounded after nor if inflicted with a critical strike. This spell has no effect on undead or constructs.

Toll of the Dead - Cast Time: 1 second, Range: 20 meters, Cool Down: None, Energy Cost: 2 Description: You must visibly see the target to cast, and they must succeed at a Wisdom save or take 1D8 necrotic damage. Cover can negate damage.

Dark Flame – Cast Time: 1 second, Range: 20 meters, Cool Down: None, Energy Cost: 2, Description: A dark radiant flame emits from you towards a target. The target must succeed at an Agility save or take 1D8 dark radiant damage.

Spells: By Level: Heal – Cast Time: 1 second, Range: 20 meters, Cool Down: 3 seconds, Energy Cost: 10, Description: Heal a living creature in need of health for 1D10 + skill level of health point.

Necrotic Ray – Cast Time: 3 seconds, Range: 20 meters, Cool Down: 5 seconds, Energy Cost: 10, Description: Produce a bolt of death and necrosis at an enemy for 1D10 + skill level necrotic damage. It also causes damage over time of 2 damage per second for 5 seconds and will stack. This spell has no effect on undead and constructs.

Bless – Cast Time: 3 seconds, Range: 30 meters, Cool Down: 30 minutes, Duration: 10 minutes, Cost: 20 Description: This spell allows you to target up to 3 allies and bless them +2 to attack and evasion.

Aura of Necrosis - Cast Time: 5 seconds, Range: 10 meters, Duration: Passive until dismissed, Cool Down: None, Energy Cost: 30 initial and a reserved cost of 10 during use. Description:

This spell emits an aura of necrotic energy radiating from you in a 10-meter circular radius. Any ally will gain necrotic resistance while any enemy will take 5 points of necrotic damage every 3 seconds while within the area of effect. At higher levels, this spell can evolve.

Purge - This spell allows you to purge and remove up to 3 afflictions or poisons from a targeted individual. Ability to purge dependent upon level of ailment being removed. Range 30 meters, Duration Instant, Cooldown 120 seconds.

Raise Skeleton – You can call upon the bones of vanquished enemies to serve you in death. You may summon a total of 6 skeletal minions and can be a pre-selected assortment of the following. Skeletal Scrapper – Level 15, Health 120, Energy 0, Stamina 70, Defense 65, Weapons: Claw (1D8 +2)(x2),. Tier 2 Skeleton, Description: These basic skeletons can understand basic commands and execute them to the best of their ability. Skeletal Archer – Level 15, Health 80, Energy 0, Stamina 80, Defense 45, Weapons: Crude Longbow (1D8+3), Description: Tier 2 minion. This ranged unit is armed with a crude longbow and arrow. This unit can scout. Umbral Mage – Level 15, Health 65, Energy 100, Stamina 65, Defense 35, Weapon: Staff (1D6), Spells: Shadow Bolt – A bolt of shadow that does (1D8 + Int Modifier), Blindness – A dark magic spell that will temporarily blind a target from seeing. Any attacks toward the target gain a + 2 attack and +2 to damage as they are considered flat footed. Targets can resist if their resistance exceeds the spell strength. Description: This Tier 3 skeleton is a masters of darkness and shadow magic. They are intelligent, capable of creative thought, critical thinking, and high-level communication.

Summon Skeletal Bulwark - Level 15, Health 155, Energy 0, Stamina 155, Defense 95, Weapon: Heavy Bone Club (1D10 + 3), Actions: Taunt – A roar that angers enemies and makes them focus on the bulwark, To the Last Bone – when injured down to 10% health the bulwark will enter a stance that reduces incoming damage to itself by 15%. This will last until either the bulwark is destroyed, or it is healed above the 10% threshold.

You may summon one bulwark at any given time. These frontline warriors focus on taking the brunt of the damage from enemies. They are equipped with armor, a club, and a shield. They have minimal intelligence but can communicate. They will follow your commands to the best of their ability.

Spells: Divine Absorption – Cast Time: Instant, Range: Self, Cool Down: 24 Hours, Energy Cost: 40, Description: Once per 24 hours you invoke the divine instinctively to prevent a death dealing blow you would otherwise normally receive. Your god looks down on you and will keep you alive with 1 hit point. Warning any subsequent successful attacks dealing damage will deal damage accordingly.

Spells: Gifted Summon Companions – Cast Time: 1 Minute, Range: Self, Cool Down: None, Energy Cost: 30, Description: As a reward for assisting your god, you are given the ability to summon up to 3 companions to aide you in your pursuit of justice for your god, Tikallnosis. May summon 1 companion at level 1, another at level 10, and a final companion at level 20.

Current companions:

Companion (Mittens): Species: Displacement Beast, Rank: Small, Rarity: Rare, Level: 15, Armor: 75, Health: 110, Stats: Intelligence -11/Wisdom – 14/ Hardiness – 20/ Strength – 12/ Charisma – 11/ Intuition – 12/ Agility – 23, Skills: Perception +15/Stealth +9, Abilities: Darkvision, Avoidance (1/2 damage on saving throws), Displacement (projects a magical illusion that creates an image of him within 10 feet of his position creating a -50% chance to be hit), Keen smell (+2 perception for issues relying on smell), Shifting Step (While displacement is active and an attack misses him he can teleport up to 5 feet without penalty), Magic Resistance +5, Attacks: Tentacles – Melee, Range: 10feet, Attack: +9, Damage: 1D6+4b, Bite; 1D4 piercing

Companion (Serenitianix): Species: Song Dragon, Rank: Very Young, Rarity: Mythical, Level: 15, Armor: 105, Health: 135, Stats: Intelligence -16/Wisdom – 17/ Hardiness – 18/ Strength – 17/ Charisma – 16/ Intuition – 15/ Agility – 12, Skills: Perception

+17, Abilities: Dragon Sense, True Sight (Passive), Lightning Reflexes, Hover (Locked), Flyby Attack (Locked), Immunity (Electricity, Paralysis, Sleep)(Locked) Magic Resistance +10, Attacks: Breath – Magical attack (Locked), Range: 30feet cone, Attack: +11 DC16, Damage: 2D6 electrical, Bite Range: Melee Attack: +11 Damage: 1D8 +4. In her human form the bite is replaced with dragon bone sword x2. 1D6 +4

Armor Set: Unliving Cowl – Armor 10, Unliving Spiked Chest Armor - 15, Unliving Spiked Gauntlets Armor – 8, Unliving Spiked Greaves Armor 10, Unliving Boots Armor – 8: Set Rarity: Rare, Full Set Bonus- Summoned companions or pets have a 10% attack speed and 10% increase in damage; Evolution Set – This set of armor was designed to be worn by the mightiest of the lords of death, but you have received this in its infancy. As you grow in skill and power this suit can be evolved to further protect and enhance you with powerful features at higher levels. Total Defense 61

Belt of Wisdom +1, Bracelet of Control (+10% Minion Damage)

Weapon: Dual Sickles of Minor Decay – Type: Simple, Hand: Both Slots, Attack: +5/+3 rating, Rarity: Uncommon, Speed: Normal, Description: Sickles designed to slowly rot their enemies upon attack, each successful attack will inflict 1D6 + Str modifier damage with a 15% chance to inflict Decay. Decay will cause 3 necrotic damage per 3 seconds for 12 seconds

Racial Abilities: As an offspring of darkened humanoid creatures from both the Celestial and Elvin bloodlines you have made your way onto the material plane from the shadows to forge a path of your choosing. Both races resemble typical humanoid creatures but with potential elven or celestial features that are a bit off from your typical kin.
Darkvision. You can see in dim light within 60 feet of you as if it were bright light, and in darkness as if it were dim light. You

discern colors in that darkness only as shades of gray.

Keen Senses. You have proficiency and +2 bonus in Diplomacy and Perception skills.

Necrotic Resistance. You have resistance to necrotic damage, charming, and sleep affects.

Night Cloud: Once per day you may cast this spell centered around a targeted point within 60 meters. This spell emits a perpetual mass of spherical darkness surrounding your targeted point. The distance emitted will equal in meters to your character level plus skill level. Enemies within this darkness are blinded and considered flat footed. Night Cloud can dispel any light spell within the same area of equal or lower level. This spell can be negated by a higher-level magic spell.

CHAPTER TWENTY

Reunion

Aerach pranced and danced her way down the path while her companions Dealz, Aurora, Endor, and Olivia walked behind her in torment. The cat-like Kitsune was being overly loud with her words especially since they were trying to meet at the designated location without dying. Endor, the wood elf monk, kept trying to be as perceptive as his new stats would allow but he wasn't able to hear much over her singing.

Aurora and Dealz were just trying not to kill her. Aurora pointed out that at the compound Aerach was a much more tolerable person. The gnome alchemist just looked at her again then turned to her husband, Dealz. He also had chosen the gnome race with Auroa so they would be the same. He opted for the arcane mentalist or as many refer to it as a mesmerist. He was a great salesman in real life, so those traits just seemed to want to carry over. The gnome race was odd as they were so short and round, but Aurora was adamant to be this race prior to entering. Olivia on the other hand tried to choke the life out of Aerach. In the real-world Olivia was a very quiet person. Here though, it would remain to be seen but Olivia was not a fan of the noise. The halfling witch finally had to put her hands over her ears. Endor heard something and grabbed Aerach to shut her mouth. As she did, Endor waved everyone around and put the group on alert.

Pint Size as an elf rogue was nimble on her feet and acutely aware of her surroundings. She motioned for Glamdring,

Farwind, Rakasha, and Bhorn to stop. Glamdring was trying to soften the sounds of his armor hitting the ground. It was a good thing the gnomish cleric didn't have to bend too far. Farwind knelt next to Glamdring, and the drow ranger did not make but a whisper in doing so. Rakasha refused to kneel on the ground and instead leaned up against a tree. She was a sun elf rashaman witch and a self-appointed princess in real life so that was a big no. Bhorn didn't give a rat's behind about the dirt and just shook his head at Rakasha. Now granted he was a halfling rogue so getting dirty was one of his jobs.

As they sat there quietly, they continued to hear singing approach. They couldn't believe how loud this idiot was. Then they heard other soft voices and suddenly, the voices clicked. They knew these people from the compound. Please tell me that isn't who I think it is, Farwind said. As the group turned to her and seemed to nod in agreement, she decided to step out into the path. The rest of her group quickly realized they didn't have an option in this, scrambled to join her. The next thing they knew was the scene got eerily quiet as Aerach finally shut up when the two groups faced each other. Then without a warning Endor walked over and hugged Pint Size. Everyone in both groups gathered around to exchange pleasantries, discuss classes, races, and where they were headed. In the back of her mind Farwind knew that trusting Mitch, AKA Dookooze, was the right thing to do when agreeing to come to the compound. Strength in numbers he had said and that seemed to be proving its worth right now. As they all began to embark on the remaining portion of the journey they made sure to tell Aerach that her decibel level was now a requirement of zero.

The closer that Jaceberlen came to reaching the town that was designated as the meeting point, he couldn't help but be excited. Even though their time in WEO had been short so far, it wasn't without challenges. They were alive in a video game simulation for goodness' sake. They had fought goblins, cleared a dungeon, leveled up, and almost died. Not to mention that in their new reality there were seven skeletons, a displacement beast called Mittens, and a toddler dragon disguised as a human called Serenity accompanying them at this moment. All courtesy of his dad's class. And they could talk. What the hell! Jaceberlen looked at his dad and just started laughing.

Unaware of what the joke was I smiled and asked if Jaceberlen was okay. He said yeah just reminiscing of our time here so far. At that point Jaceberlen noticed that his dad had cracked a smile and laughed quietly to himself. Jaceberlen deep down was seriously grateful that the system had placed his dad with him. He would have been okay on his own for sure, however being able to see what could truly be at stake was a heavy motivator for him to be as strong as his dad. They both knew just how hard this would be and he would need to have his dad's back when needed. To do that though he would need to be strong enough to enforce it.

As Jaceberlen and I walked down the trodden path towards our destination, the trip had not been a cakewalk since leaving the dungeon. I had tried to consistently learn more about our newest addition, Serenity, continue to try to understand my class and mechanics better, fiddle with the user interface, and just get a more fluid feel for the system. We did, however, figure out how to access and turn on and be able to see opponent's health bars and mechanics. We had fought several hundred enemies since we had left the Den of Bones. That wasn't near the challenge of the dungeon, but it did help with learning the group dynamics. The bulwark was solid, the archers did what they did, the scrappers had moved to more of a damage type role, and the umbral mages were just dangerous.

Over the last several hours we had also managed to gain a few more levels. I was now firmly on my way to 19 and Jaceberlen was about to cross over to 17 at any time. Neither of us liked the difficulty change to the experience modified upon reaching level 15, but we would make sure everyone in our group knew what to expect if they didn't already. Mittens was just becoming a nice little badass while Serenity could also hold her own quite well. She and I both knew that most of her powers would open as she got stronger, however we needed to be secretive about her true origins for the time being. She was very mature and wise even for a young dragon. She would be a good shoulder to bounce stuff off in the future I presumed.

Serenity and Mittens were still not warming up to each other as their backgrounds weren't exactly aligned. Both were of Chaotic nature but while Serenity being of the good aspect would do the right thing by any means she saw fit; Mittens just damn well would do what she wanted regardless of good or bad. That was something we would need to keep in check or at the very least monitor closely. Both were very young and had a lot of room to grow so I hoped that they would form a solid bond. As our adventures continued, I would anxiously wait for them both to be more open to one another.

During my moments of reflection, I heard Jaceberlen chuckle. As I looked at him to make sure that he was all good, he managed to make a statement that literally had been running rent free in my mind for a good portion of the day. I too had been trying to wrap my head around the gravity of our new life. Everything had changed. One moment I was a normal John Doe walking in a line that was headed towards cryogenic pods and then a few hours later I now feel as if I am somehow the last hope for humanity. It is a heavy burden for sure, and I honestly don't know if I can do this, but I will do everything I can to help uncover the truth. I will have my family and friends with me, and I really hope they will support or understand regardless of what I am able to divulge. I will work with Tikallnosis regarding that aspect. I took a long slow look across my immediate group. Mentally I was amazed at not only the realism of everything but just the composition. It was of course my son, but then a cat, a dragon out of fantasy, walking and talking skeletons, and then there was magic. This was certainly something to grasp.

We had been on the windy road now for several hours and by our calculations we should be at our initial destination very soon. Our party was tiring and ready to get there. Dusk was beginning to settle in and as we crested a large hill, we finally saw it. The clouds were heavy and low and with dusk rolling in and the grass was high. In the distance you could see the town and the wooden walls surrounding it. Lights were starting to emerge due to darkness creeping in for the night, but the town was still very visible. As we crossed a narrow bridge about a hundred meters in front of the outer walls, you could begin to smell a variety of scents. It was a hodge podge of pig pens, cattle fields, unwashed townsfolk, ale, flowers, and food. Certainly not the greatest smell in the world but I would embrace whatever was accosting our senses at this point.

The town guards crossed their halberds to prevent our entry as we walked up. State your business, one of the guards said. I looked at them and politely responded that we were meeting a group of friends here, looking for food and lodging, and we as a group would be heading out tomorrow. Seems to be a lot of you today the other guard said. We replied that yes there was a large group of us and we hoped it wasn't a problem. The left guard narrowed his eyes at our party and tightened his grip on his weapon. I noticed that and asked if there was a problem. He remained silent for a moment then looked at my minions and said that they were not welcome. I looked at him and advised him that they were my minions and would not harm anyone unless we were attacked. The guard said he didn't care and that they could not enter. Jaceberlen looked at me and shrugged. Fine was all I could begrudgingly say. Where can I leave them for the time being. The guard said I could unsummon them or have them take shelter across the bridge at the edge of the woods. What if I place them in my room for the night and leave them until we leave or is there a barn I could rent.

The guard took a second pondering the request. I even offered to have them patrol the area for them which was quietly refused with a nod. The other guard spoke up at this point and advised me that there was a barn just on the outside of the rear gates that they could rent from the owner Ron. It was currently unused as it is awaiting repairs and Ron could likely use the coin. I then told the skeletons to follow me as we headed over that way.

When I met Ron, he seemed to be a bit more understanding of my plight than the guards. He notified us that necromancers are extremely rare in these parts and the sight of the undead has a tendency of scaring the life out of people. He said it all depended on the necromancer whether it was a violent or civil interaction. I assured him it would be civil and he allowed my minions to stay there for 3 silvers. After the transaction was completed, I instructed the archers to patrol the area and defend the barn. If they needed me or vice versa, they could reach out mentally. They all nodded in agreement and moved into their resting spot for the night. I would grab them in the morning.

Jaceberlin, Mittens, Serenity, and I finally reached the inn and walked inside. Once we entered it was a barrage of sounds, music, and people. It was very crowded and the ale and food were flowing like a buffet line. There was what appeared to be a minstrel playing a lute and singing tales of old heroes to the yells of the crowd. I approached the barkeep and asked for a room to start then meals and drink for my party. The barkeep nodded and said I was lucky as they only had 2 rooms left. 10 silvers for the room, 2 silvers per meal, and a silver for each pint of drink. I thought it was fair, and I gave her the requested coins. She gave me a numbered key and then nodded for us to sit at one of the few vacant tables in the joint.

Moving to the table we had to dodge and avoid numerous non-player characters or NPCs as well as Earthen players we didn't recognize that were certainly using the mead as a way of escaping the recent events. Upon sitting down, we did notice quite a few of our friends sitting near us, so we decided to greet them and see how their travels had been. There wasn't enough room for all our incoming group to gather as a single unit so it would seem the visitation would have to be a table here and a table there for now. I decided to pull up my quest:

CHAPTER TWENTY-ONE

Family Time

You have been offered a quest: Gather the Followers Part Two of the Divine Investigation. This is a unique Divine Level quest and has an unspecified number of parts.
Level Requirement: None
Rewards: Experience Points; Distinguished Points; Class Appropriate Spell
Description: You are to communicate and coordinate at least 85% of your contacts list to meet you at the quest point or at your designated place of gathering. Percentage of group gathered – 53% 44/83

So far it looked like over half of the group was here, but I decided to send out a quick message to everyone letting them know we were down in the eating area. I soon got several replies stating they were also in town and either at the inn or taking care of some other business. I also got a few messages from the remaining groups as to how far out they were. From their responses I figured we would have everyone here within the hour. After speaking with Jaceberlen we decided to see if anyone in our group needed any of the items we had looted before selling the remains tomorrow morning.

Once our food came, we broke away from a few of our friends, Maverick, Piper, and Beanie, to eat our meal and formulate what we would tell the group. We sat down at the table to our food and drinks, as Mittens even had a nice big chunk of roasted meat with a nice thick bone in the middle. You could hear the purring sounds from the floor. Serenity seemed to eat like a human, so I was happy that her shapeshifting included eating etiquette. If anything, she was a bit dainty. I decided that it was a good time to summon Tikallnosis. I needed to prepare what was going to be said plus I needed to clarify a few things. I mentally brought up my summon icon and clicked it. Instantly the world went quiet and his mental image appeared in my field of vision.

Tikallnosis looked at me and as if he knew what I was thinking, he advised me that nobody outside of us two would see or hear anything we discussed. With a sigh of relief, I said, okay and began to say what was on my mind. We are in our meeting place to reunite with our group, I said. He nodded in agreement and let it be known that this was a good first step. He then looked away and then let me know that he just looked at our location and that we are a few days from the quest location. Tikallnosis then said that the fastest route was by boat from the port city about a half a day's journey from here to the south. After nodding in acknowledgement, I asked him if there was anything more I needed to know about the purpose behind Serenity's placement in my care. Tikallnosis just said it was the safest thing for them and that he trusts her with me and she would help me in my pursuits as well. A voice of reason for the future me. I decided to take it at face value and just shrugged my shoulders.

I then dove straight into the real reason I wanted to talk to him. I laid out my next series of plans and thoughts for the next few minutes while he sat there and listened. Once I was done, he was quiet for a minute longer and then he spoke. I understand your logic and can see your point, Tikallnosis said. Let's both think about this and although I think your rationale is very solid, I would like to vet it on my side. So, we agreed to pick up the conversation at a later point although we did come away with a good intro for everyone. We discussed a few more items of importance before I decided to end the talk. As we parted ways, he looked at me and said, "I believe in you. Then reality snapped back into focus as the roar of the patrons and music hit me full on like a locomotive.

Jaceberlen looked at me like I had gone crazy when he asked if I was alright. I laughed and said yes, I was just discussing some things with Tikallnosis. Ahhh okay, he said because you just looked like you were spaced out into oblivion and that he was starting to get a bit worried. He then asked if anything had changed and I just reassured him that it hadn't.

As the night progressed, we finished our meal even though Mittens was still going to town on the clean bone. She was content so who was I to argue. I mentioned to Jaceberlen that we should be seeing the remaining group members arrive anytime now considering they were basically on top of us with regards to their dots on the map. At this point we were only missing a handful and then the door to the inn opened.

This was the main group that we had been waiting for to arrive. These were mostly my main family members so I couldn't wait to see them. Raven, my daughter, was the first person through the door holding my granddaughter, Ophelia, in her arms. She was followed by Duck, Laltag Duine, my son-in-law, Mimis, my mother, Big Bear, my dad, and finally Tiger Lilly, my wife. Upon seeing them Jaceberlen and I jumped to our feet and made our way over to them giving them all hugs, welcomes, and then giving my wife a kiss. As we ushered them to our table, I gestured to the barkeep to please bring them food and drink. I gave the barmaid the required silvers and then I was about to head back to the group, but I knew that I had to somehow quickly explain to my wife why a young girl was part of my party as Tiger Lilly was giving me some of those glances asking what the hell is this. So, I tried to mentally converse with Serenity while I was standing there. Serenity responded with a light laugh and somewhat understood the predicament I was in. Thank goodness she took pity on my situation and consented to an explanation to my wife.

During the time they were eating their meals, I pulled up my interface and typed a lengthy detailed message to Tiger Lilly as to whom and why about the details surrounding Serenity's involvement in my party. Once that was smoothed over and out of the way we caught up on their adventures, starting area, as well as races and classes. I just had to tell Tiger Lilly how cute she was as a Drow. I had to get the naughty thoughts out of my head. I had family present after all, I thought.

Jaceberlen and I went over our adventures, the dungeon, our classes, and then of course Mittens, and Serenity. We didn't get into a lot of information but tried to keep their backgrounds surface level. They were all somewhat taken back at my race combo and more so the class. I once again kept this information somewhat close to the vest for now as we were not in a secluded place and ears were everywhere. I let them know my companions were hanging out on the edge of town and they would see them shortly. I did go into more of my testing specifics so they could understand that I had tested very highly which opened these possibilities.

Jaceberlen nor I went into the classless and 1 hit point period in my new life, but we did delve into the different minions that I had. Everyone seemed to be starstruck that my class and race were both Mythical ranks. My comment that the testing was extreme and felt like for days raised a few eyebrows. Everyone looked stupefied when I mentioned the bird skeleton that I swung around like a weapon. Duck just laughed and said dude you just can't make this crap up. We all had to just laugh at that remark.

Soon the conversation shifted to my mom and dad. My dad had lost the use of his arm when Raven was just a baby so to see him with a matching set of juiced up biceps was a talking point. Big Bear was all smiles as he moved it around. He then looked at us and with what appeared to be complete sincerity; he thanked us for persuading him to come to the compound. Mimis gave him a big hug and then she verbalized how scary this place was and that she hoped to avoid all this craziness. With what felt like a little guilt I told her I would try everything I could to keep her away from it, but I doubted it. I deep down knew I couldn't keep that promise but would do everything I could to protect them. Raven and Laltag Duine next discussed how Ophelia was handling it and that Raven loved her ranger class and that she had wanted a companion just like Tiger Lilly did. They then went into explaining their classes again and what their pets would hopefully be if they ever evolved into a companion type of ranger. Raven had a tiger in mind as a pet while Tiger Lilly had a drake. That is super cool, I exclaimed as I knew from gaming with them back in the real world that they were both prone to the ranger class with pets. Sharpshooters with a soft side I laughed. Raven's pet would be called Pookie and Tiger Lilly's would be called Coconut. The rest of the group were non-pet classes, but it did seem we had a very good mix in just this portion of the group. I was excited to see what the entire group makeup would look like.

The night began to wound down, and we all managed to gather down in the eating area. I notified them all that we would head out around eight in the morning. Thank goodness our user interface had a clock. A few of them had questions as to where we were going but I let them know that I apologized for the delay in information, but I wanted to make sure their ears were the only ones that heard it. I did let them know our destination however I didn't necessarily say why at this point. They all knew it was some sort of quest because I had been able to share the Homestead quest with them earlier that evening. Everyone had jumped at the chance to earn experience and the other rewards. Not to mention a possible home. I needed to talk more with Tikallnosis before disclosing more. We had a plan in motion for all of that though. This was enough for now.

As we all broke for the night, I mentally checked on my minions, and they seemed to be handling themselves just fine. Their patrols had turned up with a few dead wild animals but nothing serious. I told them I would see them in the morning and cut the communication. We all made it to the rooms and Tiger Lilly joined us in the room. We had room for one more person so Smeeeagal joined us so he and Jaceberlen could clown around and catch back up. When I laid down next to Tiger Lilly she curled up into my arms and it was certainly weird lying next to a dark-skinned, pointy-eared drow elf with red eyes. I mean I can certainly get used to it, but it was going to be something to get used to. Before falling asleep I decided to check my flashing icons in my interface.

You have completed the quest: Gather the Followers Part Two of the Divine Investigation. This is a unique Divine Level quest and has an unspecified number of parts.
Level Requirement: None
Rewards: 1200 Experience Points; 150 Distinguished Points; Class Appropriate Spell – Withering Snare Cast Time: 3 second, Range: 30 meters, Area of Effect: 10 Meters, Cool Down: 1 Minute, Energy Cost: 20, Description: You call forth spectral arms from the afterlife to grapple, slow, and nauseate your enemies in the affected area. Any target caught within their grasps will become slowed to half of their movement speed and will take temporary constitution damage. The target must succeed at an Agility save or remain in the snares for another turn. Damage does stack.

Description: You are to communicate and coordinate at least 85% of your contacts list to meet you at the quest point or at your designated place of gathering. Percentage of group gathered – 100% 83/83

You have been granted the quest: Deliver Them Home Part Three of the Divine Investigation. This is a unique Divine Level quest and has an unspecified number of parts.
Level Requirement: 18
Rewards: Experience Points; Distinguished Points; Profession Skillbook
Description: You are to escort your group to the borders of the designated township with at least 90% of your group still alive. Percentage Alive 100% 83/83
Do you accept this quest: Yes/No

Well of course I selected yes and I couldn't wait to try Withering Snare. I was inching closer to level 19 as well. Just a bit more to go. Okay it is time I go to bed I had to remind myself. I then gave my wife a soft kiss on the forehead and then I drifted off to sleep.

CHAPTER TWENTY-TWO

Landfall

The group had progressed about four hours into our journey to the coast. We were more than likely about an hour or so away from the supposed port town and had seen a regular stream of monsters on our path. Initially the group really didn't truly conceptualize my class until I had seven skeletons walk out of the woods and join us on our trip. Some of the group gave them a wide birth but most kind of just went with it. By the time we hit the two hours mark the females of the group were chatting with the mages and had given names to every one of my skeletons. Luckily the archers got to skip out on the naming session as we had them running as our perimeter scouting party.

They were operating in a semi-circle all around us as forward points to catch all sides of the pathway warning us of impending danger. Mittens tried to get involved and go hunting, however all the children latched onto her like a ragdoll. They were hugging all over her, trying to grab her tentacles, trying to ride her, and asking her questions nonstop since she was the first catlike creature they had ever seen talk. I felt sorry for her as you could see her physically cringe. Mentally she was screaming at me and kept asking me if she could eat them. After promptly denying that request she just seemed to decide that she had dealt with enough torment and whispered into my mind that she was going to see what trouble she could get into and that she was hungry. I laughed and just advised her to stay close. Then she was off.

Jaceberlen and I tried to let the minions and the other group members handle any of the enemies we faced as it would allow us to gain insight into their skills, styles, and abilities. Most seemed to handle themselves well. There were some standouts and our normal group of gamers back when the world wasn't a toxic shit pool seemed the most eager to embrace the new reality that we saw ourselves in. My old group of Tal'n, Biggus Dikkus, and Captain Ahab seemed to be in high heaven. They were the typical Min/Maxers that dissected every role-playing game to determine the best combination of skills, tactics, and armor to give the most of an advantage. I knew their capabilities, so I was eager to watch them work. We were an awesome team when we played games.

Other gamers I knew such as Atriox the Arcanist, Dartonias, Landoleer, Fandela, Farwind, Gunthar, Gundham, and Smeeeagal seemed to also be embracing everything. I looked at Jaceberlen and said, dude what is up with Smeeeagal? He is running around in insanity mode. Jaceberlen just laughed and said that when they were cutting it up last night, he noticed his best friend seemed super into the new world. On a warpath sort of Jaceberlen added. Well, I said that race and class combo of his is downright nasty. I cannot wait to learn how we can use it. The Fetchling race was a new one to me too as it was a humanoid surrounded by wisps of shadow. Aesthetically cool as hell for sure.

Raven and Tiger Lilly were coming along slower, but I expected that as they were not gamers to this stye of play. I was grateful that they had both chosen the same class and that they would potentially have pets to help them acclimate to our new life. My wife's siter and husband, Gundham and Belle, seemed to be in a renaissance fair dream land. They took roleplaying to an extreme before WEO, but this was taking it to an entirely new level. I just hoped that they would calm down with the accents, attire, and well just everything. It was either going to be that, or they would just give themselves over to WEO's culture. I just shook my head at them, but it will be what it will be.

We continued to slowly fight our way through the uncharted wild until we hit the outskirts of the port city. By this point it seemed that most of the group had gained a few levels due to our constant friction with the regional wildlife. We ran into a city patrol that advised us what was the best route to reach the docks. They took a second glance at my minions, but they were smart enough not to say a word. As our group continued to push towards the city. It looked like we were about half an hour's walk to the gates when my archers as well as Mittens alerted me to a potential threat.

We were heading into a heavily wooded area at a curve in the path that seemed to last about five hundred to six hundred yards long. According to the scouts there appeared to be a group of about fifteen to twenty brigands concealed within the forest. I motioned for the group to halt and at that point I conveyed what the scouts had seen. I asked if anyone was willing to fight and honestly all but about five of the adults were willing to fight. Mimis, Nana, Aurora, Tallulah, and Tal'ns wife were then redirected to watch and protect the children. My niece, Neelz, was barely old enough to warrant a class and as a two-handed warrior, I figured she would be able to hold the fort with them, so I redirected her there.

This was now the time to get into a strategic set up as we weren't sure what type of classes we would be facing. Tanks were placed in the front followed by melee classes to the flanks, then ranged damage classes, and finally support personnel were directed to the rear. My archers and Mittens were still ahead, gathering intelligence so I instructed them to surround the upcoming group and keep me updated on their movements.

Once we were positioned correctly, we slowly entered the forest. As we approached about 100 meters inside of the densely wooded area Mittens and the skeletons both notified me at almost the same time. It looked like the group ahead were taking positions as we were about 75 meters away from them around a curve. Tiger Lilly, Raven, the rogues, and the other ranger classes went into crouching mode as they tried to sneak to line themselves up better. Killer, Jaceberlen, my Bulwark, and the other tanks began moving in unison down the road. The magic users began buffing the group with various spells and shielding effects while the other range classes got all their stuff powered up. So far nobody had died on our journey, and I was damn sure going to keep it that way. I instructed the two scrappers to flank their way to the back of the group and offer support for Neelz and the non-combatants. Neelz was still only fourteen and this wasn't her forte.

While the group continued to slowly usher forward, we rounded the curve and were met by the group of fifteen or so ruffians blocking the road. I am not sure exactly what they were expecting but looked very surprised at our organization. You would think that they would be smart enough to realize an unwinnable situation when it was presented to them, however they decided the tough guy approach was better.

As the group marched to a stop, the ruffian leader must have figured that we were scared. He looked like he was in a rusty chain shirt, leather pants, metal bracers, and a mail coif. He also brandished what appeared to be a longsword. The next words he uttered were those of confidence at robbing people blindly without them pushing back. I showed a glimmer of a smile before I spoke. I was simple in my words but firm; If you do not move then you will not last the afternoon with a heartbeat. This is your one chance and one chance only to walk away alive and peacefully. Those words lingered in the air, and you could see both sides tense up amidst the gripping of weapons. Killing monsters was one thing but these were humans. We gave them an out although it did look like they would refuse to take it. I did not want this, not at all but I refuse to let these hooligans try to shake us down and hurt us.

I suddenly received a mental communication from one of my forward archers. Apparently, the low life leader was quietly moving some attackers to the rear of our group to attempt to flank us. Unfortunately, I knew how this would go, and I felt no enjoyment in this outcome. I warned Mittens as well as the scrappers. I told her to tell the others in the back to watch for a flank attack. I then looked at the leader and as straight faced as I could muster without showing my anger I said, you had your opportunity and now I see that you are trying to flank us from behind. Just remember that you chose this outcome and this will be your fault not ours. The leader seemed to come to a decision at that moment and signaled his goons to attack. I did the same.

In that instance the ruffians released their projectiles. Our warrior's shields were instantly raised in a protective measure, and most were blunted, however a few managed to land in non-critical locations. This would, however, cause panic. I yelled to Killer to regain formation, and Captain Ahab began his musical abilities. As we refocused, the ruffians' warriors were already in motion to charge. Our ranged attackers let loose their attacks and I gave the minions in the woods the nod to attack. Within seconds you could hear the thrum of bowstrings, an assorted crackling of spells, and the clanking of weapons. The ruffians were seriously outgunned, and I still have no idea why they had continued to press the issue. They seemed to have greatly misjudged our group, but just our numbers alone should have deterred them.

One of Tiger Lilly's arrows lodged itself right into the eye socket of a warrior. Killer used his shield to block an incoming attack and then rode the momentum downward as he parried with a deep gash into his opponent's calf. A not-so-subtle shield bash to the skull caused the attacker to stumble and then Laltag Duine appeared behind him and came downward with a pair of short swords to finish the guy off.

The Umbral mages were hard at work trying to blind any of the ruffians that they could as several of them were just swinging wildly into the air since they were unable to see. Seeing that they had an opportunity Jaceberlen, Smeeeagal, and Biggus Dikkus just opened a savage exchange of steel, blood, and death. There was no need for their cool downs or spells as it was just metallurgic carnage. A wild swing that left an enemy exposed was answered with a sword strike to a kneecap removing it entirely and then a finishing blow to the skull. Another caught a sword thrust to the chest, and another took a javelin throw to the face. Booyah, yelled Biggus Dikkus as the javelin hit home. Our healers were tirelessly trying to heal any of the wounds that occurred with our group as the front liners that had taken damage from the initial barrage of arrows were now topped off and back in the fight.

The casters of the group sensing the ruffians were almost done for, began to shy away from single target attacks to let loose with any area of effect spells they might have been holding onto. The enemies were falling one after another and were down now to just a few. The rear of the group watched the onslaught as they prepared for any kind of attack. Three enemies charged the back line and went for the unformed line at the edge. The scrappers were in the middle holding that line and Mittens was on one edge while Neelz stood on the other. That happened to be their attack path. Neelz was young and was only a freshman in high school until a few months ago. Softball was her love and not video games. Although she had adapted well enough to our new reality with the monsters, humans were a different matter. I knew she wasn't ready for this, but we didn't have a choice.

As the attackers approached, she hesitated and that was all they needed to press the advantage. She blocked the first attack, and as the bandit side stepped, she plunged her sword into the gut of one of the attacking ruffians. Both her eyes and his went wide in shock. She had just hurt another human. Neelz hesitated again at that moment and the initial attacker swung. His strike connected with Neelz and clipped her hip and sent her to the ground. She cried out in pain as the gash that was left was pouring blood. Mittens came around and engaged the enemies along with the scrappers and a few others. The bandits fell quickly with the large onslaught, however the scrappers and Mittens continued to tear apart the three ruffians into a bloody mess even after they had died while Mimis and Nana healed Neelz as fast as they could cast. As the last healing spell bathed Neelz, Mimis grabbed Neelz, her granddaughter, and wrapped her in a hug. Her mom, Tallulah, and Nana, all tried to cocoon her with safety. The rear threat seemed to be over, but the scrappers and Mittens took a defensive stance to make sure nothing else happened.

The leader looked all around at his fallen compadres and the reality of his miscalculation was in full bloom. I mean they were all experienced fighters and should have been able to handle these travelers regardless of the numbers. They were not used to bravery among their targets. He had miscalculated with what he thought were their leader's words as an apparent bluff. A bluff seemed to be the farthest thing from this group's mind. They had cut his group down in literally a few minutes and it now appeared that he was the lone standing member left.

He was strong for sure, but he now relinquished any false revelation that he would survive this encounter. He should have walked when he was given the chance but chose to call out the so-called bluff. That decision had now cost all of them their lives. For a split second he considered trying to reason with the group, however one glance at the group showed that our group's expressions were full of anger, resolve, and not an ounce of remorse. He knew there was no walking out of this.

As he hardened his nerves, he looked up at the group again. He gripped both of his axes and prepared for one last battle. The roar that came from his lungs was more for him than anything else. The opposing group didn't even flinch. The leader charged at full speed. His steps took him about twenty feet before pain erupted everywhere. When his momentum had fully stopped, he looked down at his body. Arrow shafts protruded from everywhere. He had burn marks as well as wounds from frost, poison, and shadow damage. He lost control of his limbs as he saw his health pool drop dangerously low.

At that moment a dark-haired ranger stepped forward with a bow in her hand and an arrow knocked. Raven looked behind her and then said four words to the leader before releasing her arrow; This is for Neelz. The shaft instantly slammed into the leader and lodged itself deeply into his skull. The knock back alone from the force put him flatly on his back. He was dead before he hit his back on the ground. Raven didn't make a sound as she just turned around and went to check on her cousin, Neelz.

After looting all the bodies and making sure Neelz was mentally fit to travel, we decided the best course of action was to just get to the dock and secure passage as quickly as possible.

Neelz was physically okay as she had been healed back to full health. Mentally though it was a different matter. Killer, Tallulah, and Birdz stayed near her as she tried to come to terms with the situation that was just thrown at her. It was a rough card to play but one that would continue to happen as we live in this reality. Especially with what Jaceberlen and I knew to be a possible truth.

We approached the gates of the port town and as we did, we notified the guards that we had encountered a scuffle with a group of bandits and that we had dealt with them. The guard initially looked at us with a sense of surprise but then it shifted to relief. He advised us that the group of criminals had avoided their patrols for months and preyed upon anyone that tried to come into the city from the north. The guard told us to check with the captain in the building just up the road as there was a bounty quest for them. I asked if there was a way to secure boat travel across the way towards the land to the west. The guard thought for a minute and then let everyone know that there should be a ship heading out later in the day and to talk to Rubert as the port building. I nodded and threw a few silvers his way as a thank you. He nodded and said thank you, as we began to enter the town.

I asked Jaceberlen, Tal'n, and Captain Ahab to head towards the dock and negotiate our upcoming travel. I told the rest of the traveling party to head to the inn while Biggus Dikkus, ThreeBD, Gunthar, and myself headed to the captain's office. When we entered the office there was a shrewd stout man of mid to late years. Although he looked tired there was a stoic demeanor to him. As ThreeBD closed the door behind us, the captain looked us over and asked what business we had. I looked at him and let him know that we were told to report to him since we had dealt with the ruffian gang that confronted us in the wooded areas to the north. I also informed him of their numbers and rough makeup. The bodies are still littering the path; I told him although their belongings are in our possession to do with what we deemed appropriate.

He nodded in thought and took a second to respond. When he did, however, he seemed very sincere as he told us that he was relieved that we had escaped unharmed and that he would rest easier tonight knowing that the bandits are no more. That group had been a plague to our northern routes, he said. He also let us know he would send a patrol party up there immediately to gather the bodies and take stock of the situation. The captain also confirmed that there was indeed a bounty quest for that group and that we were entitled to it. Just like that the system chimed and then an icon blinked in what appeared to be everyone's interface.

You have completed a bounty quest: Exterminate the Northern Ruffians
Proof of completion has been removed from your inventory: Breastplate of Dale the leader
Rewards: Experience Points Earned: 1000 per participant, Distinguished Points: 200, Reputation: Port town of Kinship +150, Currency: 1 Gold

Well now the reputation increase was a new one. I looked around and saw that Biggus Dikkus, ThreeBD, and Gunthar had all leveled up from the smiles on their faces. ThreeBD said he had just reached 14, Gunthar had also hit 14, while Biggus Dikkus had reached level 15. I let him know about the experience hit and he nodded in agreement that he had seen that. I was happy for them, and I expected that several others had done the same in the group. The stronger the better for our group. Now that I knew bounties were a thing we would have to learn more about them if possible.

When we left the captain's office, it was on a friendly goodbye and an offer to help in the future. We made our way to the inn and were met by Jaceberlen and company just before we reached the inn. They advised us that they had secured passage for this evening at three silvers a head. We would also need to provide security for the ship as part of the deal. Three silvers didn't seem too bad considering we still didn't have a full understanding of the economy. Tal'n, being a lawyer in our previous life, was certainly someone I wanted to help negotiate the trip. Tal'n looked at me and said yeah it was reasonable, and we would use any experience that being a security detail would provide. Tal'n even got a small quest for it providing a few hundred experience points for each member of the group.

That evening we all embarked onto the ship for our trip across the sea. The trip was mostly uneventful with only a handful of sea monsters attempting to cause trouble. When the dawn sun started to creep its way into view along the edge of the water line the next morning, we could see the distant shore of our desired path. The water was calm like a sheet of glass with just our ship creating a break as it parted the water. As we slowly made our way forward, the shore became more prominent, and we finally could see the outline of our docking point. It seemed to be a trading port much like the town of Kinship.

The ship slowed to a crawl as it nestled up against the dock and tied itself off with the moor lines. A walkway was then strown over to our ship and the dockmaster there welcomed us to the town of Mordenwain and the lands of the Lexxtenburg Monarchy. The land is more widely known as the Cold Mists due to its weather. My name is Dockmaster Martin, he said. You may exit the ship now and then identify your business in our esteemed town.

As we exited the boat, our security quest completed and we all received a flashing icon. I decided to look at them shortly as it appeared that I had a few. Once we were all off the boat, I instructed everyone to go to the inn while I motioned for Jaceberlen and Captain Ahab to stay behind. When we were alone, I asked Captain Ahab to go to the general store and make sure that we were stocked up on supplies before our journey and I gave him some money to do so. We could gather it back from the group later. I also let him know that I needed to talk to him soon. Captain Ahab nodded and then left us to head to the store, and I took that moment to look at Jaceberlen and let him know I needed to talk to Tikallnosis to figure out the next steps and see if my plan of action was good to go. He nodded and said that he would check his notifications too.

I mentally brought up the summons tab and clicked it. As before, I was suddenly in a private room with Tikallnosis. We nodded with pleasantries and I let him know that we had made landfall in the Cold Mists. He acknowledged that and said, well done. Tikallnosis then began to speak of the plan we had discussed earlier. He still found no issue with the strategy, however he advised me to limit the circle of information as to not cause panic and to have more manageable control over the flow and gossip. We agreed to limit it to eight to ten and create some sort of circle or council. With that I fully agreed. Your progress has been impressive so far, he said but don't get complacent in our goal. Lives are at stake. I nodded and agreed. I asked what the next steps were and he advised me that the quest line has been updated and will continue to be as events unfold. With our main topics covered I disconnected the call and returned to the here and now.

I once again saw the flashing icons but wanted to eat and digest the information before I did that. We headed to the inn and sat down amongst our family and friends. Aerach tried singing on stage and received quite a few tips from the local patrons before she also sat down to eat. Once we all had our fill of food and drink, we settled in to get ready to travel again. By now it was late morning, and we had another six or seven hours of daylight. Our destination was about twelve hours away, so were looking at a map for a midway resting point. Having notated a small village about four hours from here we set out for that location to the west.

CHAPTER TWENTY-THREE

Scout's Eye

When we finally departed, I decided to take my time to scroll over everything since I was in relative safety. I ordered my minions to stay around and protect me with Mittens and Serenity near me as well. I pulled up the first notification.

You have completed the quest: Security Detail.
Level Requirement: None
Rewards: Experience Points 300, Distinguished Points: 50, Reputation: +50 Town of Kinship
Description: You are to provide security for the ship ride from Kinship to its destination

You have completed the quest: Deliver Them Home Part Three of the Divine Investigation. This is a unique Divine Level quest and has an unspecified number of parts.
Level Requirement: 18
Rewards: Experience Points: 1500, Distinguished Points; 200, Profession Skillbook – Management (Level 20 required)
Description: You are to escort your group to the borders of the designated township with at least 90% of your group still alive. Percentage Alive 100% 83/83

Congratulations you have hit level 19. You have 5 free stat points to allocate.

Congratulations, you have hit Illustrious Level 5 and opened the Distinguished Paths and Perks tree.

You have been granted the quest: Final March Part Four of the Divine Investigation. This is a unique Divine Level quest and has an unspecified number of parts.
Level Requirement: 18
Rewards: Experience Points, Distinguished Points, Class Appropriate Reward
Description: Deliver your party safely to the designated location
Percentage Alive: 100% 83/83
Do you accept the quest? Yes/No

Of course, I accepted it, quickly allocated my stat points, and then refocused back on the task at hand. I looked at Jaceberlen and noticed he was still in thought so I then turned my attention to Tiger Lilly. I slipped my hand into hers and let her know that she was wonderful. As we marched forward, I felt a sense of nervousness as we all drew closer to our home for the foreseeable future. The path would be long and daunting.

The trip to our resting spot for the night was quiet. Our group size seemed to ward off most anything that would want to cause us any trouble. As we made our way into the little village that was named, the village of Lotterdam, we overcrowded the inn and had to take refuge on a good portion of their floor for the night. It wasn't the cleanest thing to do but we were covered and all together.

My skeletons didn't report anything out of the ordinary through the night, so everyone got a chance to have a good night's rest. With dawn coming up through the trees and peering into the inn in rays, we all woke up and began preparing for our final push to our possible home. The group had a quick breakfast, gathered their belongings, and made our way out of the inn into the main road heading west.

For the most part everyone was in good spirits, and morale was high even though several of them were still dealing with the raw truth about where we were now. Neelz seemed to be a little better, but she was still visibly dealing with her demons from the attack. Time would hopefully heal that wound but unfortunately time was not something that would protect her from what we knew was coming. So, she would have to heal fast and come to grips with our new world.

Marching all together gave us even more time to catch up and discuss everyone's testing, beginning areas, and classes in more detail. Most of the group had normal type builds with some notable exceptions. We did have a lot of variety within our group though, and I had a sinking feeling that we would need everyone's skills going forward. Most of our group were in the level ranges of eleven to fourteen. Quite a few had broken past fifteen with Jaceberlen being the second highest at a newly seventeen, while I was now at level nineteen. Most were very interested in our journey as it appeared to be quite different from the normal path of everyone else. So, during the journey we dove into the wonders of the dungeon mechanics and our questing heroics. I figured I would save the rest for a different time.

I moved around from person to person talking to everyone individually to really try to understand how everyone was dealing with the transformation. By the time I got to Neelz, she was talking to her mother, Tallulah, about how she was going to get used to all of this. I came up to her and without a word, I gave her a big hug. I told her I loved her and we would do everything we could to protect her but the best protection she could ever have is to get stronger. We would gladly help with that of course. Mittens came up next to me and asked out loud if Neelz wanted one of those things. Neelz looked at her as if it was still odd to hear a cat talk and asked what she wanted one of a what? Mittens seemed to tighten up like an unoiled robot and then replied with those things you call a hug. Neelz froze up for a second then relaxed and said sure if you want. I mentally told Mittens that she was starting to get soft and I got a snarky comment back like she will rip my face off if I ever say or bring that up again. I just laughed and then she started purring. Mittens walked the few steps over to Neelz, placed her head up against Neelz's leg for a minute, and then said, well that's enough and stepped away. Well, I thought it was a start.

I looked over at Killer who was watching Mittens and we nodded at each other. He motioned me over, so I stepped his way. He lowered his voice and asked if Mittens was safe. Look little brother, I said. She is in good hands with Mittens, I continued. She might be quite stand offish and testy at times, but she is a heck of a fighter and loyal to me. I will tell her to watch out for Neelz in the shadows, but I reiterated the next words; but Neelz must get past this and work on getting stronger. It will only get worse. He somberly agreed and said we will all help her get there. I placed my hand on his shoulder and smiled at him. Yes, we will man yes, we will.

Late morning to midafternoon came and went as we continued to trudge along the road. By late afternoon we finally emerged out of the foggy forest area that we had been in since this morning. The view was not what I expected. The path continued into an open valley surrounded by mountains on most sides. We were still around an hour or so away from the destination, but I was already starting to think in a strategic and logistical sense.

In the distance it seemed as if the mountains were closing in on one another to create an area that would seem to be defensible from the back but with a disadvantage in the front with maybe only having one way of escape. That is something we would need to get more intel on. The surface area seemed flat with trees in surplus, howling winds, and almost like a creepy feel. I knew we hadn't reached the border of the zone yet due to my quest not updating, however we couldn't be too far from it.

From this point on I suggested that we form up into the same formation that we had assumed in the forest before Kinship in case we ran into anything. Once we formed up and began moving again, we got a better view of the area. I walked over to Captain Ahab, Tal'n, and Biggus Dikkus, Killer, as well as Jaceberlen and asked them for their thoughts on defensive measures for this type of geography. After about ten to fifteen minutes of discussion we had come up with several possibilities, but the area was still rather large.

I ordered my archers and Mittens to begin scouting ahead along with the Rangers. We needed to know if there was anything ahead of us as well as choking points for an ambush. Thirty minutes or so later I started receiving feedback from my skeletons. About a mile ahead there seemed to be a patrol of humans monitoring the areas around the road. They counted about twelve people but were not sure about anything else. They could also not determine if they were friends or foes. Mitten's information was better but all she could add was that the patrollers were all in leather armor and were equipped with a mix of bows and swords. A few minutes later Raven, Farwind, and Tiger Lilly returned. They had managed to get a bit deeper into the path forward and they advised us that the patrol seemed to be not of any formal kingdom force but more of the bandit variety.

Upon hearing that it seemed that we were not out of the woods yet per se. Now that we had a better layout it was time to prepare for the worst yet hope for the best. After discussing the layout of our plan, the archers and the rangers along went ahead of the main group to continue to scout and set up the initial stage of what we needed to do. The bulk of us continued down the road but at a more controlled pace. The set up was as before with the tanks with the melee fighters in the front, and ranged attackers in the middle, while the support classes were in the back. I had a sneaking suspicion that this patrol might be part of the group we were sent here to eliminate. We would soon find out.

The forward group let me know that they were in position and shortly afterwards we came into view of the patrol. As soon as they heard the sounds our group walking, they became much more alert and defensive. I stepped forward without any emotion and asked the group if there was a reason why they were blocking the road. No answer came from them but a question in turn; What is your destination and you better answer quickly?

I couldn't help but shake my head at their cockiness and it did appear they saw the action. Do you know who the Ebony Cloaks are? I replied no and is there any reason I should care who they are? You could visibly see the anger surface in their expressions. Apparently, that hit a nerve. I whispered to Jaceberlen, Tal'n and Captain Ahab to get ready and funnel it down to the rest of the group. Mittens slowly moved her way to the back of the group and then went into stealth. Their leader or whatever he was seemed to hold back his disdain and rudely responded by saying, yes you should care and we run these parts. You do not travel these roads unless we allow it, he then further elaborated. Great another shakedown I barked back. Is this what we must face every time we travel? The last group didn't like what happened. As I finished that I decided to inspect the leader. Ebony Cloak Patrol Leader Level 17, Health 800, Energy 600

Watch out I said as these guys are somewhere around level 17 to the group next to me. I turned to Jaceberlen and resigned with a sigh as I asked him if he wanted honors. Of course, he smiled and said hell yes. Then without another word he channeled his Thunder spell and lit the group up. Then came the barrage from the rest of us. I had a necrotic ray slam into the leader full on and Smeeeagal looked like a lunatic out there swinging and gashing. Killer charged and parried a sword thrust from one of the Ebony Cloaks and then kicked out his foot to place the bandit off balance before finishing him with a swipe to the throat.

Biggus Dikkus hurled a javelin at one of the attackers while screaming; come get some boys. The wooden javelin impaled the enemy right above the waistline. At the sound of battle, the rangers and archers began raining down death from their hidden locations. This group was being quickly disassembled. After all this ideocracy, I am still wondering if NPCs counted numbers before starting a fight. One of their melee warriors managed to score a critical hit on Big Bear's thigh, however Gunthar caught the enemy with a right cross to the jaw that sent him sprawling. Gunthar then got on top of him and activated some sort of special skill because suddenly, his gauntlets grew spikes and his attacks took it to another level. A few seconds later, the enemy was a pulp of flesh.

The healing group had been working their magic as our many wounds or afflictions were quickly healed and our group remained in top form. One enemy tried to rush them but Laltag Duine, Landoleer, Skullbasher, and Endor made quick work of him. I mentally ordered Mittens and my scrappers to try and capture one so that we could question him. After their acknowledgements, I heard a scream and Mittens had grabbed one by the back of the neck and wrestled him to the ground. The scrappers were holding his arms down and of all things the bulwark was just sitting on him like an idiot. All I could say was good job and hold him there.

At this point there were two members of the original patrol group left. The one we had captured and one that was fighting ThreeBD, Dartanius, Bhorn, and Pint Size. It wasn't a fair fight at all as they danced around dismantling the bandit. It was over quick when Bhorn shivved him with a backstab in the kidneys. Once he fell, all anyone could hear was the heavy breathing from everyone feeling tired from the battle and then the muffled screams of the prisoner.

The battle was over and several of our group were wounded but they would be in top form shortly as Tallulah, Mimis, Nana, Duck, Tal'n, Mendor, Pope, and Glamdring all used their healing magic to get everyone back up again. We were lucky to have a healthy set of healers. It was weird watching them perform these spells as any form of this type of healing would have been a miracle in real life. It was time to have a little chat with our guest of honor.

As we approached the prisoner, the bulwark, or as the children had named it Peppermint, was still just sitting on the guy's legs essentially pinning him down. Mittens still had him by the throat and the scrappers or also as the children had named them, Clunky and Clacky, were still holding his arms. I told them to sit him up and the scrappers moved to his legs and Mittens released her grip but growled. His eyes were already wide, but he made no move to do anything hostile. Peppermint had to finally just get up.

As he finally sat up, I looked straight into his eyes and relayed my thoughts; If you answer honestly then you will live, if you refuse or lie then you will not like that outcome. Do you understand me? He nodded in understanding. There were still things I didn't necessarily want the children to witness, and torture wasn't one of them. While we did this, I just asked most of the group to go ahead and loot the bodies. That would be a good distraction for them.

Where is your base of operations being the first question I asked? The guy laughed at that and spat on the ground. I then looked around and when I only saw resolve, I reiterated to the man of what his predicament was. He smirked and said that we really didn't want to go there as we would be slaughtered. I just smiled and said that we would take our chances. I asked Dealz if he had a dominate spell and he reluctantly said yes. He then let me know he wasn't okay with that type of questioning yet. He really didn't want to have to use it. I could understand that, but we needed to know what we were dealing with if they were from our destination point. There had to be another way.

Piper came forward and wanted to try something. She was an illusionist, so she began weaving a mental image of the man growing old in a cell devoid of sunlight, communication, and freedom. He aged rapidly until all that was in the scene was what looked like elderly man nearing eighty years old. At first it looked like it might work but then the captive seemed to strengthen his will, and it broke the spell. Nice try, I said to Piper.

We tried a few other methods and weren't getting many answers that were worth it, so we were all getting impatient. Finally, Olivia came up to me and spoke, let me crack this asshole. I was like go ahead girl get it done. She smiled and not a nice smile either. It was a type of smile that spoke volumes; this guy was going to wish he wasn't born type of smile.

As a witch I was a little scared as to what she might do to him. She stepped forward and cast some type of hex or curse on him. At first nothing happened but then a boil started forming on his cheek. Then another and then another. Within a few minutes the prisoner was covered in oozing boils. The guy tried to scream but his tongue was swollen in his mouth. Olivia looked at him and smiled. Do you want me to continue, or will you be a good little boy, she said. His eyes were wide with horror and he quickly nodded.

Wonderful, Olivia exclaimed. She reached into her bag and grabbed a vial of something of a brown color. She walked over to him and made sure that he knew that this was the only antidote she had, so if he didn't talk then she would handle him again without a remedy. Do you understand, she said. You could see the resignation in his eyes and then he nodded. Once he drank the vial he became a very chatty Kathy. He answered every question we asked and once everyone was satisfied with the information, we decided to release him. I looked at him dead in the eye and let him know he is only alive by the grace of us, and it would be in his best interest to leave this area and never come back. I am not sure if he even let that sink in because he took off in a sprint before I could even get a response. As he began to distance himself, I looked at Mittens and she bowed and then disappeared.

CHAPTER TWENTY-FOUR

Not as Expected

Once we gathered everyone up and distributed all the loot that would be an upgrade to anyone within our party, we decided to get moving again. About ten minutes later the feel of the area changed and I got a notification that we had traveled into another zone which we did expect. I looked at my internal map again and tried to calculate the math. We really were not far so I figured about thirty to forty-five minutes were left. I sent out my archers and now that Mittens was back with us, I sent her ahead to scout as well. All the rangers went too so we would have a full blanket of intel to work with.

I got a message from Raven, and she let me know that they had found the town and had spotted a gathering location from which we can discuss next steps. Ping the map, I said and we will be there shortly. I sent my minions a command to meet us there and let Mittens know what was going on. We would all converge at that location. As we got closer, I noticed a subtle movement and noticed Tiger Lilly motioning at us to come to them. Soon after Mittens and the archers arrived. Everyone was in hand finally.

According to the scouting party of Tiger Lilly, Raven, Farwind, Gundham, Malgum, Ant, and Legion the town was up ahead, and it looked like a large contingent of armed individuals just left the main gate headed along the eastern valley of the mountain range. We certainly needed more information but that was a good start. We could all see the town from here and as we had already suspected it was a flat valley with some rolling hills.

The area was a bit colder than expected but that was likely due to its proximity to the mountains. The mountains were on all sides of the town in question except this valley. So, it would logically be defensible from three sides for sure. The area was mostly wooded so we should make sure the area is clear of potential enemies before doing anything rash. As it was late afternoon, we decided to send the rangers to get more intelligence about the town itself so that we can develop a strategy of what to do next. My archers would stay here and be our early warning system if anything approached. The rogues Bhorn, Flower, Pint Size, and then Mittens joined our perimeter detail as well.

Tiger Lilly, Raven, Farwind, Gundham, Malgum, Ant, and Legion set off from the meeting point with a clear description from me as to what was needed. They were to scout the surrounding area of the town and gather patterns, numbers of citizens, as well as enemies, defenses, the layout, and buildings. If possible, they could infiltrate the city but being still daylight that might be hard. I needed information to plan an attack strategy, so they were the eyes.

As they spread out into the woods, the group was able to keep in contact via messages so they could remain silent. Ant took the westernmost point while Farwind to the easternmost point. Tiger Lilly and Raven stayed closer to the road while the others filled in the gaps. The trees continued to roll along until each of them emerged in a small clearing, maybe twenty-five yards before the gates to the town. They were being patrolled by the same types of individuals that we had encountered earlier in the day. So that answered that question, Malgum decided to point out over the chat. Okay, with that question out of the way the group now needed to do some reconnaissance. Gundham and Ant would try to bypass the patrols and scope out the city from the sides which were mountainous. They would also try to infiltrate the city if possible. Legion, Malgum, and Farwind all spread out and began to climb the highest trees to gain a better scouting position. Tiger Lilly and Raven would measure out the patterns and help identify possible enemies from civilians.

Farwind reached the canopy of the eastern line and tried to take stock of her surroundings. In front of her was obviously the town landscape, while as she looked around, she noticed other pathways branching out into winding mountain paths. Those paths didn't necessarily look like military routes but rather small routes for travel through the mountain passes. Where they went was unknown to us right now, but it would need to be looked at. The locals should know what they travel to, she thought.

Even with them being small, an armed force could travel them in lines of two people. They would need to account for them in their overall plan. The mountain range seemed straight forward with cloud cover hitting a few hundred meters above the town and the tops of the mountains disappearing within them. As they had known earlier, the range of peaks covered the town on three sides and could be seen as far as the eyes could see.

Suddenly she caught movement on one of the mountain paths. As she turned towards the motion to get a better view, she saw what seemed to be a horse and cart coming over the crest. It could have been a trading cart, but she would need to learn more. When the cart emerged from the path onto the valley floor her suspicions were confirmed. The driver seemed to be a hearty looking human with a beard. He didn't appear to have any weapons on him and the side of the cart was dangling with goods. Farwind tried to get a closer look by activating her zoom skill which magnified her vision three times. With this skill active, she was able to get a more detailed account of what type of goods this trader was peddling. This cart seemed to be focused on food as there were many types of meats, cheeses, and breads hanging and partially visible under the tarps. That made Farwind ponder if this town had an issue with agriculture of just simply wanted variety. Thoughts for later she surmised.

Gundham managed to climb the western side of the mountains adjacent to the town with relative ease as he was promptly able to avoid prying eyes and anything that might have given him away. He found a little nook that would help conceal his presence until it was dark. The view from here was a clear and concise picture of the town's layout. From his viewpoint the town seemed to have a lot of promise. There was a lot of the town that was just wasted with random hobbies.

It seemed that whatever bandit gang had taken control of this place, it took joy and great humor in the mistreatment of the townsfolk as well as some not so nice vices. His eyes noticed something and immediately burned with a sense of fury. He had been scrolling across the town taking notes of anything of interest when his eyes landed on a scene playing out before him. A few of the bandits inside the town were using one of the town's elderly as sword practice as several others were watching and laughing. The old man could barely hold a sword however he wasn't given a choice. He tried to defend himself, but the younger men just toyed with him.

They would faint a thrust only to use a counter strike to cut the man. They took care not to cut him deep as they wanted to keep him alive so that he would be able to take more of a beating. The old man had cuts all over him and blood was running freely down his body, but they didn't relent. Finally, it looked like the old timer couldn't take anymore and he dropped the sword and collapsed on the ground. The bandits had other thoughts as they lifted him up and continued to beat him and inflicted more shallow cuts on his face and torso. Only when they had got tired did they toss him to the ground and look for another victim. These dudes are sick and twisted, Gundham thought to himself as he continued to recon the area over the next few hours. Only when the sun began to cast shadows in the valley did he make his way back down to their meeting point.

Ant had been in position for a few hours as she was hidden in a small cravat just above the town's walls. She had a great view of the buildings and make-up of the town. The town's design was simple. There seemed to be the main town hall at the back of the town with a few shops and service buildings in the back part of the town to be somewhat close to the hall. There were quite a few shops of various products, a few barns for livestock, and other food structures. A grain silo, a church steeple, and many other types of building were present. Several homes too but they seemed to be stacked upon one another.

From what she could see there was plenty of room to adjust and altar the town. The citizens that were mulling about didn't appear to be very happy. Nobody seemed to be conversing, and they all had their heads down. It was a very dreary sight indeed. They quickly went to and from and a sense of fear was everywhere. Once Ant felt that she had got enough intel to help the overall agenda she began to make her way back while being careful not to draw any attention to her movements.

Malgum and Legion could vaguely see each other in their respective positions within the trees. Malgum was the closest to the gates while Legion was on the outer western side. Hand signals would be tough to decipher between the two but luckily if anything was needed, they could message via the interface. Malgum tried to inspect the guards and could barely make out the data points that shown within his interface. The guards appeared to be called Bandit Defenders. They were large men and seemed to be in the levels of 17-19. Health pools were also varying from 170-300. Depending on the total number of the bandits and if these numbers rang true with the entire group, then this might be a challenge. He watched a trader come to the gate on a horse and cart. When it arrived, the guards treated the driver like a sub class citizen and demanded that driver uncover the goods for them to see. When the trader replied in a manner that was not one hundred percent subservient, one of the defenders grabbed the trader by the shirt and delivered a hard fist to their gut. The driver doubled over in pain and Malgum could hear the exchange from his location. Damn he wanted to deliver an arrow to the skull of the attacking bandit at that moment.

Legion received a message from Malgum in response to what Malgum had seen. Legion looked to his side and tried to get a glimpse and could see movement and some distortions but was out of range. He then activated his zoom ability and was now able to notice everything at a focused point. Legion also witnessed the exchange between the guards and the trader. He knew what these kinds of people were like due to his days in the military. There was only one resolution with these criminals, he thought. As he turned off zoom, he put his focus on the outer edge of the walls. Over the course of a few hours, they observed back and forth with the placements, movements, numbers, and other details. After they had both seemed to gather the proper rotations and intel, they motioned to each other that it was time to make their way back. As the duo made their way down the trees, they noticed movement on the wall. It seemed someone had noticed them and was trying to get a closer view. Malgum went perfectly still and Legion finally did the same. After what seemed like an hour passed the man left the wall and seemed to head downward. Once he left, the duo quickly made their way down and disappeared into the trees.

Raven and Tiger Lilly were in position on either side of the road. About twenty to thirty feet from the pathway in the trees, they hid and waited to scout anything that might come their way. They also looked for traps and any defenses that might have been laid heading to the walls. As they were not in view of the gates due to the foliage blocking that direction, they didn't hear the gates open. They did, however, hear a small group of bandits traversing up the roadway heading into the woods. Soft voices could be heard from the group as they walked, and they were discussing movement that they had seen on the western tree line. It could have been just birds one of them said. The bandit in front seemed to very much disagree with that comment and replied with; birds don't bend tree limbs, and I could have sworn I saw a person. The frontal bandit followed that comment with the fact that they needed to check it out since the commander was gone. Tiger Lilly and Raven knocked arrows and tightened their bow strings in preparation for a fight if it was necessary. As the group made their way down the road they suddenly stopped. The leader of this group perked his ears as if to try and catch something in the distance. It looked like when Raven had taken a deep breath, it wasn't as quiet as she had hoped. It looked like she might become exposed but at that moment some birds left their nesting spot and took to the air. The bandit group looked up and seemed to let out a breath of air they didn't know they had taken. The leader wasn't completely sure and then he had their group fan out but eventually they didn't find anything and reformed up. They gave the area one more glance over then they headed back to the town.

A sigh of relief washed over Tiger Lilly as well as Raven when the situation finally calmed down. It was about to be an absolute throw down but luckily, they were spared for the fight. Now was not the time to reveal themselves as that time was rapidly approaching. Plus, with the levels of the bandits and a five versus two, it didn't look too good. They took what intel they had gleaned from everything and promptly left to meet the rest of the rangers on their way back to the holding camp.

As they all gathered at the designated spot, the rangers all looked at each with a look in their eyes. They knew what they had to overcome but only in singular points. They were about to meet up with Dookooze and see what it would look like all together. When they noticed him, they headed that way and as they did, the others seemed to clear a path for them. Plus, since they were all given a quest to research and gather intel, they were each eager to complete that and get the needed experience.

CHAPTER TWENTY-FIVE

Preparation

I was talking with Serenity and Jaceberlen when I noticed that Tiger Lilly and the rest of the rangers had returned. I was anxious to hear what they had uncovered, and it was time to begin putting together the council I had discussed with Tikallnosis. I would not officially set it up just quite yet, but I wanted to lay the groundwork. I motioned for Jaceberlen to gather Tal'n, Captain Ahab, Biggus Dikkus, himself, Killer, Dartonias, ThreeBD, and Dealz. I instructed him to bring them to me for our debrief.

The rangers had arrived and the others were gathering now. We decided to head off about fifty feet away to get some quiet as we really didn't want to be overheard. Once we were far enough away from the group, I asked the rangers to report. One by one they each did so with the details and information they had each gathered. Once they were all finished, I asked Tiger Lilly and Raven to remain, and I dismissed the others and thanked them for this information. As the remaining group sat there, they looked amongst each other like they weren't sure why they were there, so I figured I needed to at least give them a reason. After a bit of silence, I finally spoke; I bet most of you are wondering what I called you here for. Obviously, I wanted each of you to hear the intel reports that the rangers gave, however I trust each of you with your knowledge and expertise. I know that some of you have never stepped into a game world but some of that is irrelevant with much that we will potentially face.

Each of them looked at me as if they didn't know what to say so I continued. As you all know Jaceberlen and I were given a unique quest line. I can share some of it now, but the rest will have to come later. You all will just have to trust me in this. The quest is originally mine, however Jaceberlen was added as a secondary participant. I can give quests as the rangers have already found out. The first major questline is this town. In short term this will be our home and base of operations moving forward. This road will not be an easy one but together we can succeed. Our first goal is to take the town and eliminate all bandits or criminals from the town. Initially we might have gotten a break with this as a good portion of the bandits and their leader are gone currently which means we have a timeline to infiltrate, eliminate, and occupy the town before they return.

I kept talking regarding the ranger's reports. We have all heard what the intel, levels, formations, etc. are within the town currently. I have sent Legion back into the woods to ensure that none of the current data changes. Now what we need to do as a group is to determine the best course of action to achieve our goal. I will say this. In this world we are not without risks. When each of you entered and even prior to immersion, we knew there would be fighting, magic, blood, and honestly, possibly the worst in humanity. This will be no exception. When I say eliminate, I mean exactly that. If any of you are against this then let me know now and we can remove you from this group. We will have you take on a non-combat role until we have no other option. Even so it is about a hundred percent likely that everyone will have to fight or we will all die.

The only one I really had a concern about was Dealz. With his background this wasn't really something he had to deal with considering he was a salesman at heart. I looked straight at him and asked if he was with us as we needed him to help us protect one another. Dealz looked back and forth among the group and then said he would never let anything happen to Aurora so if that means that he would have to use his class and skills to do that then he would, but he wasn't happy about it. I acknowledged that and agreed that none of us really want this but once they knew more they would hopefully understand.

I had each of the group give me their thoughts and recommendations on what to do and then we began to piece together the sequence of events that we wanted to unfold as well as contingencies in case it all went to shit. As we continued to discuss the strategies that we would like to implement, we determined that tonight was our best chance with the main force still away from the town. We also knew that no quarter could be given, however, if we captured one that might be a plus. After about an hour of discussing strategies, we diverged into what to do once we had control of the town.

Several of them perked up upon hearing that as town development entailed some of the best aspects of online gaming before the Soul Crusher came around. Dealz, Captain Ahab, Jaceberlen, and I included loved this aspect and we were excited about the possibilities. I went into only a part of my quest now per my discussion with Tikallnosis. I advised them of the part of my quest that involved taking over the town, and I will be granted the rights to it. At first, they didn't completely believe me until my son verified the same information and showed them his quest that explained that he was to assist me in claiming the town for my rulership. That got everyone's attention; however, we made sure that we didn't divulge too much at this time. I also went into my skills to a small degree that reflected the same type of synergy.

When the meeting finally came to an end, we gathered everyone up to go over the next steps. As they all gathered around, I waited for it to get quiet and then I cleared my throat. I looked at them all in the eye and told them our next steps. During the gathering I could see fear and tension in their faces. Some didn't want to fight, and I could understand that however if we were to carve out a place for us then we would have to take it. Most everyone was on board and those that weren't agreed to take on a support role.

All in all, out of our group of eighty-three that counted as the core group towards my quests, but we had more due to other people's families joining up. We needed everyone. Out of the eighty-three we had about sixty-seven that would fight. The remaining people were mostly kids that couldn't or the ones that were going to stay and watch them. The rest were formed up by class type as I had instructed. For a newbie breakdown I asked them to get into simple groups such as melee tanks which were the defensive specialist that were punished by our enemies so that everyone else can unleash hell on them, melee fighters such as barbarians, skalds, dual wielders, and two handed specialists that were more on the damage dealing side, roguish type melee fighters that used smaller weapons combined with stealth to attack for massive damage or assassinate, Ranged attackers such as rangers, magic casters, and then finally support casters and healers.

Once they were each debriefed in their individual groups we went over the night's plan. The objective was simple. Infiltrate and neutralize the guards, eliminate the existing bandits within the walls, secure the town, and prepare to defend. Now the overview was simple, but the detailed version was anything but. Not to mention it would certainly at some point go to hell, so we had to be ready for that.

Finally, we departed as a group with the scouts in the front until we got to maybe half a mile away before hitting the town's walls. At this point we waited a little bit longer for nightfall to fully take over the sky. I walked up to Jaceberlen and told him to be strong and kick their ass, He cracked a slight smile and replied that he would do his job. I responded again with I know you will. I called him puddin and he just laughed and said he would see me on the other side. Raven and Tiger Lilly both seemed a bit nervous when I approached. I gave them both a hug and just told them to focus on what their jobs were, and the rest would be okay. I reminded them to remember the goal. They both nodded. I gave them each a kiss and told them I loved them and I would be right there with them albeit a shout away. I gave another look at Tiger Lilly and softly pointed to my heart and she returned the gesture. Then I was off.

When it became fully nighttime the rangers took off as well as the roguish type players to get themselves into position for the assault. As they made their way towards the town walls, they made sure to avoid the patrols and guards. When they came within a hundred yards of the tree canopy ending, they decided to break off into their groups. Tiger Lilly, Raven, and Farwind along with assassin specialists Smeeeagal, Flower, and Pint Size took off to the western side of the town while Gundham, Malgum, and Ant along with the assassin squad of Rosie, Bhorn, and Endor broke off to the east. Legion, Arns, the monk, and Dealz, the Arcane Mentalist, continued forward at the center. The rest of the attacking force was right behind them. We were waiting for the fireworks to begin. Following the plan, I murmured to myself as I watched everything fall into position.

Tiger Lilly approached the spot where they had designated as their launch point. It was a tight little nook on the side of the cliff face just inside the walls of the town. They were in range of a few of the guards and within leaping range of the wall itself. Tiger Lilly and Raven positioned themselves with clear lines of sight for their bows. They both turned to the group of stealthy assassins and let them know it was time to drop into stealth and move into their respective spots. Flower and Pint Size seemed to just meld into the night and just like that, not a sound of them was to be heard. Smeeeagal looked at both Tiger Lilly and Raven and whispered be safe. He was practically family, so they replied the same. Hell, even Farwind replied in kind and then told him that he was a scary little shit. He smiled and said it was now time to go kill some shit. His shadowy frame moved into the night sky and then he too was gone.

Gundham, Malgum, and Ant sat quietly on the edge of the wall on top of a rocky overhang. They had already sent Rosie, Bhorn, and Endor to get into their spots a few minutes ago. They were just waiting for the other groups to get into position. They noticed that the guards were around fifty or so yards apart and in pairs at the corners. The goal was simple in design, but they all know the execution relied heavily on timing.

Legion knelt at the edge of his bow range looking at the gate and the walls connecting it. Arns and Dealz knelt next to him as they all were deciphering which sequence to attack with. The gate had a pair of guards on each side. The numbers did not add up so they would have to hope that the other two groups could sway the odds.

The rest of the group stood quietly in the protection of the edge of the tree line. I waited for every group to check in that they were in their positions. First it was the western side, then the middle group, and finally everyone in the eastern side had checked in. I looked over at Jaceberlen and Captain Ahab and let them know that everyone was in position. They both nodded in return and advised the others in chain link type format to keep our secrecy. Everything we had planned was contingent upon our three forward groups completing their tasks. I pulled up my interface and typed a single word response to all of them. GO!

CHAPTER TWENTY-SIX

Silent Assault Kind Of

Tiger Lilly, Raven, and Farwind had their targets already lined up when Dookooze sent his response. All it said was GO! And that is all they needed to see. Their part of the plan relied on a two-prong quick strike to start. Raven eyed the farthest guard and released a Power Shot. That was a skill that took a long time to set but the damage was twice the normal damage. The thrum of her bow signaled the other two to release their arrows.

Farwind took the middle guard with a Blunt Shot that did normal damage but also added a knock back as she was trying to send the guard over the wall. Tiger Lilly took the nearest guard and ripped off a Precise Shot that allowed her to hit specific parts of the body. This would give a higher critical chance and critical chance rate, with a little less damage. As they had timed their shots to hit simultaneously the guards were completely caught off guard. The farthest took an arrow to the back and fell up against the wall. The guard looked down only to see an arrowhead protruding from his chest. As he tried to muster his strength to signal an alarm, a hand visualized out of nowhere from the shadows and covered his mouth. At that moment the guard felt a sharp pain in the back of his skull. His vision started to fade and as he fell backward to the pathway, he saw a small pint-sized female staring over him. Everything then went dark.

The middle guard turned at the sound of something to his side and then suddenly he felt a hard impact on his side that spun him around and into the ledge with enough force to knock the wind out of him. He looked up to try to figure out what the hell just happened and what he saw next freaked him out. A man of shadowy wisps was smiling at him ear to ear with an axe in one hand and a dagger in the other. The teeth were white, but darkness encompassed the rest of him. The strange being cackled softly and then just said; Smeeeagal says hi. Then the two weapons came down in a flash. The guard was still reeling from the initial arrow shot and was unable to register what was happening until his blood was pooling everywhere. In a split second the guard went from thinking of the ale waiting for him at the inn to seeing the light leave his eyes. Smeeeagal checked the guard and verified his death and then he disappeared again back into the night.

Tiger Lilly's arrow sailed true but at the last minute the guard shifted. The arrow, instead of landing in its intended spot in the back of the skull, slammed into the guard's shoulder. The guard jumped in pain and almost fell but braced himself up against the ledge. His shield arm was now busted up from the arrow shot, but he was coherent enough to try to draw his sword. As soon as he wrapped his fingers around the hilt, a woman materialized out of the darkness to the side of him. She lashed out with a dagger and he tried to dodge. He leaned to the side and was able to avoid the main part of the blade, however the tip of it grazed his skin. He felt a searing pain from the wound as if something foreign was at work.

He quickly glanced down to see a green hue to the wound, and he immediately knew that he had been poisoned. He next looked up to stare the attacker in the face when an arrow shaft pierced his gut. He doubled over from the impact and that was all that the attacker needed. She came down with her daggers and thrusted one cleanly through his neck and another to his kidney. The guard tried to yell but all he could manage was a gurgling sound. He knew he was dead and rapidly became much weaker. It was hard for him to stand and then the female lowered her weapons and walked towards him. As he put his weight up against the wall. She reached up and drove one of her daggers into his heart. She then shoved him over the wall, and he never felt the impact of the ground below.

Legion, Dealz, and Arns watched as both flanks attacked simultaneously like a pincer move. Legion targeted the guard on the left on the walkway above the gate and as he released his arrow Dealz cast a hold person spell on the right guard. The spell hit home and the guard froze in place as he was unable to overpower the mental command. The guard could only stand there staring as his friend next to him as he took an arrow in the throat and was bleeding to death. In just a blink of an eye they had gone from conversation about the urges they would take out on the town's females to dying while looking into the darkness. The guard heard the whistle of another arrow hit his friend in the chest and then his friend was gone. He tried to break free but the only thing he could still move was his eyes. He then suddenly felt a hand wrap around his throat and then he was twisted into the air and thrown off the ledge. All he could see was an unarmed man looking down at him as he quietly screamed to the notice of not a single soul. He hit the ground hard and before the light in his eyes went out, he saw two shadows approaching. Then everything went dark.

Once the wall guards were down the infiltrating teams went into their next phase. The archers took up a defensive formation on the wall facing inward while the rogues made their way down to the gate itself. Luckily the noise from the initial attack had been very minimal so the rest of the bandits were still in the town and likely living it up at the inn or at the tavern. Smeeeagal and Bhorn were the first ones to go to the gate and so they began to unlock the mechanisms keeping the gate doors locked. The rest of them joined them and finally they were able to pull the gate doors apart. The gate was never made for stealth, so the noise was obvious as to what was happening. The archers were now on full alert and getting the gate open as quickly as possible was the top priority.

As the gates opened in front of us, I ordered the remaining forces inside to set up a perimeter. We all rushed in with the tanks and warriors first followed by the casters and support staff. Peppermint, my super smart bulwark tank led the charge and about fell over himself when we got inside. Once we had entered, I had the rogues close the gates again to secure our flanks and then I advised the casters to prepare. Due to the noise of the gates, it appeared to have gotten some of the town's people's attention. Belle and Bear shapeshifted into bear forms as druids. Gabby and Kibbles, both warlocks, summoned their imps to their sides, Fandela and Dawg, a demonic summoner and a fey summoner, called forth their available minions. Fandela had a pair of hell hounds while Dawg called upon a fire elemental and a dryad. The support healers began casting various versions of bless and heroism while the witches prepared hexed and damaging auras. The other casters just waited until it was time to unleash their spells.

For this battle I decided to keep the same minion lineup as I had continued to carry so far. Two scrappers, two archers, and two umbral mages, plus Peppermint, the bulwark. I decided that a well-rounded approach was best especially since we were now going to be pushed with our backs potentially up against the gate wall. I sent Peppermint to entrench just behind the tanks and the mages and archers were next to me. The scrappers took their spots just behind Peppermint. Only two healers had decided to stay back with the children and that was Nana and Mimis. They were not ready for this type of fighting so keeping them with the children seemed right. Neelz also stayed behind to help protect them. I left Serenity back as well to help protect them as she would be an added layer of defense. I had to be honest in the fact that I wasn't sure I was ready to unleash her yet as she was still very young for her race.

Mittens on the other hand was almost gleeful in the fact that we were about to engage in mass carnage. She had decided to remain next to me and had done so more often since our bond had changed in the dungeon. We were closer and I had begun to care for her more than just a stereotypical pet as she wasn't that but that was a thought for another time. I looked down at her and placed my hand on her head and scratched her ears. It will all be alright, I said to her and she pressed her head into my palm and let it sit there for a second then she shifted to her game face. All she said then was let's kill these bitches. I cracked a smile and said damn right.

I then looked up at Raven and Tiger Lilly and motioned to both with a nod and then took a lasting glance at Jaceberlen. A split second after doing so he turned as if he knew I was looking and he smiled and nodded. All I could do was nod in return. At that moment Pint Size popped out of stealth about fifty yards away from us and let everyone know that we had incoming as the gates had certainly made some noise. So, for all our stealth and coordination, it was a total lack of WD-40 for the gates that set off the alarms. Go figure.

CHAPTER TWENTY-SEVEN

Reality Check

We tensed for battle and then they were in view. It looked like around fifty or so bandits came around the corner in a rush. They didn't appear to know what caused the gates to open and certainly were not expecting a force of almost seventy in our own right to be inside of the walls and facing them prepared to battle. When they rounded the clearing, they immediately halted and quickly developed a confused and surprised look on their faces. That hesitation was all that we needed.

We had planned to limit structural damage to a bare minimum if it could be avoided so that we didn't have to rebuild. With that in mind, large area type damaging spells were mostly out of the question, so our ranged damage dealers were advised to focus on small area spells or single target attacks. This limited everyone's spell types, but it was a tradeoff I felt worth taking. I had my umbral mages cast blindness to as many targets as fast as they could in the area that the bandits were standing in and while some resisted or escaped the spell, several were caught in its effects. Once that was down the arrows and spells released.

The enemies that weren't affected by the spell tried their best to defend and counter the attacks. Shields were raised and magical barriers appeared to protect who they could, but several attacks got through. Suddenly screams echoed and shattered the silence of the night. At this moment our forces fully engaged the enemy bandits. Jaceberlen, Laltag Duine, and the other melee class members charged while Gunthar, Killer, Illistar, Thor, Da Man, Squasher, Cheeda, Amedeus, Bear, and Belle led the group as our tanks. Peppermint, my bulwark was right behind them followed quickly by all the melee damage dealers.

The tanks began using their various taunting skills to draw the attackers to engage them for the damage classes to begin their assault. The bandits seemed to engage the same tactics to draw the damage focused classes away from flanking maneuvers. And now it was on! Now that the battle was in full swing. I commanded my minions to engage and with that I joined the fray as well. I spotted a healer in the back of the group and directed the umbral mages to target him as well as the archers. I then followed that up with a necrotic ray.

Their spells landed up against a magical shield and so did my first spell, but I continued casting toll of the dead until my necrotic ray came off cool down and then I would cast again. On the fourth volley from my minions and myself, the shield shattered and the cleric's armor was first slammed by a shadow bolt. Then the necrotic ray hit and an arrow was after that. The cleric was now completely on the defensive as he was trying to heal himself from the barrage of attacks. A dark flame hit him square in the chest and then he fell backward.

He was barely moving when out of the darkness, Smeeeagal came down with an axe to his head cackling as he did so. Then the cleric was no more. Smeeeagal laughing maniacally rejoined the fight with the others. For a while it was an even matchup as most of their group was of a higher level, however, we were more organized and had a wider variety of classes to counter their makeup. My aura of decay was not quite reaching the main battle so I came forward until I could feel the radius edge about five feet within the melee groups.

Peppermint was fending off a dual wielding warrior and as his shield blocked what appeared to be a faint the warrior gouged his left femur and left a very deep groove. ThreeBD arced a swing with his two-handed weapon and caught the dual wielder in the back and dropped him with another downward thrust to the skull. Big Bad Booty Daddy to the rescue, I thought. The rangers up on the wall were sending a steady stream of arrows into the crowded battlefield from both sides and injuries were mounting up. Gunthar, our brawler, had taken a nasty sword cut to the abdomen and was bleeding profusely. He was still throwing punches left and right, but his speed had slowed and one of our clerics threw him a quick heal to help. Gunthar seemed to look more energized, and you could see that the wound was starting to visibly close.

Big Bear, my father, looked like a reborn sugar addict out there swinging his two-handed axe in circular motions and if there were any questions about his arm, they had disappeared now. Suddenly a thunderous boom sounded throughout the landscape as lightning seared into several of our opponents and stunned some of them. I looked over after casting another necrotic ray to see Jaceberlen in the thick of the mix lowering his sword hand from the sky after casting the spell. He was still uninjured as it would seem. Music began to play behind me as Captain Ahab began playing his lute that seemed to energize our entire group with a certain aura, and everyone began to fight with more vigor. I noticed one of Utha's totems on the ground to the left of the main battle as it pulsated with what appeared to be a debuff to our enemies. I wasn't sure of its type, so I identified one of the closest enemies to the totem. What I saw was a negative ten percent to attack. That was a nice added touch. That is where my distraction cost me.

I took my eyes off the battle when I wanted to casually check out Utha's totem effects, and I didn't see it until it was too late as an enemy rogue come out of stealth next to Manerva, the witch. One second, she was channeling a hex spell and then her eyes were wide with a dagger being removed from her throat by the rogue. It was at that moment when the momentum shifted. We had never had one of our own group members die, and upon witnessing that series of events, several of the team froze. In that moment of hesitation, Penny and Magster, two of our wizards, and Lady Jane, a sorcerer, were cut down by arrows and spells.

We were winning the momentum of the battle until that point, however when four of your damage dealers go down it can shift the battle in a blink of an eye.

Once they were down, we had to regain our emotions and work to curb the momentum swing of the battle. We still had the numbers, but they had the levels and now the flow of the engagement. I began recasting with vigor and I told Mittens to reinforce the melee lines. I yelled at the group to refocus and push to end this. Every summon and minion that we still had attacked with a new ferocity. I was down to my bulwark, one scrapper, and a single mage and archer. The tanks in unison seemed to refresh their taunts which shifted most of the aggression towards them again. With that in place, Jaceberlen, Smeeeagal, and the other melee attackers reengaged their flanks. Ducks and the other healers tried their best to keep everyone up, but she soon voiced their concerns as their energy was running low. I nodded in understanding and decided to take a risk.

I pulled up the interface and placed an icon on their healers. This was a relatively new function that we had discovered so it caught some of them off guard, but they soon recovered from the surprise. I yelled at the remaining archers and casters up top to focus left to right on the marked targets. Suddenly a barrage of magic and arrows shot towards the bandit healer on the left side. He appeared to have some sort of summoned shield and withstood several of the attacks but after a few seconds the barrage seemed to be too much. An arrow got through the shield and slammed into the cleric's shoulder. Then another arrow hit and then an ice bolt crashed into his face. That was followed by an energy bolt, more arrows, and finally he was taken down by a magma bolt that left a smoking crater in his chest as he crumpled to the ground dead. The group then moved to the next target and systematically worked their way through the healers until none remained.

The next icons found their way to the casters. We were in a groove now and no matter what their defenses were, they could not withstand the bombardment of so many attacks for any great length of time. One by one they kept falling into darkness. We weren't, however, the only ones trying to end the battle though. A few more of our melee party members fell due to being targeted and flanked by their rogues and casters. This was becoming a battle of attrition and that was something we could not afford.

Finally, the last of their casters fell and now we only had to take care of the melee fighters and the stealth enemies. Farwind took over placing the icons on the melee fighters, so I signaled for all our stealth combatants to search and locate their counterparts within the battle area. I continued to focus my fire on the battle still raging in front of me. Necrotic ray, dark flame, and toll of the dead were being spammed as fast as I could and even looking at my energy, I knew this was about to have to turn to an unsheathing of my scythes as my energy was running dangerously low. I decided to use the last of my mana to refresh Bless on Jaceberlen, Mittens, and myself and I followed that up with another necrotic ray to one of their tanks. It splashed against his arm, and the necrosis instantly took. He glanced down at his arm in surprise and that was all that Belle needed as she clamped her bear jaws around the man's neck and ripped his head clean from his shoulders. Blood spewed everywhere like a fountain and to add insult to injury, she tossed the head with her mouth, and you could see it rotate end over end until it hit a wall.

Even though we had the goal to preserve as much of the town as we possibly could, the bandits being notified that there was something afoot minimized that realistic goal. By now the front part of the town had been utterly devastated. Building lay in ruins and others were burning causing the whole area to resemble the remains of an area of effect spell. The town residents were clearly nowhere present, which was a big plus if we won this. We needed to keep it contained in the front part as anything can be rebuilt and we didn't want the townsfolk to completely resent us.

As another building fell, we were in danger of the conflict spilling into the market area of the town. I didn't even try to think about it, and instinctively I summoned my night cloud spell behind the fight just in front of the area of the market. With that summoned, the entire zone behind the bandits went into complete darkness. Hopefully that would deter anyone from entering that part of the town.

The bandits were down to a handful of combatants left as most had now been destroyed by the battle and focused fire. By now most of the caster classes had run out of energy as everyone had unleashed everything they could as quickly as humanly possible, which had now shown me a visible weakness in our strategy and one honestly, we wouldn't have really seen it unless we had encountered this. If we made it out of this then we would work to rectify that glaring whole. The remaining forces on their side seemed to notice they were on the losing end and frantically tried to disengage and regroup. I never said that was the smartest move, but they tried too, nonetheless. The archers now had more room to attack and began in earnest while our tanks reformed their lines as well and created a wall of steel.

We still needed to account for the missing stealthies, and I took a second to look at my quest count. The number of bandits slain showed fifty-one, but it didn't give an overall count so I couldn't see how many had left the camp nor how many remained here in the town. As they were reforming into a group, we marched forward and attempted to encircle them. Our tanks closed the area and left nowhere for them to retreat too. I told the damage melee to protect the healers and casters as I sent a quick message to Bhorn to let me know how the hunt for the stealth-based enemies was going. He responded a few seconds later stating that they had taken down four of them but two remained. Pint Size, Flower, and Smeeeagal, and himself were on their trail now and about to engage. Shifty little bastards, he said with a laugh, but he assured me they had it in hand. He would update me very shortly.

You could hear close quarter battle nearby with daggers flying around and the grunts of pain as attacks landed. We weren't too sure of where they were, but we could hear two sets of fights happening simultaneously. With a two versus one we had the odds in our favor. Then the sounds softened and then a few moments later it went quiet. I received a message from Bhorn stating that the enemies had been killed and they were all accounted for albeit with some nasty injuries. They were heading back to flank the remaining forces.

Finally, we could see the light at the end of the tunnel. I motioned for the tanks to begin creating a semi-circle around the enemies. The bandits tried to counter by backing up towards the darkness however they were met by four of their damage dealers taking sneak attacks in their kidneys as our rogue type warriors emerged from stealth behind them and did devastating damage. Two of the bandits fell dead from Pint Size and Smeeeagal while the other two who were damaged turned around only to catch arrows in their now exposed flanks. They too dropped to the ground dead and now there were only seven bandits remaining.

The bandits, knowing they had lost immediately tried to whine and wail to the effect that they wanted to surrender and that they were just following orders. One however had no such notion and just spat on the ground saying that the commander would deal with us. This response was more typical of what I expected considering the intel we had on them. I stopped and looked at the man and raised my voice; and when should I expect the commander and his entourage of about one hundred plus bandits to grace us with his presence?

The bandit looked surprised at my comments and the information I had on their numbers. He then seemed to solidify his resolve and sneered at me stating that he wouldn't tell us anything. I looked him dead in the eye and just said then you die first. I looked to my left at Biggus Dikkus and nodded and then suddenly a javelin soared through the air and slammed into the chest of the bandit in question. He died instantly as the point protruded from the back of his armor. Biggus Dikkus laughed and uttered in his bad boy voice; I got that silly goose. I just sighed and murmured, how is that resolve treating you fellas now? I then looked at the remaining group of bandits and asked if anyone else had anything they wanted to share? Most of them decided that they weren't going to survive the night anyway and took the same approach that the dead bandit did, however there was one that just yelled out; in two days.

I nodded at the one who responded and asked where they had gone. He began to respond that they went to raid a nearby village, but before he could finish his statement, a blade was seen sticking out of his chest in a spray of blood. His eyes went wide and a bloody foam came from his mouth as he turned around only to see one of his friends holding the blade. The man looked at him as he called him a snitch and then yanked the blade free in another spray of blood. He fell to the ground in a pool of blood, and his eyes went blank with the peace of death.

It was obvious that this conversation was over and I signaled to the group. The circle began to close. I got a few looks about the decision but considering what we had just witnessed there were no verbal complaints. The group began marching forward, closing the circle as the bandits pulled up their shields and brandished their weapons. Five remained as three were of the defender or tank class while the remaining two were dual wielding warriors.

Raven released an arrow that seemed to slip through the shields and hit one of the dual wielders in the arm that spun him to the side and with great timing, Pint Size came up to meet the spinning man with her blades. A soft grunt of pain exited his mouth as she withdrew her daggers, and he looked down at the gushing wounds. Then his neck snapped back as another arrow this time from Tiger Lilly crashed into his skull. The bandit's eyes rolled into the back of his head as he crumpled lifelessly to the dirt. The remaining four bandits tried to defend themselves valiantly, but their fates were already decided. As the final one fell from a hammer strike to the skull from Tal'n the area finally quieted down.

CHAPTER TWENTY-EIGHT

Clean Up and Prepare

As we stood there with the adrenaline starting to simmer down, I knew that we were not out of the woods quite yet. I immediately advised the group to remain on guard until we had secured the town. I noticed that my stats had started regenerating, so I know this part of combat had ended. I looked at Captain Ahab and asked him to put a group together to secure the town and notify the residents that the bandits had been dealt with. He nodded and grabbed about fifteen of our group and headed further into town as I dispelled the dark cloud.

I motioned to Duck and told her to grab a few and head back to the group that had stayed back at the edge of the woods and bring them inside of the walls. She nodded and had a few others accompany her as well. With those two tasks taken care of, I got another group to begin sorting out any loot and items and then place them in a pile. I told Altriox to have them gather the bodies and burn them to the side as soon as we were able to. He took to looting the bodies as well to help expedite that order.

Jaceberlen looked at me and whispered well that was intense. I responded in kind and I also mentioned that I was worried how the group would handle some of us being killed as this was a real thing here in WEO. He also agreed and then he smiled. Hey, we won the first round big man, so we now get to come a step closer to having our own home. I couldn't help but smile in agreement but we were not out of the woods yet. I told him that I needed to check on how the death process worked with our members that had fallen and asked him to check on the others to make sure they were okay. We needed to set up a watch on the wall and secure the area.

I pulled up my interface and checked for the quest update and noticed the number of slain bandits had reached sixty. The total number of bandits was still a question mark for the time being, but that was for another time to delve further into. I saw that my experience bar had certainly ticked up and was getting closer to twenty. I couldn't wait for that. I then pulled up my group list and saw that the team members that had fallen were still greyed out like before, but they now had a timer attached that seemed to be ticking down to their apparent respawn time. Their dots however were located at the inn we had stayed at on the route here. That seemed to give a bit of insight.

Was the respawn location at your last designated rest stop? I made a mental note to ask them upon their return. Now this also posed an issue. The group was a solid half a day away and would need to make a hastened trip here to make it by the time the commander and his troops arrived. We would need every person we had to win this. I couldn't send them a message that I could see but I will have to research that soon. Their timer was listed at close to twelve hours, and I assumed that the more you died, the longer that would be. Not to mention any experience loss.

I looked at my energy level and saw that I had enough energy now to summon my minions. I immediately did that considering I had only one mage left by the end of the battle. Once again, I really had to get them stronger. They quickly reappeared at my side, and I kept the same composition as I had since it still seemed to work well. For the battle with the commander though I will need to look at a different mix. The bulwark was next and the hulking box of bones stepped forward and stood there. Mittens came up to me, and she was covered with blood. I looked down and she was licking her lips like she had just finished up at an all you can eat buffet. I asked her, "Did you eat those guys? She looked right back at me and smiled. "I'm hungry," she said and when I am hungry, I eat, she continued. I just shook my head at that, and she pressed up against me leaving a blood smear on my pants leg.

About ten minutes later the bodies were all in a pile off to the side and being taken care of by a massive fire thanks to Altriox. There was also a pile of loot stacked neatly at the base of a semi standing building. The wall was covered by the archers and a few casters. About another ten more minutes, the archers let us know that the remaining group led by Duck were approaching the gate and motioned to open the gate doors. I must admit I was a bit hesitant as to what their reaction would be to the destruction and carnage. Luckily Altriox worked fast.

As the group led by Duck entered, you could see the worry and surprise on their faces. Obviously, the children acted how we expected them too but Mimis, Nana, and Neelz took me off kilter a bit. I knew Neelz might have a problem considering what she had just been through, but Mimis just looked at us and asked us if we were okay. I nodded and then she gave me a hug. Her days as a nurse must have helped her deal with this type of scene. Nana looked at Tiger Lilly, Gunthar, and then Belle and noticed that they were all okay. With them being her children, she seemed to release a small amount of tension she was holding. Priest, their father, immediately hugged them but then knelt and checked on Neelz. He was a very religious man, and the sight of all this death was not something he relished or even agreed with. I walked over to him and just looked at him and nodded somberly. The message was understood.

Once everyone was inside of the walls, the doors were closed and secure. The group that had remained outside of the town during the skirmish finally noticed that we were missing some people. We then had to explain why quite a few were with the party that was securing the inside of the town and that others had to be explained as temporarily dead. We all knew that death was not permanent, however we also knew that it would be very costly and painful. Mass murder was not a trait the system wanted instilled into people's behavior unless they were willing to pay the consequences.

I tried to explain to them what information I had gathered about the process from the interface. For the most part it was understood and accepted. The rest we would have to hear firsthand from the people that were currently in respawn. All in all, it seemed that we had lost about ten people not including any of the summons. We really were unable to do anything about that now so we will have to defend this place with what we have. Everyone will need to do their part when the commander arrives with their remaining forces. I did have an idea on how to use the ten but for now we will handle other things.

A while later I was notified that Captain Ahab was approaching and was accompanied by a large group. As I headed to meet him, I noticed an apprehensive look in his eyes. I guess we will find out what is going on. He met me and he placed his head to my ear and whispered that I needed to tread carefully here. I nodded and moved to see what appeared to be the leader of the group of residents accompanying Captain Ahab.

The elderly man looked to be in bad health. There were bruises everywhere across the man. His cheeks were sullen with what looked to be malnutrition, and he had cuts and dried blood all over him. He barely had any clothes on and walked barefoot. Honestly the man and everyone that had joined him looked awful. I knew the intel reports that the archers provided were bad, but this was even worse than I had expected. I looked at them all and then I introduced myself.

The group looked up at me and then the old man lifted a frail hand and gestured at all the devastation around us. He then asked me if this was our handy work. I felt bad in the overture, but we needed to have an honest and open dialog. I responded simply with a yes although it wasn't our goal. I continued; We came here to rid the town of the bandit menace and make a home here with you. He looked at me silently for a few moments then retorted that he was worried all we did was make matters worse when the bandit leader returned. I nodded and could perfectly understand his meaning, and I honestly didn't know if we could take the commander's forces when they arrived at least initially, but we would do everything we could too. I looked at him and explained what we were trying to do and with their help we can make this town a prosperous place for all of us.

The ragged man looked at us again with determined eyes and just advised us that we would see, and we could start by giving them some healing. He then introduced himself as Jim. I extended my hands and when we gripped each other's hands, I could tell just how frail they were. I looked at Mimis and asked her to gather the healers to help take care of the residents. We would need all of them as there were a few hundred of them and everyone looked as bad or worse than Jim.

As the healers went over to the residents to begin the healing process, I motioned for Jaceberlen, Captain Ahap, Tal'n, Biggus Dikkus, and Bhorn. As we gathered, I looked at them with a serious look. My next words were straightforward and to the point. "We need to secure the area and prepare for the commanders forces as we have less than two days". Bhorn nodded and said he would look for the unseen entry points from the reports into the town, Tal'n said he would grab some help to scour the town to see what can be of use, Jaceberlen would walk the town to see what buildings there actually were that we could use to set up a strategy, while the rest were going to run through the towns structural aspects and defenses to see what can be fixed and or enhanced. I advised that group to grab Dealz to go along with them. Time is of the essence I said again as they all left. I let them all know we would reconvene in two hours.

Tiger Lilly and Raven came over to me once the group broke off and they both wrapped their arms around me and even though no words were spoken the sentiment was clear. We were all safe for the moment. Raven moved off to embrace her husband, Laltag Duine, and their daughter, Ophelia. Tiger Lilly gave me a kiss on the cheek and then moved off to check on the rest of her side of the family. I looked down at Mittens and Serenity and smiled. I am glad you two are okay, I muttered. Mittens being the overly sarcastic smart ass just scoffed and said always, while

Serenity was a bit more realistic to the situation. Thank you and same to you she replied and I gave them both a hug. I knelt and looked them both in the eyes and let them know we couldn't hold back when they return and as afraid as I was to have Serenity join the fight, we really didn't have a choice. She just nodded and said that she knew the stakes and would help how she could. I nodded and then looked at my minions. I ordered them to go up on the walls and keep watch with the rangers and let me know if they see anything. They sharply nodded and marched off.

CHAPTER TWENTY-NINE

Panic

Once the groups all reconvened, we included the elder, Jim, in the discussion since it was his home after all, and he would know it best. We covered various topics and tactics. They all gave their assessments of their respective tasks that they had completed and together we were beginning to form a plan of action to take down the remaining forces when they arrived. We continued for about an hour going over all that we were planning to put in motion as well as the starting plans for post battle acclimation.

Jim said that we could all stay in the inn tonight, so we didn't have to stay out in the elements. Finally, the discussion ended and everyone seemed to be checking all their notifications since most of the group appeared to be staring out into space. I was glad to see that everyone had gotten some possible levels and some of that sweet loot we had piled up earlier. Most of the bandit's gear was an upgrade to most of our group so anything we could upgrade with was a win. The tank classes made out the best as the bandits seemed to focus on that type of warrior with heavy armor. Most of ours were in medium armor still so it would be an upgrade for sure. It was all still in the common or uncommon rank but hey; loot is loot. The rest of the items we decided to give to the townsfolk as they flat out needed everything they could grab.

I went off to the side and sat down near one of the partially standing buildings. I pulled up my interface and summoned

Tikallnosis. After a few seconds he appeared in my vision, and I explained where we were at currently and what was expected to come. One question had been nagging in the back of my mind for quite a while, so I finally decided to ask it. So Tikallnosis; How exactly will you be able to do your thing once these targets are defeated? I mean I know you aren't going to be stalking me twenty-four/seven, are you? Tikallnosis just laughed and said, well that is kind of my job but all joking aside, I am giving you something after this conversation that will appear in your inventory. Once each of these entities are killed you will need to stab the creature with this special dagger of sorts. This will disable the firewall and help pull the file out and place it in a secure folder for my review.

You are more than welcome to ping me before you engage each one, but this will do the trick regardless. Once he finished talking, I got a notification that an item had been placed in my inventory. I decided to look at it, and it pretty much was what I thought it would be. Shiv of Retrieval – This blade will assist in securing necessary data when plunged into a dead foe. This item is of no other use and cannot be traded, looted, or sold. Yep, pretty much what I needed I replied.

After a few more minutes of conversation the call faded, and my vision warped back into reality. I looked around and noticed that I was still alone although Serenity was looking at me from across the way. I smiled at her and began walking her way. As I approached, she nodded and asked if my communion with Tikallnosis went well. That caught me off guard, so I asked how she knew. She just snickered and advised me that the last time I talked to him I did the same thing. Plus, she is a dragon and smart at that. Not like it was a hard assumption, she commented.

It was getting very late and I knew we had a long day tomorrow preparing for the upcoming battle. I let Serenity, Mittens, and my minions know that I was heading to the inn, and the group gathered up behind me, but my ranged minions remained as a security detail. As we walked, we could see the destruction and the fear in all the residents' demeanors that were still outside in the streets. One woman walked up to us and grabbed my hand. Although the sight of skeletons walking around made her more than a bit nervous, she still managed to have the courage to tell us that she was grateful that we had come to help them. She said she would pray for us in the upcoming battle and if we failed then the town would fall as well. The commander's rage was well known to them and losing most of his forces would mean death to most if not all the town's residents as payback.

Thomas leaned back in his chair once he had taken off his headset and disconnected from the chat with Dookooze. He still wasn't sure if all of this was a colossal mistake, but he had gone this far and he wasn't able to back out now. All he could do now was wait and see what the first piece of the puzzle gave him as far as information. Thomas was extremely nervous about what he was trying to achieve with all of this, and it would surely cost him his job and reputation if that even meant anything anymore with all the chaos in the world. Something was off and his gut had never let him down before. The algorithm was precise and thought out. The chosen one, Dookooze or Mitch, seemed to be a solid choice so far to justify the selection. Thomas was deep in his thought process when one of his team members knocked on his door and reminded him of a meeting that they were about to have. Startled, Thomas locked up his drawers and headed out to the conference room.

When Thomas and his coworkers entered the room and sat it seemed upbeat. The process of integrating all the world's citizens into WEO had been completed mostly without a hitch and everyone's neuro link seemed to be operating smoothly. Thomas was calm on the outside and even friendly, however internally he was a hurricane of tension. The last thing he could have happen now was the scheme that he had put into motion to be discovered. As the final members of his team took their seats, his boss advised them that today's update meeting will include a special guest, Igor Romanovichky. Thomas' blood went ice cold with the mention of that name as he was the creator of the simulation itself and was located far away from their location.

He just told himself to keep his answers simple and to the point. The rest would take care of itself.

As the meeting progressed the topics ranged from maintenance to updates and all the customary discussion points within this type of game environment. When the meeting seemed to be ending it took a sudden turn when Igor Romanovichky asked a blanketed question about how it was going so far and what some of the milestones that had been achieved? That took everyone inside the room by surprise but most had information to share. Classes and the variety of races were mentioned as well as some of the test results. It was at this point that the results began to go under scrutiny and as the top scorers were brought up in discussion, a name that Thomas was desperately trying to avoid came up.

One of his colleagues mentioned that a man by the name of Dookooze had scored in the upper echelon and seemed to be very well rounded when based against his peers in the same grouping hierarchy. Igor asked the man to explain, and the colleague went into Dookooze's results and that he managed to score high in all categories. This got Igor Romanovichky's attention and he asked what class and race the man chose. The man obliged and when the information was shared, Mr. Romanovichky sat back in his chair while rubbing his chin in thought. The first to level fifteen and a patron of a god already, he murmured. I guess it should not be too out of the ordinary for this considering his scores but nonetheless keep an eye on progression levels for all the top scorers so that we have a baseline. That was when Thomas inwardly gave a huge sigh of relief. So far so good he thought. Once the meeting ended, Thomas quickly ran back to his office and shut the blinds and the door. He needed a drink.

Manerva sat in what appeared to be dimly lit room. Her interface was grayed out so she was unable to communicate with anyone however she was able to have access to online information and her character. This was a weird experience; however, the time of her death was anything but weird. It hurt like absolute hell. The pain was insane when she was stabbed and instinctively, she put her hand to the invisible wound mark. It left a mark for sure but just not a physical one. Now she understood the warnings about dying and if she was honest with herself; this was something she never wanted to feel again. Putting aside the trauma from dying, she now had to accept the consequences.

Realizing that she needed to get much stronger was glaring at her right in the face as she looked at the penalties that she had incurred from dying. Not only was she unable to respawn for twelve hours but she got hit with an experience penalty of ten percent of her current level. She was about to hit level sixteen when the assault happened but now, she had taken a large step back. The ominous notification only made matters worse. "Further deaths will face increasingly more serious repercussions. Get strong and don't die" There was nothing she could do about it now but mentally prepare herself to get back in there and become more powerful. She would not be denied power. She just hoped the rest of the fallen members of her group handled it that same way.

CHAPTER THIRTY

Groundwork

I awoke the next morning and immediately checked in with my minions. Before we went to bed, I had resummoned my skeletal minions to have them all as archers. I needed them to assist in keeping watch and look out for anything out of the ordinary. I woke up in fear as I had not heard even a peep out of them, so I wanted to make sure they were still around. All six responded in kind that nothing was afoot, so I finally relaxed. I advised them to check with the leader on the wall which should be Farwind and let her know that they would be going into the woods in all directions to scout. That way we would be notified if anything would alter our timeline.

I rolled over and shook Tiger Lilly to awaken her and then I noticed my bulwark, Peppermint was just standing there guarding us. It was a bit creepy but hey I would live. I let her know that I needed to check on some things and that I would see her in a bit. She whimpered and gave me a kiss then she went back to bed. I then messaged Jaceberlen, Captain Ahab, Dealz, Tal'n, and Biggus Dikkus to meet me in the courtyard in half an hour. When they all replied to the affirmative, I headed outside.

The air was a bit heavy, and a light fog was hovering over the area. The temperature was crisp like an early winter morning. This would have been a great time for a jacket but that wasn't a luxury we had now. As I walked through the town, I noticed that the residents seemed to have a bit of a brighter outlook over what I had seen last night. A sparkle of hope maybe or just maybe the fact that nobody had been tortured, raped, or beaten so far today. Either way I would take the win. I was ready to get this meeting over with as I had another plan for today. First, we needed to secure and prepare the town for what was to come.

I stood at the base of the gate looking at what had already started and then I asked Farwind how things were going and she just nodded and let me know that so far all was quiet. She also noted that my minions had disappeared into the woods about twenty minutes ago. I could see them on my map, but it was good to know that her keen eyes were able to discern their movements. I looked around for a few more minutes at all the rustle and bustle of the town cleaning up and setting anything aside that can be reused.

The group finally arrived and we all decided to take a walking meeting as we went over the defenses. Dealz had an architecture background so his input would be well received while Captain Ahab was a min max specialist and tactical guru from our online gaming days. Tal'n and Biggus Dikkus were also part of our online group and had their own specialties while my son, Jaceberlen, was a wealth of strategy from all his strategy gaming days before we came here. We continued to talk about what we could feasibly meld together for a defensive platform in a day. We weren't sure exactly when the bandits would arrive, but I would rather prepare for an early morning encounter and be pleasantly surprised then vice versa.

We discussed our plans for the next hour or so as we put together our strategy. The walls and gate were still perfectly intact, and it was mostly the inner buildings at the front of the town that were damaged. The bandits had relied strictly on defensive cover by numbers while we would need more. I mentioned to Biggus Dikkus about the pathways we used to enter the city and he thought for a second and then said he would shore those up before nightfall. Tal'n would lead the citizens and unassigned group members to prep the city for an incursion with traps and choke points. Captain Ahab would work to develop troop placement and tactics for the assault, while Jaceberlen would help train the troops that were citizens that volunteered to fight. Dealz would take all the town's builders and begin constructing anti-siege equipment and simple defensive structures. My part at least for the next few hours was all agreed upon. When the battle commenced, I would lead the defense with this group commanding their respective groups.

With the meeting out of the way, I mentally contacted my scouts and asked them a few questions about the creatures out in the woods. After their responses, I asked Mittens and Serenity if they were ready to head out, and we then set out to the northwest as there were some things that I desperately wanted to get taken care of before tomorrow's battle. We all met up at the gate and as the gates were open, I looked up at Tiger Lilly and Raven who were up on the wall and nodded.

As we made our way from the valley into the deeper woods, I looked at Mittens and Serenity and thanked them for helping me. Everyone knew how important this would be if I could get it. In our meeting this morning, we discussed all options as far as duties for today when Captain Ahab asked how far I was from level twenty. I pulled up my sheet and gave them all the amount of experience that was needed. We all knew that level twenty was the first major evolution of a sort for all Earthen and entities within WEO. What that entailed nobody knew, however we all were aware it could be a game changer and could do nothing but help. So that was what everyone decided that my goal would be for the day. Jaceberlen had been insistent that he would come along and as much as I wanted him there, the town would likely benefit more from him giving instructions on warfare. I recalled all my archers except for the two closest to the path that the bandits took. That left me with four of my archers, the bulwark, Serenity, Mittens, and myself. We should be okay, I hoped.

As we made our way through the woods, we heard what appeared to be rushing water. Our group led by the archers continued to move forward as they were looking for anything that might seem aloof. After about another hundred meters in the area, one of the archers advised me that we had come upon a den of some sorts and there were large creatures mulling around near a waterfall. The trees and underbrush had completely isolated this area. It felt weird as if there was an aura of some sort of energy. It felt heavy but not oppressing.

When we stopped in the last bits of cover, I looked out and I noticed a stone pedestal surrounded by rocky steps leading down to an outcropping. It was all covered with moss and the smell of earth was in the air but the energy this place was giving off was insane. I finally inspected the creatures and noticed that we had stumbled into a large den of weird looking salamanders. They were reddish in color and had fur from head to toe. This was certainly different.

There seemed to be over two dozen of them with what appeared to a level range of five to twenty. There was a gigantic salamander that had a different name altogether was listed as 'The Queen of the Waterfall'. She might need to die last because if she was already level twenty, then this would be a tough fight. I decided to watch their patterns for a bit, and the queen was mostly immobile now, the rest of them were anything but. The very low-level ones were likely offspring being cared for as the middle-level ones were gathering food or resources for their den. The ones that were gathering food used some sort of fire-based breath attack as they would cook anything they were after and then bring it to the queen. From there it was devoured and the cycle would repeat.

I realized that the group makeup was not ideal for this fight as the mages would have been a much better option instead of the archers however, I couldn't afford to dismiss the ones that were scouting for the bandits so I would need to get a little creative. I glanced over to Serenity and with the unspoken words she just nodded and pulled out two small swords, twirled them around a skosh and then said it was time to level. Mittens purred and I knew that my little murdering kitty was thirsty for blood. I smiled and whispered "Let's go kill some salamanders.

CHAPTER THIRTY-ONE

Growth Spurt

I cast Bless on us as we were about to engage the salamanders. Mittens went into stealth and we were holed up at a choke point in the trees with a few rocks blocking them. In this fight, positioning would be everything due to the numbers. The bulwark took up its defensive stance in front of the archers and on my command, they released their barrage of arrows at one of the mid-level salamanders. All four arrows struck the one to the far right and it fell without a sound. Before the beast even hit the ground the second round of arrows had been sent to the one on the far left. The salamanders noticed the death of one of its own and lifted their heads, but the next round slammed into their target before a sound could be made. Now there was alarm within the group of beasts. Hissing sounds were echoing throughout the base area of the waterfall. A third salamander dropped from a barrage of arrows as they finally realized where the attack was coming from. I then released a necrotic ray toward the group, and it too hit home as the blackish green bolt washed over the fur of another foe. Now the fight was in full force.

As I continued to cast spell after spell, the salamanders charged the direction from whence we were located. As they hit the choke point, the salamanders started lighting up the area with their fire attacks. The bulwark slammed his shield down right before they unleashed the fire and it was mostly blocked by the bone shield. Not all of it though as his white bones began to char and show scorch marks. How much damage the fire attacks could cause was still up in the air, so we needed to take these bad boys out.

Mittens appeared to the left flank and used her projection to draw a few of them from the bulwark and then she pounced. Her tentacles moved like whips through the air striking enemy after enemy. When an attack hit, Mittens would follow up with a swipe of her claws. The blood of the salamanders was everywhere in the wake of the attacks. Serenity appeared on the right of the cluster, and she used her two swords to carve a path. Even for her size, she was still technically a dragon. Her breath attack had not evolved yet to where she could use it on a mass scale and was essentially locked away in her human form, but it was still something she could utilize on a small, singular scale. She had exhaled a small breath on her dragon swords, and they began crackling with electricity. When she connected with the salamander's flesh it would begin to spasm slightly and create openings with its small stunning effect for her to attack again. Smoke began coming from the fur of each salamander as she attacked.

With the flanks being fully engaged and drawn away from the middle, the archers were able to focus on a singular target at a time. Picking off the edges was the plan until the boss of the riverbed remained. My focus was to keep the queen occupied while the others took out the other beasts. I continued to cast toll of the dead and necrotic ray. I had initially tried a dark flame and although it wasn't technically a fire spell as it was a shadow-based attack, when it had connected, I had received an icon above the queen saying that it was partially resisted. So, with that I focused more on the necrotic side of my menu of options.

I followed up the disappointment of a partial resist with a nice helping of withering snare in the middle of the salamander group ¡and that was fun to watch. Bones began grabbing at the enemies and siphoning their health. As the necrotic energy began stacking up, I pressed my attack even harder. The necrosis was spreading throughout the queen's body as the fur surrounding the attacks was wilting away and falling off. Bare splotches of skin were appearing everywhere. My energy kept dropping at a steady clip, but I would not be denied. I took a few steps forward to stand just a few feet behind the bulwark so that my aura could finally wash over the front attackers.

Suddenly I heard a mental scream and as I jerked from the scare, I lost my rhythm and my focus waned. Just then a fire bolt hit me on the side, and a searing pain ran down my shoulder to my thigh. I glanced down only to see where an area of my side had melted away to where my ribs and open flesh were exposed. Part of my flesh had charred and was burnt. I tried to give myself a quick heal to stem the injury, but it was so painful I couldn't concentrate long enough to get it cast. I knew that if I didn't get myself taken care of and then address what the scream meant, that we would be done for.

I began to feel the effects of the injury as the blood began to flow unabated from the burnt ends of what used to be my rib cage. I knelt and refocused on my efforts, and I was finally able to stabilize myself to at least determine what had happened. I looked up and saw that Serenity had taken a nasty series of gashes from the claws of two of the salamanders and she was bleeding profusely. She was limping while trying to dodge the multiple attacks. Serenity no longer appeared to be dishing out any offensive attacks as she was solely on the defensive. Her parries were slowing even now, so I immediately cast a heal on her since it had just come off cool down. The relief was evident in her eyes and as soon as the three second cooldown was off, I then cast another one to help her get back to as close to a hundred percent as I could. I saw that her health was back to eighty-five percent, so I turned to Mittens and noticed that she was still at seventy percent, but I threw her a heal regardless.

With those two healed up for the moment, I cast another heal on myself and saw the opening in my rib cage stitch itself back together. It was very unsettling watching strands of flesh mend itself in an active battle or honestly at any time but now was not the time to process that sight as I had to get back to fighting. I turned my attention to the bitch that gave me that wound. An anger began to build inside me and I screamed. I then unleashed a rage filled necrotic ray and as it hit the queen, she was noticeably rocked back by the force. A toll of the dead bolt followed, and the attacks resumed in earnest. I really had to develop a broader attack strategy considering one of my three spells was resisted albeit partially.

My aura seemed to be affecting the front line of salamanders as their fur was bald in many spots and their wounds from the arrows were now leaking greenish red blood. The bulwark was doing all it could to stem the onslaught of the creatures as it swung its club back and forth to hit anything that came close. It roared another taunt and like clockwork the remaining salamanders charged him. A club managed to smash the skull of one salamander and when it fell another one climbed over its corpse. The foe slashed its tail like a spear at the bulwark but a timely move to bring its shield up to block it, saved it from being pierced in the chest.

The archers continued their onslaught and slowly dwindled the number of salamanders down to below five. They showed some initiative when that happened because they shifted their target to the remaining salamander that Serenity was squared off against. As Serenity blocked a claw attack and combined that with a sword strike against one of its legs, four arrows slammed into its back. The salamander screeched from the pain and then it dropped lifelessly to the ground. A winded Serenity turned to the archers and nodded in thanks, but that shift of focus was a mistake as the queen slammed her tail into Serenity's side, and she flew in the air only to land hard against a tree several meters away.

I felt it before I saw it. I noticed the health bars of everyone were still good and then it happened. A split-second flash of movement from the queen in a sideward direction and then my eyes went wide as I saw Serenity fly across the battlefield only to slam into the base of a tree. Her health bar immediately went below ten percent, but she was alive and as I looked at the queen, she didn't seem to try to go in for the kill. If she was stable, she would be okay if we survived. I threw her a quick heal for insurance, but she was essentially out of the fight.

Mittens and the archers took down her target and now there were only three left. The queen and the two frontal ones that were currently dismantling my bulwark. It was in very bad shape from the fire attacks, and I currently had no way of healing it. Its bones were charred and brittle as cracks were spidering all through its body. I immediately shifted my casting to take out one of the ones attacking my tank and the archers joined. It finally fell after a few rounds as they were of the higher-level salamanders in the group.

It was at this time that my beloved Bulwark had finally seen enough. The queen unleased another fire attack with the lone remaining salamander protector doing the same and the intense heat damage was too much for the bulwark to withstand. Both attacks slammed into its shield, but the residual fire wrapped around the shield and kissed my tank squarely in the face. Its body made a loud cracking sound and then it just crumbled into a pile of shattered bones. The archers simultaneously released their arrows at the suspecting protector and when they landed, it arched back in pain as a necrotic ray slammed into its unprotected underbelly. It shook violently and tried to turn its attack on the archers but then another duo of arrows hit it in the skull. It stumbled and tripped as it lost its footing with all the blood on the ground. As it finally hit the ground another arrow tore into its neck for good measure. I mean why just become dead when you can be extra dead is a great motto to live by.

My energy was running low so I needed to conserve as much as I could while still killing this damn thing. The archers were behind me which suddenly made me the defacto tank. That was a big no can do as that is not my way of surviving this. I didn't have enough energy to recall the bulwark and even if I did it would leave me exposed to the queen's attack for too long. No this would have to be a battle of attrition. She was down to about forty percent health so if we were smart, we could do this. I took a snapshot glance at the team, and the archers were consistently standing at about seventy percent health. I was standing at sixty three percent, Mittens seemed to be holding okay at about forty three percent, while Serenity was holding at about seventeen percent.

The archers released another round of arrows pot shotting the queen while my aura and spells hit it repeatedly. Mittens popped out of stealth as she apparently had popped a cooldown with one of her skills letting her enter stealth mid fight. Her claws and tentacles mercilessly shredded the back of the huge salamander queen while she continued to try to dodge the tail attacks. The queen was down now to around thirty percent and was dropping rapidly. When it hit around twenty-five percent health, the queen hit some sort of mechanic in which a fire storm came down from the sky with a radial effect.

This was some sort of area of effect spell that triggered with a low health threshold. The fire balls crashed everywhere around us. I had to roll out of the path of one ball only to have to instantly readjust and jump out of the way of another. The splash damage shaved off five percent of my health, but I mostly avoided the main part. Two of my skeletons were not so lucky. The two most left ones took a face full of fire as they looked upward just as the fireball descended into their faces. They were taken down to single digits in their health pool and as they stumbled with the force, they staggered into another attack that quickly ended their existence. The remaining two archers just continued to shoot like nothing happened and I quietly thanked them at that moment for their low intelligence.

The queen had now fallen into the single digit percentages of health due to the constant attacks, my spells, and the aura of necrosis. That honestly had been the game changer so far as it was a damage overtime effect that was ongoing. As we were down to the final stretch, we all pressed with everything we had. I had enough energy for a few more spells, so we had to make them count. Mittens continued to duck and dodge attacks while striking when she could. As if on cue, I noticed something in the air was hurling towards the queen. A little girl with two electrified swords somehow had rejoined the fight and without being noticed, had made her way unknowingly to an elevated outcropping behind the queen. She was attempting a type of execution move.

The queen never saw it coming as she was about to unleash her attack, when Serenity landed with a thud. Her twin swords crackling with electricity sunk into the skull of the queen with more force than a girl of her size should be able to muster. The electricity jolted the queen and she then reared up on her hind legs with a twisting thrash. Blood spewed from her mouth and the spasms threw Serenity off the queen and back onto the ground hard. Serenity was moving slowly to get back up however her swords were still profoundly wedged still in the enemy. A quick glance at the health pool told me the queen was at one percent and then in a split second it greyed out at zero. The area went still as the queen's eyes seemed to glaze over and then she crashed into the riverbed as water splashed everywhere. It was finally over.

CHAPTER THIRTY-TWO

Evolution and Discovery

When the queen fell still, I immediately ran over to Serenity. She had fallen to five percent health after being slung into the air after her insane attack method that ultimately killed the foe. I looked at my energy bar and noticed that my regeneration had now begun as we were technically no longer in combat. I gave her a quick heal to stabilize her and quickly felt bad for what I said next. "Serenity you could have gotten yourself killed for what, a superhero coup de grace. "Don't ever do that shit again" I had apparently gone fully into dad mode as she looked up at me with shameful eyes. I knew my comments were out of fear, but she scared the crap out of me. My tone softened and when I spoke the next words, she just leaned her head into me. "I can only protect you if you let me and I know there will be danger, but we don't need to be reckless with how we seek it out" Her reply only made it worse as she said against my chest. "At some point you will have to trust me and know that I am very capable of handling myself. As I grow and become stronger you will see." I just hugged her tightly and said that she was right and we just need to be smarter.

It was at that moment that the mood took a one eighty shift as Mittens jumped over to her like a crazed lunatic. "That was the sickest shit I have ever seen. We can be friends now. As those were the next sentences out of her mouth, she added. You are one bad bitch! I looked down at them both and just laughed as the mood was totally broken. Don't encourage her, I said. Mittens just scoffed at me and smacked me with her tail in return. That was with love she said. I just laughed again.

Now that the danger was over, we sat on the ground at the base of the riverbed looking at all the carnage. There were salamander carcasses everywhere. Mittens did notice that the babies were still alive in the cove and she took it upon herself to go over and have a meal. I tried to ignore that and looked at her and just asked her to just not make it gross. She growled back in return, fine. I looked back at Serenity and softly murmured; you did good and I'm proud of you.

I looked back at the carnage and noticed all the sparkles lying around, and it hit me that we still have all that sweet loot to get. I jumped to my feet and noticed I had several notifications to go over but that could wait as it was time to see the fruit of our labors. I had the two remaining archers begin gathering the loot from all the salamanders while I headed towards the queen. When I got to her corpse, I touched her and the familiar message appeared asking if I wanted to loot her corpse. That was a no-brainer as I selected yes and I immediately smiled.

There were four items to take, and I looked at them one by one. You have looted; The Heart of the Waterfall Queen. This heart is what remains of the death of a Firemander Queen, and this item may be consumed for a permanent fire resistance gain. You have looted salamander meat times twenty-five. This is an uncommon cooking ingredient and may be harmful if consumed raw. You have looted; Egg of the Firemander Queen. This egg is the final offspring of the Queen of the Waterfall and can be a tamable companion to the Earthen that calls it to hatch or it can make a delicious spicy omelet. Your choice. The final item was very interesting. You have looted; Schematic: Firemander Pen. This schematic allows the construction of a Firemander Pen. This pen will provide a food supply and defense. You must place live Firemander infants into the pen to begin this cycle. This schematic will be destroyed upon use.

I quickly realized what the hell Mittens was doing and I yelled for her to stop. I looked over and she was covered in blood and was about to chomp her maw down on the last few infant salamanders. She looked up at me with irritation, and I quickly had to inform her of the new plan. Mittens didn't quite catch on at first, so I had to just explain it. She dropped the wiggling salamander in her paws, and it rolled to the ground. There were a few left and luckily so. I could have used the egg, but I had another plan for that little sucker. The schematic was very interesting, and I began to imagine a horde of these things charging our foes like a horde of calvary. I was getting ahead of myself, but it did have potential.

I had a weird feeling as if something was telling me there was more to this area than met the eye. I wasn't sure what it was, but my instincts were screaming at me, so I decided to investigate the area within the basin. As I got up and began to slowly walk around, I had Mittens and Serenity do the same. My archers were still gathering up the loot, so I just let them be for the time being. I couldn't detect anything in the surrounding area, so I headed towards the stone pedestal.

The moment that I placed a foot in the stoney area surrounding it, I knew this was what was giving off the weird vibe. I made my way closer to it and after a second of questioning what this was, I decided to trust my gut and placed my hand on the pedestal. As soon as my palm touched the mossy stone, a wave of energy burst out for about a hundred meters. I immediately jerked my hand away and everyone stopped and looked at me. I wasn't hurt so I decided to place it back on the stone.

I instantly received a prompt when my hand settled on the pedestal; You have discovered an unclaimed shrine. Would you like to dedicate this altar to your god, Tikallnosis? Yes/No? Well, I'll be damned blurted out of my mouth at the sight of the altar. I didn't immediately know the benefits from this as I had only done this once before at the start of all this mess, but he had initially stated that he was a forgotten god and as his chosen, I now could spread his name. I had already awoken his faith when I touched the first one at the dilapidated temple with Jaceberlen on our first day. What the hell I said, and I selected yes.

The system accepted the answer and suddenly the pedestal began to shift. The mossed turned into shadowy wisps of energy, the stones began to come apart and reshape, the area took on a darker feel, and the dirt, carcasses, and terrain flew up into a tornado like cone. The wind picked up all around us and my clothes were flapping against the currents of the air. Mittens and Serenity ran to my side, but the archers remained stoic. Luckily the loot was already stored away for review. The stoned landscape disappeared into a sea of shadow and then one second later, the wind subsided. What was in front of us was nothing that was there a few moments before.

Before me stood an onyx archway with a glossy black type of altar. All around the altar seemed to be a cloud of moving dark shadow. As Tikallnosis was the god of undeath, darkness, and chaos, I suppose that all made sense. The darkness was symbolic to the onyx structure while the chaotic aspect I could only assume was represented by the ever-shifting cloud. As I stared at the now sanctified altar, another few messages appeared in front of me. Due to this altar now being dedicated to Tikallnosis, it will radiate an aura of darkness, undeath, and chaos for a radius of two hundred meters. Any friendly allies or companions within this aura will gain +5 to the resistances of Shadow, Chaotic, and Death damage, while enemies will receive a negative to these affinities via the same margin.

You have discovered a hidden quest; Spread the Fluidic Night. Find secret, hidden, or otherwise locatable places of divine power and turn them to your deity's path. This is an ongoing quest. These places of power can also be used as means of sanctuary or transportation. You must have at least two places dedicated to Tikallnosis to activate that function. Congratulations as you have uncovered two locations: Waterfall Basin and Inkwood Region Church. Look at you stumbling onto religious power. You go boy! 1,000 experience points earned. 250 Distinguished Points earned.
Title earned: First Seeker of Enlightenment Description: You

gain an innate sense of locations to places of power when in a proximity of one mile.

I looked around and everyone was just looking at me. I asked Serenity if she knew what that had been and she just shrugged and said no. She knew it was something but not that. I just looked at her and replied, "Communicate please" and then I decided to just leave the altar. The area had promise as far as a potential population area. Now it was time to go over all the notifications, rest up, and see if our goal was accomplished. I asked the crew to sort and identify all the stashed loot, gather up the hatchlings and as I looked directly at Mittens I uttered; "Do not eat them", and I then recalled the bulwark for an additional sense of protection. I then sat down and pulled up my interface. There were several notifications awaiting my attention, so I just went down the list.

Congratulations: your bond with Tikallnosis has increased and will continue to strengthen as his faith becomes stronger in the known regions of the universe.

Congratulations you have slain the Queen of the Waterfall. You have slain twelve Firemander Protectors. You have slain thirteen Firemander Gatherers. You have slain six Firemander Servants. You have slain five Firemander Hatchlings. The location is now under your deity's influence. Total experience earned 3400

You have discovered and claimed a new area: Waterfall Basin 100 experience earned. Resources available. Now that was a new take on a location. I will have to look more into that.

Congratulations, you have reached level 20. You have 5 free points to allocate.

At level 20 you have unlocked your first Earthen evolution. Based on your actions, class, race, and style you can be offered up to four options to choose from. You have also unlocked potential racial evolutions if the requirements are met. Please see your character screen for character and racial evolution options.

Congratulations! As the first Earthen to reach Level 20, you have been granted an upgrade to the title: Megalomaniac. It has now evolved into Driven Megalomaniac. This title will not only give a +5% increase to any Distinguished Points but it will also add a random modifier to Distinguished Pathways. Wait was that a thing, I thought. What the hell is this immediately came into my mind.

Congratulations you have hit level 6 in Distinguished Levels. Whether your path is infamous or illustrious you may now chart your destiny with the stars as new pathways have opened to you. To choose your path select the Distinguished tab and select upgrade. Oh crap, I had forgotten to look at that when I hit level 5.

You have new abilities, skill upgrades, class evolutions, or spell modifiers to decide. Your armor set is now available to upgrade. Please select your evolution options as your spells, abilities, skills, and pathways could change.

Congratulations, your companions have evolved. Please see interface for more details.

You may now summon your third companion.

Global Alert!!! The Earthen, Dookooze, is the first player to hit level 20. May you continue to evolve and grow.

CHAPTER THIRTY-THREE

Decisions

I just stared into the void trying to process what had just been explained. Not only had I finally hit level 20, but now there was an evolution archetype, a possible race evolution, and now a distinguishment path. What the heck. This had so much potential and could really be a game changer in the upcoming fight. I looked over at the crew, and they were still busy sorting through everything. So, I sat down and chose to grow.

I sat down on the cold stone at the base of the altar and pulled up my interface. I figured that going through the character screen and choosing that evolution first was the right move. The screen jumped into the character tab and an icon appeared asking me if I wanted to begin my evolution. Yes/No? I no longer could contain my excitement, and I mentally hit the yes button. The world went black and then I was staring at another screen.

Welcome to your first character evolution. Please see the available options to choose from. You have acquired the maximum total of four options

Option 1. Expert Moon Cleric: Rarity: Mythical
This is a direct upgrade to your current class and will allow you to grow in your initial path of both a cleric and a necromancer. Stat increases per level upgraded to +2 Wisdom and +2 Charisma. Well, this was the standard upgrade to what I was already doing

although it did come with an increase to the level allotments with Wisdom and Charisma. I must say that I think the is extremely boring. I thought with the Mythical rarity every option would be insane, but I suppose I was wrong. I already knew this class and although it wasn't completely vanilla, it was still very strong. I passed on this for now to go to option 2.

Option 2. Lunar Spiritwielder Rarity: Rare
This variation allows the character to denounce the ways of the necromancer and reaffirm their commitment to the aspects of healing. Even in darkness life emerges and this class uses the power of darkness and shadow to heal companions, minions, and allies alike. Stat increases per level are +3 Wisdom and +2 Charisma. Warning choosing this evolution will remove all necromantic spells or summons but will greatly enhance your healing capabilities. This looked to be the clerical shift to this class. From a healing route it looked good but sacrificing all my minions is just something I refused to do. The healer in me wanted it but the summoner part was stronger, so I decided to pass.

Option 3. Putrid Dimachaerus Rarity: Rare
This option brings forth your expertise with dual wielding weapons in an ability to shred enemies up close using necrotic weapons and auras to a devastating effect. There are many types of two weapon warriors, and many elemental applications are commonplace, however one such warrior utilizing necrosis is rare indeed. Using your blades dripping with death to mutilate and desecrate the enemy is your destiny. Stat increases per level altered to +3 Strength +2 Agility +1 Hardiness. Warning choosing this evolution will remove all necromancy spells except Aura of Necrosis which will remain. This will also remove any healing spells. This was interesting and it looked like it was the melee option. It was a pure focus on close combat but if I was able to keep my aura then that could be a nasty type of fighter. The stat shift could be a problem but with six stat points a level plus the normal five, I could make that up quickly. As cool as this sounded

it just wasn't what my heart was in. I didn't want to write it off just yet as I still had one more option.

Option 4. Necro Lord of Darkness Rarity: Mythical Forgoing any further clerical growth, this option embraces the full potential of a true champion of Tikallnosis. This option cuts off any further clerical growth but does allow the simplest of healing spells to be cast on living flesh. By embracing your necromancy and necrotic skills, you will be allowed to dominate the landscape with potential armies at your command. Be the champion of bone and undeath. Stat increases per level +2 Wisdom +3 Charisma +1 Intelligence. Warning choosing this evolution will block any further growth in healing magic. Now this was something to tell mom about. I wasn't a fan of forgoing any growth as a healer and I truly did love the option to help my team members when needed but this option still allowed me to cast bless, purge, and a small heal. I could be used in a pinch as a healer, so I still would get to scratch that itch. Besides the thrill of commanding possible armies of minions was something I had always loved as a gamer in the real world, so that should be no different here. I couldn't wait to see where this would lead. I reviewed the options just one more time but, in the end, The Necro Lord won out. I chose my option and selected yes at the prompt.

Suddenly, my view changed and it was as if I was being spun around. I could feel my connection to the healing part of my class close a door and my necromantic path widen from what seemed a door to now be the size of a warehouse. I felt so many possibilities awaited me. Glaring me right in the face seemed to be some sort of menu option.

Congratulations Necro Lord of Tikallnosis. You have been given the following spells:
Summon Golem: Allows you to summon a Bone Golem to aid you in your endeavors. Golems focus on a primarily defense role. Limit of number allowed depends on level and abilities.

Raise Skeletons has evolved into Advanced Raise Skeletons: Allows you to summon stronger versions of your current spell plus alternate variations. They may also perform special abilities and skills. They now have a heightened intelligence. Control limit depends on Charisma modifier.

Aura of Necrosis has been evolved to Deadly Aura of Necrosis: This upgraded version is tougher to heal and has an extended radius of 20 meters but has a higher energy reservation of 20 while on.

Summon Bulwark has evolved into Advanced Bulwark: This upgrade heightens the intelligence of your bulwark, and it now has special abilities and skills. Limit of number allowed depends on level and abilities.

Withering Snare has evolved into Pull of the Dark: Allows you to now call forth bone hands in a designated area that reaches for and grapples enemies in its 20M radius effect. The bones will slow, nauseate, damage constitution, and cause piercing damage to enemies in the affected area. Spell may evolve with abilities and effects.

Bone Cage: Summons a cage of bones to protect the summoner. The amount of damage it can withstand is dependent on the skill level. The caster cannot move while this spell is in effect.

Advancement points can be gained with each level attained or via special circumstances. You will begin with five advancement points and will gain one additional one per level depending on points.

You have gained +10 points allocated to each stat.

CHAPTER THIRTY-FOUR

Synergy

I wanted to take a deeper look into the advancement options since I had five points to spend but before I did that, I wanted to see if the Distinguished path would help in that decision with any possible synergies. With that thought, I decided to focus on that first, so I mentally brought up the Distinguished tab, and it looked very different. Before it was just showing whether your choices were infamous or illustrious, your current level, and a bar growth to the next level. Now it was different as it showed a list of options. Each were very different in comparison to the evolution I had just gone through, and these seemed to be centered around a global interaction and such. I noticed that I had a total of four options which was the maximum allowed so I dove right in.

Option 1: Motivated Speaker
No longer will you be an unknown commoner not allowed a voice at the table as your fame has begun to earn you the eyes and ears of the universe's leaders. You gain a +5 to charisma checks when dealing in political negotiations with other population centers, diplomatic parties, summits, or the universe at large. Your words have meaning and an effect on those that hear them. Be careful with how you use these words. +1 Charisma per level. If you are a lord of a town then special buildings can be built. So, this one was a political path. Not my favorite but I do see the perks of it

especially with what we have to achieve. I decided to hold off on my judgement until I read all four of them.

Option 2: Favored Trader

Your name has spread to the outer reaches of the land and traders from all over the world desire to establish business relations with someone from your station. Trading routes have an easier time being established. Yours and your settlements wares sell for +10% while you and your settlements receive a -10% reduction on the cost of any purchases. Additionally, some traders might have a private stock of merchandise only fit for someone of your level. What that merchandise is depends on your level. +1 Wisdom per level. If you are a lord of a town then special buildings can be built. Okay, this is an economic pathway, and I can certainly see the benefits of this. Trade is an essential part of any thriving economy and with what we will need to rebuild it could certainly be a boon. Still two more to go though so I didn't want to get too excited.

Option 3: Kindral of Battle

Your achievements have brought your name to the very lips of not only your enemies, but potential subjects as a general in the most militaristic sense. Your allies and subjects gain +2 strength and +1 wisdom within your sphere of influence as they will fight stronger for you until their last breath. +1 Strength per level. If you are a lord of a town then special buildings can be built. So, this is the combat side of the coin it would seem. The bonuses are great with the added strength, and I can see the wisdom addition coming into play with fear effects and the like. I'm not sure I want to focus solely on combat though. There are a lot of moving parts to consider, and this just doesn't necessarily feel right. Before I decide though, I need to see the final one.

Option 4: Bastion of Justification

Your legend grows and with its power, many seek to join your cause. You have a higher chance of attracting beings to your land and cause. Any buildings in an area you control has a +5% hardiness factor. Your allies also have a 5% decreased spawn rate, and a 10% rate decrease if it is at an inn in which you control. +1 Charisma +1 Intuition per level. If you are a lord of a town then special buildings can be built. Well, this one is interesting as it focuses on defense but also recruitment. The defensive aspect wouldn't matter for the upcoming battle but going forward it would for sure. The spawn rate doesn't mean a lot now but with no idea how long a respawn rate will be down the road it could be crucial. Recruiting people is something we will need as we expand and grow. My normal mode of play in the old games where resource management is a main gameplay factor, I would always focus on defense and try to weather the storm until my defenses were strong enough. If I were able to survive that, then I would shift to a 100% offensive nature, and nobody could survive an attack against me. I know that method and it has always worked if I was never bum rushed from the start. Hopefully that pattern will hold. I made my selection and hit yes.

Congratulations you are now a Bastion of Justification. No longer will your lands be weak and idle citizens stand by. Many will flock to you for protection and safety. +1 Charisma, +1 Intuition.

Now it was time to go back and check out the advancement options. I had three points to spend and one going forward with each level. I pulled up the Bastion of Justification tree and noticed that I had four points to spend as I had hit level 6. The selections were very tame in scope versus the other selections that I just went through.

It was set into defenses, respawn aspects, and buildings. These, however, did have synergy between them as some of the selections in higher tiers required a set number of points in other trees. I would cross that bridge when I needed. Upon reading the descriptions I found an interesting aspect.

Towns and buildings had tier scales with the town hall being the trigger point for upgrades. Each tier required a set number or building types from that tier to be built before it allowed for an upgrade. That reminded me again of some of the resource strategy games from old. With four points I put one point to up the hardiness factor of all buildings by another five percent. I then put a point into building types and the tier zero building that was now available was something called a Recruitment Hall. Now I was able to see the next building that was a tier one building called a Trader's Bazaar, which is certainly something we would need. I immediately placed a point into that selection.

With my last point I looked at the next building on the list, but it had an X over it as it was a tier two building and I did not have the prerequisites with a tier two town hall. I did not have the tier one building yet either, so it allowed me to select up to one higher tier. I looked over the respawn tree and it reduced time even further and later down the line it would reduce experience loss. Certainly, it is needed but not my priority now. I decided to put the last point into defense to bring my bonus up to fifteen percent defense.

Now that the Distinguished arc was done, I navigated back to my evolution screen. I willed up the advancement tree and immediately fell in love with it. It had a few options in the first tier and as I read how it worked when one option was selected in its tree then the next tiered options would be open for selection. The options seemed to focus on a few of the key mechanics of my new evolution. The first tab was Minions, the second tab was Golems, and the third option was Aura/Spells. I decided to pull them up each individually to see what the trees entailed.

The Minions tree seemed to branch in three directions once the first was chosen. The initial selection was the key to the others, but it would make any summoned minions stronger. One tree focused on a smaller group of considerably stronger minions, the second was mainly about the control limit of how many I could have at a given time, while the third tree focused on alternate minion types like wraiths, ghouls, and swarms, etc. That tree just looked damn awesome.

Next, I moved to the Golem tree. Same as the first tree, the initial selection would make any golem currently active more durable and stronger. After that It looked like a continual focus on strengthening the current golem or going into other types of golems such as a Shadesteel, Blood, or other types. Pretty straightforward. Either stay focused or broaden up.

The third tree was about Auras and Spells. As in the other two, the first slot and the first tree would just strengthen the damage and resistance threshold of my spells. The second arc would break off into adding modifiers to spells such as bleed effects, stuns, etc. The other break in this tree granted new spells like Bone Storm or Blight Cloud. All looked very cool.

This would be a tough decision. I needed survivability but I also wanted more of an offensive variety, and more minions. Did I say more minions? In truth I was at the crux of the issue. As a necromancer, my minions are my instrument. My spells and such were great, but I relied mostly on my minions. I thought about my auras and how they could enhance my minions but to start I might need to just make them more badass. So, I pulled that branching tree arc up again.

I knew already what the first selection would be so I looked at the second tiered options and then at a few more levels above that to try to get a sense of the arc I might want to traverse down. The control tree looked initially to be +1 to whatever my max limit was with a few enhancements sprinkled in. Finally, when so many points were dedicated to it then it gave a burst increase of allowable minions. Fairly straightforward. I looked up the initial pathway, and it was described to just put an emphasis on strengthening my current minions by certain percentages with each selection until a few special skills opened for them. The final arc in the minion tree was the additional minion's type. This was rather intriguing as it really put an emphasis on versatility of minion types that did a variety of things. Kind of like a minion for each situation. It had area of effect damaging minions, swarms, wraiths, etc. Some of these minion types had a higher control limit cost but were exceedingly more powerful. This tree however did allow for a lot of flexibility. I really liked it to be honest. There really wasn't a hard level cap to my character so in theory I could end up with a vast army if it was managed right with the different arcs.

I looked back at the Golem tree and as I went through it, I really liked some of these options. I was tempted to go this route, but I hadn't seen my beginning golem in action yet so I didn't know how powerful they would be. It might be a smart idea to just wait and see what the bone golem could do before allocating these rare points into it. I tried to think about what would help me the most as we had a major battle for the town looming over our heads. As much as I wanted to give this tree some love, I lowered it on the priority list. I then moved back to the Aura/Spells tree.

I knew that this tree would ultimately play a vital role in my overall playstyle as I could immediately see area of effect spells all around the large battlefields with my minion army delivering justice to all our enemies. That was certainly down the road but for the immediate short term, I needed to see if any of the upgrades were worth investing in with my initial lump sum. I could easily see where adding multiple effects to a spell would have great benefits. This aura tree ended with the ability to do a wide area aura based burst attack. It also put a focus on strengthening and expanding my aura abilities with the forementioned modifiers while the next arc opened different necromancy spells up to me and increased spell strength in between the spell options. The later spells in this tree were just insane and very dark but that didn't bother me so much. There were spells such as Blight Fog, Locust Plague, and several others that would expand my spell options. Overall, they were very enticing and could potentially have an immediate use. The other arc was boring as it just strengthened the effects of everything.

As I reigned my mind back into the task at hand, I reminded myself that I only had five points to start with and I needed to chart out a path. I sat and reviewed my tree arcs a few more times before deciding. I placed one initial point into the minions' tree, then a point into the control arc, and another into the additional minions' type arc that allowed the ability to call forth the Animate Dead spell that would summon three zombies at the cost of 1 control point. Now that three points were used, I looked at where to go next. I didn't know how some of these minions would fare in battle so I was hesitant to allocate more points in a place I would be better off waiting on, but I know for sure I wanted another in the control limit, so I put another there. That left a final point to go. So far, my minions had done well except the scrappers were relatively weak however with the spell upgrading to advanced I wasn't sure what they would look like going forward. I read the arcs a final time and then just said screw it and I slammed my final point into making my minions stronger and hit the submit button. I could always use stronger minions.

Now that the fun part was over, I had a few things left to look over before I reformed our group and we headed back. The first was to go over the race evolution icon as that was something that I totally did not expect. The second was to summon my third and final companion, the third was to see about the upgrade to my armor set, and finally the allocation of my stat points.

I brought up the race evolution screen, and I wasn't sure what to expect. The first version was a Chosen Necrolyte Undead. I guess that shouldn't have been a surprise. The perks were +2 Hardiness, +1 Agility, +2 Wisdom. There was also immunity to poison and unable to be exhausted. It was cool but I wasn't ready yet to go this route and turn undead. I liked the makeup of my current race and its benefits. I decided to move to the next one. It was a race I had already seen. It looked to be Smeeeagal's race, A Fetchling Lord. I already knew they were of shadow and how he has utilized it so far. This type was a Lord variant though. It wasn't really a good fit for my class as its benefits were +3 Agility, +1 Charisma but a -2 to Wisdom. That would hurt my energy pool, and it just didn't feel right. The third one was my exact class but of a Noble upgrade. The difference wasn't huge, but it did extend my Darkvision to 120 meters and added a fear effect to my Night Cloud ability. +1 Charisma would be well received on top of my other stat bonuses. So, in all actuality, it was just a slightly better version to my current race and no losses, so I decided what the hell and selected it. I must admit I was hoping for a bit more, as I only felt a slight tingle as the increases took hold, but I will gladly take any gains I can get. I was hoping for a bit more but ultimately it was what it was and I was no worse. Talk about a tease, I smiled and thought to myself. Now for the armor set.

I mentally pulled up my character screen with the armor displayed in the images and I noticed a blinking light next to each upgradeable piece. I perused through each piece and decided to start with the cowl. When I selected the upgrade option It told me that I needed two pieces of leather and three pieces of cloth. Well shit I thought. I then scrolled over all the other pieces and discovered that I would need a total of twenty pieces of leather, ten pieces of cloth, and 4 ingots of metal of uncommon quality. I just looked and thought to myself that this would have to wait, and I hoped the town had someone that could help. This development would likely not help in the upcoming battle, however there is a path and a hopefully easy one. I decided to swap screens to the free stat points, and I just went ahead and slapped every one of them into Charisma to increase my control limit.

Now was the time to summon my 3rd companion and I could only assume my last from that spell description. I had been extremely lucky with a Mythical and Rare creature so far in Serenity and Mittens. I was hoping for something good as it was a totally random pull from the universe. I closed my eyes, centered my mind, and began the spell incantation. When the spell was complete, I opened my eyes to the familiar black vortex that had been part of the last two summons.

By this time, Mittens and Serenity had directed their full attention to the scene playing out near the altar. They immediately came over as we were waiting to see what would happen. What came out was something that I could just say was something indeed. The portal opened and what I can only describe as a flying hog appeared and landed next to the portal. It was jet black in color with grey feathers. It stood about two and a half feet tall and looked to be around four to five feet long This thing was the size of a small riding lawnmower, had plated armor, a singular horn protruding from the middle of his forehead and wings that were just not quite proportionate to its size. They were a bit smaller but somehow, they lifted its bulk. It turned to us very astutely with its greenish eyes and introduced himself. "My name is Cadet Major Theodore Cyril of the Space Swine Defense Force reporting for duty." I was given a top-secret mission by high command so please forgive me if I ask said who are you and what alternate reality did I get pulled into with this symmetrical vortex you call a portal."

Upon hearing this introduction, we just stared at him and no words came forth. He just looked at us and uttered more. "I take your silence as non-comprehension so please let me rephrase my statement, and as he restated his comment again, I finally snapped out of my stupor and replied. Yes, you are on mission. What parameters were you given as I tried to think from the top of my head as quickly as possible. My name is Dookooze. The space swine looked up at me and seemed to come to some reconcilement in his head and he just replied, "I was told to report to you, and the mission is to help defend you from any and all enemies as you complete a top-secret mission." I am here reporting for duty as my high command ordered for me to graduate and become a fully-fledged Major, the swine said.

I said nothing for a moment or two then I looked at him, knowing this would be very interesting. At ease, I said as this is a nonmilitary unit for the time being so, please relax. He did not move and just stated that he is relaxed. What do we call you as this is Mittens and Serenity. The Cadet Major looked at them both and then turned back to me; Cadet Major Theodore Cyril is sufficient. No, it isn't I said so give me a name. The other two hid a smile but he was stone-faced in his reply. Cadet Major will do. Alright Cadet it is. The Cadet Major started to protest as I cut him off promptly stating that we don't have the time to argue.

Out of battle Cadet Major is fine but otherwise Cadet will need to suffice. The Cadet Major looked like he was in an internal battle but then seemed to deflate and said fine sir; Cadet it is. Thank you, I replied and then asked; did they give you any other parameters of just what you already stated? Cadet looked at me and just told me that he was advised I would disclose more details which honestly, I was glad to hear. You are correct Cadet.

Can you please give me a more detailed description of your class and abilities? The Cadet suddenly flapped his wings and propped up onto his two back legs and saluted with a yes sir. It was everything I could do to not just shake my head. Cadet then proceeded to tell us that he was an excellent tracker, of noble birth, possible to achieve winged combat as that is still being practiced, a defender, and a sense of smell that is unrivaled in all his home of Wild Space. He noted that his attacks were a bite attack along with his horn and weight distribution. Anything else, such as being a beast of burden, is now considered uncivilized and below him as a creature of great intellect, he added. Nobility of his race preferred to only be in the presence of like-minded individuals. AKA geniuses" Duly noted was all I could muster up currently as I processed everything and I just replied thank you cadet. At ease.

CHAPTER THIRTY-FIVE

Totally Upgraded

Now that we had Cadet in our group, I looked over at the other two and saw that Serenity was studying Cadet with interest. She looked like she had some questions or knowledge of his race, but I decided to ask her later if she didn't bring it up first. I turned to Mittens and she just looked at me all doughy eyed and I could hear her purring. This seriously caught me off guard and I looked at her as she said the one thing I did not expect; Oh, my I love a man in a uniform and then she wriggled. Her eyes then turned back towards me and whispered, what? Can't a young lady have urges too? I really had no response, so I just decided to quickly avert my eyes and tell myself that I was in the middle of a pubescent teenage situation. I am too old for this shit, I said out loud and then just told them I had a few more things to do then we could be off.

I wanted to resummon my skeletons, but I needed my scouts to continue scouting for the bandits so that I would have to wait. I was very happy to see that my control limit had expanded all the way to twenty-four. Now we are talking, I thought. I looked at the spell and noticed that there was a new and most welcome addition. This was some sort of cleric class minion. Undead Bone Mender – Level 20, Health, 80, Energy 180, Stamina 30, Defense 80, Weapons: One Handed Mace (1D8) + Bone Buckler, Tier 3 skeleton, Spells: Heal – Healing magic for 3D8+ Wisdom modifier, Desecrate – Applies a heal over time for 1D4 per second for six seconds, Description: These undead skeletons tap into the unnatural void to bring forth eldritch divine power to heal all forms of undead, Special Ability: Mass Heal.

I also noticed that the other units had improved as well. The scrappers were upgraded to the following: Skeletal Warrior – Level 20, Health 180, Energy 0, Stamina 100, Defense 85, Weapons: Short Bone Swords (1D8 +2)(x2), Tier 3 skeleton, Description: These basic skeletons have evolved and can now fully communicate, Special Ability: Power Strike. The archers were also improved. Skeletal Archer – Level 20, Health 100, Energy 30, Stamina 100, Defense 55, Weapons: Black bone Longbow (1D10+3), Description: Tier 3 skeleton. Description: This ranged unit is armed with a black bone longbow and arrow. This unit can scout and track. Special Ability: Penetrating Shot. The Umbral Mage was next. Umbral Mage – Level 20, Health 85, Energy 130, Stamina 65, Defense 45, Weapon: Staff (1D6), Spells: Shadow Bolt – A bolt of shadow that does (1D10 + Int Modifier), Blindness – A dark magic spell that will temporarily blind a target from seeing. Any attacks toward the target gain a + 2 attack and +2 to damage as they are considered flat footed. Targets can resist if their resistance exceeds the spell strength. Description: This Tier 3 skeleton is a masters of darkness and shadow magic. They are intelligent, capable of creative thought, critical thinking, and high-level communication. Special Ability: Shadow Storm. So, all three now have special abilities and the mage had an area of effect spell now too. Awesome.

I went ahead and dismissed my bulwark and then recast that spell. I then also cast the Animate Dead spell. The bulwark was obviously a stronger version as it seemed to now have much larger bleached white bones and a more enhanced version of the dark chain armor and now horns protruding from its head. He also now had a spiked bone club instead of the previous one he had. As he was now semi-intelligent, he turned to me and spoke really for the first time. He stood up straight and said what are my orders sir and I must say thank you for giving me the ability to speak. I just looked back and nodded. You're welcome and take up your usual position as our guardian. Introduce yourself to Cadet and it saluted and stomped off toward our newest companion.

I then turned around to see three zombies crawling out of the ground with milky white eyes and they were wrapped in blackish dirty cloth. Their claws were long and even though they stood about average height, their reach looked like they were going to extend a bit further. As one they turned to me and asked how they could serve. I wasn't a fan of that type of comment, but I decided to let it go for the time being. I let them know to fall in and protect us. That was all for now.

Now for the golem. As the spell finished, I noticed that the area seemed to shift with the wind and bones seemed to appear out of nowhere to begin forming this thing. As the pieces began to coalesce the finished product was a bit scary. Standing before me was a giant bone construct standing about ten feet tall with blackened chain mail over white bone. It had soulless black eyes and hands the size of dinner plates with claws extending about six inches long. It had a tail reaching about six feet in length and I swear it was a damn scary ass monstrosity. I decided to look at its character screen later but holy shit this was a frightening son of a bitch. Its special ability was something that really didn't need an explanation, Shockwave. It just nodded at me and all I could say was protect us. It nodded again without a word and just stood there.

Before I could get into the character screen, I heard Serenity call my name. It broke me out of my concentration, so I turned to see what she needed. They were staring at me as their eyes were asking a question that wasn't spoken. What do we do with this loot? I laughed and asked what all we had gotten and Serenity let me know that we had accumulated a total of sixty-seven leather strips, fifty-one strips of Firemander fur that could be woven, and one hundred and ten chunks of Firemander meat that seemed to be a cooking ingredient. A pretty good haul if I say so myself. I just told them to put it in my pack, and anything left over we would carry. Mittens just grunted but nobody objected. Now that was over, I could wrap things up so we could leave. I decided that there was too much data coming into my field of view, so I decided to mess with the interface and clean it up a bit. I played with it until I was able to minimize all the meta data and just have the summary unless I wanted to focus on a specific entry. I also just wanted to see percentages of health, energy, and stamina while in battle, and I just wanted to view percentage bars on experience for next levels. I changed a few other things and then I decided to pull up my character sheet to look at it before we rolled out and holy hell I loved the upgrades.

Name: Dookooze Darkbringer
Level: 20 (38% experience gained to next level)
Class: Necro Lord of Tikallnosis
Race: Half Aasimar/Half Shadar-Kai Noble
The Chosen Champion of Tikallnosis
Stats: Intelligence – 24, Wisdom 86, Hardiness 24, Strength 21, Charisma 90, Intuition 28, Agility 23.
Health: 290
Health Regeneration Rate: 80 Per Minute (Non-Combat)
Energy: 860
Energy: 230 Regeneration Rate Per Minute (Non-Combat)
Stamina: 290
Stamina Regeneration Rate: 80 Per Minute (Non-Combat)
Distinguish Level: Illustrious Level 6 Bastion of Justification - +15% Town Building Defense, -5% Respawn Time, Tier One Building Access
Skills: Structural Construction, Conceptual Research, Lore-Ancient, Leadership, Lore-Religion, Herbalism, Skinning, Knowledge-Divine Spell Craft, Agriculture, Administration. You have 25 open skill slots remaining.
Abilities: Higher Education, Over Skilled, You're A Secretive Lot Aren't You
Titles: First Dungeoneer, Driven Megalomaniac, First Seeker of Enlightenment
Divine Action: Prayer

Spells: Cantrip
Spare Death – This spell can no longer be advanced
Toll of the Dead
Dark Flame
Spells: By Level:
Heal – This spell can no longer be advanced
Necrotic Ray
Bless – This spell can no longer be advanced.
Deadly Aura of Necrosis
Purge - This spell can no longer be advanced.
Summon Golem
Advanced Raise Skeleton
Summon Advanced Skeletal Bulwark
Animate Dead
Pull of the Dark: Allows you to now call forth bone hands in a designated area that reaches for and grapples enemies in its 20M radius effect. The bones will slow, nauseate, damage constitution, and cause piercing damage to enemies in the affected area. Spell may evolve with abilities and effects.
Bone Cage: Summons a cage of bones to protect the summoner. The amount of damage it can withstand is dependent on the skill level. The caster cannot move while this spell is in effect. Advancement points can be gained with each level attained or via special circumstances.
Spells: Divine
Absorption

Spells: Gifted
Summon Companions: Current companions:
Companion (Mittens): Species: Displacement Beast, Rank: Medium, Rarity: Rare, Level: 20, Armor: 90, Health: 250, Stats: Intelligence -12/Wisdom – 16/ Hardiness – 25/ Strength – 16/ Charisma – 12/ Intuition – 13/ Agility – 35, Skills: Perception +15/Stealth +9, Abilities: Darkvision, Avoidance (1/2 damage on saving throws), Displacement (projects a magical illusion that creates an image of him within 15 feet of his position creating

a -50% chance to be hit), Keen smell (+2 perception for issues relying on smell), Shifting Step (While displacement is active and an attack misses him he can teleport up to 10 feet without penalty), Magic Resistance +5, Attacks: Tentacles – Melee, Range: 12feet, Attack: +14, Damage: 1D8+7b, Bite; 1D6 piercing

Companion (Serenitianix): Species: Song Dragon, Rank: Young, Rarity: Mythical, Level: 20, Armor: 125, Health: 160, Stats: Intelligence -18/Wisdom – 20/ Hardiness – 22/ Strength – 22/ Charisma – 20/ Intuition – 18/ Agility – 16, Skills: Perception +20, Abilities: Dragon Sense, True Sight (Passive), Lightning Reflexes, Hover (Locked), Flyby Attack (Locked), Immunity (Electricity, Paralysis, Sleep) Magic Resistance +15, Attacks: Breath – Magical attack, Range: 30feet cone, Attack: +11 DC16, Damage: 2D6 electrical (Locked), Bite Range: Melee Attack: +15 Damage: 1D10 +6. In her human form the bite is replaced with dragon bone sword x2. 1D8 +4

Companion (Cadet Major Theodore Cyril): Species: Space Swine, Rank Cadet Teenager, Rarity: Uncommon, Level 20, Armor 180, Health: 300, Stats: Intelligence – 20/Wisdom – 18/Hardiness – 30/Strength – 22/Charisma – 14/Intuition – 18/Agility – 14, Skills: Stealth -1/Perception +10, Abilities: Death Squeal Taunt, Charge, Enduring Stance, Flight, Immunities: Charm, Magic Resistance +5, Attacks: Bite 1D6+6, Horn Strike 1D8+6, Weight Distribution 2D6, Aerial Attack (Locked)

Armor Set: Unliving Cowl – Armor 10, Unliving Spiked Chest Armor - 15, Unliving Spiked Gauntlets Armor – 8, Unliving Spiked Greaves Armor 10, Unliving Boots Armor – 8: Set Rarity: Rare, Full Set Bonus- Summoned companions or pets have a 10% attack speed and 10% increase in damage; Evolution Set – This set of armor was designed to be worn by the mightiest of the lords of death, but you have received this in its infancy. As you grow in skill and power this suit can be evolved to further protect and enhance you with powerful features at higher levels. Total Defense 61

Belt of Wisdom +1, Bracelet of Control (+10% Minion Damage), Cloak of Protection +10 Defense

Weapon: Dual Sickles of Minor Decay – Type: Simple, Hand: Both Slots, Attack: +5/+3 rating, Rarity: Uncommon, Speed: Normal, Description: Sickles designed to slowly rot their enemies upon attack, each successful attack will inflict 1D6 + Str modifier damage with a 15% chance to inflict Decay. Decay will cause 3 necrotic damage per 3 seconds for 12 seconds
Profession: 0 of 2
Racial Abilities: As an offspring of darkened humanoid creatures from both the Celestial and Elvin bloodlines you have made your way onto the material plane from the shadows to forge a path to your choosing. Both races resemble typical humanoid creatures but with potential elven or celestial features that are a bit off from your typical kin.
Darkvision
Keen Senses
Necrotic Resistance
Night Cloud

I dismissed and then recast my Bulwark spell and well damn that was a noticeably bigger version. The spiked club had bone spears all around the ball that were about three inches long and the tips looked like they were razor sharp. I looked at his health pool and wow I liked what I saw. A massive upgrade. What I really didn't expect was for it to look at me and thank me for making it smarter so he could talk. It then advised me that it was so sweet of the children to name him Peppermint and wanted to thank them. I once again just sat there and finally just said cool well you can tell them when we return. It just nodded and fell in line with the golem.

So, for the trip back I had my three companions, the golem, the bulwark, and my two remaining archers who had not upgraded yet so it would likely not occur until I recast the spell. We had a tough enough party to handle just about anything if we ran into a confrontation during the trip back, so I got the minions to carry the excess loot, and then we started our trek back to the town as our main goal was done. I was eager to return and see if they had an armor smith or leatherworker. I mentally checked in with the archers, and they still were monitoring their assigned areas with nothing to report other than beasts. So far that was good. The more time we had to prepare the better.

CHAPTER THIRTY-SIX

Return Trip

Our trip back to the town was uneventful. I had the golem and the bulwark take care of the few little miscreants that tried to attack us just so I could see them in action. As an exercise it was overkill. The golem was impressive, but I knew the upcoming battle tomorrow would really test us. On the way back I sent Jaceberlen, Tiger Lilly, and Raven a message letting them know the goal was achieved and my estimated time of return. They all replied with the fact that a global alert had gone out so they already knew that I had evolved and were happy for me. They were also excited as to the town's progress and to see what level twenty was all about.

Night had already fallen and as we exited the tree line into the open valley facing the town I received a message from Manerva. She had said that the group had spawned a while ago and they also had received thirty-six-minute reduction to the timer due to some sort of perk and that they were headed back to us, but it would take a few hours. I was apparently correct in that they had respawned at the last inn we stayed at. I advised her the perk was mine and I could explain it when they returned. She went into the actual death timer and experience she had lost which made me wince, but we knew there would be some sort of penalties. All you can do is get back, prepare, train, and don't die. She laughed and then she said they were on their way and then she ended the message. That was useful information to have going forward, and it was great to hear an immediate benefit to my Bastion selection.

I made my way to the gates, and I could hear the group members on top of the wall yell to the group below that I had returned. As the gates opened, I saw the wide eyes from everyone when they saw the ten-foot-tall monstrosity rolling in behind me and then confused looks as they also noticed a five-hundred-pound pig with wings marching in formation like he was practicing for the military parade championships. To make matters even more comical he was even mumbling with a cadence. It reminded me of some nineties animated movie involving a lion.

We entered the town and as the staring continued, Cadet roared for a halt. He of course introduced himself to the entire town using his full name as Cadet Major Theodore Cyril of the Space Swine Defense Force reporting for duty. It made everyone jump and I once again just face palmed myself. He would have to stop that but now wasn't the time for that conversation. Soon though and very soon. I looked around and noticed that Jaceberlen. Tiger Lilly, Raven, Ophelia, and Captain Ahab were walking towards me. I greeted them all and then I was bombarded with questions about what happened at level twenty.

I figured I might as well heed that off one time so I advised everyone to gather around and then I proceeded to go into an in-depth explanation of what we fought, the loot we received, the crafting and cooking materials, how the evolution took place, the upgrades, skill trees, how classes and races can evolve based on factors, the Distinguished tree, etc. When I finally finished, I decided to introduce my new party members to everyone, but of course Cadet had already done that for himself, but I did it again and I explained that we will have a full complement of minions after the archers reported. It was a very successful venture.

Cadet just went full on military mode to everyone with flaps of his wings, salutes, and the whole nine yards. You could tell he was in his full stoic demeanor. He even explained he was on a top-secret mission. The group came up to just welcome him in as part of the oddball family dynamic that we were and started giving him hugs. I swear the pig freaked out screaming no hugs allowed repeatedly as they swarmed him. He finally decided it was a futile attempt and just stood there and accepted the affection. Hell, even the kids got involved. Golem just stood there, and the townsfolk just stared at him. No sound came from him at all, but I guess it was just the way it was. I received a ton of questions from those that were in the upper teens of levels. When that concluded, I got the morning group together and we went over the progression from this morning until now. I also mentioned the altar and that it was now a possible location for us to annex since it did technically belong to me. Plus, the transportation ability I decided to keep quiet until we were more secure

By the time we had finished our ad hoc meeting, the town had resumed the preparations for tomorrow. Everyone was tired so I wasn't sure how much more could be accomplished but we needed to try. I ordered the golem, bulwark, and archers to assist Captain Ahab with the preparations and they marched off with their new tasks. I looked at Cadet and asked if he could help in any way. Cadet looked at me like I was about to ask him to pull a wagon in disgust but then I decided to clarify. As part of the defense force do you have any information that might prove useful for tomorrow? He noticeably relaxed and then thought for a second. He replied with the fact that he might have a few ideas and then he proceeded to explain his thoughts which I had to admit were not bad at all.

Once everything had concluded, I asked if the town had a leatherworker or armor smith. After a few minutes an older man that looked frail and weathered approached and identified himself as Gus. He apparently was the town leather worker. I shook his hand and introduced myself and then asked if he would be able to enhance some armor for me as mine needed to be upgraded. He smirked a bit. After a moment of unhappy looks, he without a word just began to manhandle me and my armor. He was pulling, stretching, and looked like he was examining it.

He rose up to meet me with a questioning look and let me know that he hadn't seen the likes of this armor before, but it could be upgraded given I had the materials. I told him about the leather and fur that I had looted and he seemed genuinely surprised. Firemander fur has a great affinity for fire, and the leather was not too far behind, he stated as a fact with a grin. Great materials indeed he stated. I smiled internally and then remembered that a small amount of metal was required. Oh, shit I blurted out and then let him know about the metal. Luckily, he brushed that comment off and said that he can get some on loan from the smith and just charge me for them.

I breathed a sigh of relief as that was a big worry. I asked him what a rush job by tomorrow first light would cost. He gave me another one of those deep smirks and advised me that I was a bit unreasonable, but his pride wouldn't let him say no. The next words spoken let me know I had him. Fifteen extra silvers and you will have it by sunrise. I didn't even care about haggling as I knew asking him to work all night was a tough ask. I gave him a smile and said deal. I then added a bonus: If the set is of your best craftmanship then there is an extra five silvers in it for you. Gus seemed to puff out his chest at that comment as pride once again got him. Sold and unequip your amor now sir was all that was told to me, so I did so without complaint.

Gus walked away with my armor, and I realized I was almost butt naked except for a long under shirt and linen pants. My cloak was still on thank goodness, so I wrapped it around my body to stop the chill from hitting those spots that become a turtle in the cold air. The rest of the group just laughed at me and let me know how super cute this moment was. Screw you all, I need my armor upgraded. I couldn't help but laugh too as we headed towards the ramparts.

The night was quiet until around two in the morning when my archers informed me that a group of people were approaching the town gate. I immediately thought we were under attack until I remembered Manerva and the rest of them. I decided to double check and mentally told the archers to ask for identification. Manerva and the group were caught off guard when the skeletons told them to halt and identify themselves considering the minions were still kind of stupid. They had not been upgraded yet, so I am sure it came out in an irritating fashion. The group stopped and Manerva being Manerva just replied curtly; hey you idiots stop standing around like skeletons and let us in before I beat you back into a graveyard. It's Manerva. After a few seconds of them relaying the info to me, the gate began to open from the golem and bulwark.

I met them inside of the gate and greeted them back into the town. I let them know the situation and they also received the global alert and congratulated me. The archers are about six miles out and will report immediately upon seeing them, which depending on their speed, will take them about six hours from that point to reach us, I told them. Get some sleep as you will need it for the upcoming battle and hopefully, we will prevail. They had made good time from the respawn point, so it was a huge win for us as a group. My alternate plan for them wasn't needed now and for tomorrow, we were now almost up to our full fighting force.

The rest of the night was peaceful and as dawn came so did the apprehension for the day. Everyone in the town knew what impact the events of today would have on the future of the town. Kids were nonexistent in the streets as the teenagers and adults ran around frantically to make any little bit of progress the extra time would allow. Everyone was nervously trying to get stuff done. As I walked around checking all the various project's progress, I heard a man calling my name. It was Gus. I swear the man looked like he hadn't slept but truthfully, he likely hadn't and it was my fault. He had a bundle of items in his hands as he finally stopped running towards me. He was out of breath from exhaustion, but he managed to quickly let me know the job was done and I owed him forty silvers. He handed me the bundle and I inspected it.

Armor Set: Unliving Cowl (Tier 2) – Armor 15, Unliving Spiked Chest Armor - 25, Unliving Spiked Gauntlets Armor – 15, Unliving Spiked Greaves Armor 15, Unliving Boots Armor – 15:

Set Rarity: Rare, Full Set Bonus- Summoned companions or pets have a 15% attack speed and 15% increase in damage; Evolution Set – This set of armor was designed to be worn by the mightiest of the lords of death, but you have received this in its infancy. As you grow in skill and power this suit can be evolved to further protect and enhance you with powerful features at higher levels. Total Defense 85

That was a very nice upgrade. The armor wasn't a major boost, but the minion damage and attack speed would certainly be. All in all, it was fine work and the price was more than worth it. I gave him the money and let him know that he did a great job and after this battle is over, he will have more work than he can shake a stick at. Go get some sleep, I added as you will need it in a few hours. Every able person is needed.

It was at this moment that I received a mental message from one of my archers. A large group of people were headed in our direction and were about six miles out considering the location of the archer. It tried to give me numbers, but it was unable to give accurate accounting since it was you know not so smart in its tier two form. I told it to stay close and report every thirty minutes as to their movement. I ended the communication and then notified everyone that the group had been spotted, and we had less than six hours. Time to get ready and the group hit another gear as the pace quickened all around me.

CHAPTER THIRTY-SEVEN

Final Preparations

The progress within the town continued and as the projects wrapped up their completion, the archers continued to give reports. At this point they seemed to be an hour away and were steady in their march towards us. We still didn't have an exact number but after some interesting attempts it looked like there were about one hundred and twenty of the bandits plus the commander. Give or take a few of course. Either way we had a massive fight on our hands that didn't look good for us.

The mood was tense and you could cut it with a knife. We had flexibility, variety of classes, defenses, and the will to defend our future home on our side, while they had power and numbers. I didn't know the level of the commander, but I was positive he was at least level twenty. He was a boss of some fashion after all. Which means an evolution for him and a power spike like I went through. We might just have to adjust things if they didn't go as planned. We always must make an alternate plan for when it inevitably goes to complete shit. I knew it was time. I dismissed the remaining skeletons and decided to finally cast my new advanced raise skeleton spell. Everyone turned to stare at me as I did so, but I suppose it would be entertaining to watch. With a control limit of now twenty-four, It allowed for more flexibility.

When the spell completed the group moved away as a large group of skeletons emerged from the ground. The kids were in awe and thought it was a game while the adults just stood there in curiosity. From the cloud of dust rose five new warriors who had obviously changed due to their new glistening medium armor and dual bone short swords. Then came the eight umbral mages which had new robes covering every aspect of their bodies and carried with them an aura of shadow and ebony black staves. The eight archers then appeared with their new matte black bone bows, matte black leather armor, and black daggers to each side. The final addition was the new option. Two undead bone menders emerged wearing black medium armor, a bone mace, and finally bone buckler. Their eyes glowed an eerie light green as they oozed with Eldritch magic. With the twenty-three minions and the zombies that maxed out my control limit of twenty-four. I still wanted more. As if on cue they all snapped to attention with the bulwark, golem, and zombies in line with them, turned to me, and said as a single unit, Orders sir!

The area surrounding us went quiet and from the crowd I heard someone mutter, holy shit. I had to agree with the speaker as it was truly a sight to see. A small army of twenty-eight that did not include bulwark, golem, my three companions, and myself stood before me awaiting commands. This was just the beginning if I had anything to say about it. Now we just need to see how they hold up against a true enemy. With the minions and zombies, we certainly had mostly closed the gap between us and the bandits. With my minions, companions, and the rest of our group we had around close to one hundred of a true force. Every able Earthen in our group that could fight was there. Only the children were not included. If you include the townsfolk assisting, we had close to one hundred and thirty. I did not want the townsfolk to get involved unless necessary since they could not respawn like we could. Once dead they were gone for good. That was an unacceptable loss in my book. Even with them sitting out only as a last resort we appeared to have equalized the playing field.

The group in charge of all the preparations approached for the final time. Every group was able to complete their respective tasks. It was all we could have done with the time allotted, so I could only hope that it was enough. I trusted each of them and if they said that they were ready, I had to believe them. Dealz felt confident enough in the defenses that a day and a half could provide and he was reluctant but ready for the next part. Captain Ahab felt the strategy and tactics would be sufficient not to crack without it all going to hell, but he felt confident. Jaceberlin and the others nodded in agreement with their assignments too. Knowing the answer before he asked it, Captain Ahab smiled and asked what I would do if it hit the fan. They all laughed and I just exclaimed; what I always do; Leroy Jenkins the shit out of it. It was the comment that broke the underlying tension within the group and we all just laughed. Knowing what was coming, we all just knew it was time to take positions and get ready to enact our strategic plan. We nodded and said good luck to each other and we separated.

I looked around and noticed that Gus, the leather worker, was approaching and when he reached me, I saw that he was wearing leather armor, a shield, and a long sword. The last time I saw him at dawn he looked like a sick little child, but now he was staring at me as a proud defender of his home. I could not help but feel proud for the determination of a clearly tired and beaten old man. Reporting for duty sir, where do you need me, he spoke with a voice I did not hear before. Resolve was clear in his voice. I looked around to see that other town elders had joined up behind him. The man we talked with after we cleared the town was now next to him, several others too and they were all dressed for battle. In all there stood about twenty of them and I had not placed them in the town regiment, but I was now clearly aware that I was wrong by not doing so.

You all have done your duty by helping to get the town ready for battle. Are you sure you want to do this? They all looked at me when a short old man I hadn't met spoke. His words were soft but had power behind them. Son, he said, we were spanking monsters when you were sipping on the tit. Just tell us what you need us to do. I just stood there for a split second and replied, yes sir. What I need is a defense force protecting the town residents and children.

The children and a few of our group will be back there too.

Protect your families and my group with everything you have. My group back there outside of the children are not fighters but will do whatever it takes to defend themselves and the residents. Please join them was all I could say to their request. I do not want any of you to die was the comment I ended with. Death comes to us all the old geezer said but they all nodded in understanding. You are our last line. Pride came upon their faces with that remark and as they left, I noticed respect from them.

I walked over to my parents, wife, and kids that were waiting for the talk with the older fellows to stop. It was a surreal setting, but I took the time to hug them all and tell them to stay strong as only together can we do this today. If not, we just march back after we respawn repeatedly until we windle them down like the little bitches they were. That got a laugh from everyone except my mom, but she still needed to get used to this new world. Mom, I said, and Mimis looked at me, it will all be okay just keep us healed as best you can. I love you was all she said. Big Bear wrapped his arm around her and said, "Look, I now have two hands so how can we lose? Plus, I am super sexy now." Mimis looked at him like he was an idiot. Dale or I guess it's Big Bear now you are a moron, but I do love you. Don't' think you can be a teenager again just because your arm is now useful. You're still in your seventies. I was, he said but now I feel twenty. Mimis just shook her head and laughed. With the conversation now having a lighter tone, at last we said our goodbyes as we broke to head up to our respective roles.

Jaceberlen was right behind me as I headed to the ramparts. His job was straightforward. Use his thunder spell as many times as possible before he needed to join the melee fights below at the gate entrance. He looked at me with eyes knowing we were in trouble. Have faith young one, I said and he shared a slight grin. I then added, you know what time it is don't you? His grin grew even wider and replied yes, I do. What time is it poo bear, I replied? Its ass kicking time he greedily admitted. Yes, I retorted and may the blood of our enemies soak the ground and cover our blades. It's time to bring the pain sir, I added.

We looked out onto the valley as the bandit group emerged from the tree line. Upon seeing them we tried to do a quick count, and we were not too far off in our estimation. It looked like there were about one hundred and twenty of them, but the commander was clearly noticeable. They were still about a half mile from the town, and it didn't look like they had been tipped off as to the town not being in their current control, but I wasn't sure. I looked over at Captain Ahab and let him know that he had control of the defenses.

Captain Ahab walked off and began barking orders to begin formations. We were going to try a new tactic within the group dynamic. We had always been able to form groups but now we were attempting to convert it into two forty-person raid groups with some to spare. We had eight tanks, so we developed groups around each one. We had seventy-eight combatants from our group alone without any minions or townsfolk, so we were close in numbers to the bandits. We changed our plan a little by taking everyone except the children that were part of our initial group, which was a little scary as we had to completely trust the townsfolk to protect our children. Thank goodness I had sent Gus and his group to do that specifically. When they were advised of that the resolve and pride seemed to swell even more, which made me relax a little for sure. A minion was not as strong as a person so we would see how they stacked up today. I would not want to face my golem for sure.

The tanks formed up into their groups with Killer being the brother that he was, taking the lead there. I decided to form the last and smallest group as there would be only eight of us as my minions would more than make up the difference. My group consisted of the skald tank, Thor, my good buddy the warrior, ThreeBD, Jaceberlen, my mom, Mimis, Dubi, the ritualist, Jackaboo, the artificer, the Occultist, Moovadeeb, and myself. We were caster heavy but if you included the minions we had plenty of firepower. All the group compositions overall were well balanced but as we enacted our tricks that might shift. Now we will see if all our preparation and little surprises would be the difference.

I ran a quick double check of everything I had summoned and the placement of my minions as they were currently hidden below the wall as to not tip our hand. Skeletons would kind of do that you know. In fact, all the summons across the party were down below until we were ready to bring them up for battle.

The bandit army continued to move closer and were now only about a hundred meters away from the gate. One of the front-line bandits seemed to be casually talking to one of his comrades when he thought he had seen something out of the corner of his eye but figured it was just his imagination after a long trip. The man wrote it off and picked back up the conversation with his friend. That would be the first of many mistakes made today by both parties but hey such is the swings of momentum in battle.

CHAPTER THIRTY-EIGHT

Party Time

When the bandit commander hit around the seventy-five-meter mark before the gate he realized something was off. First, the gate was manned now by too many guards, and they didn't even look like guards. In fact, he didn't recognize anyone on the walls. The commander immediately halted the group, and red flags went off like crazy. He scanned the walls again and didn't see a single member of his group that he had left behind. He issued a few commands for the army to form as he tried to figure out what was going on. It was at that moment that a figure in all black standing at the wall seemed to move forward and began to speak.

I saw the moment the commander realized the view was not what he expected. He then formed up his army, and I could see the confusion turn into alarm as he realized the bandits he left behind must be dead. I decided to get the party started and stepped forward and addressed the commander. You must be the commander of the bandit group, the Ebony Cloaks, that has been terrorizing the town and surrounding region? You are a menace and a coward and honestly just need to die.

The second I finished those words. Captain Ahab signaled the triggering of the ritual spells that had been laid by Dubi. Explosions went off across the area and several of the bandits were caught in the spell's attack. They weren't extremely powerful, but it did create chaos. Bandits were taking damage from all around the areas of effect when arrows, some form of bottles, and spells began to rain down into the ranks of the bandits. The commander looked up to see even more ranged attackers, including wait what? How the hell? How in the fuck did skeletons get here he screamed internally as he had never seen a necromancer in the flesh? He had to get this under control, or it would be over before the battle even began.

Phase one had been a success with catching them off guard and taking several out with the ritual and ranged attacks. The ranged attacks would continue and Dubi was currently trying to develop another ritual behind the wall. The tanks were shielding the ranged attackers from return fire so it was about as good as it could be so far. Dealz with his mental magic and Piper with his illusions went to work to sew even more chaos. A few of the bandits started staring dumbfoundedly into the horizon due to whatever they were seeing, and another one was held in place as more attacks drove deep into their ranks. A thunder spell and several other area spells such as fireball and shadow storm began to hit them in mass. Several others fell to the carnage of the spells. We did not get by unscathed though.

Throughout the chaos and carnage befalling his members, the commander finally got his troops back into attack formation. They had mostly been returning fire sporadically but now it was time to thin the herd. He ordered his casters and archers to attack the wall while the warriors created a shield wall to protect them from projectiles and spells. The tide began to turn as he noticed several of the enemies' ranged attackers had fallen due to precise shots slipping by the town's tanks. He needed to have the gates bashed so that the warriors could enter the town and lay waste to the town's defenders. He ordered a few of the mages to focus on the gate with fire attacks. Shield our casters at all costs, the commander yelled, and the warriors shifted their shields to do just that.

I noticed the shifting of the tide as the commander finally got them organized properly. Then as they began to pick off a few of our ranged attackers, he ordered a few of the casters to attack the gate. I was expecting this move as he assumed that once inside, he could make quick work of us. We still had a few surprises in store for him though. Captain Ahab signaled for the next phase as my mages began blinding the casters going for the walls and any archers they could target. Our bards began playing their instruments for those extra sweet buffs. First it was the lute granting us extra defense against fire-based attacks while the other was a cittern of some sorts causing a healing aura to permeate the area. Together it was an odd mix of music, but I didn't see any Queen or Metallica music playing around so we would work with it. Immediately the party began to heal albeit slowly. Now for the suicidal surprise of phase two.

Just for the record I was not a fan of this part of the plan although I did see its merits. My main concern was to keep as many alive as possible to offset their larger numbers and strength. Well, some of us would rather a bloodbath instead, be damned the cost. So, in the end I reluctantly agreed and now was the time to see if it was worth the risk. Those damn assassin classes.

From the back of the enemy's line, the group in stealth had maneuvered right behind the casters bombarding the gate. They were all waiting for Captain Ahab's signal for them to attack. As soon as it came, they burst into action. Pint Size backstabbed one of the casters bombarding the gate while Aerach and Bhorn got the other two. Flower and Rosie helped finish off the three fire mages before anyone knew what had happened. From there they attempted to move to the archers but by then they were spotted.

An archer fired an arrow at Rosie, but she was able to mostly dodge the shot as it grazed her shoulder as it went by. Then the assassin group was on the archer. It wasn't a fair fight with five against one, but nothing is fair in war. As the archer fell from the onslaught, the commander turned and as if he had finally decided enough was enough, he engaged the assassin corp.

The commander was tired of this fight and there would be hell to pay for the townsfolk and the leaders of this damn group trying to take the Ebony Cloaks down. He was the king of this region, and nobody would take his spoils. He moved faster than the group of assassins could see and before anyone knew there was a sword sticking out of the back of Aerach's Kitsune frame. She looked down in shock as a large broadsword ripped her insides out. When the commander withdrew the sword with force, she just dropped straight up dead to the ground. Her raid icon just greyed out to zero.

The commander now looked like he could get them down quickly so he could get back to the task of leveling the gate. He swung his sword in an arc, and it seemed to crackle with a hint of fire as it made its way through the trajectory. Bhorn managed to deflect the blade to his side and then Rosie tried to block as well but her injured shoulder came into play when she did so. The rogue winced when she lifted her shoulder and that split second delay was ultimately her downfall. The blade passed cleanly through her neck and severed her head from her shoulders in one attack. The fire from the blade even cauterized the blow so there wasn't even a drop of blood. Just a flying head and another of us gone.

Thomas sat at his desk watching at his computer screen with a drink and some popcorn watching the battle unfold at the town that Dookooze would use ultimately as his base of operations. In talking with Dookooze, he knew the battle would be today and he had followed the bandit commander's pathway back to the town, so he knew when it would happen. So far, he had to admit to himself that the strategy and tactics being used by Dookooze, and his group had been effective. A knock on the door showed that another programmer named Ben was at the door and he ushered him in.

The battle was no secret, so Ben pulled up a chair and was instantly enthralled. Thomas offered Ben some popcorn as the commander decided to fully engage in the battle. Within a few seconds, two of Dookooze's friends were dead. The tide looked like it was about to turn. Thomas, trying to play it cool, just advised Ben that he was scrolling through the world and saw this conflict begin and decided to watch if to see how it ended. After a few minutes, Ben said he needed to get some more work done but told Thomas to catch him later for a beer. Great in game battle you have going there Thomas, Ben ended with as he left the office and let me know how it turns out. Thomas readjusted his seat and went back to seeing just how his chosen would fair in his first major obstacle. Not to mention the commander was the first piece of the encrypted file puzzle. He had to be ready to work as soon as the bandit lord died.

As the battle raged on, I could clearly see that the commander was every bit of a boss monster that I had feared. He did carry the first clue to the whole questline so why would I think it would be a cake walk. Attacks were flying back and forth, and I could see through the raid screen that many of our casters were low on mana despite them all being conservative with their attacks. I looked over at Jaceberlen and Captain Ahab and they seemed to realize the same thing. I looked back at the commander, and he was still in full health. The assassin group did manage to take out four of their backlines, but a one-to-one trade is not what I would call a win. One thing that was certain was that I was getting a very good look at how we looked as a fighting force. Not to mention that several of our total group had yet to engage in the battle. I think it was time for that to change.

Attrition was starting to take a toll on both sides. We had already lost about thirty of our forces while the Ebony Cloaks were down about sixty. Area of effect spells were still going full scale on both sides, and the walls were starting to show damage. I continued to cast spell after spell. I cast pull of the dark in the area around the commander to help the assassin group and cause some damage with my mages focusing on shadow storms stacks on him as well. Eight Penetrating Shots flew towards the commander and as they struck him, he hesitated a second and you could see his health bar drop. The break in his swing allowed Pint Size to land a critical hit on his hip. A necrotic ray splashed up against his back as they had continued to do ever since I had shifted my focus to him. At this point, the commander's health bar had dropped to about eighty-five percent. I was waiting to see what the first mechanic would be and if it was at the eighty or seventy-five percent threshold. I continued to focus on helping the remaining rogues which were now at two with Pint Size and Bhorn struggling to stay alive. They were no longer offensive as every blow by the commander seemed to throw them both off balance. As another blow was coming towards Bhorn, he attempted again to divert the blade however this time the attack was too strong, and the impact pushed his own blade back into his chest. Following this attack, the commander landed a frontal kick to the midsection of Bhorn, knocking him to the ground.

Bhorn hit the dirt hard and lost the grip on the two daggers he was holding. He tried to roll to get to his feet, but the commander executed some sort of charge ability that placed him within two feet of Bhorn. Before the rogue had a chance to do anything the commander's blade pierced his throat. In a state of dismay, he looked up at the grinning bloody smile of the commander and then he faded into blackness.

Pint Size, at the sight of Bhorn being eviscerated lost her ever-loving mind. She felt a rage build within her gut and said screw stealth and charged the commander. As she reached him, she popped a cooldown called, Blade Fury, and her blades danced around the back and sides of her enemy leaving piercing holes all over her target. When the attack finished, she noticed that she had done quite a bit of damage, but the commander seemed to shrug it off and turned to face her. Pint Size didn't have time to pop her last cooldown for an enhanced evasion ability before the commander grabbed her chest and head butted her in the face. Blood gushed down her face as she screamed in pain. Pint Size struggled to get away but his grip was too strong. She saw the killing blow land before the pain registered as the blade slowly entered her abdomen. The pain of the cold steel blade was excruciating and as he continued to slowly push it in, he again was grinning at her. The commander spit into Pint Size's face in disgust and then tossed her to the side with the blade ripping lose in a spray of blood. Pint Size was dead before she hit the ground. Now the commander could focus on the real threats.

I saw the attack that Pint Size went with and although it did cause a lot of damage, it was anything from a finishing blow with the commander still above seventy-five percent health. I continued to attack him as well as my other ranged minions and the damage was slowly ticking away at his pool of health. I noticed Captain Ahab give a signal and I could see several contraptions looking like miniature catapults unleash a slew of rocks down upon the remaining forces of the Ebony Cloaks. The rocks hit several of them and finished a few that already had taken several major wounds.

By this time the commander hit seventy-four percent, and as expected he hit some sort of mechanic threshold. The battlefield was blasted by a roar of anger from the commander and then he turned to face the gate. His hand turned a deep orange and he aimed it at the gate. A magical chain shot from the tip of the sword and slammed into the gate embedding itself into the metal. The commander then yanked the sword back and the gate flew off its hinges and landed with a thud out in the field about thirty feet from the walls. With the gate free it was time for phase four. Captain Ahab signaled the phase, and our remaining troops went into motion.

With the gate finally open the commander and his remaining troops came for the town opening. There appeared to be about twenty troops left and every one of them was injured. The commander was down to about seventy percent and dropping. A well-placed pull of the deep spell landed right in front of the opening which sent a barrage of boney hands grappling and slowing the enemies as they moved. The damage also helped but it gave our ranged attackers another chance to take a few out. More area of effect spells landed on top of my zoned spell, so it was a radius of death for any bandit coming through. What the enemies didn't notice was the movement created by the new phase.

When Captain Ahab called for the phase four shift, the tanks on top of the walls abandoned the casters to their own devices and quickly made their way down below to the gate opening to join up with my warriors, Cadet, golem, and the bulwark. The rangers along with my archers and mages also moved down the ramparts leaving the casters alone up on the ramparts. The casters were about to run out of energy so they wouldn't necessarily have an impact in the battle below once their energy pools were dry. Geezz, I wish there was a regeneration of some sort for energy or health. The warriors whom to this point have been mostly a non-factor began to move to their new assignment.

These secluded pathways that we had identified as points of entry into the town would become a vital part of our plan. Every non tank class warrior as well as Smeeeagal and a few others made their way through the path onto the side of the town with the intention of flanking the remaining troops and attacking the commander. We still had one more surprise left in this phase that the bandits would soon see.

CHAPTER THIRTY-NINE

Final Confrontation

The bandits charged the gate as fast as they could to avoid the spells raining down on them only to hit several areas of effect spells layered on top of each other. What they also didn't see was the new ritual of poison that was activated by Dubi. What happened next was that they ran headfirst into was a radius of death and hindering effects. The bones grappled and pierced them while fireballs, ice storms, and a poison cloud assaulted them at every slow painful step. Several of them dropped to the relentless damage but those that survived got to the gate only to encounter a new surprise.

Before the gate went down, Piper had constructed his illusion which was simple in effect but convincing. Dealz also aided by helping ensure the mental aspect of these bandits were confused to the point where they wouldn't necessarily believe anything. The second they crossed into the town wall the bandits at the front were plunged into three-foot-deep holes filled with spikes. To them it looked like normal ground thanks to the illusion magic, but it was a pit trap. With the tanks arranged in an arc around the pits the bandits had nowhere to go.

As the first few bandits fell into the traps the ones behind them finally saw what was in front of them. Spike filled pits, an arc of tanks blocking their path, archers and shadow mages behind them releasing attacks, a damn golem standing ten feet tall, a god forsaken armored pig, and a plethora of spells going off behind them. They were utterly screwed. Attacks were released into the crowd of bandits down in the spike traps and after a few seconds they were quickly eliminated.

A few bandits tried to jump across and land safely only to come face to face with shields and steel as they tried not to fall back into the pits. The commander hit the spell barrage and was caught just like everyone else in his party, but he pushed through. When he emerged from the attacks into the open sky, he was furious at what he saw. He had underestimated this group of usurpers and now he only had a handful of men left and they would be dead soon. He once again saw those damn skeletons, but this time he saw more and a bone monstrosity that looked like a damn demon. He paused for a split second as a barrage of arrows peppered him all over his body. Shadow bolts hit him at every turn, and he saw the man who had initially spoken on top of the walls. He was the necromancer, he figured. If he died, then they still might have a chance.

Both sides had lost many combatants. We were down to less than half of our force while the bandits only had about five remaining plus the commander. With him being a boss the odds were still about fifty-fifty. I looked at the health pool of the commander and was at fifty-one percent, so I shouted that another mechan; I was cut short and not able to finish that comment before a pulse wave emerged from the commander in a circle. Everything that was an enemy of his on the ground was sent flying backwards. The remaining bandits took this opportunity to jump the pits and take advantage of the disarray. A few of them began cutting away at the prone bodies of the tanks. Steel pierced armor and blood was everywhere.

Golem was staggered from the ability but not down. It looked around and saw the enemies coming over the pit trap and it went into action. As he was clawing and attacking two bandits he heard his master call for a Shockwave. Golem didn't hesitate and repaid the commander's ability with one of its own. Golem jumped high and as it hit the ground the sequence activated. A wave of force erupted from its center just like the commanders, albeit a weaker version. The bandits had taken advantage of the stunned troops and killed a few of them but now they would feel the same. The bandits flew back into the walls, and one even fell back into the pit. This allowed the remaining tanks to get up and form back up. The archers remaining and umbral mages regained their footing as well and went on the offensive once again. Cadet rolled onto his side and got up with a snort.

The commander thought his ability would render the usurpers useless for a short period while his forces cleaned them up. He didn't take into an account that that big ass demon had a similar ability. What the hell was that thing. He heard the man he believed to be the necromancer shout something right before it acted so his beliefs were confirmed. Just then the two large skeletal creatures leaped over the pit trap and came to engage him from another command from the necromancer. They were followed by a few of the tanks as some had apparently stayed to engage the Ebony Cloak's remaining forces.

After the shockwave spell hit the battlefield, it had become even again. I saw from the top that the surprise was closing in, and I ordered Golem and the bulwark to engage the commander. It was now time to show this bastard not to mess with me or my friends. I yelled at the commander, and he turned up to see me. I pointed my scythes at him and screamed; time to die you bastard. The commander grinned and gripped his sword as my minions closed the gap.

Killer and Belle went to join Golem and the bulwark while the remaining tanks stayed to finish the bandits before joining the rest of the party. All four of them charged the commander with Killer opening with the initial taunt. The commander faced Killer and attacked. I came down off the wall, dodged the ongoing battles, and leaped over the pits to also join as it was time I got more up close to this asshole. I wasn't stupid but I wanted to be on the ground level. The commander was down to nearly forty percent now and still dropping. His attention was completely on us when the surprise party arrived.

All the melee damage class fighters had quietly made their way around to flank the commander. We needed focused damage to bring him down. The tanks were now in position to taunt and keep his attention while we all could unleash hell. As soon as they had established threat and would rotate taunts to keep it, the commander was land blasted from behind by twenty-one of our melee fighters led by Jaceberlen, several summons, my warriors, Smeeeagal, Maverick, Tal'n, Mittens, and Serenity. In total the commander was about to get intimately familiar with over close to forty damage dealers. They hit him like a tidal wave. Luckily enough threat had been established since it spiked heavily and just as it looked like the threat by Killer would be broken, Belle roared to grab threat again as Killer lost it. I continued to cast spell after spell and giving orders as necessary to the minions.

By this point the necrosis had been continuously building as it continued to ravage the commander. His health was dropping rapidly now and was close to thirty percent. The other troops within the walls had finally dispatched the last of the Ebony Cloaks, so now all that remained was the commander. Every fighting and healing asset we had jumped the pits and engaged the boss. It was now a race to the finish. This was going to be a battle.

As the rest of his forces were eliminated, the commander noticed that all the enemies' party had come to engage him. Seeing all the minions and summons, he knew there was more than a single summoner here. There had to be a total of what, fifty or sixty total troops engaging him but maybe even higher. He knew he was in trouble, but nobody would take his town. The commander lashed out at the bear urging him to attack. He knew he was getting annihilated from behind but was unable to attack them as he knew he needed to eliminate the bear. Arrows, spells, steel, and many other types of attacks continued to pelt the commander as he lashed repeatedly with his sword. A swift cut to the bear's side caused a deep gash and a blood spray. The commander lost his urge to fight the bear and went to attack a warrior behind him only to be yelled at again from the smaller skeleton with a spiked club and shield. Having to shift back to the skeleton costs precious time he needed to eliminate the attackers from behind.

I had been keeping an eye on the commander's health bar. He was about to hit the twenty-five percent mark, and I yelled the mark out and not a second or two later he seemed to hit his third mechanic. Large pulsing circles began appearing all around the battlefield as the commander began chanting. The circles started pulsing faster and from experience we had an idea of what was coming. I yelled at everyone to clear the circles now. Most of them cleared it in time but a few were not quite fast enough. Belle was still in bear form when she disengaged from the commander.

The chanting by the commander finished and the circles exploded with extreme heat. Fire spewed up into the air and engulfed everything within the circles. In the matter of three seconds, we lost seven party members due to not moving fast enough. Belle was gone as well as Endor, Honey Badger, Utha, Carno the Great, Beanie, and oh shit, Raven, my daughter. Just like that we lost several damage dealers and a tank.

Golem immediately used a taunt to establish threat once again and this became a slugfest as its claw attacks and tail were relentless in its assault. Once that was done the damage dealers charged back in and everyone else reengaged. I yelled out to everyone to pop every ability and cooldown they had as the commander was now below twenty-five percent. Every remaining caster with an ounce of energy also hit the boss with anything they could muster. Summons popped abilities or just flat out attacked. My archers dialed up penetrating shots, and the mages unleashed shadow storms and shadow bolts. All the skeletal warriors utilized power strike in unison and the damage spike shot through the roof. Smeeeagal could be heard cackling as he lashed out repeatedly like a shadowy blur. Smeeeagal kill could be heard all through the battlefield. That idiot of a boy I swear. Jaceberlen connected with attacks left and right. Biggus Dikkus hurled a javelin straight into the chest of the commander and Tal'n slammed his war hammer into the boss' knees. I yelled that he was down to eleven percent and then ten.

Once the boss hit ten percent, the shit hit the fan. The commander began to glow red and his sword became covered in a swath of fire. Once we saw that, anyone that was a gamer prior to WEO knew instantly what this was; he was now enraged and will likely one shot anyone he hits. I yelled again to attack with everything you have left. You must avoid the hits at all costs, I yelled. I redoubled my spells and tried to slow him again with pull of the dark. I held off on the night cloud since I wasn't sure who could see in it or not.

Just at that moment the Commander charged and took out one of our archers, Ant. The boss left that corpse and ran towards Chedda, who was one of our remaining tanks. One hit and his icon greyed out dead. The health bar kept dropping as it was now down to seven, wait no six percent but his charge attacks kept increasing in speed. Another damage dealer was down and now he was approaching Duck. She tried to move but took a kill shot to the side and was instantly dead. We were losing people every few seconds. Now the commander was down to three percent, and he then looked directly at me.

I saw the stare immediately and began to move. I had a purple hue develop around me and needed to get it off me although I knew it would not happen. Before I could take two steps I felt it. The fire hit me with searing pain. I just knew I was dead, and the momentum of the blade swing knocked me back about ten feet. Damn that attack hurt like hell but then I realized that if I could still feel it then I was still alive. I looked at my health bar and I would be damned; I had one hit point left. A notice appeared telling me that my special ability, divine absorption, had activated. Hell, yes, I shouted as I got side glances of shock considering I was still alive. I just yelled out it's an ability and then I quickly cast a heal on myself to bring me above one health point. My minions had not died either so that was a huge relief but unfortunately my healer minions could only heal undead, so I was out of luck. If I were hit again though, I would be toast. The enrage mechanic moved to another party member but this time it was a healer. I got up to my feet and saw that the boss was now at one percent and ticking down.

Jaceberlen struck with his sword as fast as he could and Serenity had continued to cut the commander repeatedly with her electrified swords. Cadet let out a loud cooing sound like a damn bird and then charged with his horn and impaled the commander. As he withdrew the horn, he snagged a bite on the boss' leg. Wait did I just hear Cadet cooing when he charged. What in absolute hell was that. I would have to ask about that. I heard a comical outburst from Biggus Dikkus as he yelled, Anders this, and smacked the commander with his axe. That is an inside joke for our online group from a game that we played weekly. I could not help but smile as I began to attack again. I yelled out a half of a percent now drop him and the attitude swung to high anticipation as we were about there.

I was down to half my minion count now, as most of the warriors and archers had fallen and the casters were not looking good. The bone weavers were spinning their eldritch healing as fast as possible, but it was hard to keep up with the damage from, well a raid boss. They were minions after all. Our party icons were graying out left and right as the enrage mechanic was getting faster with every second.

Gundham knew the boss was about to drop as he pulled back his bow. He activated sniper shot as it had just come off cooldown. He released the arrow and its green energy rocketed toward the commander. The attack struck true as it lodged itself in the commander's skull. The commander wobbled a little as several other attacks hit it as well. He saw the boss drop to his knees and Gundham knew it was finally over. For what seemed like a few hours of battle, it was at an end.

I continued to attack as the party continued to be one shot by the boss. Out of the corner of my eye I saw my brother-in-law, Gundham, activated some sort of ranger ability and the arrow turned green. The streaking of the shaft soared through the air as it hit home in the boss' head. I had just released a necrotic ray and as it hit I saw that Neelz had seemed to connect with a two-handed sword strike as Mittens got in another attack too while many other attacks arrived concurrently.

We attacked with one last push and then the commander stopped all movement as his health bar hit zero. He just stood there and began to sway. I realized what I had to do and equipped my golden shiv and ran towards the creature as fast as I could muster. As I closed the distance to him, he fell and then he collapsed to land on his face. I rushed past the party members still alive and to their shock, I plunged the dagger into the skull of the boss. A bright light erupted from the impact point and a beam shot up into the sky. This continued for a second or two and then it vanished just as quickly as it had started. I received looks from everyone except Jaceberlen and my companions as they knew what was going on. I just looked at everyone and said three words: for a quest. Then it was over.

CHAPTER FORTY

Intel and Discovery

Thomas was watching the battle in earnest as it was nearing its conclusion. This battle had been one of epic proportions and he had been extremely impressed with his choice and their strategy. Thomas had ditched the popcorn and drink for the keyboard as he wanted to be ready for when the first boss fell. Suddenly, he saw the commander target Dookooze with his enrage mechanic and what looked like to be a killing blow left Dookooze with one hit point. Thomas internally thanked the maker for deciding to give him that saving ability, divine absorption. It had saved Dookooze's ass. He saw the man rise and without missing a beat continue the attack. As the boss hit zero, he saw his chosen rush with the golden dagger. When the dagger plunged into the boss, Thomas had his window.

When the dagger landed it created a window of time where the firewalls were down on the encrypted file within the commander's coding. A golden beam of light shot upwards in the simulation from the boss as it ate away at the security and Thomas did not hesitate. He typed some commands into the simulation and then he reached in and took the file. The dagger could have done it without him, but he was very anxious to see what it was. He would do it manually this time. The first thing he did was copy it onto a private secure server only he could access. As soon as the file was copied, he placed the file back into the coding of the boss so as not to cause any suspicion.

Within seconds it finished and he had his first bit of information to analyze. Thomas then created a thumb drive. And placed it within a lined slot in the sole of his shoe. He had to be extra careful here. It was time to get to work.

When the beam dimmed and then distinguished, I withdrew the dagger and placed it back in my inventory. Cheers went up from all the remaining party members as we had taken out the trash which was the commander. This had been a hell of a battle with only about twenty of the original seventy-eight in our group still alive. Of my minions I still had three warriors, two archers, two mages, and both of my bone menders. Luckily, all my companions survived, albeit wounded badly. We were all a hot mess though.

I noticed a slew of notifications but decided to wait until after looking to see what the boss had dropped. Before I could touch the glittering corpse, a global alert hit. Global Alert: The first wandering regional raid boss in WEO has fallen. To all participants in that battle you have earned a new title, Slayer of the Elite. You will gain +5 to damage against all enemies within a raid setting. On cue, everyone saw the title appearing within their screens and the cheers became louder.

Everyone standing there, who had been a previous gamer, knew what was next and the ones that were new to this were excited once the concept of rewards were explained. It was time to see that super sweet loot. I reached down to touch the corpse and when I did, I received an icon asking if I wanted to loot the commander's corpse and how I wanted to set the loot system. I set the system to a roll mechanic and decided to separate the items by class or usability. As I looked through the rewards, I saw everyone with that greedy look on their faces. There was a total of ten items that were lootable. I took everything that was there, and the system advised me that even the dead would be notified of the items and they could also roll. They would immediately receive the items when they respawned. Okay that was a relief to hear as I did not really want to wait a day to pass out the loot.

I continued to look at the items, and it was identifiable as to who could wield the items so I decided to place one item at a time with the marker on who could roll. So, I threw up the first piece in the group chat. Great Sword of Flame: Rank – Rare, Description – A great sword that can be ignited with a constant flame dealing 2D6 Damage plus 1D8 fire damage; Chest piece of the Fire Nova: Rank – Rare, Description - Plate Mail Chest Piece that can erupt in a fire nova 10M 3D6 damage; Chain Ring of Heave: Rank – Uncommon, Description - Can emit a magical chain to a target and then forcing them to your location; Necklace of the Volcano: Rank – Very Rare, Description - Creates magical fire volcanos spewing molten lava in a max of 3 targeted areas. 3D6 damage; Leather Gloves of the Sadistic Mind: Rank – Legendary, Description - When worn allows 1D6 extra damage from melee attacks in the form of psychic pain. There is a 10% chance of fear; Elixir of Aggressive Casting: Rank – Rare, Description - When consumed grants +3 to Intelligence; Cloak of Protection +15: Rank – Rare, Description – Cloak granting +15 defense; Longbow of the Bandit Commander: Rank – Very Rare, Description - Attacks have a 20% chance to inflict a will save or become frightened. If target fails, they cannot move for 5 seconds; Class Evolution Book – Fire Warrior of the Cruel: Rank – Very Rare, Description - While In possession of this book this class will be an extra evolution option. Melee with fire magic; Greaves of the Bandit Commander: Rank – Rare, Description – Grants wearer +20 Fire Resistance; 200 Gold; Schematic – Training Yard: Rank – Uncommon, Description – Allows the construction of a military training yard in a settlement; Head of the Bandit Commander: Trophy Rank N/A, Description - When placed at an inn will grant morale boost to anyone that spends one hour there. +5%XP for 12 hours; Conquered Town Deeds of Ownership: Quest Item, Description - Town Deeds of ownership from regional towns overtaken by the Ebony Cloaks. When read, it will begin quest – Return or Rule!

As the items went into the chat bars the rolls flooded in. It was good to even see the folks that had fallen include their rolls. The flaming great sword went to ThreeBD. The chest piece was taken by Biggus Dikkus. Chedda claimed the roll for the Heave ring.

Altriox the Arcanist took home the volcano necklace. Oh, hell I immediately thought as Smeeeagal claimed the sadistic gloves and I must admit, that is a perfect fit. Lady Jane took the Elixir while the cloak went to Amedeus. The Longbow went to Raven, so I was incredibly happy about that. The class evolution book was rolled by several people, but it went to Skullbasher. Honey Badger took the greaves, while I took the schematic, trophy, and quest items. The gold dispersed evenly among everyone.

With all the items distributed, you could see all the winners that were alive immediately trying to equip the items. Most needed to be level twenty, but some were able to be worn. I let the group know that I was about to check all the notifications before I went back into the town. With that in mind everyone else decided to do the same. I pulled up my interface and started looking at them all over.

Congratulations you have slain Raid Boss: Ebony Cloak Commander Wrex. Level 23 Elite. Experience Earned: 1000, Distinguished Points earned: 300

You have completed the quest: Final March Part Four of the Divine Investigation. This is a unique Divine Level quest and an unspecified number of parts. Rewards: Experience Points - 1700 based on percentage alive 21/83 = 28%, Distinguished Points – 150, Class Appropriate Reward – Ring of Regeneration, Description – Allows 35 Energy regeneration per minute during combat. That was the first time I had seen anything allowing an active regeneration during combat. This would very well be a damn game changer if we could locate and farm these types of items. A must have in our new world if you ask me.

You have been granted a quest: Solidify your Rule. Part Five of the Divine Investigation This is a unique Divine Level quest with an unspecified number of parts. Rewards: Experience Points, Distinguished Points, Class Appropriate Reward, Description – Claim rulership, name the town, advance the town from Tier 0 to Tier 1.

You have Completed the quest: Homestead: Description - Head

to the designated town, eliminate the brigands terrorizing the citizens and assume direct control over the town and its population. Brigands defeated 184/184, Ebony Cloak Commander Wrex defeated 1/1 Rewards: Experience Points – 5500, Distinguished Points - 1000, Class Appropriate Spell – Vampiric Attack, Description – Upon hitting a target with a melee attack you will deal 3D6 instant decay damage but will be instantly healed for half of the damage inflicted. Bonus Reward - Appointment of Lordship over town

Congratulations you have defeated Ebony Cloak Bandit Levels 17-20 x 123. Experience Earned – 1800, Distinguished Points – 200

Congratulations, you have hit Level 21 and have 5 free stat points to distribute and one free point to assign into your evolution tree.

Congratulations, you have hit Level 22 and have 5 free stat points to distribute and one free point to assign into your evolution tree.

Congratulations, you have hit Level 23 and have 5 free stat points to distribute and one free point to assign into your evolution tree.

Congratulations you have reached Level 7 in your Distinguished Path: Bastion of Justification. You have one free point to assign in your tree.

Regional Alert: Dookooze of the Earthen is now the lord and ruler of Anchorin!
Title Earned: As the only Earthen lord and ruler of a settlement you have gained the title, Nobility; You gain a +10 percent increase to NPC loyalty that are under your rule.

When that finished, I decided to go ahead and allocate my stats and then recall all my advanced minions and zombies. I split the stats between Wisdom and Charisma. I needed more energy even with the new regeneration ring. For the last few battles now, my energy had run extremely low to the point where I almost had to change to melee. Every point helps. I also now noticed that my control limit had increased again. Awesome sauce, I muttered to the delight of those around me. As the minions resurfaced, I decided to keep the same line up, but I added five more warriors and another bone mender due to having a new control limit of thirty. I stopped the spell at twenty-eight skeletons as I still needed a point for my zombie spell. That left me at twenty-nine of my possible thirty control limit as I wanted to wait and see what I could do with that extra point after looking at my class trees. I then directed them all plus the bulwark and Golem to loot everything from every single enemy and bring it inside the town to take an inventory. As the thirty-three minions went off to take care of that business, I turned to hear the cheers and roars of approval from all the party members. Every single one of them had gained a few levels and it looked like hopefully one or two of them had finally hit level 20, which gave them their first evolution. I was certain that Jaceberlen had done so. I could not wait to see what they all would select. It's amazing what a modified quest for them and taking down a regional boss will do for levels and morale. I did notice several look my way due to the lordship regional alert, but nobody seemed to complain.

I entered the town and the first thing to do was to fill in these spike traps with dirt so that nobody else would get hurt. I then send Dubi to fetch the town elders. We did it, we survived and won and they were safe, I thought to myself and then I realized I had forgotten to do a few things. I immediately recalled the Heart of the Firemander Queen into my hand from out of my inventory. I had been an idiot and completely forgot to consume this prior to the battle. That fire resistance enhancement miscue almost cost me everything. I quickly consumed it and saw the percentage increase show up on my character screen with the ten percent addition. Now to see how this whole Lordship thing worked. Secondly, I decided it was high time I absorbed the profession book, City Management. Once that was absorbed, I realized just how uneventful it was as it just let me know that one of my profession slots had been filled and asked me to verify my choice. As I said yes, it appeared and I saw where there was now a profession tab within my character data so I assumed that the meta information and branches or trees would be there and that was it. I did not have the time to go looking for more info so I would do that at another time.

One question I really have been pondering for ever since we came into WEO was the issue with skills. I have not seen any upgrades, levels, or really any prompts to use any of them so what was going on with that? I needed to ask the townsfolk or even Tikallnosis. I also needed to ask the group to see if any of them had any answers. Since I had a few more minutes before Gus and the rest of the elders arrived, I selected the prayer tab and mentally hit it. Just like the last time, I arrived in a semi dark room which looked more like an altar. A few seconds later Tikallnosis arrived but he looked like he was in a distracted craze. I had to get his attention, so I just said, hey man you alright. That broke him out of his focused stupor, and he looked back up at me and quickly said yeah man just trying everything I can as quickly as possible to decode this file to see what is in it. I could completely understand that so I told him I would keep it brief. I went right into it asking him when we would know what the file consisted of and I made a point of emphasis to state loud and clear that I needed one hundred percent disclosure on what these files contained and what this all meant. Not the abridged version, not the cliff notes, not lies, but full disclosure. He looked up at me for a second and seemed to come to a decision in his head. He then nodded and said of course you need to know what you are fighting for and against so I will show you everything I know. Plus, I said two minds can be better than one. He could not help but agree with that.

After telling me that he had already started a decoding program on the file he then told me that it could take up to a few days to unlock it. Then he would need to piece the data together to see what it could contain but he would get with me at that point so we both could see what it meant or at least a way forward. He was also in the middle of gathering other entities within the simulation game that contained other files. They could include any boss, monster, or hell even a king. We would put a path together for that. For now, though he said, you have done great.

Now we went back and forth on the earlier plans we had discussed about giving people something to fight for and creating a council of sorts. I told him who I wanted, why I did, and the number. He rubbed his chin in thought and made a few suggestions which I could understand and then we agreed on the final decision. Over the next few minutes we discussed the town aspects, how to navigate that, would there be any push back from the townsfolk, altars, churches, how religion worked, were guilds a thing, and then the final two questions I had. The first was simple and I just asked; man, what is even your real name? Tikallnosis can be a bit hard to pronounce. He looked at me like he was scared but he surmised that his name might lend a little credence to our goal. My name is Thomas was his response. Nice to meet you, Thomas. I am Mitch but you already know that. Now that the formality of that awkwardness is over let's get the last question out of the way so you can crack that code. He seemed to relax and cracked a smile.

I finally asked him what was up with skills as it really had not been explained in the testing. I explained that there were no prompts, upgrades, or even signs of its usage. He looked confused and just frankly blurted out; you mean you all do not know how to use them? I explained I can only speak for myself now, but that we all had skills, but I had not seen anything to show they have been used or growing or anything. Tikallnosis or aka Thomas pondered that for a moment and then as if talking to me like I was a baby he asked; have you opened the skills tab and applied them to your character? I sat there slack jawed like I was an idiot. What do you mean, don't they just work in the background?

Tikallnosis seemed to understand my conundrum at that point and understood. No, he said. Tikallnosis then went into it deeper and said that unlike most or honestly all online games in the past they were, but although abilities were innately passive the skills had to be manually selected and applied to your player code. No wonder they have received so many complaints so far, he softly murmured. He then showed me how to go into the skills tab and select everyone and then hit the apply button. Once that was done, I began to see a series of overlays encompass my screen and then disappear. Tikallnosis then let me know that now they would mostly work in the background like the abilities but many others like skinning it would give you a prompt to use when applicable. Now I feel like a complete moron. Tikallnosis continued and advised me that yes, they will level to open higher tiers of abilities and craftsmanship options. Thanks for the information man I said, and he nodded and said anytime bro. He followed that up with letting me know he had to get back to work but I asked him one more thing on the religious part and after that brief conversation, the communication was ended and I warped back into reality with an irritated Gus looking straight at me.

CHAPTER FORTY-ONE

Anchorin

Once I finished apologizing to Gus and the rest of the elders for the delay as I was speaking to my deity, they seemed to calm down. It was in their eyes that shown awe regarding a deity and of course if I were a chosen champion, then they would be wise to respect that. They understood per Gus and we decided to get to the points at hand. We surveyed the damage and with the help of Tal'n, Dealz, Captain Ahab, and Jaceberlen we walked them through what our plans were for rebuilding. I went over some of my skills. I also disclosed my lone profession and that seemed to click in their eyes as to the alert. They had already mentioned, without any animosity, that I was the newly appointed lord and they would serve under my leadership. Gus did ask, however, what my intentions were as they did not want to go from a cruel torturer to the same. Everyone looked at me, including my own friends as I responded. I then disclosed my Distinguished path and their eyes went wide. That was an extremely rare thing in their eyes, but I really didn't know any better. I then went into our vision and then my own vision. My thoughts on the matter seemed to satisfy them completely.

I did ask them how this all worked and they let me know that to run a town in the lord capacity, I needed to access the top floor of the town hall. It normally is only accessible to those in a recognized leadership role. Gus went into more detail that their old leader was killed a few months ago with the arrival of the

Ebony Cloaks so we could only maintain buildings or just build basic tier ones. I asked him to show us this floor and then I let him know I already had a few schematics ready to use for construction. We will make this place a beacon of imperial strength, security, and stability. I channeled my inner interstellar dark lord with that comment for a split second. I laughed aloud for a moment but then I had to reel it in since I was the only one that got my internal thought. My friends snickered a little though.

We decided to make our way to the town hall to see the top floor and on our way, you could see the townsfolk finally realize that they were free from the Ebony Cloaks. Cheers and even crying could be heard through the streets and Cadet seemed to stiffen with pride as he marched behind us like only he could. I looked back at him and smiled; The Space Swine Defense Force would be proud of your courage today, Cadet. However, we must have a conversation about what was it that I heard, cooing? Cadet seemed to inflate with pride to immediately deflate with embarrassment. Yes, sir he said, lowering his head and I just smiled and let him know it was all right. Mittens then smacked him on the backside with her tentacle and purred loudly. Both Cadet and I went stiff with a sense of awkwardness. She seemed to feed on the silence as she purred louder and licked her lips. Good lord woman, I exclaimed can you please act like an adult? Well, I could but I am not yet an adult if you remember, and kitty likes what she sees. I just shook my head and pleaded with her to keep control of herself. Serenity just placed a hand on her shoulder and shook her head. That is an interesting dynamic you have Dookooze, Captain Ahab stated with a laugh. I just laughed in return.

When we reached the top floor, I placed my hand on the door and that granted access to us. I opened the door and what looked like a normal large office appeared before us. It certainly needed a deep clean and some serious reorganization, but it had the capacity to handle what I needed it to. Gus let me know the map of the town was on the desk and access to the town's management system would be granted through my profession interfacing with the map. I decided to try it.

The moment I touched the map; a 3D interactive map populated my vision. The first thing I noticed was the resource tab as it listed all available resources and the quantities of each. It also gave me the option to allocate access to other individuals so they could interact with this part as well. Those people could be like a mine foreman, master lumberjack, head farmer, construction manager, and several others. There were resources like food, meat, grain, ores, wood, etc. Some of the resources were greyed out due to the buildings being not high enough in tier to require these resources or that we had a zero inventory of them. It made perfect sense to me as they would need information on their respective resource pools to manage it properly. The construction manager also made sense as they would need the scope of all the resources for their current and future projects.

I then went to the construction tab and wow. At the bottom were all the tier 0 buildings available and currently within the town. I opened my inventory and decided to consume both of my new schematics and immediately the Firemander Pen was an option as a tier 0 building and the Training Yard appeared as a building available in the tier one portion. I could also see that the Recruitment Hall had now populated as an option and that would be a priority. As I investigated the higher tiers the options were cool. Glancing over the Tier 0 buildings I finally got to see what the town's makeup truly was. Several of the buildings were damaged or destroyed. The buildings needed to gain access to the Tier 1 upgrade seemed to be repairing or rebuilding the ones already there and creating four more buildings of the Tier 0 tier so I would discuss that with the new council when we met but I knew what I wanted to build.

I looked over at the population screen and noticed that the population seemed to be around two hundred twenty of what I can only read as a previous population of around two hundred and seventy-five. A population minimal requirement of three hundred was needed for a Tier 1 upgrade so with our current party adding to the current population we should be good. I do want to bring in many more though. It did seem that I had the capacity to assign certain people within the city to separate roles and allow the option to create roles so that would be great for creating a council. I would need the townsfolk details to effectively use this plus the Recruitment Hall would play a pivotal role here. Ahhh, that was what I was looking for as I finally found the tab allowing me to invite people to join the town. This would take a while as we had eighty-three people with our current party and more would come with their family members or friends for which we had not accounted.

This seemed to be a rabbit hole of epic proportions, but then I noticed I could just send a mass invite to all my party members, and I jumped all over that. I then received a notification that I have been invited to take rulership as lord of the town, Anchorin. Yes/No? I of course selected yes and then I noticed the invite at that moment was sent out to everyone. Soon everyone that was still alive accepted so I assumed the others would get it when they respawned. I then pulled out the deeds from the quest item I got from the commander and read them. Immediately the quest Return or Rule updated.

You have read the deeds of the conquered towns and must decide. You may either assimilate these towns to your rule as annexed vassal locations, or you can return the deeds to their rightful leaders and try to develop diplomatic or trade alliances with them. Every decision has consequences. The choice is yours.

I shared the quest and updates with the room, and they had a mix of reactions. Gus was the first to speak and let us know that these towns, before the Ebony Cloaks provided trade and safety as an alliance pact to help defend each other. There were five locations mentioned and four of them fit into this category. There was one over the mountain path to the east that conducted trade but never wanted anything more.

I asked Gus what their opinion would be if we annexed them to our town's control. He pressed his lips together and looked at the other elders for a second. Hard to say he said, that was never something our town considered due to our size and fighting force. They were mostly in the same situation, so we tried to benefit from one another. This was certainly more information than I had minutes ago. This would also be something I wanted to bring up and think about. The decision was mine in the end and I needed to think of the long-term goal I had.

I then thanked Gus and the elders for their help. We decided to leave the room and head back down into the town. I went over everything I had seen and informed them we can delegate roles and responsibilities within the system interface. I let them know about the schematics and other possibilities based on the Bastion tree. Everyone was upbeat with the possibilities, and we even discussed who had what skills they knew of and how we could properly and effectively use them.

By the time we got back to the gate entrance, the hole had already been filled with dirt, and the loot had been categorized into separate piles. There were tons of items separated into weapons, armor separated into what slots they took up, resources, and finally other items such as jewelry. There was so much loot. I went over to identify some but wanted to wait until everyone was back here to properly distribute the stuff to everyone and especially the ones that did not get items from the commander. I placed my skeletons as a guarding force to protect the items from anyone with sneaky hands. I then let everyone know that the rest of the group will be back by tomorrow night at the latest and we will go through everything then and hand out presents. Everyone groaned as if they were licking their chops for some sweet loot, but they understood.

I walked over to Neelz as I wanted to check on her. She was handling the recent battle okay and even as she had fought like a warrior, I could tell something was troubling her. Killer and Tallulah looked at me with concern, but they were both proud of her for overcoming her fear of what had happened on the trip. I had already thought heavily about what I wanted to do next and Killer and I had discussed it as well. I placed my hand on her shoulder and leaned into her whispering something in her ear. Sweetheart I have a present for you, but you must promise to protect it and take care of it. If you do this it will protect you in kind and you will be far more prepared when something like what happened on our trip occurs again. Do you want it? Neelz looked up at me quizzically while Tallulah did the same. Killer just patted his wife and urged her to just watch. Birdz, her younger sister, on the other hand kept trying to insert her eyes into every angle to see what was going on.

I pulled the Egg of the Firemander Queen out of my inventory and into my palm. I told Neelz this was an exceedingly rare item I got off a Firemander queen. It is hers to hatch and nurture to be her companion and teammate if she chooses. As it grows, you two will form a bond and a team to battle together. Neelz looked up at me with a tear in her eye and asked what if it dies out there? I was so happy she asked that as that was a key to getting her back on track. I simply said that she would have to get strong to protect it and it would have to be strong to protect her. Killer nodded at me in agreement. Do you want it and will you grow strong to protect it I asked again? After a second, she nodded yes and I handed it to her. As she grabbed it, I informed her of the incoming prompt and to select yes when she was ready. At this point we had gathered a crowd of interested people wanting to see this thing hatch. A sense of rebirth and new beginnings here in WEO. Neelz accepted the prompt and the egg began to glow a reddish color. As the color grew, movement was seen within the egg. Neelz about dropped it but wrapped her arms around it at the last second. A moment later the egg began to crack and what emerged was, I must admit, cute as hell.

A reddish-brown little thing crawled its way out of the egg leaving a trail of slime behind and moved into the awaiting arms of Neelz. She seemed a bit repulsed by the slime, but she appeared to get over it when the next thing happened and it was something even, I did not expect. Neelz has accepted the bond with the last of the Firemander Queens. All her race's ancestors have poured their legacy, knowledge, and potential into this legendary queen and she is the last of her kind. She will need time to grow and become strong and quite possibly the fiercest of the Firemander race. Only then can she secure the species' bloodline and future.

Do you accept the responsibility/ Yes/No? Neelz looked up in shock as we all were in the same state. Hell, now I was jealous, but she needed it more than I and I was happy as it could compound Neelz's resolve. I nodded to her that it was okay and to go ahead. You deserve it honey, I said.

Neelz accepted and then there was a glowing light that made everyone place their hands over their eyes. It quickly vanished and when I looked back, the Firemander had opened its eyes, leaned in, and slapped its tongue on the side of Neelz cheek in affection. Everyone came to see the new addition to the town, and I knew this would be a town of people that would protect her from danger. I just slapped Killer on the arm and the words were unspoken; Family means all my brother. Thank you was his reply.

After the excitement of Daisy, which is the new name of the Firemander, faded people went through their notifications and levels. Out of the twenty plus of the people still alive, several had hit the level 20 evolution. That surprised me but we were not the only ones trying to level up on the way to reunite. It was quite possible that some currently in respawn had hit the mark too. I was close to 24 so I needed to keep pushing if I wanted to dominate the landscape. Watching them reminded me that I had points to allocate into my trees, so I decided to get right on that.

I pulled up my class arc and as I had three points I decided to review the trees again. It looked like my control limit would increase naturally due to the charisma boost I got per level, but it might not be enough. Overall, my golem and bulwark held their own admirably; however, the boss eliminated the warriors from the battlefield with ease. Expected but they could be stronger. I also wanted to see if there were minion types that could counter the types of attacks we faced. I decided to put one point into improving my minions and the increased percentage went up to a ten percent improvement. I then shifted to the other minion tree and the golem tree. I wanted to see if there was anything that might alter the scope of my bulwark since the golem would be the primary tank. An off tank was perfectly fine but a heavy warrior or something more damage related was preferred. I found what I was looking for but unfortunately it was a few levels in the tree ahead of what I could access currently. I decided to go on that route, and the first selection was Specter. That was an incorporeal type of minion that had a life drain ability and could phase through objects. It was resistant to most elements, but sunlight would make it a little weaker. Humm, I noted but I decided to go with it anyway. Besides, I could summon two for the price of 1 control point. That would be a nice addition. I would cast that in a little bit as I wanted to check out the Bastion tree.

With my last point I decided to delve into the golem tree. There were different varieties of golem that were more powerful. I wanted the best I could get or at least the best lineup of minions. There was one golem that I thought would be ideal. It was still a few levels up, but I would like to try it. If anything, going to that selection would make my golem stronger no matter the type. I put my last point into the golem tree and like the other arcs; it would make my golem stronger. Now however I had the path I wanted. I decided to wait on that too as we were currently out of danger and I wanted to take care of some other items too.

As I brought up the Bastion tree the respawn rate arc was still the same and honestly all of them were. Until I unlocked higher options, I would play with the options that I had. I felt that with the new deed quest that it might not be a bad idea to continuously improve Anchorin's defenses, so I decided to throw a point into that and hit yes. It brought the town's defense up to a total of 20%. I did also notice that on the building arc, a few of them now glowed with a green checkmark as one of their qualifiers had now been met. I still had one more point, but I decided to hold onto it until we upgraded the town to Tier 1. That way I could possibly place the point into the building tree. There were some really optimal buildings I wanted us to have access to. Interesting indeed and I will need to spend more time going through all of this to make a proper progression plan.

CHAPTER FORTY-TWO

Aftermath

The rest of the day went by as I had hoped. We had begun cleaning up the town, repairing old buildings with the help of the town, and started removing any trace of the Ebony Cloaks' brutality. That was something the townsfolk needed so we were happy to assist with that. We had collected all the bodies and placed them outside of the town. It was honestly nasty and gross work but needed. We did finally discover to our surprise that if a body lay there long enough it would start breaking down and begin to disappear. That was great to discover so we would not have to burn them all. It took a few hours, but they ended up disappearing on their own.

We spent the evening celebrating and getting ready to receive the rest of the group tomorrow. Tiger Lilly and I spent the night playing with Ophelia, the other children, and watching Neelz go all mommy mode on her new companion, Daisy, which was quite good to see. Daisy had developed a crowd of adoring fans, so she was in great hands. Even the elder women of the town were giving Neelz pointers. Neelz looked like she was in a state of mental overload, so we just laughed.

With the morning came a sense of newness. We continued to get ready to receive the rest of our group and the recovery was still in full swing. It would take several days but we should be able to make progress enough today to begin other construction tomorrow. I sent a message to every person that I wanted to meet with tomorrow morning after everyone returned. It will be our initial council meeting and there was plenty to go over. I hope that everyone chosen will be ready to accept that responsibility. We will certainly find out.

By the time noon came around, I started receiving messages from the people that had respawned. As a group they had already started making their way back and I even got several replies about the looted items that were claimed as rewards. Raven was happy as a toddler with candy as she had won the bow, and I was happy to see her elated.

When everyone arrived at dusk we welcomed them with open arms, cheers, food, drink, and congratulations. Tonight was cause for another celebration as we were all back together. There were still groups of people in other parts of WEO that we wanted or needed here, but the entire group from my homestead in Mississippi was now all in Anchorin. We finally had a home to grow, build, and call our own. We would make this place something we could defend and dominate through.

As the night wound down, I received an icon informing me that Tikallnosis was asking me to accept his commune request. I was hoping this would occur before the council meeting, but neither of us knew how long Thomas's task would take. Or at least I hoped that this message was about. I walked up to the room that Tiger Lilly and I were currently using as a bedroom, and I sat on the bed. As I laid down, I hit the accept button and as normal, I reappeared into a semi dark room, and I immediately noticed Tikallnosis sitting there on a bench made of bone. His demeanor was not that of someone that had happy news, so I walked over and sat. I then looked him squarely in the eyes and said, "OKAY man what did you find?"

Tikallnosis, AKA Thomas the developer, looked up to meet my gaze and just softly said he might have underestimated the depth of how far this might go. I looked at him with a puzzled look and retorted, and? Man, you got to give me more than that. He looked at me with an even more serious look and said that he had discovered a few things in this file with something called

Project Overhaul as well as portions of the file referring to the Soul Crusher pandemic. The project had to do with the nanite injections that every person uploaded to WEO had currently running through their bodies and a secondary programming function to the nanites that were currently dormant. He was still deciphering the file, he said but verified he did not like the looks of that. What would the pandemic have to do with that, Thomas said to himself mostly, but it was said aloud? He also discovered references to something of a group or entity called Viper. What in the hell was that I asked and Tikallnosis shrugged his shoulders adding that he did not have the foggiest clue.

He did note that from what he had detected so far that the secondary program functioned as some sort of control override feature, but he would continue to investigate. This is not good man, I replied and he nodded in agreement. If they have a coding within their functionality that allows control over the subject and as my words died in the air as the implications, were evident. Could the Soul Crusher and these nanites connect somehow, I added? Could they be a progressive cure or was it something far more sinister? If this were a cure Thomas said, then it would not be encrypted behind a raid boss's firewall he snapped back with.

So, I replied after a deep breath; we have mentions of the Soul Crusher pandemic, the nanites with a secondary protocol that mentions something called Project Overhaul focusing on possible human control, and something called Viper. Not much to go on but it certainly raises concerns, I added. He replied frankly and verified my concern. None of this makes sense, he uttered and then added that more files were needed to put more of a clear picture together. Tikallnosis then said that he had the location and name of another file, but it was a level 30 dungeon boss and you and your group cannot manage that yet.

The goal was simple then. Get stronger, train, and grind until we are. The name of the dungeon was the Catacombs of the Sundered Crimson King. Well, that sounds just damn ominous I said, without hesitation. Tikallnosis nodded and added that it is going to be a tough bastard and it was a forty-person raid dungeon with a level 30 requirement. You need to make your people stronger and please do it quickly. I agreed and asked if there were any smaller dungeons close that we could party up and repeat to gain experience and gear. Tikallnosis pondered that for a minute and then let me know he would see what he could find and get the information to me as soon as he was able. He would also include the location of the raid dungeon as it was a good way to the south from us. For now, grow this place, dominate, and get stronger, he finally said. With the conversation at its end, I told him that we would talk soon and then I ended the communication.

After returning to the world of living, I returned to the downstairs area and rejoined in the festivities, but now my mind was very deep in thought. How could all of this be intertwined, I kept wondering? A few of my family noticed I was off in deep space, and they asked what was wrong. I played it off as nothing but just said that we could talk later maybe. Jaceberlen looked at me from across the table, and he knew something was wrong, but he knew better than to ask now. This would be something to dissect and ponder for now as that was all we could do currently. Now it was time to enjoy what we did have.

The next morning, we as an entire town went through all the massive piles of spoils that my minions had collected and sorted. Most of the gear was equal to what we already had but there were quite a few of us that came out with a winning hand. Between the weapons, armor, and the rest of it, everyone came away with at least something for their efforts.

The townsfolk, however, cleaned up house as they had nothing beforehand. This was great for goodwill, and it would also enable us to train them to fight and defend the town better going forward. We would also have plenty of items to trade with soon, and stuff that we could melt down and reuse. Finally, the people that I had asked for arrived at the top room that we were now calling the Summit. As they entered I had them sit at the rectangular table that I had arranged for us. One by one they sat looking as if they were wondering what this was about. Even

Jaceberlen did not know everything yet, but he was about too. Before me sat Jaceberlen, Raven, Tiger Lilly, Killer, Tal'n, Captain Ahab, Biggus Dikkus, Dealz, and my oldest friend, ThreeBD. It was time to begin our crusade of sorts.

I stood up and introduced the easier parts of the meeting by advising them this would be a council of sorts to help govern and build the city into what we know it can be. Each has my trust and by the end of the night they must swear to a few bylaws for this to happen. Dealz would help oversee the completion of our construction and growth efforts. Tal'n would be the political advisor, ThreeBD would help oversee trade, Captain Ahab would be our man overseeing defensive and military strategy with a caveat that we can always Anders that shit. Tiger Lilly had farming or agriculture skills so she would help oversee food production. Biggus Dikkus would assist in leading the mining and ores production and exploration. Killer would assist in the city management from where to place buildings, waterways, etc. Raven would lead our scouting forces for recon, espionage, and exploration. Finally, Jaceberlen would oversee training and leveling our forces both Earthen and townsfolk. We needed someone to manage the laws, security, and police, but I wanted to see what the recruitment hall had before we tried to delegate that out. Right now, Jaceberlen will handle that too. As we would not always be there, we needed the townsfolk to be professionally trained to defend it. I would oversee it all and would have the final say in everything.

When the different duties were covered, I went over the ideas I had about the new buildings, priorities, and prompt upgrade to Tier 1. I also went deeper into the Bastion of Justification tree arcs and what the future choices could be as well as the open buildings and perks I had currently. They were all amazed at what this could mean as far as an edge. Everyone agreed with the Recruitment Hall, Firemander Pen, and everyone started drooling at the Trader's Bazaar. They were excited about the Training Yard too, but we needed to upgrade to Tier 1 before we could build it. After setting priorities, we discussed everything dealing with the city, as well as needing someone to keep track of our people and their growth with evolutions. Since Jaceberlen was going to lead the training, he volunteered for that.

Now with everything out of the way there was only one thing left to go over, and it would be a bombshell. In my previous meetings with Tikallnosis, we had discussed how to keep people from discussing this potential issue. We produced a sort of non-disclosure document that had to be voluntarily signed. It would then create an ability within the system to prohibit the topic from being spoken unless allowed. The punishment would be enforced somehow by the system, and I did not really want to know. With that in mind I had the room quiet down as I began somberly. "All of you in this room have asked what the quest was that I received and Jaceberlen was subsequently brought into. I will now tell you about it in detail and what has been updated since we took down the commander of the Ebony Cloaks"

The room went very quiet as I continued and the room got heavier the more information that I disclosed. When I finally finished everyone in the room sat in stunned silence. Worry was apparent by everyone at the implications, but that was all we knew so it could be nothing. Nobody in the room thought that and I knew Tiger Lilly was having an internal panic attack. I continued with the fact that the unknowns will become clearer the more we uncover but our purpose remains. Get strong, grow, build, and take down the next raid boss. I went into the dungeon and the requirements, which was a great short-term goal to build upon outside of the town. We needed focus and the next challenge would provide that.

We continued to talk late into the day as we broke down troops, groups, and anything else you could imagine. We decided to meet again the next day once everyone had the opportunity to gather information on their respective duties and I encouraged them to enlist the aid of the townsfolk for their knowledge and experience. The Recruitment Hall, I added, will be a great boon for managers, troops, and many other things, if it was what I thought it would be.

After everyone agreed to the non-disclosure issue, we revisited the deeds quest and what my plans were and that they were on board. We would need to be ready for that fast. We did cover one more thing that Tal'n mentioned at the end. The creation of a formal guild or faction. With the way WEO was operating, we decided that a faction made more sense until we knew more of the mechanics around it. We decided to get more information. A few names were already in consideration though.

EPILOGUE

The figure sat in his current office located in the highlands around Minsk, Belarus. He was going through some encrypted information that he had put into a secure file and uploaded into the server when he received an alert. As he turned to review the system alert, he noticed that a group had taken down the commander of the Ebony Cloaks. That was not an easy feat as the digital raid boss was a roaming one that traveled in a certain path repeatedly. What was difficult about it was the fact that it was one tough bastard, and he had made sure of it considering what the coding entailed. It would take a large decently leveled group at the initial stages of the simulation to take it down, so this piqued his curiosity. That should not have been possible at this early stage, especially since it had only been several days since the mass upload had taken place. He immediately became extremely cautious as his training had created an innate response mechanism, but he later dismissed it as random stance.

The man decided to monitor the situation but determined that it was just a random event trigger by a group of people being aggressive in growth. He did, however, look at the alert more closely to view the group that had taken it down. Interesting indeed, he whispered to himself as he recognized one of the names but could not remember where. This was probably just a chance encounter, but maybe it was not. How could anyone know was what his mind kept telling him. He decided to let it go for now but would follow back up in a week or so to see if there were any flags. That name he would have to remember.

Thomas sat at his desk sweating even though the temperature inside was set at a cool sixty-five degrees. It had been two days since Dookooze had met with his so-called council and from that time, their progress was impressive. The discussion that he had with Dookooze was very disturbing indeed as Thomas now contemplated the newest and latest information that sat on his secure screen. He had a large lump form in his throat at what this could mean, although it was still very much a working theory that needed to be figured out.

What are we a part of, he began to internally question and what the hell is Viper? He decided that he would continue to worry about this until he was sick if he let himself. He also wondered what this might mean for his life and what the possibilities were. He removed the thumb drive, cleared his screens, and shut down his computer making sure everything was clean and safe.

Thomas made his way to his room within the complex, jumping at the slightest sound within the halls. He entered his room and closed the doors with a final click of his lock. He was sweating badly now and grabbed a washcloth with bottled water to wipe his face and neck clear of the perspiration. Why am I so paranoid? He kept asking himself this repeatedly. There is nothing to fear. It is just a random batch of information; he kept thinking to himself even as his conscious knew that was a lie. Thomas finally decided to lie down in his bed and tried to close his eyes, but sleep would mostly evade him this night. His thoughts would run rampant.

Deep within a cave on a continent far to the north of Anchorin, an entity awoke anew by opening his lone eye and seeing the world for the first time. Power radiated from it as it flexed its muscles and limbered up its extremities. It did not need anything other than to grow and kill everything that crossed its path. This cave was its domain and everything inside. Standing over forty feet tall inside of the cavern, it looked around at its new realm as it was close to a few hundred feet in height and covered in a misty green ice that reeked of toxic fumes. The creature inhaled the sickly-sweet scent as if it were candy and exhaled the same thing. Ten beings approached and knelt before the creature. Lord Iogus, how may we serve you? The creature looked down at the congregated group and intuitively knew its name, and they were there to serve him. Yes, that is who I am, he decided and stood tall. Time to feed. Secure my domain it gutturally replied.

The current King of the Lexxtenburg Monarchy sat at his throne when the royal messenger arrived. He motioned for the servant to approach, and the messenger handed him a sealed roll of parchment. As the king ushered the royal messenger away, he cracked the seal and unrolled the paper. The communication was not long and was to the point as it was an update to the current lords within his fragile realm. His power had been waning for some time, and he desperately was holding on to what control he had. Bandits had taken over portions of his land and disrupted trade and taxes. Six of his towns were under the criminal's control. Or at least they had been. From what he was reading there was a new player in this game. Someone he would need to have words with to determine if this new player was a threat or a loyalist. Dookooze was his name and he appeared to be an Earthen which is a new species of settlers that are now rapidly migrating from a faraway land.

Deliver a message to this Dookooze, the king ordered the royal messenger. As the message was scribed and sealed with the king's signet ring, the messenger was dismissed. The king sat there in pondering silence as he calculated scenarios and the plethora of chess-like possibilities. Was this new player a threat that would finally break his fragile hold and end his family's monarchy or be the catalyst that secures it? Soon we will know but the royal forces need to be ready just in case.

The altar at the Waterfall Basin began to pulse with a shadow array of darkness. Once a haven for the Firemander Queen, it was now a growing willful presence loyal to its new owner, the Champion Dookooze, and of Tikallnosis. It wanted to aid its new owner and the best way it could accomplish that was to help him and his people get stronger. The will of the alter was not strong enough to speak to Dookooze just yet, but it did have the strength however to do something else. The essence spiraled into a point and focused itself to reach out behind the waterfall and touch the rock. The rock resisted at first but then it relented and the point pierced the substance and began to claw at it. As the rock gave way a little bit at a time the essence continued to push until the beginning of a dungeon formed. The altar's presence stopped for a moment to smile as if that was even a possibility. Then after a brief second, it began with renewed interest. This would help Dookooze his people achieve their goals and make us a part of his kingdom. Soon I can contact him to spread his domain and serve. Tikallnosis and his chosen entity, Dookooze.

Thank you for reading World Evolution Online Book 1 Apocalypse. World Evolution Online Book 2 Vigilance is currently in development.